MW00880502

CONDO COMMANDEAUX

Alan Wolford

Copyright © 2016 by Alan Wolford
All rights reserved.

ISBN: 1530511658
ISBN 13: 9781530511655

No part of this publication may be reproduced, stored in a retrieval system or transmitted in any way by any means, electronic, mechanical, photocopy, recording or otherwise without the prior permission of the author except as provided by USA copyright law.

This novel is a work of fiction. Names, descriptions, entities, and incidents included in the story are products of the author's imagination. Any resemblance to actual persons, events and entities is entirely coincidental.

Book design copyright © 2016 by Alan Wolford. All rights reserved. Third edition.

Published in the United States of America.

For Gwen

ONE

Ahalf hour before dawn, Mark McAllister woke to the loud intermittent drone of the Delmar fire alarm. He'd last heard the sinister-sounding alarm when it was tested right before the luxury condo received its certificate of occupancy a year earlier. Groggy from a late night of partying, he distinctly smelled something burning as he slipped on his aqua-colored Bora Bora running shorts to find out what the hell was going on.

Still half asleep, he stuck his head out his penthouse door just as three shouting men dressed in heavy-duty firefighting gear rushed past him carrying armloads of emergency equipment. They stopped two doors down in front of Mrs. Seidelbaum's penthouse and began banging on the door.

"Boca Raton Fire Department! Open up, Mrs. Seidelbaum!" yelled the lead fireman over the drone of the alarm. "Mrs. Seidelbaum, Boca Fire Department. Open up!" More uneasy neighbors opened up to peer out and assess the danger. As Mark stepped into the travertine hallway, one of the firemen turned to him.

"For your own safety, sir, please have everyone in your unit exit the building," he said. "We don't know how bad this is yet."

"All right. Break it down," said the fireman facing Mrs. Seidelbaum's door. "She may still be inside." The door gave way to the second heavy "thud" of the battering ram, flying open and releasing a cloud of smoke that spewed into the hallway as the fire-rescue crew rushed inside to check for survivors.

Mark peeked out to see more of his penthouse neighbors standing in the hallway and gawking in disbelief. He could tell what they were thinking. Things like this weren't supposed to happen in three million dollar Boca Beach condos. He made a decision to exit the building, let the Boca Fire Department do their thing and hope for the best. As he stepped outside and shut his door, two firemen rushed past him carrying a stretcher piled high with a smoldering black material that smelled disgusting.

"I hope that's not what's left of Mrs. Seidelbaum," he quipped.

"No sir," said the trailing fireman through his oxygen mask. "Victim's pantyhose. From her dryer," he shouted over his shoulder as they rushed to exit the building carrying the smoldering pile of pantyhose.

As he reached her open doorway, Mark got a clear view of Mrs. Seidelbaum inside, sitting up and being administered oxygen. Reassured to see his eighty-eight-year-old neighbor still in the land of the living, he stuck his head in the smoky entryway.

"She gonna be okay?" Without taking his eyes from his patient, the fireman gave him a big thumbs up.

Happy that no one was burnt alive, Mark continued down the corridor toward his dumbfounded neighbors as he shrugged nonchalantly. "Guess her dryer runs a little hot." Nodding in agreement, they all went back inside, relieved to know they were no longer in danger of being cremated today.

It was now twenty minutes before sunrise as the only son of the most successful developer in Boca Raton made his way to the north stairwell in preparation for his four mile beach run. He felt it prudent to look back one last time to make sure nothing else was burning.

Mark wanted to forget the haunting image of Mrs. Seidelbaum's smoldering pantyhose being carried out on a stretcher from the luxury condo that was the crowning achievement of his company. Instead, the unshaven, slightly hungover forty-year-old President of Mizner Park Development tried to focus on the details from last night's wild Fourth of July boat party on Lake Boca.

There had been a dozen souls aboard for the celebration, and he was feeling lucky to have returned his forty-four-foot catamaran "Multiple Ohhhs..." back to the marina in one piece. He'd seen some rowdy boat parties during his twenty-seven month circum-navigation years earlier but couldn't remember one quite as wild as the one that celebrated America's birthday last night.

Needing to clear his head, he was anxious to hit the beach. Physical fitness wasn't just a hobby for him; it was a lifestyle. Extreme fitness was the best way he'd found to balance the excesses of late-night partying, and the endorphins always made him feel better. The natural painkillers his body produced held more healing powers than any prescription medicine he knew, and his addiction to physical fitness was a habit he embraced with both arms. As an extreme fitness junkie, he could remember applying sand-infused epoxy to the bottom of his running shoes to provide traction in the ice years ago when he lived in a Tribeca loft. Back then, his resourcefulness had paid off, keeping him on schedule for his early morning runs as he hopped over the winos on Manhattan's icy sidewalks and dodged the hookers returning home in their knee-high leather boots.

As his thoughts drifted to women who were attracted to lean athletic men, he came across a used condom draped over the stair-way guardrail. Disgusted, he propped his foot up on the railing to adjust the fit of his Surf Walkers as he eyed the dangling party favor, wondering why someone would lack the decorum to dispose of it.

While many of the condo commandos at Delmar were too old to have much interest in sex, they liked living vicariously, consuming vast quantities of alcohol while safely ensconced inside their pricey Boca Beach condos. Mark's best guess was that the party favor belonged to Jason, the condo president's drug-addled son. He remembered their portly president bragging that Jason had just returned home after completing his sixth session of rehab. Chalk it up to the list of reasons why he'd never had kids of his own.

Bounding his way down eleven more flights of stairs, he stopped to stretch his legs on the ground floor and thought about what kind of home life Jason must have with a heavy-handed mother like Sarah Glitzsky. Real parenting seemed to be in short supply, often defaulting to the virtual reality of the web and the violent video games that kids often confused with real life. Mark felt like the perfect armchair parent, bouncing from one relationship to the next like the game ball in a pinball machine. He kept telling himself he just hadn't found the right girl yet. Along the way, parental responsibilities seemed to have escaped him like sand streaming through an hourglass.

Reflecting on his childhood, he thought about how far he'd come. The sole heir to a ninety million dollar trust fund, Mark was born in Key West, where his father had started out selling commercial waterfront lots. Known as Little Lloyd to his family, his dad was a waterfront real estate specialist who would buy and sell beachfront property in an area until there were no more beachfront lots left. Then his dad would pack up the family and move to another coastal town, ensuring that young Mark got to explore even more of the hundreds of miles of Florida's sandy beaches.

His childhood memories were of building sandcastles and chasing dogs on pristine shorelines of mangrove and sea oats stretching from Key West to Sanibel Island, from Jacksonville Beach to

Ft. Lauderdale. During his adolescence, Mark hadn't yet made the connection between his father's job and the changing Florida coastline. But as he grew older, he began to notice the wildlife, coastal dunes and native vegetation giving way to the towering concrete hi-rises at an alarming rate.

Mark's mother had always dreaded direct sunlight and wasn't crazy about the humidity, but she put up with the heat and constant moving, given the plentiful money Little Lloyd was making. Sarah McAllister often felt disconnected from the social fabric that a developer's wife was expected to embrace. She stayed mostly indoors for sixteen years, trying to fill the void in her life by looking beautiful for a husband who was seldom around. She obsessed with her skin and complexion, and occupied herself with obscure hobbies. She took up the oboe, grew wild ginseng plants, immersed her fantasies in dirty martinis and began writing a romance novel. Later, she became fascinated by Japanese culture and grew bonsai trees, practiced Geisha dancing and took up yoga. Meanwhile, little Mark was free to run wild on the beaches while his parents had no idea of what he was getting himself into.

When Mark was three, Little Lloyd moved the family to Naples, a city famous for its pristine sugar-sand beaches and mid-western affluence. The unspoiled shorelines were decorated with an over-abundance of tropical seashells which young Mark collected and used to adorn his dresser, headboard and even his Dr. Seuss books. He had shoebox after shoebox filled with seashells, mementos of the picturesque seashores he remembered as a child. Before long, Little Lloyd was doing well enough to hire a nanny who often accompanied Mark to ensure he didn't wander into the Gulf of Mexico and drown.

When he was eighteen, he spent a night anchored off Naples Pier on a small boat with his first girlfriend, Melinda. Much to his delight, Melinda spent the entire evening patiently training him in the art of French kissing. When he awoke the next morning, it was as if Mark was suddenly confronted with the ugliness of the concrete and glass hi-rises for the first time, and he began to truly grasp what his father's job involved.

Reluctant to confront his feelings over the role his father played in such a radical transformation, Mark was nonetheless conflicted about the gradual disappearance of the mangroves, dunes, turtles and sea-birds. As his rebelliousness grew, years later he went against his father's wishes by embarking on a divergent career path.

While it was obvious that his father didn't want him to succeed at anything other than real estate, Melinda was very pleased that he'd succeeded at mastering the art of French kissing and introduced him to her very private repertoire of more French-inspired intimacy. Her patient tutelage ensured that eighteen-year-old Mark would develop the skills that came to endear him to his future wives and girlfriends.

By the time he was in his thirties, he had taken more than his share of walks on the wild side, especially during his tumultuous twelve years on Wall Street. After freeing himself from the tyranny of cocaine, he realized it was the chronic drug abuse and constant carousing that undermined his success as an institutional money manager. Trying to live a life that was both productive and gratifying within a culture fraught with deception, he found himself wandering through the smoke and mirrors as the façade of Wall Street seemed to crumble around him.

He thought about the lessons learned. Half of the traders refused to share Wall Street's secrets, and the other half of what investors were told was just misdirection that often disguised a classic pump-and-dump scheme. Analysts were forced to issue positive reports and go along with the crowd while the incentives for telling the truth were all wrong. By the time the terrorist attacks of 9/11 were inflicted on the heart and soul of America and New York City, the honeymoon was over. Caught up in the quagmire of drugs and the unending stress of managing a billion dollars in global equities, he found himself foundering on the stormy seas of Wall Street and drowning in the aftermath.

After a dozen years of watching his son's self-annihilation as a Wall Street party animal, Little Lloyd finally convinced him to confront the carnage and spend a month in detox. The way his seventy-eight-year-old father saw it, everything except family was transient. Alzheimer's was slowly ravaging his brain and it was time to groom his successor while he still had enough marbles left to plan his estate.

So, Little Lloyd threw his son a life line and pulled him into the family business by installing him as his right-hand man at the real estate firm founded when Mark was only thirteen. Boca Raton was where he crash landed, and it felt as right as rain.

Vulnerable to the world and a little beat up, Mark was still in the game, and an environmentalist when it suited his sense of fashion. But not to the point of playing the role of the proverbial Earth biscuit that attended only the tofu and broccoli dances. Except for the years he modeled for GQ, he was leaner than he'd been for most of his life. Partly out of vanity, he began to pay more attention to his health, and his fitness regimen was a discipline he pursued faithfully, even when hung over.

Mark took a moment to reflect on his Achilles heel; a tendency to fall in love with girls who were nice enough to sleep with him on the first date. This meant he fell in love often. One such girl was Christa, a bi-polar Las Vegas-bred dancer and a real show-stopper. He would have likely married her sooner except for the fact that her divorce wasn't yet final from a violent man with mob ties up and down the East coast.

When Christa's estranged husband found out about her new love interest, he hired a guy named Luigi to break into Mark's condo one evening and discourage his romantic inclinations. As luck would have it, Mark wasn't home when it happened, and Luigi was apprehended after snorting an entire box of bath salts, drinking a bottle of rum, and running over the neighbor's dog in his attempt to flee the scene.

While Mark was a man who fully immersed himself in the elixir of love, his marriage to Christa was a stormy one. They fell hard for each other, and in her quest to regain control of their relationship during their last year together, one-by-one she took away the joys they once shared.

She became so bereft of joy that it made him wonder if love was just some cheap trick of nature intended to propagate the species.

On her manic side, she would thank God for 'making her feel like a woman' after hours of passionate lovemaking, but her depressive side would condemn Mark the next morning for 'loving her and making her feel so damn good.' Christa claimed that her hypersexuality made her vulnerable, but it was her habitual cyber-stalking that helped to erode their love. To counter her criticisms, he would remind her that all saints have a past, and all sinners have a future.

After years of teeter-tottering between love and madness, his prayers were finally answered when Christa left him for a wealthy heavy-set country clubber who wined and dined her at Trattoria Dario and all the most exquisite restaurants, took her on shopping trips to Worth Avenue, and catered to her every whim.

Saddened by the failure of their marriage, Mark took it as a sign that he should up his game and leave the strippers, dancers and head cases behind. Christa had reigned like a queen on the throne of his memory for a year before he began an earnest search for an intelligent, professional woman worthy of bearing his children-a woman who was not only beautiful, but sweet, ambitious, and spiritual. And, of course, willing to sleep with him on the first date.

It was a few minutes before daybreak as he made his way outside and down the steps of the walkover. Putting aside his thoughts of Christa, he paused to inhale the ocean air and scan the shoreline in the pre-dawn light as the mournful sound of a freight train's horn drifted across the Intracoastal. Boca Beach was waking to a new day, and facing the huge expanse of ocean always gave him a sense of awe. The panorama momentarily took him back to the picturesque islands of French Polynesia where he'd dropped anchor and hunted seafood on the reefs while hanging out with movie stars during his circumnavigation years ago.

The loud throaty roar of big diesel engines jolted him back to reality as he watched the big Boca Raton firetruck depart Delmar after coming to rescue Mrs. Seidelbaum and her smoldering pantyhose. The firetruck turned north on Ocean Boulevard, reminding him to look in on her after his beach run.

Now, he focused his eyes on the beach and searched for evidence of last night's storm. The shoreline looked deserted except for the ghost crabs darting in and out of their sandy hideaways and the cry of gulls floating on the incoming breeze. He relished the faint sea breeze on his face as the gentle morning sway of the sea oats seemed to deny there had even been a gale. His reverie was interrupted by the distressed call of a seagull coming from underneath the walkover. Unable to ignore the high-pitched trill, he descended the stairs to search for the stricken bird.

Mark found the gull lying under the walkover, tangled in a ball of fishing line as it struggled to free itself. The seagull's plight brought to mind the last volunteer coastal cleanup and the huge ball of discarded fishing line they'd pulled off the reef that day. The gull continued to trill loudly and flap its wings in a plea for help as it tried to break loose. Mark reached to untangle the line, and in a minute the wounded bird was free. He watched the gull stand up with a limp, chirp a thank you and fly away toward the fast-approaching sunrise.

A flat summer ocean greeted him this morning, a huge lake of softly lapping waves as he stretched one last time before his four mile run south to Deerfield Beach. It was then he noticed a large bulky object floating at the edge of the surf, trapped between two large coral formations. Curious, he edged forward between the rocks to get a better look.

He could barely make out what looked like a giant rectangular duffle bag floating just below the surface. His pulse quickened. Was it the Mother Lode? He recalled the stories from his friends about the 'square groupers' that often floated up on the beaches in South Florida, but he was never lucky enough to have found one himself. Sometimes they would float up on the beach in groups worth millions, the lost caches of pot and narcotics that often broke loose in stormy seas or abandoned by smugglers as they fled from law enforcement.

He noticed a speeding police car racing south down A1A, lights flashing but with no siren. As the car's blue beacon pierced the pre-dawn haze like a revolving laser, something seemed out of place to him. He was surprised to see a uniformed Boca Raton police officer standing to the north and pointing at something in the surf as he spoke into his shoulder radio. Looking south, he could make out the silhouette of yet another police officer walking down the beach toward the surf in the distance. It *had* to be the Mother Lode. The adrenaline washed over him like a powerful tsunami as his imagination raced with the possible scenarios of what his find could be worth. And, the penalty for getting caught.

An avid skydiver and admitted adrenaline junky, Mark thought it would be a hoot if he could pull it off. His heart pounded as he began to weigh the possibility of ten years in Federal lockup against the likelihood of scoring a boatload of cash from the sale of a hundred pounds of pot. It was less about the money and more about the thrill. As he leaned in closer to the coral outcroppings that hid him from view, the far-off thump-thump-thump of a chopper's rotating blades momentarily stayed his snatch-and-grab plan.

As more light began to fill the sky, he knew things would liven up as soon as the sun peeked over the horizon like a giant searchlight. He checked his watch. If he went for the bale of pot, he would have less than five minutes to hide his treasure, so he had to move fast.

For a moment, he considered doing the sensible thing and taking off like a scalded squirrel, but the ego trip of getting away with such a big score in the middle of a police search outweighed his fear. It was the thrill seeker in him that often displayed an unhealthy disregard for his own safety, and he felt compelled to ride the action to its conclusion.

Mark waded in and grabbed the huge package with both arms, but the heavy bale slipped from his hands. He tried again, using all the upper body strength he could muster, grabbing the bale in a bear hug and muscling it out of the water. He threw it onto the sand where it landed with a loud "whack". He glanced in both directions to make sure the officers on the beach hadn't heard. The sky was getting lighter now and the sun would be peeking over the horizon in less than three minutes. This would be his only chance. Scrambling in the loose sand, he dragged the heavy package higher on the beach as fast as he could, like a crab with its quarry, up past the high water marks where the seaweed line defined the limit of high tide.

He picked a secluded spot near the bottom of the dune to bury the pot. Like a dog on speed burying a bone, he dug a hole in a blur of energy and flying sand. Within seconds, the hole was deep enough, and he pushed the black package inside and quickly covered it up.

Nervous as a bag of rats in a burning meth lab, he looked left and right to see who was watching, relieved to see the Boca police cruisers moving away in opposite directions as their blue strobe lights rotated eerily in the twilight. Heart pumping wildly and out of breath, he took a moment to rest and re-evaluate, looking for a handle on the moment. For camouflage, he tossed some strands of seaweed and a few pieces of driftwood onto his freshly-dug burial mound. Pleased with his artful camouflage, he straightened himself up and reflected on his work, amazed that he'd been able to conceal the bale in the middle of a full-blown police search. He did a slow 360-degree scan of the beach to check again for onlookers and took a deep breath of sea air as he faced the rising sun. Lucky, lucky, lucky.

When the sun peaked over the horizon, the surreal scene gave way to a normal Boca Beach sunrise. Mark brushed the sand off his body and started his run, trying to pretend it was just another ordinary morning. Lengthening his stride, he fell into a rhythm and started a mental checklist of wealthy potheads to call. There was a guy he knew who owned a medical marijuana facility who could identify the chemical compounds in the bale. Ironically, Mark didn't have much use for the whacky weed himself; the stuff just made him feel silly and gave him the munchies, but a lot of his friends sure liked it.

It didn't take him long to compile the list in his head. The potential buyers he knew who had enough cash to take the whole load off his hands was a short one.

TWO

C onflicted over what to do with his bale of pot, Mark hadn't accomplished much at the office. After a few morning meet- ings, formulating a new ad campaign, and a business lunch at The Boca Resort and Club, he took the time to make some inquiries to see about unloading his new-found treasure. After a few conversa- tions, he concluded there was enough interest from two potential buyers who were both principals in legitimate medical marijuana facilities, and who could pay him in cash. The latest research on the benefits of medical marijuana had sparked a new liberalism toward the merits of cannabis, and it was clear that the nation's attitude had changed.

It had been seventeen hours since Mark buried the bale on Boca Beach, and it was time to recover his treasure. He stood on the deck of the walkover, stopping to scan the beach in the light of a full moon for any signs of late night passers-by. Minutes ear- lier, he had enjoyed a second glass of Beringer Private Reserve to steady his nerves. He'd been saving the vintage for something special, and he figured the likelihood of scoring fifty grand worth of abandoned weed seemed sufficient cause for celebration.

Descending the wooden steps, he could hear giggling from an amorous couple in the sea oats on the far side of the dune as he approached the spot he marked that morning. Even this late at night the heat was unbearable, and he could feel the perspiration saturate his black Under Armor workout suit. Reaching the burial site, he was relieved to see that his treasure trove looked undisturbed.

Mark was excited at the thought of what he was about to unearth as he knelt down and unzipped the two empty black duffle bags draped over his shoulder. After clearing the sand away from the bale's black plastic wrapping, he unsheathed his dive knife and cut it open. The compressed pot popped out of the opening like a jack-in-the-box, and he knew there was more than he could carry in one load. He estimated more than a hundred pounds of premium-grade, six-inch Jamaican buds were compressed inside the package. Stuffing as much as he could into each of the duffle bags, he tried to avoid breaking the buds, but the gooey resin was making the stuff stick to his hands and clothing.

Mark made his way back to the elevator lobby with two duffle bags stuffed with pot hanging from his shoulders like luggage from a wild Jamaican junket. He prayed no one would be around this late on a Monday night to get a whiff of what he was schlepping upstairs. When the brass elevator doors opened on the penthouse level, he stuck his head around the corner and peeked down the marbled hallway. Making his way to his kitchen, he unloaded fistfuls of weed into the brown paper grocery bags he'd been saving, never expecting to see them stuffed to the brim with Jamaican buds. As he separated the damp clumps of weed, it occurred to him to dry the moist grass by placing several pounds on broiler pans. Sliding them into his stainless steel Viking oven, he turned the setting to "warm" and kept the oven door ajar to prevent burning.

The building was quiet as he rode the elevator down to the first floor lobby for his final trip to retrieve the rest until the condo president's sixteen year old son appeared out of nowhere. Spotting him with the empty duffle bags, Jason confronted him with wide-eyed excitement.

"Hey Mark, ya see that?" asked Jason like he'd just won the lottery. The lanky kid had a habit of adjusting the fit of his baseball cap like a pitcher about to hurl a fastball.

"See what?" Mark froze like a deer in the headlights in the elevator doorway and went with his best dumb blonde act. His face felt funny and he couldn't stop thinking about diving into a huge bag of cheese-flavored Doritos.

"Six-inch buds all over the elevator lobby, man! Check it out," blurted Jason as he held out a fist full of grass to make his point. "Look! I got enough for everyone in my rehab class!"

"I'm happy for you Jason," hoping to calm him down. "Merry Christmas and Happy Hanukkah!" He thought about an angle. "Don't worry. Your mom doesn't have to know. It'll be our secret." He knew he was going to have to get his act together to pull this thing off if he wanted to stay out of the Palm Beach County jail tonight. Medical marijuana or not, possession of a hundred pounds of pot was still illegal in Florida.

"Thanks, dude," responded a grateful Jason with a fist bump. "She don't have to know." The kid adjusted his cap with a quizzical look. "What's with the duffle bags?"

"Getting' ready for a trip is all." Mark nonchalantly pushed the glass lobby door open hoping Jason would let it go.

Looking for more reassurance, Jason followed him. "Promise you won't say anything to my mom, right? She'll put me back in rehab if she finds out."

"Don't worry. I won't say a thing," patting him on the shoulder. He thought about what a messed-up life Jason must have at home to have gone through rehab six times. With a mother like Sarah

Glitzsky, it didn't take much to figure out why his dad had flown the coup. Mark watched the clueless kid disappear into the elevator lobby, hoping he would stay inside so he could finish harvesting his treasure without any more interruptions.

Minutes later, after listening to the couple in the sea oats finding God again, Mark finished stuffing the rest of the pot into the duffle bags and slung them over his shoulder, this time making sure they were zipped tightly. Not wanting to leave any traces, he filled the hole in the sand and collected the plastic wrappings for disposal down the condo trash chute. Checking the beach one last time, he was alone, except for the two in the sea oats who were now cooing to each other like a couple of love birds.

After making his way into the elevator with another heavy load, the doors opened on the penthouse floor and Mark was hit with the strong odor of baking cannabis. Paranoid over whether his entire condo could smell it, he rushed down the hallway in a panic, feeling like an idiot for forgetting about the damp dope in the oven. When he opened the door, he was greeted with a cloud of smoke so thick he couldn't see his Roche Bobois leather furniture twenty feet away. Grabbing some potholders, he pulled the smoking pot out of his oven and set it on the granite countertop, dumbfounded at his own stupidity, so stoned he wasn't even sure of what planet he was on.

Yet another brilliant idea popped into his pot-ravaged head; he would air dry it on his window screens! He set about removing all five screens from his bedroom windows and placed them over the stacks of marble tiles left over from his kitchen upgrade. As he spread the damp dope evenly across the screens, he realized he had more damp pot than screens, so he stumbled down the hall to see if he could borrow some from his hot-looking neighbor. With any luck, her sugar daddy would be busy in New York at his Park Avenue townhouse counting his money.

One of the most ambitious, intelligent and beautiful women at Delmar, Carol Nutter was a senior designer and manager for Venus Sportswear, studying for her PhD in Business Marketing at FAU. During their first encounter at the pool two weeks ago, it was obvious there was a strong attraction between them. After standing in the hall and ringing her bell for the fourth time, she finally answered the door dressed in a cashmere bathrobe with a black sheer teddy underneath. Mark greeted her with a grin, his black Under Armour outfit soaked in perspiration, sprinkled from head to toe with bits of Jamaican bud.

"Honey, you know what time it is?" Carol looked half-asleep as she peered out from her half-open door. Still, she looked stunning. Looking him up and down, his stealthy outfit was decorated with little bits of buds like it was a pot-sampling smorgasbord. Curious, she stepped up, picked a piece off his chest and gave it the sniff test.

"Nice, Mark." She licked the sticky pot from her fingers like it was ice cream and smiled at him with a mischievous look. "Mmmm. Good stuff. Whatcha been up to tonight, handsome? Speed gardening on the beach again?"

Doing his best to sound casual, he lowered his voice and leaned against her door jamb as if borrowing a cup of sugar. "I just need to…uh…borrow your window screens." She opened the door all the way, stepped past him into the hall and inhaled a lungful of smoke.

"Hmmm. Smells really nice out here." She got up close and peered into his blood-shot eyes. "You looked totally baked, Mark. Ya wanna come inside, tell me what the hell is going on?" Her robe fell open as she reached for him. "Oops," she said, smiling mischievously. Mark felt himself falling under her spell, transfixed by her beauty, his willpower beginning to melt away as the high from the pot steered him toward more hedonistic thoughts.

"I, uh…really can't stay, sweetie. I just, ah…need to borrow your window screens. That okay?" He smiled sheepishly, trying to stick to his plan, but it wasn't working. "Nice outfit," he said appreciatively. The potent pot had him thinking with his smaller head. He couldn't help himself, his prior agenda yielding to one of a more primitive nature as he felt the blood rushing to his groin. Slipping inside, he kissed her on the neck and nuzzled her earlobe as he eased his way into her warm entry hall.

"Ooooh," she cooed from his kiss and dragged her nails across his chest. "Honey, you can have all my screens, but you're gonna have to pay the toll." Her cashmere robe dropped to the floor to reveal her sheer teddy as she shut the door and took his hand. Leading him inside, she reached for his groin and teased him with her fingertips. Giggling, she said, "I can see you *do* like my idea."

With her hand on his tiller, she steered him to her bedroom. Mark's hopes for a quick getaway went up in smoke.

After ringing Carol's chimes a few more times, he awoke two hours later, handcuffed to her wrought iron headboard and badly in need of a massive dose of Viagra and vitamin E. The vague memory of falling out of bed onto a pile of her textbooks during their lovemaking made him realize just how stoned he'd gotten. Then he remembered Carol begging him to handcuff her, which got him excited all over again and sparked another encore performance. After a few more momentous moments, Carol snoozed while he slipped out of her condo with the handcuffs dangling from his wrist. He held all of her window screens, his clothes draped over his arms and the key to her cuffs clenched in his teeth.

Less than a hundred feet from his own front door, Mark tiptoed naked down the cold marble hallway as he tried to balance the armload of screens and clothing. Seconds away from a clean get-away, the window screens tilted and banged against a light fixture. As he reached to straighten the sconce, the screens slipped out of his grasp and clattered to the floor. Cursing under his breath, he bent over to gather them up as he heard a door open down the hall. Uh-oh, he thought. He could see a familiar shriveled face and nose protruding from the opening.

"WHO'S MAKING ALL THAT RACKET?" demanded Mrs. Seidelbaum as she peered out in her negligee at a naked man wearing handcuffs and carrying an armload of clothes and window screens. It was three in the morning, and in her haste to confront the culprit, the eighty-eight-year-old widow had forgotten her eyeglasses.

"It's just me, Mrs. Seidelbaum," squeaked Mark in a mousy voice as he continued to sneak down the hallway, hoping like hell he could make it inside before she found her glasses. His door was locked, and he fumbled desperately through his pants for the keys. "It's okay. Go on back to bed, now, ma'am. No escaped convicts out here."

Shocked at what she thought she was seeing, Mrs. Seidelbaum went back inside to retrieve her eyeglasses to make sure she wasn't dreaming. Mark worked feverishly to open the door and get inside before she returned, fairly certain that his outfit was not only against the condo rules but might even give the elderly lady a stone-cold heart attack.

He managed to get all the screens and his clothes inside just as she returned to her doorway wearing her eyeglasses. This time, she saw no one, but something was still very fishy. She sniffed the air like a bloodhound, certain she smelled something burning. Concerned that something might be on fire in her own condo again, she closed her door and went back inside to make sure she hadn't left her pantyhose in the dryer.

By now, the whole place smelled like a ganja frat house party. Locking the door behind him, Mark stumbled back inside his smoke-filled condo, unloading his armload of screens and imagining the hefty fine the condo commandos would have levied if he'd been caught naked in the hallway.

He threw his bathrobe on and took a quick inventory of his body parts, confirming that his person seemed intact but his mind felt like it was melting away like Velveeta cheese in a microwave. As he distributed the rest of the damp weed on the balcony screens, he was so out of it he managed to bruise his nose walking into a wall. He couldn't honestly ever remember being quite this stoned before. As a matter of fact, in his current state, he couldn't honestly remember much of anything.

When he caught himself trying to check his cell phone messages from his TV remote control, he decided he was too messed up to function and passed out face down on his bed. Within minutes, he was back in ganja land dreaming of giant brownies, huge bags of Doritos, crunchy Jiff peanut butter and Carol playing Alice in Wonderland in a sheer teddy as she pranced up and down a yellow-brick road of butterscotch candy.

⚔️

Mark woke the next morning still wearing his bathrobe at a quarter past eight, his head pounding from the Jamaican ganja fest. He was getting a late start to his morning as he tore open a packet of Emergen-C and washed it down with a glass of carrot juice. Stepping into the hallway to grab his copy of the *Boca News*, he spotted Carol locking her door, looking hot in a leather mini skirt, high heels and blue halter top.

Spotting Mark, she smiled from ear to ear as she recalled their erotic night together. For the first time since moving in to her Delmar penthouse, she was secretly entertaining the idea of ditching her sugar daddy for a younger man as she felt her maternal instincts kicking in.

"Hi honey!" she said. "Hope we didn't break your fun meter last night!"

"Trust me. It still works great," Mark said with a grin as he fantasized about nuzzling her neck. "Like your outfit." His pounding head had magically begun to feel better a she stepped closer.

After stopping to adjust a crooked wall sconce, Carol made her way to him. With her bag over her shoulder, she surprised Mark with a hug and a lingering morning kiss that got his motor running all over again. "Wow," she said. "Who knows more about a girl's anatomy than you do, baby?"

"Well, there's Jack Nicholson, Bill Clinton…Rosie O'Donnell…"

"Funny, Mark," she said, prancing down the hall in her high heels, putting on a show as she twirled her finger in the air. "I love your sense of humor," in a melodic voice that sang of happiness. When she got to the elevator, she did a perfect pirouette and winked at him. "Got a meeting with our creepy condo manager. Call me later?"

"You're insatiable," pointing playfully. "Okay. Sure." After waving goodbye to Carol, he stepped back inside his condo, stooping to pick up a Post-It from the floor. On it was a note he'd written to himself last night that presumably described a way to fax a fruit roll-up from one fax machine to another.

"Wow!" he said out loud as he squinted and tried to make sense of the note for a second time, "…was I messed up. I am *never* touching that stuff again!" He stuffed the note in his pocket as he unfolded the morning paper and stared at the front page. The headline read:

"21 POT BALES FOUND ON BOCA BEACH"
"Shrimp Boat Captain Charged"

Mark chuckled to himself, knowing that much of bale #22, which was notably absent from the story, was *not* mentioned in the morning news. Part of bale #22 was spread all over five window screens on his balcony drying out on this fine morning.

Good luck with finding that one, you sunny beaches.

THREE

B efore his passing, Mark's father had high hopes that he would settle down and find the right girl, maybe deliver him some grandkids while his Alzheimer's still allowed him enough brain power to remember their names. Mark was attending a developers' convention in Las Vegas at his father's request when he met Christa. Though she stole his heart years before, it was clear she had some changes in mind. Especially fond of Cohibas, he smiled as he thought about the box that he'd persuaded her to smuggle across the border from Tijuana two summers ago. Smuggled Cohibas always just seemed to taste better.

Mark was comparing the dangers of tobacco and dating girls from his own condo. While cigars were easier for him to pass up, it was difficult for him to be without the comfort of female companionship ever since his mother's passing years ago. Her battle with cancer had left a huge void inside him, and in a more forgiving world, Mark was sure his mother would still be alive today.

I remember watching her fading. She was thin, pale, all shriv-eled up. Remember asking her if she felt frightened. Ignoring the pain, she silently shed a tear and shook her head. Tore my insides out watching her slip away. How can I put aside this darkness?

Dear Lord, help me collect the pieces of my life and mold them into something wonderful to better serve her memory.

It was Saturday. He leaned on the weathered railing at the walk-over, took another draw on his cigar and reminisced about Christa's wacky antics. The ocean breeze felt good on his face as he remembered scenes of her wilder manic side that always came out after a few glasses of wine. She always said she loved riding in his BMW without a stitch on because the sensual feel of the plush leather seats on her skin and the excitement of watching Mark maneuvering in and out of traffic at high speed got her so hot she just had to strip down. To see how far she'd go one night, she emerged from his car on a dare wearing only her Jimmy Choo high heels and a black boa when they'd pulled up to The Plaza after an evening out. Her unforgettable high-heeled sashay up to the valet station had cost him a hundred bucks in hush money, but the look on the valet's face was priceless.

He smiled. Nostalgia just isn't what it used to be, he thought, taking another puff on his high-dollar smoke.

He thought about how he'd squandered so much of his youth hooking up with models and showgirls. Today, he yearned for an ambitious professional woman of intelligence and high moral fiber; one who was capable of being an outstanding mother to his children. Was he growing up? He was at a stage where he was losing interest in the meat markets and bikini contests.

Christa continued to occupy his thoughts. As pretty as she was, she was saddled with more baggage than twenty skycaps could manage. She was high maintenance, and he'd accepted the fact that it was only a matter of time before all that baggage sank their love boat. His pursuit of her was not just about passion, but had a lot to do with how his relentless ego would take center stage and demand satisfaction. It was the way he went after things. After Hurricane Christa, Mark found himself hard aground, stranded between wives and sailboats, which made the drop-dead gorgeous girl standing next to him on the walkover this morning all the more tempting.

Covered from head to toe in a pink ski outfit, Desiree Stone continued to stare out to sea as if she were expecting someone near and dear to return from the briny blue and sail up at any moment. From all the condo scuttlebutt, Mark knew she was thirty-one-years old, single, a former Dallas Cowboys cheerleader and a fellow fitness fanatic. And a rumored adult film star. Mark knew he was playing with fire, but he just couldn't help himself. Adjusting his fedora, he had it set for maximum protection from the rising sun as the orange orb peeked out from behind the blue-grey masses of cumulus clouds. Checking her out furtively with his peripheral vision, he was determined to get her to smile and pay homage as he took another thoughtful pull on his Cohiba and looked for a way in.

From his neighbors, Mark knew that Desiree's former boyfriend was serving a fifteen-year sentence for defrauding hundreds of shareholders in his mob-backed pump-and-dump investment schemes. Although she had no knowledge or experience in business or finance, Mr. Ferraro had seen fit to make her an unwitting Director on five of his twenty-two shell corporations. When she'd asked him about the Federal investigation into his business practices, Antonio told her "…it was all just a few unfortunate misunderstandings. Nobody got hurt."

But earlier that same year, Federal Magistrate Frank H. Prikhower strongly disagreed, ruling that Mr. Ferraro had to pay back millions of dollars within ten days or face additional charges. As part of the settlement ordered by the judge, Ferraro agreed to pay over $58 million in reimbursements for bilking senior citizens out of their life savings when the SEC charged him with selling millions of dollars in bogus charitable gift annuities to over 500 retired people in Florida, Tennessee, Texas and Colorado. Ferraro had claimed that the money would help Ebola victims in Africa while generating "lucrative financial benefits" for the investors.

But, said the SEC officials, "only a small percentage of the funds were actually used for charitable service" or paid to the investors. Instead, Ferraro "siphoned off most of the funds for personal use." Documents and court records showed that Ferraro chartered private jets (Desiree loved to fly!) for vacations and trips to Las Vegas (Desiree loved to travel!). Ferraro bought a $950,000 condo in Boca, and a $2 million high-speed luxury Excalibur motor yacht (Desiree loved yachts!) while he helped himself to over $3 million in bonuses and salary.

The suit said the money came from "inexperienced elderly investors" who were "coerced, often at gunpoint, or under threat of cutting off their portable oxygen supply" to handover their life savings-including homes, real estate, stocks, pensions and cash-all to Friends of Africa, Inc., to "manage the charity and produce income" for the elderly.

"Instead," said SEC officials, "the main purpose was to distribute the money to Ferraro, fund his lavish parties, including the purchase of cocaine and Percocet, distribute cash and drugs to his female companions, pay third party sports promotors, prostitutes and fund pornographic productions." Months later, the SEC barred him from the securities industry for life.

Following the SEC's investigation, the FBI had leveled additional felony charges against Ferraro and his cohorts, and there were rumors that Desiree had turned state's evidence in exchange for immunity from prosecution for her complicity. As a security precaution, she purposely kept a low profile, and the word around Delmar was she was very particular about who she spoke to. Knowing something about what she'd been through, Mark decided to be patient as he eased his way into her world.

"Penny for your thoughts there, Desiree," coaxed Mark. Pretending not to hear him, she stared out across the ocean, unblinking, wrapped tightly in her trademark full-length pink ski parka that covered almost every inch of her body. Only a small part of her face was visible, her eyes hidden behind aqua-tinted sunglasses. His intuition told him she was hiding lots of secrets, so he played it cool, checking the weather app on his cell phone along with his messages while he waited for her to respond to his overtures. Bewildered by her imitation of Mt. Rushmore in the face of his irresistible charms, it bugged him to be ignored by such a beautiful woman-especially a former Cowboys cheerleader and adult film star. It never occurred to him that his ego was writing checks that his talents couldn't cash.

He thought of another way in. Smiling, he extended the smoking Cohiba in her direction, imagining her sensuous lips around it. "How 'bout a puff? It's a great cigar-very smooth." There was a crack in her façade. Amused by his gesture, there was the hint of a smile as she continued to look out over the Atlantic Ocean, vigilant and unyielding in her gaze.

Looking down from their perch on the walkover, she said; "I don't think Mike would approve," shifting her hips and re-crossing her legs, elbows resting on the railing. Again, she fixed her gaze on the roiled waves on the horizon.

"Who's Mike?" asked Mark in a casual tone of feigned indifference, concerned about competition for her affections. She was ignoring his question, unrelenting in her fixation on the turquoise water, her expression offering no clues about her feelings. Matching her coolness, he turned his gaze to a sailboat heading south on the horizon and took another puff of his high-dollar smoke, still mystified by her immunity to his boyish charms. Determined to get her attention, he thought of yet another approach.

"Wait here," said Mark. "There's something I want to give you." He turned and strode down the steps to the hibiscus hedge nearby, picked a fresh pink blossom and returned to her side. "Here. This is for you, Desiree." Holding the flower so she could admire its delicate beauty, he earned the response he'd been craving. She had a smile as dazzling as the sunrise as she grasped the pink hibiscus with French-manicured nails, but her smile faded far too soon as she returned to her unflinching fixation on the incoming waves.

For a brief moment, she finally dropped her gaze from the horizon and indulged his curiosity. "Mike's my uncle and bodyguard."

Her response surprised him. "Your bodyguard?" asked Mark. More intrigued with her than ever, he wanted to dig deeper, but something on the beach caught his attention.

Their interlude on the walkover was interrupted by a barking dog barreling down the beach dragging his leash, while a slender clean-cut man in white linen shorts and a Navy polo tried to catch up. The man looked exhausted as he stopped to catch his breath with his hands on his knees. The golden retriever was racing toward a flock of gulls that had taken flight, the birds wanting nothing to do with the barking four-legged menace heading in their direction with mayhem on his mind.

"Mitzvah, no!" yelled the man. "Get back here! Mitvah!" Mark remembered meeting the man on the beach in front of the Arroganza two condos further south when the man was walking his retriever last week.

Without warning, Desiree's entire mood suddenly changed. Agitated by the sight of the dog, she pulled out her phone and dialed a three-digit number. Mark could hear the conversation through her speakerphone.

"911. What is your emergency?" asked the female dispatcher.

"Yes! Hi! There's a big vicious dog running loose on our beach illegally and he's coming right at me! Can you send an officer right away?" blurted Desiree with heavy drama. Though the City of Boca Raton was notoriously anal about their ordinances, Mark was thinking that her behavior might be a little over the top for a dog running loose on the beach.

"Desiree, the dog's only playing. Let the guy grab him and take him home, for God's sake," pleaded Mark. "You really think we need the cops?" Ignoring him, she turned her back, determined to incite police action and have the man and his retriever arrested.

"People like that ought to be put away," she said heatedly, "...or publicly flogged at the mall." Confused by her sudden mood shift, he pictured the dog and its owner with their heads and paws sticking out of a locked wooden stockade at Town Center Mall while being flogged by a huge man in a leather mask.

"Ma'am, what's your location?" asked the female dispatcher on the phone.

"1901 S. Ocean Boulevard. Delmar Condos."

"The tall round building that looks like a big gold vibrator?" asked the dispatcher.

"That's it! I'm on the beach walkover. The dog's threatening the birds and everyone on the beach. Please hurry!"

The dispatcher said: "I need your name, honey."

"Desiree. Desiree Stone. I'm on the Board here."

Everyone's on a condo Board in Boca, thought the dispatcher, who wondered just how far astray this particular display of petty condo power would take everyone. After the police radio squawked a few more times in the background, the dispatcher was back on the phone with her condo victim.

"We have a motorcycle officer in the area right now on South Ocean Boulevard, Mrs. Stone. He'll be there in two minutes. Just stay put. I've informed him of your exact location."

"Please hurry," she pleaded. "He's trying to eat everything!" Desiree stood with Mark at the railing watching the dog dispensing all manner of mischief on the beach. The retriever was having a blast scaring an elderly couple who were now hastily leaving the beach and acting like they might need to change their undergarments. The canine continued to gallop after sandpipers and seagulls as the man chased after, yelling commands that were blissfully ignored as he tried in vain to corral his pet.

Then they heard the sounds of a Harley, followed by the approach of measured heavy footsteps on the walkover behind them.

"Mrs. Stone, are you the one that called 911?" asked the muscular officer. With his chiseled face, perfect buzz cut, carefully polished knee-high leather boots, leather cross-strap and custom-tailored uniform, the motorcycle cop looked like he'd just stepped out of a photo shoot at GQ Magazine. Mark recognized him from the gym and stepped forward.

"Hey, Rod. It's Mark McAllister from Gold's Gym."

A flicker of recognition passed over the officer's face. "Oh, yeah, with the development firm," said Officer Rodman as they did a fist bump. "How's it hangin'?"

Temporarily forgetting she was in mortal fear of her life, Desiree removed her sunglasses and smiled seductively, making no effort to hide her overt pleasure with Officer Rodman's appearance. "I'm *Miss* Stone," said Desiree in a melodic voice, redirecting the officer's attention. "*I* was the one who called. I got bitten by a dog last summer and had to have cosmetic surgery," she explained. Giving him her profile, she puckered her lips. "Whaddya think?" she asked.

"Gorgeous, Miss Stone," said Officer Rodman, quite captivated by her beauty. "Don't worry, we'll handle it from here. Are you two together?" he asked, nodding toward Mark.

"Oh...no, we're just neighbors here at Delmar," explained Mark, stepping back to give his buddy more room to conduct his investigation. He wondered if Desiree suffered from multiple personality disorder. Curious about her choice of a skin-tight pink ski outfit on a hot summer day in Boca beach, Officer Rodman eyed the outfit.

"Here's my card with my number and website," said Desiree, smiling seductively at the officer. "In case you have more questions for me later, officer." Rodman pushed his *Terminator*-style shades up to read the card.

"Stallion Productions?" he asked. "Desiree Stone, Producer/Director. Adult films, huh?" He cocked his head and smiled as he stuck the card in his pocket and pulled out one of his own. "Call me Rod," said the officer. "My direct line at the station is right there."

"Sure, Rod," she responded. "Check out my website with a glass of wine or some of your favorite bath salts tonight. You won't be disappointed," she said with a wink. The officer looked blankly at her before heading down the steps to confront his second big bust of the morning.

Amazed with their off-the-wall conversation, Mark suppressed a twinge of jealousy. He was less concerned about the pitfalls of dealing with Desiree's multiple personalities and ever more curious about uncovering her other secrets.

Descending the stairway, Officer Rodman pointed toward the golden retriever frolicking on the sand. "That the dog you called about, ma'am?"

"Sure is. Oh, thank you so much for taking care of this, Rod," she cooed, pandering to her new-found boy toy, completely fixated on her muscle-bound hero trudging through the sand in ninety-degree heat. Her heart skipped a beat as she admired his leather boots and cross-strap, the motorcycle cop pursuing justice for her, the damsel in distress. Rodman was focused like a laser beam, duty bound on citing the dog's owner as he flipped open his black citation book and pulled out a pen.

Shoulder-to-shoulder with the man in the blue polo and linen shorts, he asked, "Sir, are you aware there's a Boca Raton city ordinance against having dog's on the beach?"

Dr. Yana flashed his celebrity plastic surgeon ID like it was a get-out-of-jail-free card, expecting a warning. Certainly not a citation. "Well, yeah...but I'm Dr. Yana, Cosmetic Surgeon," he said,

"...from the TV show. You may have heard of me. My dog Mitzvah and I live just around the"-

"Well, Dr. Yana, if this is your dog, I'm gonna hafta write you a citation," said Officer Rodman as he dutifully began filling out the ticket. "He's upsetting a lot of folks here," pointing his pen at Desiree watching from above the beach on the walkover. After a short but futile conversation with the no-nonsense officer, the doctor pocketed the ticket and glared over his shoulder at Desiree as he stalked down the beach toward his house.

Done wreaking havoc with the birds and old timers in his path, Mitzvah did what every retriever does following a half hour of romping and disobedient chaos; he followed his master home, expecting more affection, tasty treats, and a nice long nap. And more rib eye steak.

Content with having completed her personal vendetta against the evil dog and his owner, Desiree turned and headed toward her ninth floor condo, pleased that the encounter had uncovered hot new talent for her next adult film production. As he watched the seductive sway of her hips, Mark made up his mind he wasn't going to give her up.

"So Desiree, wait a minute. What about your bodyguard, Mike?" he called out. "He okay with all this?"

"He's out of town 'til next week, working on his new TV show. You know...while the cat's away..." waving her hand over her shoulder, her melodic voice trailing off as she descended the stairs toward their high-rise. Strolling past Officer Rodman's Harley, she smiled as she read his card again. Perfect, she thought. Ascending the steps to the side entrance, she entertained herself with the image of her new-found boy toy in a starring role opposite her in Stallion Production's new erotic presentation of "Beach Cops Gone Wild". It would be a hoot to do a real live Boca motorcycle cop onscreen.

After Officer Rodman had left, Mark was alone on the walkover as he continued to enjoy the last half of his *Cohiba*. With Desiree's departure and his buddy's noisy exit, the motorcycle's loud throaty roar could still be heard reverberating up and down the concrete canyons of Ocean Boulevard. He'd gotten used to hearing the raucous sounds of Harley's running up and down A1A. On Boca Beach, there was never a lack of entertainment.

But there was something about Desiree that aroused a man's most primitive innermost desires. Not quite ready to give her up to his workout buddy, he decided to visit her website and see if he could get an idea of what baked her cake.

⚒

Early the next morning at his waterfront home two blocks west of A1A, Dr. Zane Yana roused his golden retriever before sunrise and fed him a special treat; bite-size chunks of ribeye steak with pieces of Ex-lax wrapped inside. He thought about the dog-hating girl in the pink ski suit who called the cops the day before, anticipating that she'd be up early on the walkover to watch the sunrise. Deciding that she needed a lesson in canine tolerance, the rest of his plan was coming together nicely as he finished his second cup of espresso. He was pleased to see Mitzvah excited about getting up earlier than usual for his special breakfast. The retriever had ferociously gobbled up every last morsel of ribeye steak laced with the laxative. Now, he sat begging for more, licking his chops and pawing his master while his tail thumped the floor expectantly.

"You ready for another romp today, boy?" he asked, scratching the underside of his jowls. The retriever raised his head appreciatively and barked. "Yeah, I'll betcha you are. It's payback time, boy! We are gonna have us some fuuunnnn this morninnn'." In preparation for his early morning beach escapade, the plastic surgeon went over his checklist: hair styled and gelled, check; white linen shorts ironed, check; Under Armour tank top pressed and tucked in just right, check; Mitzvah's leash, check; Armani designer sunglasses, check; Ex-lax digested, check.

Dr. Yana had a feeling this escapade was going to be even more fun than the implants he did for Sofia Viagra in his Boca clinic last year.

⋙⧾⧿⧾⋘

So many fascinating smells that required sniffing! It was heavenly! Mitzvah delighted in the romps on the beach; sunrise, at the edge of the surf, where clearly everything-shells, rocks, crabs, birds, humans, even garbage-was spiked with curious, astonishing new smells that begged for investigation as the sun peeked over the top of the horizon just like yesterday.

While most of the odors that reached his sensitive snout were too weak to reward with more than a half-assed sniff or squirt of pee, a single scent was of particular interest, one that cut through the others that hung in the salty air. Was it a large animal? A human possibly? Mitzvah wanted to tear loose and track it, but his master's hold on the leash held him back.

The fragrance was clearly female, not that of another dog or cat. Nope, definitely not that of a seagull or crab. Scratch raccoon, possum, sand flea, fish, turtle, sandpiper and snake. Absolutely girlish, but unlike any other he encountered before. The kind of aroma that was heavy in the air when his master had made that girl squeal and moan on his leather couch that night. Mitzvah yearned to chase down the feminine creature exuding this intoxicating scent, if only to bedevil it until something better came along.

Up the beach, a bunch of boys carrying flat short boards were laughing and jumping into the surf, and soon Mitzvah was detecting other smells-wax, sunblock, Axe body spray, condoms, alcohol and cigarettes. But it was that intriguing, distinctly female scent hanging in the air that drove him on, reigning supreme in his olfactory senses. He had to find this extraordinary creature!

Mitzvah hunched forward and dug his paws deeper into the sand, gradually, then eased up, testing the tension on his leash. His master hadn't looked up, so Mitzvah did it again, measuring his master's resolve to rein him in, taking the slack out again and preparing for his move. Until all he had left to do was The Bolt-the most reliable escape maneuver ever conceived by a golden retriever. The intoxicating scent grew stronger, filling his nostrils as they neared that big wooden platform with the girl.

This time, it went off without a hitch. Mitzvah charged forward, executing The Bolt perfectly as his tether came loose. He became a golden streak hurtling lustily toward the pungent scent coming from the hysterical girl that wore the pink ski parka. She was acting crazy. *That's* where he remembered the scent! From her! He heard a bunch of bad words from his master, then a series of familiar angry commands as he barreled full speed ahead, no longer restrained by the dragging leash.

Suddenly, Mitzvah felt his bowels clench tightly in the excitement, the familiar spasms in his canine innards becoming too intense to ignore. Unable to hold it in, he stopped and squatted down, forced to heed the mightier call of nature and unload his huge pile of nasty right in front of the girl. She was speechless as she held the phone, a look of horror sweeping over her face. Blissfully, Mitzvah continued to empty his bowels, looking for approval from the girl for his good deed, her exhilarating scent filling his nostrils. It felt wonderful to unload on this beautiful summer morning!

"Good boy, Mitzvah! Good boy!" shouted Dr. Yana, delighted at the sight of his dog pooping so close to the walkover, tickled pink with the timing. Winded from the chase, the cosmetic surgeon tried to catch his breath as he watched Mitzvah unload his monster cargo ten feet from Desiree. A crooked smile crept over his face as he crossed his arms and locked eyes with her.

"Fifteen minutes?" she shrieked, glaring at Dr. Yana. "That's too late! His damn dog is crapping all over our private beach right now!" Angrily, she spun on her heel, shooting daggers at the two trespassers who dared to spoil her sunrise with such vulgarity.

Doctor Yana was enjoying the sheer joy over the turn of events from the day before. Between belly laughs, he yelled, "Now you can tell the Boca cops there's a steaming pile of dog poop on your precious beach! For all you do, this poop's for you!" In a mocking theatrical bow, Dr. Yana gracefully extended his arms like he had just finished a scene from Shakespeare.

Beside herself over the unacceptable police emergency response time, Desiree glared angrily at her antagonist from her perch on the walkover. She turned her back on the bizarre scene and continued to berate the dispatcher on her cell phone. "I don't care if your officers *are* tied up with a five-car accident with fatalities on Glades Road! This is urgent! This guy's dog just crapped all over our condo's private beach! And they're getting away!" A scene from her next video production popped into her head. "Wait. What about Rod, that hunky motorcycle cop? Is he available today?"

"No, ma'am. He's not on today," responded the dispatcher checking the duty roster. "This is Officer Rodman's day off."

"Well that's just great," said Desiree with added sarcasm. "I'm on the board here, and we have a sworn duty to put a stop to this wild dog crap," she explained. "Can you at least give me his cell number?"

"We're not allowed to give out cell numbers, Mrs. Stone, but you can"-

"It's *Miss* Stone."

"Okay, *Miss* Stone," mimicked the dispatcher. "You can leave him a voice mail message if you like. His direct line is"-

"I have it." With no further use for the uncooperative dispatcher, she hung up, outraged by the callous treatment and fully intending to file a complaint with the Chief of Police over the half-assed way they prioritized the allocation of their human resources in the face of her dire emergency.

Certain that a man and his dog couldn't possibly spend more quality time together other than what they'd just shared on this beautiful summer morning, Dr. Yana grabbed the leash and gave Mitzvah a pat on his head.

"C'mon, Mitzvah, wipe your ass and let's get out of here. We're done with Delmar!"

Barking in approval, and feeling five pounds lighter, Mitzvah obediently trotted toward home behind his master as visions of more ribeye steak danced in his head.

FOUR

U sually the testosterone levels in men dropped off in their sixties, slowing their sex drive and making them less inclined to
commit acts of sexual perversion. Then there was sixty-four-year-
old Dyson Stampaugh, who spent much of his day trying to keep a
lid on his unwholesome fantasies. His hormones had gotten him
in trouble before, making even George Michael's infamous sexual
exploits in public restrooms pale in comparison.

Once, as a condition of his probation and a lighter sentence,
Dyson Stampaugh had been ordered by a judge to attend a course
on sexual addictions. The class was made up mostly of young-to-
middle-aged men, although there were women in the group who
had also been arrested for sexual misconduct-the kind of deviant
behavior that interfered with their ability to function normally.

The instructor of the sexual addictions course presented
himself as a psychotherapist trained in the treatment of abnor-
mal sexual behavior, and who was-at one time-addicted to por-
nography. Having once been an offender himself, the therapist
claimed to have an uncanny insight into the mind of sex addicts
from all walks of life.

On the first day of class, he asked everyone to compose a short essay on "What Triggers My Sexual Addiction." While the students were busy writing their stories, Dr. Doff was busy reviewing the stack of file folders that had been sent over from the courthouse. After he familiarized himself with Stampaugh's file, he set it on the edge of his desk for special attention. Disgusted that a white-collar professional of Stampaugh's years would stoop to such perversion, Dr. Doff put down his reading glasses and decided to address the oldest perv in the class first.

"Mr. Stampaugh," he said. "We're going to share our stories with our classmates. Would you mind going first?"

"Well, I'm in the middle of a sentence. Why me?"

"We're going to go in reverse chronological order by age, and you seem like the, ah…well, we would hope, the most mature person here, so please stand and tell us about your addiction."

As he finished writing, Stampaugh managed to buy himself just enough time to end the passage. He set his pen down and stood up, still reluctant to address the class full of fellow sex perverts.

"Now…please share your story with the rest of the class," intoned Dr. Doff.

"It's kinda involved"-

"We have an hour."

"I don't know if the class is gonna like my"-

"Mr. Stampaugh, just tell us why you're here."

"I showed my junk to Arianna Granda when she was sunning herself on Boca Beach", blurted Stampaugh. "I had no idea she was only sixteen," shrugging to the class like he'd forgotten the lines in a school play.

All of Stampaugh's classmates straightened and turned in their seats to study the oldest perv in the class, relieved that there was finally someone who could actually make their own behavior look less onerous by comparison.

"Thank you for sharing, Mr. Stampaugh," said Dr. Doff, trying to hide the disgust he felt for a man in his sixties who would stoop to such twisted behavior. The pride of Boca Raton, Arianna Granda was one of Doff's all-time favorite performers, and to think his innocent, donut-sniffing angel was subjected to such disgusting behavior tormented him to no end.

"Mr. Stampaugh," lectured Doff, "...a person can be so afflicted with sexual addiction that they completely ignore what is socially appropriate. Lust is one of those complicated emotions that can be easy to recognize or buried deeply, so deeply that we fail to recognize it for what it is. That's what makes it so dangerous." He paused to make his point. "You must have had an inappropriate experience with a young girl in your past."

Stampaugh's face brightened in recognition of the unvarnished truth. "My eighteen-year old year old niece. You're saying she's the cause?"

"I'm saying"-

"Laying out by the pool in her skimpy bikini," he complained, "...teasing everyone. What more did I need?" There were sympathetic nods from some of the men in the class as a sort of *comraderie perverte* seemed to emerge in a show of misplaced empathy. Now the class was snickering, and it was Dr. Doff's turn to control his anger.

"Okay, enough," he said, waving his hand. "That is completely inappropriate. We get the picture. Your own niece, Mr. Stampaugh? I won't bother to ask you what you did to encourage her."

Stampaugh sat down and dutifully resumed work on his essay, which Dr. Doff never acknowledged reading, nor did he ever call on him to speak again. At the end of the course, Stampaugh received a certificate for successfully completing the counseling, which he promptly returned to his probation officer at the Palm Beach County Courthouse. His probation officer later commended him on his excellent progress in conquering his sexual addictions, and the authorities considered the matter closed.

A few weeks after stumbling through his addiction course, Stampaugh hired an attorney to expunge the records, paving the way for him to submit his Community Association Manager resume to any condo association in the state without having to explain the charges for lewd and lascivious conduct. To ensure the list of future employers included the most prestigious of Boca's condos, Stampaugh had greased the skids with a few well-placed bribes to certain administrators who had the most influence.

A week later, Stacy Miller, the Community Association Manager for Delmar, was unexpectedly stricken with angina and took an extended medical leave of absence, which allowed Stampaugh to get his foot in the door and submit his resume. After two interviews, he was hired, beating out a field of four other candidates.

Unfortunately, the Delmar Board of Directors had no idea of the quagmire of corruption they were about to fall into.

⚊⚌⚊

On a sunny summer morning at Delmar, Dyson Stampaugh was gloating with his feet propped up on his onyx-topped desk. If only Dr. Doff could see me now, he thought. As the newly-chosen manager, he was anxious to make a killing at the condo, proud of himself for having come such a long way since completing his court-ordered sexual addiction course.

The portly sixty-five year old manager was on the phone with Sarah Glitzsky, the Delmar board president, as she sat at her vanity mirror and applied a generous layer of mascara to her eyelashes. Preparing for her power lunch, the board president was not in the best of moods after catching her son rolling large sticky buds of marijuana into a six inch Philly blunt before leaving for school earlier this morning. Planning to use her condo presidency as a springboard to higher office, the condo president had an irrational fear that her reputation would suffer from adverse publicity and her presidential tenure at Delmar would be unnecessarily tarnished.

"That's right, Dyson," she continued. "Jason said he found it in the condo elevator, and I believe him. Did you do a check of the grounds this morning?"

"Every morning, Sarah. A thorough inspection, and no, there wasn't any pot on our grounds. Have you read this morning's headline in the *Boca News?*"

Sarah paused mid-stroke with her mascara. "Why?"

"Paper says Boca police found twenty-one bales of pot. I'm thinkin' someone here may have come across some of that stuff."

Glitzsky grew concerned. "Dyson, I want you to re-check the grounds. Put Jorge on it, too. We need to be sure we're in the clear. We don't need any adverse publicity. And, for God's sake, we've got to keep it out of my son's hands. Last time he got stoned, he hit a palm tree and wrecked my car. My insurance *tripled*."

Stampaugh responded with a lame imitation of Jim Carey. "All righty, then! I'll do a double check for square groupers!"

"Square groupers?"

"That's what they call 'em Sarah." Given her son's perpetual drug problems, she seemed remarkably naïve about the vernacular, he thought.

Glitzsky changed the subject. "Now, what about those storm window bids. You sure they're right? I don't want to be embarrassed at the meeting, Dyson." Finished with her mascara, she started on her lipstick.

"Yep, those figures are correct, Sarah. I have all the written bids right here in front of me."

"Three million for hurricane-proof electric storm shutters?" she asked. "Really, Dyson? What are they, gold-plated or something? Shouldn't we get another bid?"

"Well, they're motorized, they exceed the latest Florida wind damage specifications, built to resist the salt air, and they come with a twenty-five year unconditional replacement guarantee." Stampaugh could tell she was stressed out about the bid and would need a little more coaxing, so he sweetened the pot for her. "I've already taken care of preparing two higher, uh...*bids* for the board, and Steinberg Storm Windows *is* certified by the state of Florida. Oh, by the way, the owner did say they could be pretty generous to the key players who, uh...*agree* to his bid."

Glitzsky paused for a few moments as she pondered the idea of a large bribe coming her way. "*How* generous?" she asked.

"One percent apiece," said Stampaugh, knowing full well that Steinberg would go as high as five percent to snag the job.

Glitzsky thought for a moment. She was still bitter over being forced from her lucrative management post at FEMA years ago when the scandal erupted over charges of government corruption during the Hurricane Sandy cleanup. Now, she was desperate to replace the lost income and really didn't much care how she did it. Three million dollars was a big construction contract, and she figured there had to be some fluff in it.

"Tell him to make it two percent and we've got a deal," said Glitzsky. "I'm gonna have to pony up to put my son back in rehab."

Stampaugh paused. "I think I can get that done, Sarah, but where do Stone, Anatolla and Wasserman stand on this? Do we need to worry about their votes?"

After surviving the previous board president, Stampaugh had prided himself in his ability to manipulate condo board members who lacked sufficient experience in condo drama and political subterfuge. Smirking, he re-crossed his feet, knowing the contractor would agree and still secretly pay him his eighty grand bonus. Knowing Anthony Anatolla and Desiree Stone usually voted with Glitzsky on major contracts, Stampaugh continued to let her think she was in control.

"They're both on board for five grand each. Cash," said Glitzsky. "I spoke to Desiree yesterday, and as long as we let her continue to shoot her adult videos inside her condo, she'll vote with me on anything. Wasserman's in it for five grand, and Anatolla's still undergoing treatment for prostate cancer"-

"Yeah, I heard he's having a rough time"-

"Better for us 'cuz that Vicodin makes him *sooo* agreeable," said Glitzsky with cold indifference. "Thank God for hydrocodone," she added, smiling to herself. "That stuff mellows him out like you wouldn't believe."

"Just so he lives long enough to cast his vote. Right?" he replied, matching her callousness. He could hear her chuckling in the background. Stampaugh had been at odds with Anatolla ever since the manager refused to support the vice-president's bid to install concealed cameras in the ladies restrooms under the guise of security.

"The votes are in the bag on this one, Dyson. If you want to continue riding the gravy train at Delmar, make sure we get paid on our deal. All of it. They can damn sure afford it," she said emphatically. She didn't have to remind him that most of the residents were multi-millionaires and trust fund babies.

"You can take it to the bank. I'll bring all the bids to the meeting next Wednesday." Stampaugh uncrossed his legs and leaned forward in his chair, looking to wind things up. "Anything else, Sarah?"

"Yeah. Promise me you'll make sure there's no pot lying around our private beach and common areas from that drug shipment. We definitely don't need the publicity, and I can't afford to let Jason get his hands on any more dope." With a flourish, she finished applying her lipstick.

"Okay. Promise I'll take care of it, Sarah." As they hung up, Stampaugh tried to contain his giddiness over putting himself in scoring position for the monster kickback. As he stamped his feet in childish glee, his secretary knocked on the door and stuck her head in. Maria was a dead-ringer for the Columbian actress Sophia Viagra, and always a welcome interruption for him.

"Dyson, Carol Nutter is here to see you. About her fine." Maria watched for some flicker of recollection on her boss's face as he continued to fantasize about what color of new Corvette he was going to buy himself. It took him a moment to shift gears and recall what he'd said in the voicemail he'd left for her a few days ago.

"Oh...yeah, okay. Give me sixty seconds, then bring her in."

"You got it, boss." With her husband currently out of work, and her expired green card and questionable employment status as a Columbian national, Maria Diaz was doggedly loyal to her boss and completely dependent on his good graces. As a result, she turned a blind eye to all of his philandering, legal or not. Her Customs and Immigration hearing was coming up next month and Maria needed him in her corner to sign off on her application for permanent resident status.

Stampaugh couldn't help obsessing with the image of Carol Nutter reclining in her lounger at the condo pool as he checked his toupee in the mirror, straightened his tie, dabbed his eyebrows, and took a shot of Binaca before standing to greet his attractive guest.

"Okay, Maria, have her come in."

As she stepped in, he extended his hand. "Carol, you look ravishing today. C'mon in. Have a seat." Stampaugh took her hand and raised it toward his lips, but she withdrew it before he could plant a kiss.

"How are you, Dyson?" Always uncomfortable with his creepiness, she wanted to get right to the point of her visit and get out fast. "Your message said you had an idea about how we could make my five hundred dollar fine go away. Whole thing's kinda ridiculous if you ask me," she said, rolling her eyes. She sat down in one of the suede chairs and crossed her tanned athletic legs expectantly. Stampaugh was so taken with her leather skirt and halter top that he stumbled and almost missed planting his ponderous rear end in the office chair behind him.

From across the table, Carol appraised Stampaugh as if he were a silly comic book character. His hands danced back and forth like a mime and his mouth was moving, but nothing he said was reaching her ears. She evaluated the pot-bellied manager with the reddish-brown eyebrows that didn't match his cheesy toupee. He had a crooked, skeptical smile, and a nose that seemed too small for his roundish baby face. Apprehensive after hearing rumors about how he liked to trade his managerial influence for sexual favors, she'd already resigned herself to some unwanted attention. Then, his voice faded back in as she refocused on the words that seemed to emphasize his impish face and animated gestures.

"...and so, Carol, the board considers drinking bottled beer at the condo pool a finable offense," he was saying, "...and, unfortunately, this is your third fine in less than two months. I'm just doin' my job, dear."

She paused, looking for cracks in his facade. "C'mon, Dyson. Drinking a beer at the pool? Really? What will they fine me for next? Drinking milk a day past its expiration date? Floating an air biscuit?" she asked. Stampaugh smirked.

"Okay. What's it gonna take to make this ridiculous fine go away?" Irritated with his twisted agenda, Carol was looking to turn the tables. Her feminine intuition told her he was after something of a more personal nature.

He stood up and closed the door. In a low voice he said, "Well, Carol, I was...uh...thinking maybe we could have a drink at your place, maybe spend some private"-

"I think I know what you want, Dyson," she said flatly, "...and *that* isn't going to happen." She was having a tight month with her finances, and for five hundred bucks, she decided to work with the creep. "Look. I'm a manager and senior designer at Venus Sportswear, and I've got to think about my future there-as well as my professional reputation." Stampaugh looked disappointed, and she knew she had to throw him a bone.

"Tell ya what I *can* do, though." She leaned forward invitingly and uncrossed her legs to keep him interested. "Get rid of these silly fines and I'll, ah...I'll give you a backstage pass to our next swimwear show at The Boca Resort and Club next week. But no lap dances." Stampaugh's eyes lit up, and she was already having regrets about her offer. Carol raised her finger. "But, on the condition that you behave yourself, young man. No funny stuff."

Although the idea of sharing her models with Dyson Stampaugh creeped her out, she gave out fashion show passes to eligible bachelors all the time, but usually drew the line at lecherous old men. This time, it would save her enough money to make her BMW payment. She forced herself to smile and extended her hand. "We got ourselves a deal here?"

"Okay, Miss Nutter, ya got yourself a deal," he said.

Carol prepared to leave, still a little skeptical that Stampaugh would behave himself. "Look Dyson," she reiterated, "...my derriere is on the line here. You better behave yourself backstage." Stampaugh nodded sheepishly, staring at the very same referenced derrier as she stood with her hand on the doorknob.

"Oh...and let's leave all the little spy cameras home, too," she intoned. "No pictures. We don't need to see any of this on You Tube or your Facebook site, right Dyson? Like I said, I've got a professional career to think about."

Preferring to stay seated to conceal his growing excitement, Stampaugh nodded again in acceptance of her conditions as she flounced out of his office. Both were confident they'd struck a good deal.

"Maria, bring me some coffee, will ya honey?" he shouted through the open door. "And get me David Steinberg on the phone."

⊷⊶

Mark stared out his third floor office at the couple sitting on the edge of the fountain below. It was mid-afternoon as he watched them laughing and taking photos, and he thought about the last time he and Christa sat in the same spot one evening and shared a kiss. It was more than a fond memory. The foot massage he gave her and their amorous weekend together had been a prelude to her acceptance of his marriage proposal two weeks later.

Mark left his daydream behind and shifted his attention to his conversation. He was on the phone with a former roommate from his University of Miami days. As the CEO of a new budding medical marijuana dispensary that was ready to go public, his buddy Dave was anxious to score an unbelievable deal on a bale of pot that somehow had magically appeared on Boca Beach recently. Mark's former college roommate was doing his best to try and characterize the bale of buds as "difficult to move", but he wasn't buying it.

"How much weight ya got there, bro?" asked Dave, dabbing his toe in the pool behind his twenty room Tuscan-style villa overlooking Biscayne Bay.

Mark hesitated. Dave used to have connections with the Mexican cartels and he was a little unsure of how much detail he should share. "How much weight can you handle, Dave?" After hearing about his company's pending I.P.O., he knew cash wouldn't be an issue.

"Well, how much will twenty-five grand buy me?" countered Dave.

"Twenty-five pounds."

Dave sighed. Sounding disappointed, he said, "C'mon, Mark. You *found* the damn stuff. A grand a pound is hardly a wholesale price. How 'bout a break for your old college bud?"

"Look, I put my butt on the line," he reminded his former roommate. Now he wanted all the money on the table. "If you can handle all of it, Davie boy, I'd let ya have all hundred pounds for sixty-five grand. Work's out to six-fifty a pound. How's that for a giveaway, once-in-a-lifetime deal at wholesale prices?"

"And you said it's all buds, right?"

"Yup. A hundred percent pure, super-sticky, resin-soaked buds," said Mark, knowing he was describing a dream come true. "Worth every penny of sixty-five grand, Dave. You can easily triple your money." He had a hunch that Dave wanted all of it, so he forced himself to be patient.

"Forty-five grand," said Dave. "That's it. Take it or leave it."

Mark thought about it and smiled. "Tell ya what, Dave. Since we're college buds, Hurricane fans and all, and you were about the only friend who *didn't* come on to my ex, I'll meet you halfway. Make it fifty-five large. Otherwise, I've got two more calls to make here." Mark held his breath. It was a bluff; he'd already made the two calls and had come up empty handed.

Dave sat upright in his pool lounger as he calculated making four times his investment. This time, he didn't hesitate. "Done. I'll pick it up tonight."

"Cash, of course. Can you make it small bills? Tens and twenties?" asked Mark.

"What're you, Al Capone? Sure," said Dave. "Might be a few fifties in there," figuring he had enough time to stop off at four or five of his family's Public Storage facilities to pick up the cash. It was Thursday afternoon, and the coffers should be full. Plus, he had programmed the combinations to every safe in the chain right into his cell phone.

"Eight o'clock work for you, bro?"

"Eight works fine. You remember how to get here, right?"

"Yeah. Same place you had that crazy pool party for your ex-wife. Delmar, wasn't it? The one that looks like a big gold, uh... vibrator? You're in the penthouse at the end of the hall."

"Considering how wasted you were at the party, ya got a pretty good memory there, pal. Penthouse Eight. You're coming alone, right?"

"I might bring my cousin Eddie to help"-

Mark remembered that Eddie suffered from a severe case of uncontrolled flatulence and had driven all his guests out of the hot tub at his last party. "Dave, do me a favor and leave Eddie in the car. Just bring three of those really large suitcases with wheels. I'll see you at eight," said Mark.

"All right. Eddie can stay in the car. See you at eight."

Mark hung up and did a big fist pump. "Yes!" he shouted out loud, drawing the attention of his secretary, Miranda. He gave her a big thumbs up through the glass to reassure her everything was fine, ecstatic at the thought of what he could do with his new-found play money. Fifty-five large and tax free should take care of fuel, insurance and maintenance on his forty-four foot twin-engine cat-amaran "Multiple Ohhhs…" for the next few years. Unless he ran over another floating oak pallet like he did last summer.

With his square grouper deal almost behind him, Mark was as eager as ever to get out on the beach at sunrise for his morning runs, always amazed at what the tide would bring.

FIVE

Wherever he was introduced, people remembered meeting Mike Rosenberg. With the body of a lean Bulgarian weight lifter, Big Mike was a statuesque six-foot seven and three hundred twenty-five pounds. He spent ten hours a week working out at the gym, and his physique hadn't changed much since he boxed professionally in the heavy weight division twenty years ago. With a ruggedly handsome face that carried the reminders of every glove that cut him, his thick forehead, chiseled facial features and imperfect nose had borne the brunt of many a fighter's punch. After twenty-five years around the ring, his experiences had sculpted him into the successful fight promoter that he'd come to be. His brawny physique also made him an intimidating body guard for his niece, Desiree Stone.

It was midday on a sunny afternoon at the Delmar pool, and Big Mike was nursing a hangover. Lounging at the condo pool with his laptop, he was busy conjuring up some new scenes for his Spike TV reality fight show he named *My Family's Greatest Hits*. For scrappy preschoolers, his staff had proposed the spin-off of a less violent, sanitized version called *KOs For Kids*, and his teleplay writer was preparing it for debut on Nickelodeon next month. When Big Mike had questioned the viability of the spin-off, the writer explained that networks were so hungry for content that quality was often irrelevant. So far, he'd been right. As he straddled the lounger with his laptop between his knees, Mike noticed their ponderous board president waddling in his direction and wearing what looked like a clear shower curtain painted with cheap gold-leaf fish.

"Hey, Big Mike. Soakin' up some rays there, huh?" Glitzsky inquired loftily in an effort to ameliorate him after their last confrontation over multiple rule infractions. The self-appointed condo queen of rules was conducting her rounds in the daily inspection of her kingdom as she held court among her subjects, some loyal, and some not so much. She noticed Mrs. Palumbo standing in the pool reading the paper. Without waiting for Mike to answer, Glitzsky went over and confronted her with her hands on her hips.

"Mrs. Palumbo! Some of our residents complain that you don't get out of the pool when you hafta go. Please make sure and use the restroom when you swim in the pool." Shocked, Mrs. Palumbo looked up from beneath her floppy hat and sunglasses.

"Whatever are you talking about, Sarah?" she asked indignantly. "See if you get *my* vote next time you're up for president." Haughty over the president's insinuation, Palumbo pulled a purple plastic wrist bracelet out of the pocket in her suit with the letters "DNR" on it. "Here, why don't you join our DNR club?" handing it to Glitzsky.

Glitzsky looked puzzled. "What's DNR?" she asked.

"Do not resuscitate!" she said loud enough for others to hear. Palumbo stood in the pool grinning as the intended insult sank in.

"Whatevah," responded Glitzsky, tossing the bracelet back to her. Looking for someone new to pounce on, her gaze drifted back to Big Mike on his lounger as the portly president continued toward him, stopping at the foot of his lounger. "Nice cap. Nike, right?"

Mike decided to have some fun with his favorite antagonist. He removed his cap and pretended to check the spelling of "Nike" on the front.

"Oh, this?" pointing at the lettering. "Well, no…actually, it was custom ordered and they misspelled my name, so I didn't have to pay for it," said Mike straight-faced, testing her gullibility. An older man two chairs down chuckled in amusement. Mike thought he had her for a moment as she crossed her arms, clearly not amused as she misinterpreted his condescending humor as a demeaning shot at her fashion sensibilities. As a lifelong J.C. Penney's Gold Card member, Glitzsky was pretty certain she knew what high fashion was all about.

"Yeah, good one," she replied under her breath as she turned to walk away, secretly wishing Big Mike had been born with a mute button. Her desire to retaliate took center stage as she turned to square off with him again, this time shaking her index finger at him contentiously.

"Don't forget to shower before entering the pool. And you need to put a towel down over your lounge chair. And, don't forget, no wet bathing suits will be worn in the clubhouse." As if those rules weren't enough to digest, she added, "And you know shirts are required in all common areas. These are the rules here at Delmar, Mr. Rosenberg."

"Wow. Think you got enough of them?" he responded. The heat and perspiration were making Glitzsky's mascara run as she dabbed at it with a Kleenex, causing it to smear. Mike thought it made her look like a character from *Walking Dead*. Always jealous of Big Mike's popularity, she welcomed any opportunity to cut him down to size. After laying down the law, she turned on her heel to complete her inspection of the grounds, a flash of gold-leaf-on-plastic in the sun.

"Are we allowed to fart?" shouted Big Mike as the condo president continued her pompous stroll. Ignoring his taunt, she made her way toward a group of supporters more sympathetic to her cause. Annoyed with all the petty rules, Big Mike made a face behind her back that most third-graders would've been proud of as the condo president continued on her queenly stroll. She conveniently chose to overlook Mr. Paulen sitting in his lounger and chugging on a liter bottle of Cuervo Gold at the far side of the pool. A big supporter of Glitzsky's, Paulen liked to tell everyone that glasses and cups were for sissies.

The portly president's gaze fell on senior condo resident Myron Schlotzsky, passed out on the lounger as he blissfully snored away. At first, she was put off by the sight of Mr. Schlotzsky's privates peeking out the sides of his bathing suit in full view of everyone at the pool. The sight reminded her of the time her son's pet snake had escaped from his cage and had found its way into her bed one night, scaring the crap out of her.

"Myron...Myron, wake up," shaking him by the shoulder. "Tuck yourself in, for God's sake," she pleaded. "Your anaconda's getting away."

A startled Myron Schlotzsky came to life. "What? Oh, sorry Sarah," he said apologetically. Red faced, Myron tucked himself back in as he looked sheepishly around the pool. Ever the enforcer, Glitzsky stood over him with her hands on her hips, eager to make sure that Myron had put his toys away. Widowed years ago, it had been a long time since Glitzsky had experienced intimacy, and the unexpected sight of a man so well-endowed made her momentarily yearn for fulfillment.

Giving in to temptation, Glitzsky leaned over and whispered in Myron's ear. "Myron, if you ever wanna give that monster a good work out, call me," winking at the speechless man.

Witnessing the bizarre encounter from the other side of the pool, a disgusted Mike Rosenberg winced and refocused his attention on his laptop. Hard at work editing his teleplay, he was oblivious to the condo dwellers drifting past him as they looked for an empty pool lounger to settle into in their search for sunlight strong enough to cultivate their next group of squamous cells. An attractive middle-aged woman in a bikini and floppy hat caught his eye as she sashayed toward him. Delighted to see him out by the pool again, she gave Mike a big smile.

"Hi, Mike", said the shapely woman as she took the lounger next to his and spread her towel out. Peering out from under a huge floral beach hat that matched her bikini, she extended her hand to him and smiled. "It's Lillian...Lillian Peltz...from that wild cookout last week. How are you?" fluttering her eyelashes flirtatiously. Big Mike looked up, a little confused, unable to recall the event. "You were showing me the video clips of your TV shows from your phone and licking chip dip off my belly. Remember?"

"Oh, yeah...Mrs. Peltz...good to see you again," said Mike, trying hard to recall if he'd done anything really embarrassing. "Sorry, a little distracted...working on some new scenes to my TV series." He remembered he'd had a lot to drink that night and hoped he hadn't said anything too terribly indecent.

"Sure, go right ahead, honey." Lillian smiled and made herself comfortable on her lounger as she stretched out and slathered sun tan oil over herself. Thinking that perhaps her hint had been too subtle, she glanced furtively at Big Mike and continued smoothing the oil suggestively over her legs.

"Ever since my husband passed away last summer," she said, "...I've been hoping to find someone with strong hands to do this for me. Murray didn't like getting his hands greasy," she explained. "He said it made it hard to hang onto his walker."

"Uh huh," responded Mike absentmindedly, eyes still focused on his laptop as he reworked one of the scenes. Desirous of his full attention, Lillian was getting flustered, now more determined than ever to become the focus of his fantasies. After all, she was an attractive widow with a great body and healthy libido. Why shouldn't she be able to have some fun with a big strong man? Murray sure as hell wasn't going to give her what she needed, buried under two tons of granite at Beth El Mausoleum.

"So, Mike, do you think it's unusual for a doctor to fondle a woman's breasts during an examination?" she asked.

Big Mike was slowly warming up to her and went with the flow, entertained by her creativity and her unquenched need for his attention. "Well, yeah, unusual if he's a podiatrist," he quipped. "Why? Did your doctor cop a feel, Mrs. Peltz?"

"Yeah, that's what I'm trying to tell you, Mike. I think he's a perv." She smiled mischievously. "I gotta admit, though, I kinda liked it."

"Ya goin' back for another check-up?" Mike was enjoying teasing her as he pretended not to be interested, preoccupied with the video edit app on his laptop.

"Dear, dear Mike. Since you've slurped chip dip off my belly, I think you know me well enough to call me Lillian." She continued applying a heavy coat of sun tan lotion on her legs in exaggerated strokes, hoping she wouldn't have to spell it out. When she was sufficiently oiled up, she reclined on the lounger, getting more comfortable and covering her face with her floppy hat. To ensure she had his full attention, she pressed her finger tips suggestively against her bikini bottom. In a sultry voice she said, "Let me know when you're ready to get wild with that chip dip again, Big Mike. It was the most fun I've had since my kids spilled Murray's ashes on the floor at the Haagen Dazs store."

Not sure if he'd heard her correctly, Big Mike stopped in mid-keystroke to study her. She'd finally succeeded in getting his full attention. He paused to admire her glistening body stretched out on the lounger, thinking *crazy was the price of that ride*. Amused with her idea, he decided to play along. "Uh…sure, Lillian. And here I thought cougars were an endangered species. What flavor chip dip do you like, honey?"

"Guacamole," she said in a muffled voice from under her hat. "It's on sale this week at Publix. Two for one."

Mike chuckled. Women and their two-for-ones. "Bet you even have a brand in mind-like maybe, what? Chernobyl Farms? You know, for that after dinner glow that never fades?"

"Yeah, sure. We could serve it up with the four-pound Three Mile Island scallions," quipped Lillian. Impressed with her wit, Big Mike made a mental note to add guacamole dip to his shopping list, certain that he wouldn't find Lillian's suggested use of the condiment anywhere on the container.

After a few minutes, he closed his laptop to take a quick dip in the pool. Feeling rebellious after his testy conversation with their president, he purposely skipped the required shower. Secretly, he hoped the old battle axe was still hovering around somewhere in her garish gold-leaf shower curtain. Stretching for his swim, Mike was thinking his private little rebellion against condo rules just might take root. Maybe a little revolution from time-to-time *was* a good thing, he thought.

In a willful and wanton violation of the regulations that prohibited diving, Big Mike dove in and swam a few laps, feeling a new-found effervescence in his defiance of the condo queen's heavy handedness. As he waved at a couple across the pool, he began to feel the inevitable pressure building in his bladder from the three beers he had earlier. Stepping out of the pool dripping wet, shoeless and shirtless, he headed for the men's room in the clubhouse to heed the call of nature. Pleased with himself, he was shooting for a new record, on his way to his sixth condo rule violation in less than thirty minutes. But who was counting? He was on a roll, feeling his oats, and badly in need of bladder relief.

After entering the code on the key pad, he pulled the clubhouse door open and stepped inside the air conditioned room, letting his eyes adjust to the darkened interior.

"Not so fast, Mr. Rosenberg!" Glitzsky stood at the entry to the billiard room ten feet away, glaring at him with her hands on her hips like a burly traffic cop waiting to corner a robbery suspect. She launched into her abrasive reprimand. "Didn't I *just* remind you of our rules here a few minutes ago? No wet bathing suits are allowed in the clubhouse! Where's your shoes and shirt? Have you no respect for our condo rules here, Mr. Rosenberg?"

Big Mike scowled at her. He was sick and tired off all the silly rules at Delmar. She'd gotten on his last nerve, completely annoyed with her constant haranguing. "No wet bathing suits in the clubhouse, huh?" he retorted angrily.

"Them's the rules, Mr. Rosenberg," she replied heatedly, "and you damn well know it."

"Screw your petty-ass rules," countered Big Mike angrily as he jerked his bathing suit down to his ankles, pulled it off and kicked it across the room where it lodged in the branches of the silk ficus tree standing next to Glitzsky.

Horrified, she stared incredulously at his wet bathing suit hanging only inches from her nose, gasping at his outrageous act. Turning beet red, she shrieked, "Mr. Rosenberg! How dare you, you, you," stammering at the sight of the muscular, well-endowed man standing in front of her with nothing on, "...you naked gorilla!"

Big Mike grabbed his manhood and held it out in front of him as he strutted past her toward the men's room. "You know what your problem is, Glitzsky? Your mother had one of *these*!" he blurted.

"Oh, for God's sake, Mr. Rosenberg! How dare you! You think you're too pretty for jail? I'm calling the Boca police!" With that, Glitzsky bounded for the clubhouse door to find someone at the pool with a cell phone, catching her garish cover-up in the door. As she yanked on it to pull it loose, Big Mike made his escape.

Not wanting to stick around for the cops to show, Big Mike vaulted for the men's room to finish what he came inside to do, stopping first to retrieve his swimsuit from the ficus tree. Half hopping and half stumbling down the hallway, he struggled to get his feet back into his bathing suit. Desperate to pull it up and cover his privates before anyone else entered the clubhouse, he wobbled on one leg while struggling to get the other foot through the opening as he pushed the men's room door open. A shocked Al Wasserman stood at the sink, watching Big Mike in the mirror as he hopped naked into the men's room with one leg in his bathing suit.

"A little wardrobe malfunction with your suit there, Big Mike?" he asked calmly.

"Oh, hey, Al. Yeah…I think I got it on backwards." Embarrassed, Big Mike hopped into the nearest stall and shut the door, thankful that Al had not witnessed his balls-out confrontation with Glitzsky a few moments earlier.

"Hey, while you're gettin' your suit straightened out there, big guy, when's your new TV show start?" asked Wasserman with his face in the mirror as he doted over his thinning hair.

Big Mike answered through the partition, casually draining his distended bladder as if nothing had happened. "Spike TV's got us programmed for their new season line-up starting in September. We just inked a deal with Nickelodeon for the spinoff called *KOs For Kids*. That one starts in October," he added, tucking himself back into his swimsuit.

Unfazed by the big guy's wardrobe fiasco, Wasserman thought for a moment. "You know, Mike, we need a guy like you on the board here. Have you thought about running? A celebrity like you would be a shoe-in."

"Thanks for the thought, Al. I might, if I could stand being in the same room with that over-stuffed pompous condo queen of ours." Big Mike smiled, pleased with himself, picturing the shocked look on her face as she came face-to-face with his swimsuit hanging in the ficus tree.

"I hear ya, Mike. Folks on our floor call her 'Your Immenseness'". Wasserman chuckled. "She seems incapable of understanding the basic arithmetic of our condo's budget statements." Wasserman checked his hair again in the mirror, looking for new sprouts and any signs the Rogaine might be kicking in.

Big Mike tied off the drawstring on his swimsuit as he emerged from the stall. Standing shoulder-to-shoulder with Wasserman at the bathroom counter, he cocked his head and smiled at his friend in the mirror. "Yeah, just a wee wardrobe malfunction."

"Yeah, good one, Mike." Wasserman deliberated for a moment as he continued to fuss with his disappearing hairline in the mirror. "Hey," said Wasserman, "...you hear the one about the ninety-year old vet that just completed a bunch of lab tests at the VA? The doc says to 'em, 'Got some bad news for you, and some more bad news. Bad news is you have terminal cancer, and you're gonna die soon.' The vet curses, then he says 'What's the other bad news?' Doc says, 'You have Alzheimer's, too.' The vet thinks for a minute, rubs his chin and says, 'Well, at least I don't have cancer.'"

Big Mike chuckled. "C'mon, Al, let's grab a beer. I hear they don't allow drinking by the pool either."

⚞✛✛⚟

Mark's feet glided swiftly over the beach as he reminded himself this was the day they poured the footers for the new ten floor office building at Mizner Park. Over the past week, he'd watched the construction crew from his third-floor office ready the huge footers as they prepared for the fresh concrete going in today. Stepping around the larger shells and pieces of coral that were in his path like he was on autopilot, he thought about what else was on tap for the day.

His reverie was interrupted by the English bulldog that came galloping out of nowhere. The barking dog sped past him, then turned back, clearly wanting to play. Mark stopped to say hello and squatted down to make a new friend, petting him behind the ears as his tail wagged excitedly.

"Hey big boy, watcha' up to today?" He looked up to see a scruffy-looking middle-aged man with a beard wearing tattered cargo shorts, tank top, shades and a floppy fishing hat trudging toward him in the sand.

"This your dog?" asked Mark as the bulldog jumped up on two legs, tail wagging, looking for more attention. The man nodded. "What's his name?" asked Mark.

"His name's Dub, short for Doubloon," said the man, looking down the beach. "He's missing his buddy, Butch." The man paused, seeming to recognize Mark. "Ya know, I see you running past my house here almost every day," he said as he watched Dub barrel down the beach after a group of sandpipers.

"Part of my triathlon training. I'm Mark," he said, extending his hand. The word 'doubloon' triggered the memory of a news article he'd recently read in the local paper.

"David. David Callahan," said the man, shaking Mark's hand. The man removed his sun glasses for their introduction. Mark was spooked by his eyes, the black, lifeless eyes of a shark. Mark diverted his gaze, looking down the beach like he hadn't noticed.

"Is Butch that brown French bulldog I always see Dub running with in the morning?" asked Mark.

"Yeah," said Callahan somberly, slipping his glasses back on. "You have a good memory for details, Slick." He lowered his head sadly and dragged his toe in the sand. "Somebody took him from the beach behind our house last week." Mark had often run past the two bulldogs as they romped on the beach together like a canine tag team.

Being called "Slick" bugged him, but Mark let it slide. "Hey, sorry to hear that. Think I saw the article in the paper. I'll keep an eye out for him," offered Mark. There was something else that was oddly familiar about Callahan that he couldn't quite put his finger on. "That your house up on the dune there?" pointing at the huge stone and terracotta villa. There was a large bamboo double swing positioned on the edge of the dune. "That's the old Greenwood Mansion, right?"

"That's what the locals call it. My girlfriend and I rented the old house a few years back. I like getting up early and taking photos of the sunrise from up there," he said, gesturing at the swing at the top of the dune. "We upload the photos on a blog post on the net. I've been doing that for a few months, just for fun."

"What's your site called?" asked Mark.

"BocaGlitSea, spelled s-e-a."

"Catchy." Actually, Mark thought it was a little lame. "I'll take a look at your site when I finish my run," he said diplomatically.

Callahan was curious about his new-found friend. "What do you like about running so much?" he asked Mark.

Mark felt like messin' with him a bit, testing his sense of humor. "Well, I'd rather walk seven miles on the beach than run for office," quipped Mark. Callahan continued to look at him blankly, his face devoid of humor.

"Yeah, well...photography's just a hobby," said Callahan. "I like collecting guns even more."

Mark was growing more curious about the man who lived at Greenwood Mansion. "What kind of guns do you collect?" he asked.

Callahan was proud of his assault rifles. "Got a couple of AK-47s, two AR-15s with night scopes, and a fifty caliber Barrett. A man can't be too careful." Relishing the momentary look of fear on Mark's face, Callahan was well-practiced in concealing the fact that he was a demonic soul who, for many years, had managed to blend in quite well in Boca.

The strange man who collected assault rifles looked down the beach for Dub. The bulldog was now busy scaring the wildlife as he romped on the beach, first chasing down a flock of seagulls, then a couple of ghost crabs. He whistled loudly. "Dub, get back here! C'mon, boy!"

"Well, David, nice meeting you and Dub. Hope you find Butch. Those two dogs belong together." He squinted at the beach ahead.

"Got five more miles to go, so gotta run." A little skittish with his new acquaintance, Mark felt like putting some distance between them.

"Literally, right? See you again, Slick."

There it was, calling him "Slick" again. Mark thought about this and the missing French bulldog. The man's preoccupation with assault rifles bugged him, especially with the cold, black lifeless eyes. He decided to keep his feelings to himself until he could vet this guy.

Mark bolted past Dub like a hundred meter sprinter, egging on the dog. The bulldog turned and gave chase, nipping playfully at Mark's heels before Callahan whistled him back again. As Mark's stride slowed to a more measured pace, the scruffy-looking man's image with the black lifeless eyes surfaced again in his mind. He made a mental note to google the article about a fugitive treasure hunter when he returned to his condo. Before he could give it any more thought, he was distracted by a gorgeous brunette in a yellow bikini standing on the beach looking his way. He picked up his pace in anticipation of an introduction.

—⟩⟨—⟨⟩—

Ten years ago, no one in Boca seemed to know who Tommy Tomlinson was. But real estate agent Lance Meyer knew he could count on a once-a-month visit from his strangest customer ever. Going by the name David Callahan since he absconded with all the loot, the treasure hunter was one of the most wanted fugitives in the country.

To keep a low profile, Callahan liked to ride his black and beige Nel Lusso beach cruiser to drop off the $5,000 rent he paid for the beachfront villa. For years, he and his girlfriend Andrea rented the Greenwood Mansion from Mr. Brinkerhoff, Meyer's client. Callahan had first contacted Brinkerhoff the year before the last big hurricane, and the eccentric real estate magnate had referred the inquiry to his agent at Nautilus Realty. Nautilus had the rustic mansion listed for lease ever since Brinkerhoff bought it four years before the destructive hurricane had hit, well before the fugitive had selected it as an ideal place to hole up. Lucky for Callahan, it was vacant when he called.

Callahan could always be seen wearing his tattered khaki cargo shorts on the short bicycle ride to drop off the moldy cash at Nautilus Realty. With his scruffy beard and slight build, he worked hard to look like the proverbial beach bum as he pulled up on his beach cruiser to pay his rent.

But he wasn't just a beach bum.

Over the last thirteen years, many of his adversaries had met an untimely "accidental" death, and their demise was often shrouded in mystery. Now their voices were silenced, unable to speak of the horrific injustices associated with the $170 million cache of gold that he would do anything to protect.

Few knew the origin of the money, a huge stash of gold recovered from a shipwreck resting in 3,000 feet of water. It was a bold salvage mission that had focused on a U.S. documented vessel that went down in a savage hurricane off the Carolina coast in September of 1857. In a deal arranged by a major Wall Street banking group, Callahan had sold the pure gold bullion he recovered for a cool $70 million to a precious metals dealer in New York and decided to hang onto the $100 million in rare gold coins for their numismatic value. His colossal windfall triggered a series of tangled civil law suits that he avoided by hiding and staying on the run, always one step ahead of the law.

In one of those tangled suits, a circuit court judge in Illinois issued a bench warrant for the treasure hunter's arrest, and the state police had placed his photograph on a billboard advertisement portraying him as a fugitive. As soon as Callahan had heard about the warrant, probably from his attorney in Illinois who called him on his burner cell phone, he left the state in a big hurry with Andrea. He took the rest of his millions in cash and gold coins with him and left behind grocery bags full of cash wrappers, all marked 'Federal Reserve Bank of Miami-$100 bills', with the cash wrappers once containing $10,000 each. Authorities estimated there could have been as much as $90 to $100 million in cash in those wrappers, but all the cash had disappeared along with the fugitive and his girlfriend.

What was not widely known at the time was that the outlaw treasure hunter had previously located the wreckage of the 'ship of gold'-the *SS Central America*-at the bottom of the Atlantic in 3,000 feet of water in the late 1990s. This was why the group of Illinois investors had given him over $29 million to finance the treasure salvage operation for a share of the loot.

There was a colorful, hour-long special presentation on National Geographic that documented the details of the lucrative salvage operation, but the total value of the huge discovery was as unclear as the dark waters that hid the wreck for so many years. Much of the gold that Callahan recovered was being shipped by individual prospectors in the California gold rush back to large banks in New York, and there were persistent rumors-never officially confirmed or denied by the U.S. government-that the *SS Central America* was also carrying fifteen tons of gold coins owned by the U.S. Army.

When the Illinois State Police had raided the house that Callahan was renting in Chicago, they found a book he left behind on how to change your identity and live completely off the grid. There was a lot of speculation that the outlaw had changed his appearance while on the run, but there was no general agreement from the authorities on this in spite of the clues left behind. They knew their fugitive was clever, often leaving red herrings that led nowhere.

Now in his fifties, they knew he liked to appear scruffy-looking, with a curly beard, slight build, medium height, and worn, tattered clothes. It was rumored that he was holed up somewhere along the

Atlantic coast, not too far from the site of his spectacular $170 million dollar heist, accompanied by his former assistant Andrea. The trail had turned cold when authorities and private investigators ran out of leads a few months after his disappearance.

There were still 170 million reasons why Tommy Tomlinson's list of creditors would leave no stone unturned in their effort to apprehend him. And, it was rumored that the insurance company who underwrote the performance bond for his salvage operation was looking to cash in on the substantial appreciation in the value of the gold during the last ten years.

But first, they had to find it.

SIX

The Olympic-size pool deck at Delmar was crowded with sun worshippers who were busy exchanging all the hottest gossip about the most recent scandals, bar mitzvahs, dating news, BOGO deals on Metamucil and Depends, chronic rule breakers, condo corruption, kickbacks, special deals at J.C. Penney on hearing aids, who was cheating on their wives and husbands, who was still physically able to cheat on their wives and husbands, who had a new shrink, and who just had surgery, as well as who didn't make it out of surgery.

Enjoying a day off, Officer Rodman was eagerly spreading SPF-50 all over Desiree's back, shoulders and thighs as a few residents stared from across the pool. Relaxing sunny-side down on the lounger, Desiree was enjoying yet another of her hunk's many skills as she savored the strong hands and fingers that expertly kneaded her hamstrings and lower body.

"Oh, Rod, that feels so good," she whispered. "Keep that up, honey, and we may need to head back upstairs and film a sequel."

"Ready when you are, honey. Viagra's good for two more hours." Rodman smiled confidently as he continued with her poolside massage. After covering her body with the protectant cream, her new-found boy toy sat back in his lounger and applied sunscreen all over his massive pecs. He snapped the cap closed and grabbed his plastic drink container that displayed the Viagra logo, a gift from a friend in the pharmaceutical business. He was happy he'd been the one to answer her doggie distress call on the beach that day as he took a greedy sip of his margarita and kicked back.

Desiree turned over, raised her knees to her chin and checked to make sure her bikini bottom was on straight. As she caught Rod's eye, she grinned and snugged up on the straps to her thong, wanting to give him a taste of his own teasing.

Some of the older residents watching from across the pool were staring, but Desiree couldn't tell if they were just gawking, asleep, or in a coma. Sometimes she would get so disgusted with the gawkers that she would run upstairs and change into her pink ski parka to insulate herself from the stares. Today, she was content to tease the man lounging next to her, and the playful adjustments to her thong hadn't gone unnoticed by her motorcycle cop.

"So, Des, what's with you and Mark," ventured Rod. "You guys got anything goin' on?"

Confident that she was in control again, Desiree pulled her hair back, leaned over and gave the motorcycle cop a big kiss. "What are you worried about? You're so fine," she said, tracing her fingertips over his six-pack abs. "You're not jealous, are you, honey?"

"Hell no," said Rod defensively. "I work out with him at Gold's. Seems like a nice guy," he said matter-of-factly. "I know his family's practically built half of Boca."

"Well, I'm just glad my Uncle Mike likes you," she reassured him. "It isn't just about the money. He's very particular about the men I hang with. Plus, you're very well-endowed. I'll bet you could paint a face on it and ride in the HOV lane," she joked. Desiree settled into her beach lounger, adjusted her Forty-Niners cap, lifting her sunglasses to give him a seductive wink.

"Where's Diego?" she asked from under her cap. "I thought he said he was coming downstairs to join us."

"He said he wanted to finish editing," answered Rod as he put his hands behind his head and flexed his eighteen inch biceps. "Probably upstairs spanking the monkey." Desiree chuckled at the idea.

Done with their morning shopping at Bloomingdales, a few of the cougars from across the pool twittered in approval at the results of the many hours he spent working out at Gold's Gym. Used to such attention, the beefy police officer ignored their banter with an air of indifference, only having eyes for Desiree.

At the other end of the pool, Anthony Anatolla was fascinated by a pretty young girl who he hadn't seen before as he drained his fourth daiquiri, ignoring his doctor's orders not to drink with the painkillers. The heavy-set balding condo director couldn't figure out why the girl was thrashing awkwardly from one side of the pool to the other in her own klutzy version of doing laps. Anatolla watched as she made the shorter side-to-side laps, making loud groaning noises with each lumbering stroke, drawing the attention of many of the Q-tips around the pool. He noticed that she wore a white wrist cast and her top was about to come off as he took a moment to wipe his prescription Ray Bans for a clearer view and walked to the edge of the pool.

This morning, Crazy Tracy had the distinction of being the prettiest hophead at Delmar. As she swam her laps, she was feeling no pain, under a doctor's orders for oxycodone four times a day until the fracture in her wrist was healed. As Anatolla stood over her, she stopped her backstrokes at the pool's edge to study his swimsuit, perplexed by the odd-shaped bulge.

At that moment, Gary Rollings emerged from the clubhouse. "Anyone seen the clubhouse TV remote controller?" he shouted across the pool deck. Several condo residents gave him blank looks, shaking their heads as they watched the strange drama unfolding between Anatolla and the young girl.

"What's that in yer Shp…Shpeedo?" Crazy Tracy asked, treading water and eyeing the odd-looking shape in his bathing suit.

Encouraged by the attention she was paying to his groin, the inebriated Anatolla started down the pool steps to join her in the water, failing to factor in the effect of water on the circuitry of the TV remote control.

As the water reached his crotch, Anatolla suddenly grimaced in pain and let out a loud yelp, and the drunken board member yanked out the short-circuiting TV remote control like it was a red-hot piece of steel. Discarding it onto the pool deck, the device popped open, spewing batteries and printed circuit boards all over the concrete deck as fellow residents looked on in utter disbelief.

Disgusted, Gary Rollings stood glaring at him in his blue Ralph Lauren walking shorts and matching polo shirt. "Thanks, Tony. Now, how am I gonna watch the big game today?" he demanded to know with his hands on his hips.

"Damn!" exclaimed Anatolla. "How the hell *that* thing get in there?" Crazy Tracy was treading water and laughing so hard she was making snorting sounds.

From across the pool, Big Mike couldn't believe his eyes. "Anything to impress the girls, right Tony?" he chided as Anatolla cupped his privates.

Shocked at her board member's repulsive behavior, Naomi Wasserman turned to her husband lying beside her. "*Now* I know why you wipe that remote control with disinfectants before you use it, Al."

For once, he was agreeing with his wife. Nodding at her words, Wasserman shouted across to Anatolla. "Ya never know where that remote control's been, right Tony?"

Just then, Glitzsky arrived at the scene of the crime, out on her queenly stroll to inspect all that ought to be magnificent. She eyed the scattered pieces of electronics littering the pool deck. "Was *that* the TV remote control from our clubhouse, Tony?" she demanded to know.

Anatolla shrugged and tried to explain. "I forgot"-

"You forgot you stuck it down your bathing suit?" Glitzsky asked incredulously. "That's a fifty-dollar fine, Mr. Anatolla, board member or not. Throwing debris on the pool deck is strictly prohibited!" She scanned the deck for agreement from onlookers, some nodding in support. "What do we hafta do *now*, Tony, pass a rule prohibiting having sex with an electronic device?" raising her hands up in a dramatic appeal to a higher power.

Anatolla smirked at Glitzsky and shrugged. "If we did, Sarah, *you'd* have to give up your favorite toy, right?"

"M…M…Mr. Anatolla!" stammered Crazy Tracy. "I th…thought you wa…yer…dis…gusting!" With that, she squirted a mouthful of water and flipped onto her back as she awkwardly backstroked away, totally creeped out by the inappropriate behavior of a portly man three times her age.

Embarrassed by her loud rejection, a dejected and embarrassed Anatolla climbed out of the pool and entered the clubhouse, passing the condo janitor who had just arrived to clean up the mess. As Jorge swept the pieces into his dustpan, curiosity got the better of him and he leaned over to ask Al Wasserman about the mess. "So, Meester Vasserman, wot happen here?"

"Well, Jorge, Anthony Anatolla is what happened here. He got drunk and stuck the TV remote down his suit to impress the ladies." Naomi nudged him with her elbow to keep quiet.

"No sheet!" exclaimed Jorge. The Delmar janitor scratched his head in bewilderment at how badly the multi-millionaire board members behaved. It seemed the more money they had, the worse their behavior. Jorge chalked it up to the effects of alcohol on heavily-medicated geriatrics.

Looking for a new audience closer to her own age, Crazy Tracy spotted Rod Rodman lounging thirty yards away and backstroked her way to his end of the pool. She stopped in front of the officer's lounger and adjusted the top to her bikini, propping her arms up on the pool coping to check him out. Resting her chin on her forearms for a moment to catch her breath, she extended her legs behind her in the pool and began a casual scissor-kick as she studied the hunky police officer, locking eyes with him.

"Arshew a Boca pleeshman?" she asked, batting her bloodshot blue eyes.

Desiree sat up in her lounger to get a better view of the girl who was slurring her words and putting the move on her man. Rodman leaned forward to get a better idea of just how drunk the girl was, concerned that she might slip underwater and drown.

"Do I know you, young lady?" ventured the officer.

"You...you...gave me a tick...ticket onetime."

"What's your name?" he asked.

"Trayshee," she said, playfully squirting a mouthful of water toward him.

"Trazie?" he questioned, confused by her slur.

"No, TRAYSHEE. FR...FRIENDS CALL ME CRAYSHEE TRAYSHEE," she clarified in a voice so loud that folks in Utah could hear. "You gave...gave me a ticket wunsh...time fer shpeed... shpeeding." She pulled her strawberry-blonde hair back from around her face and studied him as she struggled to make a favorable impression and jog his memory. "I gave ya...my shell mumber, buttcha nev...never called," she said, her face turning pouty.

Officer Rodman wasn't quite sure how to respond, a little off balance with the attention from such a drunk underage girl. "Well, thanks Tracy. Uh, honey, you know your top's falling off, right?"

"'So kay," she slurred with a crooked smile. "Shappens awe the time. Wesh yer name?" After witnessing the bizarre scene at the other end of the pool earlier, Rodman was a little embarrassed by her drunken flirtation. Then he remembered pulling her over about a month ago on Palmetto Park Boulevard when she got out of the car wearing the same aqua-colored knit bikini after competing in a beauty contest. Instinctively, he reverted to handling the situation as if he were on duty making a traffic stop.

"I'm Officer Rodman. Have you been drinking today, Tracy?"

"Jesh a wee bit, offisher," she slurred, pressing her finger and thumb together to show him what she meant by a wee bit. "Zer any la…laws againsh…shwim…shwimming and drinking?" Tracy smiled mischievously and unexpectedly pulled her top off in one motion, holding it up for him with her good arm. "Here, tay…take dish…not shposta drink with oxy…co…codone." Suddenly, she lost her grip on the pool coping and hit her chin on the tile, still managing to hold her top above the water as she sank.

"Oh my God! Who's the nut job, Rod?" Shocked by the young girl's antics, Desiree leaned forward and peered over the pool ledge to see where the girl had gone. Rodman jumped from his lounger and lunged for Tracy's wrist as she sank, but the sunscreen on her skin caused her to slip from his grip. Rodman stood at the edge of the pool holding only the top of her string bikini as condo residents stared.

"Hey, Tracy, you okay?" yelled Rodman into the water. "Maybe it's time for you to get out and dry off, honey." With no response, he squatted and reached into the water for her. Horrified, he watched as Tracy sank deeper, trailing a swirl of pink bubbles as she drifted to the pool bottom six feet under.

Springing into action, Rodman jumped in to bring her to the surface. Diving to the bottom, he grabbed her around the waist and pulled her up. As he broke the surface he yelled, "Dez, call 911! Tell 'em we need a suction unit and defib. Stat." Grasping her chin, he pulled his unconscious mermaid toward the shallow end of the pool as scores of older residents watched.

Those that weren't confined to wheel chairs or heavily sedated stood for a better view, captivated by the life-and-death scene playing out. Unaware that Desiree was already notifying the authorities on her phone, Anthony Anatolla barreled down the pool deck and yelled, "I'm calling 911!" Jerking the loggia screen door open, he pushed the call button on the wall-mounted EMS box and spouted information to the dispatcher through the two-way speaker.

"911. What is your emergency?" asked the dispatcher through the box.

"We have a girl drowning in the pool here at Delmar," exclaimed Anatolla. "She's either drunk or on drugs, or both. We need an ambulance sent to 1901 South Ocean Boulevard right away!"

The male dispatcher responded. "Please confirm your city and location," responded the dispatcher.

"Boca Raton, 1901 South Ocean Boulevard, Delmar condos."

"The one that looks like a big gold vibrator?" queried the dispatcher.

"Yeah, that's it. Hurry. We're not sure if she's breathing," blurted Anatolla as he hung up and rushed back to assist.

At the other end of the Delmar pool, Desiree was in the middle of her own frantic 911 call from her cell phone as she watched her boyfriend bring Tracy to the shallow end. She could see the girl was unconscious and bleeding from her mouth and chin as Rodman pulled her up to the edge of the pool where Anatolla and two others waited. The three men lifted her up and placed her on a lounge chair as the oldsters tried hard to remember their CPR training.

Rodman checked her carotid artery. "She's got no pulse," he said to Anatolla. "You know CPR?"

"It's been awhile." Anatolla squatted down and waited for instructions.

"Okay, you do the chest compressions with both hands, one on top of the other, one compression a second. Go!" commanded Rodman. After clearing her airway, he grabbed a nearby towel to clean her mouth before beginning CPR. As he drew back for a third lung full of air, he studied his patient for signs of life. "Paramedics will be here in five minutes. Hang in there, Tracy."

Pressing on her chest, Anatolla thought she looked a lot like that lead singer from Paramore, Hayley something. He looked around at the group that had gathered. "Anyone know who Crazy Tracy is staying with?"

"She told me she's the Karcass's granddaughter," said an older resident as he leaned on his walker. "You know, those big bullies on the second floor."

"Someone call her grandmother," said Anatolla. "She needs to know what's going on." Nobody moved as they all stood gawking at the young girl lying motionless on the pool lounger. Pumping on the young girl's chest, he glanced over at Mildred Seidelbaum. "Mildred, will you call her grandmother? You can ring her up on the house phone in the clubhouse-number 204, I think."

Caught up in a *déjà vu*, Mrs. Seidelbaum was momentarily unable to take her eyes off Crazy Tracy. The young girl reminded her of her own granddaughter as she thought back to their last visit to the emergency room at Mt. Sinai last New Year's Eve. She'd been injured in a bad accident in the city, and the blood test that night revealed that she'd been driving drunk. But the biggest surprise was the heroin that showed up in her tox screen. This is how these kids live now, she thought, shaking her head.

"Okay. I'll call her." Mildred headed for the clubhouse to give the Karcass's the bad news, reminding herself to call her own granddaughter later.

Trying hard to revive their topless mermaid, Anatolla continued to perform CPR, now wishing he hadn't embarrassed the young girl earlier with his stupid remote control stunt. They could all hear the ambulance getting closer as the siren wailed down the canyon of condos on A1A.

"Hey, does our condo insurance cover us for this kind of liability, Milton?" asked Anatolla of the former board member. "Are we liable? I mean, if she dies or something?"

"Hell, I dunno, Tony. Grab her legs and put that pillow under her knees," he said. "Why don't we focus on saving her life first?"

Beside herself with worry, Desiree sidled over to Rodman. "Think she's gonna make it, Rod?" Before he could answer, they heard the clatter of gurney wheels over pavers and looked up to see two paramedics pulling a stretcher piled high with emergency equipment. As they set up for treatment, one of the medics reached over to check Crazy Tracy's pulse. Feeling no heartbeat, he broke out the defibrillator and proceeded to charge it.

Just as the paramedic was about to apply the defibrillator to her bare skin, Officer Rodman spotted a weak heartbeat. "Guys, we've got a pulse! Hold off on the defib!" He stood to make room for the youngest member of the EMS team who squeezed in and positioned the resuscitation bag over her airway as he evaluated their drunken mermaid.

"Let's get her to the ER," said the paramedic with his fingers on her neck. "She *does* have a weak pulse." As they lifted her onto the gurney, Crazy Tracy suddenly coughed, expelling a mixture of water and blood onto the pool deck.

Officer Rodman grabbed her hand. "How much oxycodone did you take, honey? Can you hear me?" He squeezed her hand, trying to evoke a response. "Tracy?" Feeling his grasp and hearing the sound of his voice, she struggled to emerge from her stupor. Slowly, she opened her eyes and focused her gaze on her knight in shining armor.

"How you doin', girl?" he asked again. Weakly, she pushed the resuscitation bag away from her face and strained to speak.

"Mu...mush beher..." she slurred. "Don't le...leave me, pl... pleash." As they began to cart her toward the pool gate and the ambulance waiting in the parking lot, she lost her grip on Rodman's hand. Lifting her arm weakly, she crooked her finger as they wheeled her away, pointing at her favorite motorcycle cop.

"Wear yer boots...whe...when ya come ta...see me. 'Kay?"

SEVEN

I t was early on Monday morning as Jorge Hernandez stood on the roof of the twelve story condo admiring the azure sky and turquoise water. Once a month, the portly forty-seven-year-old custodian inspected the sealant and roof flashing for signs of leaks, taking the opportunity to climb to the top and enjoy the panoramic views from the rooftop. The beautiful vistas of South Boca Beach always seemed to help when he was troubled, and today he was trying to get his mind off a pile of gambling debts.

Looking out over the Boca coastline made him feel like he was on top of the world. He wiped his glasses with his shirt and thought about what he was going to do to get himself out of the mess he was in. After admiring the architecture of the Boca Resort and Club a mile further north, he turned to face south toward the skyscrapers that defined the Ft. Lauderdale skyline twenty-five miles away.

After the threatening call from the bookie's muscleman, the janitor wished he hadn't put that stupid parlay on the 49ers game two weeks ago. The former pro cage fighter who moonlighted as a bill collector and had given him until Wednesday to cough up the thirty-five hundred bucks. In the four years he'd been the Delmar custodian, he couldn't remember ever being in a worse money crunch, and this time he was facing a trip to the emergency room if he failed to come through.

The two brand new exhaust vents that poked up through the roof from Penthouse Ten at Delmar caught his attention. Finished with his roof inspection, Jorge walked with his bucket of sealant over to the new vents to get a closer look. From the bright galvanized flashing and shiny turbine blades inside, he could tell they were newly installed. But by who, he wondered? As he bent down for a closer inspection, he grimaced from the pungent smell of ammonia fumes. Something seemed out of place, and he decided to pay a visit to the owner in the penthouse situated beneath the vents.

⇥⇤

The penthouse with the new roof vents belonged to a guy named Dominick Martorono. Dominick was an ambitious man, a staunch Democrat, and the spitting image of a bald version of Walter White from *Breaking Bad*. Before he was forced to wear the label of a sexual predator, he was a hard-working high school science teacher who paid more than his fair share of taxes. Still angry at the authorities for unnecessarily wrecking his life, Martorono was entertained by the irony that he'd created; a meth cook who contributed thousands of dollars in campaign money toward the reelection of the Palm Beach County Sheriff.

Dominick's campaign contributions bought him some influence, and he sought as much protection for his illegal activities as his money could buy. He considered his meth business payback for the horrible twist of fate that had been dealt him by the authorities. It was indeed ironic that the Sheriff had taken such a strong stance against drugs, and that Dominick was one of his

most ardent supporters. It was his way of proving to all those bureaucratic buffoons that they'd never be able to keep him down.
Not content with making a measly half a million bucks a year from
his meth business, he was putting a plan into motion that would
move him up the food chain.

The chip that rested squarely on his shoulder was created when
he was arrested for having sex with a minor three years ago, and the
unfortunate event ended his career as a high school science teacher. Dominick was then engaged to Margeaux, the beautiful young
lady whom he later married. When they'd first met, Dominick
knew that, by law, an employee of a Florida business serving liquor
in Florida had to be at least eighteen years of age. He had mistakenly assumed she was of age when he brought Margeaux home
from the club to spend the night.

As it turned out, the stunning young lady who had performed
the most sensual dance he'd ever witnessed at Club Flash Dancers
had lied about her age to her new employer. It was a situation made
far worse when her jealous ex-boyfriend followed them home that
night and called the Palm Beach County sheriff. The sheriff called
in the SWAT team, ironically on a night when Margeaux was only
a week from her eighteenth birthday, and the escapade turned out
to be a nightmare for Dominick.

When the seven heavily-armed members of the SWAT team
broke his front door down, not only did they rough him up and put
him in handcuffs and leg restraints, they confiscated his computer
and all of his personal financial records. Even worse, he would be
forced to wear the label of a sex offender for the rest of his life,
making Dominick an unemployable thirty-nine-year-old teacher
and college graduate.

After serving six degrading months in county lock-up with a
bunch of two-legged animals that were intent on molesting anything with a heartbeat, he now had to suffer the added humiliation
of having to report to his probation officer every week. Dominick

vowed revenge on the screwed-up system that had destroyed his career by putting his knowledge of chemistry to work in the most lucrative way he could imagine. An outlaw for the past few years, he was enjoying the irony of proving the adage that living well was the best revenge.

It was the skyrocketing expenses that provided the motivation to up his game. Dominick felt he was getting squeezed from all directions; Margeaux wanted a larger closet with enough room for at least a hundred pair of shoes, his dealers were demanding an increase in their cut from twenty-five percent to thirty-five percent, and it was getting more expensive to pay his smurfs for collecting the key ingredient in his product-the decongestant pseudoephedrine. Even the condo fees were going up from forty-six hundred a quarter to fifty-three hundred because of all the new upgrades and security measures. So, the super-secret meth cook needed more cash, and he was exploring an idea that would dramatically increase his income.

His dealers had convinced him that if he could increase the purity of his meth by just ten percent he could increase his price from seventy bucks a gram to over a hundred. By using ten gallons of methylamine in his cook instead of the more common pseudo-ephedrine, the purity of his product would increase from eighty-four percent to ninety-two percent and his yield would jump to a hundred twenty pounds, worth over five million bucks. After paying for his dealers cut, cost of raw materials, protection for security and the extra cost of the methylamine, he figured to net around two and a half million, potentially quintupling his income. The only thing he had to figure out was how to score the methylamine.

Through all the hardships he faced with Margeaux, they had remained inseparable, the star-crossed lovers that so many couples aspired to be. Today, he was waiting patiently as the former star attraction from Flash Dancers finished applying a clear gloss coat to her pink toenails as she sat in the leather chaise lounge.

Dominick was insisting that Margeaux show him the cash from the day's take at the "Hot Bikini Dog" stand she ran. He had stuck his neck way out to finance the new roadside-stand-on-wheels, and he needed to know it was paying off.

"You don't believe me," said Margeaux without looking up.

"I believe you."

"No you don't." She looked over at Dominick as he stood over his cook dressed in the hazmat suit he bought on sale at Home Depot. "Do I ask you how much you make selling your meth?"

Stirring his cook with a glass rod, the former high school science teacher studied her through his safety goggles, careful not to create any stray sparks around his cook area. "Honey, you don't pay for any of this. I set *you* up. Remember?" Cautiously, he moved the bottle of acetone on the stainless steel counter further from the heat, placing it next to the Erlenmeyer flask of anhydrous ammonia.

"It's your business, baby," adjusting his goggles. "I just wanna see you make some money." She was usually in the mood to play around after her nails dried, so he would be agreeable. Setting the cook timer for two hours, he turned the overhead fume hood to medium and reached into his pocket for a Viagra before wriggling out of his hazmat suit.

Margeaux knew how to push his buttons, teasing him with her knee pressed against her breasts as she put the finishing touches on her toe nails. "There. Perfecto Garcia," she said with a feminine flourish. After screwing the top on the bottle of clear polish, she blew on her nails, grabbed her purse and pulled out a thick wad of tens, twenties, and fifties. With her back to him, she held it over her head for Dominick.

"There. Satisfied, Dom?" waving the cash over her head. As she stuffed the bills back into her purse, there was an ominous knock on the door. Expecting no one, Dominick froze as he stood in the kitchen in his tidy whities. With a new cook underway, paranoia swept over him as he motioned for Margeaux to see who was at the door. Stepping across the marble foyer to the guest viewer, she took a peek and studied the man outside their condo door.

"Honey, it's that fat custodian-you know, the one that's always tryin' to hit on me in the garage when I leave for work."

"Baby, stay in the bedroom. I'll handle it." Dominick gave her a reassuring pat on the rear and stepped toward the door. "Who is it?" he yelled in a manly voice.

"Meester Martorono, it Jorge. Dee custodian. Sorry to bodder you, but dee manager ask me to take a look at dee permit for dee new roof vents you install."

Annoyed at the interruption, Dominick threw his velour bathrobe on and checked the pocket for the wad of cash he kept for emergencies while Margeaux blew on her nails and tip-toed into the bedroom. Before answering the door, he grabbed a can of peach-scented Renuzit and sprayed himself down from head to toe to cover up any scent of lingering ammonia.

"Meester Martorono?" asked Jorge, still waiting in the hallway.

"Hold your horses, Jorge. Looking for my construction permit." Dominick reduced the fan speed on the fume hood to quiet the noise and checked his cook. Then he unlatched the three deadbolts on the front door and stepped into the hallway to reach an understanding with the condo custodian.

"Hey, Jorge. Margeaux's sleeping. Can we talk out here?"

"Sure ting," said the custodian as he sniffed the air. "Wow, Meester Martorono, you smell really fresh." He leaned forward and sniffed again. "Peachy."

"Yeah, thanks," trying to hide his irritation over the surprise visit. "Some new after shave Margeaux got for me," anxiously running his hand over his hairless head. With his hand on the cash in his pocket, he faced Jorge and sized up the portly custodian. "Last time we spoke you said you were gonna start working out there, Jorge."

Jorge shot him a questioning look. "What chew mean? You tink I fat?"

Purposely putting Jorge in a defensive posture, he sidestepped the custodian's question and cocked his head to read the stitched lettering on the front of his uniform. Curiously, it read "HORGAY". Dominick tried hard to contain his amusement

"Never seen Jorge spelled that way before," said Dominick.

Embarrassed, the custodian shuffled his feet. "It was my boss idea. He said we should tank Discount Uneeforms for dee screw up. Day do dee work for free."

"Okay. Whatever." He thought of an angle. "Hey, got an idea if you can use some extra cash, Jorge. I need someone to keep an eye on things for us at Delmar when I'm not here and kinda watch our backs. Margeaux and I *really* enjoy our privacy, if you know what I mean," pulling a fat roll of hundreds out of his pocket. "So, I want you to let me know about any unwanted attention, uh...you know." Dominick counted out ten of the Ben Franklins and dangled them in front of the custodian as he watched Jorge's wide-eyed reaction. "Think we can forget about the vent permit and keep an eye out for each other?"

Jorge studied the bills and thought about the sum he owed his bookie. He was in a tight spot, but the cash in Dominick's hand just wasn't enough to cover his marker plus the vig. "Uh, well Mr. Martorono, I appreciate it, but what about dee extra roof vents? Day smelled kinda funny when I on dee roof."

Dominick was prepared for questions like this, warned about it by his buddy who had made a special midnight visit to install the vents. "Oh, that. I have really bad asthma. It was my doctor's idea. You know, all those toxic vapors from the carpet fibers and insulation. Formaldehyde. Crap like that."

Jorge had a feeling he was getting played, but decided to go with the flow if it meant he could get his bookie off his back. Rubbing his chin, he thought there might be more money in it for him and pretended to need more convincing. "Uh, sure. Long as yer not doin' nut ting *illegal*." Jorge fidgeted, waiting to see how much he could squeeze him, knowing that just about everyone at Delmar was addicted to something or other.

"Are we good here?" asked Dominick holding up the cash again.

Jorge took his shot. "Well, you tink you could swing a coupla months advance, Meester Martorono?" he asked without taking his eyes from the cash. "I got a beeg familee."

Dominick knew a buying question when he heard one. "All right, Jorge. What's it gonna cost me?"

"I got fi kids and I owe my bookie three grand plus fi hundred vig." Jorge looked down at the floor, shuffled his feet again and looked up at Dominick like a puppy-dog begging for a Milk Bone.

Jorge had him over a barrel. Dominick was far more concerned with keeping a low profile at the condo. He reluctantly peeled another twenty-five hundred off the wad of cash, holding it out expectantly. With a stern look and a firm voice, he said, "You gonna take *good* care of me now, right, Jorge? Treat me right, and there's more where that came from. So, here's two months in advance. No more questions, right?"

"Okay. I watch your back like you won't believe," he said, grabbing the cash and waiting for a fist bump. "We gotta deal!" Ecstatic about solving his debt problem and avoiding what would likely be a painful confrontation with his bookie's collector, Jorge headed for the elevator with enough cash to keep him out of the hospital.

Dominick took a deep breath as he watched the custodian pocket the money and walk toward the elevator, happy to have Jorge on his payroll. Stepping back inside his penthouse, he methodically locked all three deadbolts on the steel door and turned to find Margeaux. He was treated to a view of her laying spread-eagled and buck naked on the leather chaise, smiling seductively. The former star attraction at Flash Dancer knew how to work her magic, confident that her affections were exactly what Dominick needed after suffering through the janitor's shakedown.

"Honey, I got a fresh wax. You wanna take a closer look?" she asked in a little girl's voice.

Not needing a second invitation, Dominick grinned as he wriggled out of his bathrobe, kicked off his tidy whities with manly vigor and stepped eagerly across the living room to his teasing wife.

"Pucker up, baby! Daddy's comin' ta get some!"

EIGHT

Looking like a heavy-set flower child from the sixties, Sarah Glitzsky was all decked out in her orange and black floral polyester pantsuit as she sat at the Board of Directors' table ready to preside over tonight's meeting. Clearly a victim of the easy living at Delmar, Glitzsky had packed on quite a few pounds lately, and several residents were wondering if her outfit came in her size.

The few friends and supporters that she could count on usually sat in the very back of the room, and the ones with an ax to grind usually sat in the first few rows where they were better positioned to take their shots at the queen of the condo commandos. Her major supporters seated at the directors' table included condo manager Dyson Stampaugh, secretary/treasurer Desiree Stone, vice president Anthony Anatolla, and director Al Wasserman. From where the board members sat, the dead fly that adorned Glitzsky's nose looked more like a large blackhead, so they avoided saying anything that might embarrass the president.

Condo politics Florida style was the order of the day as Glitzsky's opponents were ready to pounce, including the big-boned Margaret

Karcass and her husband Craig. Sitting in the front row, they were busy preparing a list of embarrassing budget questions for the condo president. Always at odds with Glitzsky over their characterization of Delmar as a "dysfunctional nursing home", they couldn't help snickering at the sight of their president ready to convene the meeting with the dead fly stuck on the bridge of her nose. While Glitzsky searched the room for supporters, Craig Karcass was busy snapping photos of her Haight Ashbury outfit with his cell phone camera and uploading the photos to You Tube.

Margaret Karcass had just finished making her third unsuccessful bid at being elected to the Board, and the obese couple had quite an unsavory reputation among the Delmar residents. Rarely sober, Margaret had rightfully earned her nickname as the "Wicked Witch of Delmar", and residents knew better than to disagree with the couple or express an opinion that differed from their own-especially when they'd been drinking. Their fondness for fried food, jelly donuts and funnel cakes was difficult to disguise as Margaret weighed in at a hefty three hundred forty-five pounds, while hubby Craig tipped the scales at a whopping four hundred and five. Margaret had a masculine way about her, and many of the residents would whisper that she had the testosterone of ten men in her system. Rumors were flying about their frequent visits to the liposuction clinic, and the joke around campus was the visits were so numerous that they had a couch in the waiting room named after them.

Lending even more color to the couple's bizarre profile were the local press reports. According to the local paper, Craig Karcass had become embittered when he was passed over for a pay raise at the chemical company where he worked. To even the score, he decided to tip off the Environmental Protection Agency over what amounted to minor air pollution infractions, which caused the company to be fined a whopping three million dollars by the Feds.

When their CEO had gotten wind of the costly information leak from internal emails, Karcass found himself demoted from plant manager to plant grounds keeper and forced to work in the demeaning position for the duration of his service in order to qualify for his reduced retirement benefits.

Sitting directly behind the Karcass couple in the meeting tonight, Mr. Calkings was joined by his son after spending the afternoon setting up a revocable trust. Calkings wanted his son in attendance to prepare him for the raucous condo politics that he might one day have to deal with. A podiatrist's assistant, the dutiful son sat quietly, adjusting his eye glasses as he took a perverse interest in Mrs. Karcass's grotesquely fat toes protruding from her size twelve Birkenstock sandals. Finding the sight of her huge toes immensely entertaining, Calkings was unable to tear his eyes away from what seemed like a colossal medical abnormality.

Gesturing toward the Karcass couple, Stephan Calkings leaned over and whispered to his father. "Dad, aren't these two the ones who make all that noise? The ones you always say sound like two dinosaurs playing basketball upstairs?"

"Yeah, that's her," he answered in a low voice. "They call her the 'Wicked Drunken Bully Witch of Delmar', but please don't say anything to embarrass me, Stephan."

After listening to his dad complain for months about the couple's abusive lifestyle, Stephan sat back in his seat and prepared to have some fun with his parent's antagonists. After purposely watching the clock tick down on the start to the meeting, he tapped Margaret Karcass on her shoulder.

Pointing at her feet, in a loud voice he said, "Mrs. Karcass, I had no idea that the *Elephant Man* was living in your sandals! Who could have known?" With a grin, he sat back in his chair to enjoy the chuckles from those sitting within earshot. Annoyed, Karcass abruptly turned in her chair.

"What did you say?" she demanded, reeking of Wild Turkey. Feeling smug about his remark, Calkings sat silently, enjoying the comments.

"Craig and Margaret, what a lovely couple," said a resident with unmistakable sarcasm. "Let's just hope they make it back to the AA meetings."

"I heard she sets fires to feel joy," commented another neighbor.

Not to be outdone, another quipped, "Well, I heard they did their whole condo interior in IKEA for thirty-seven dollars."

Before Karcass could mount a comeback, there was a loud "BAMM!" as Glitzsky brought the gavel down hard on the table. "Meeting will come to order," she pronounced loudly. "That means you too, Margaret and Craig Karcass," pointing her gavel.

A stickler for following Robert's Rules, Glitzsky got the meeting off by calling for a roll call. "Please answer if you're present. Or here. Or whatever. Vice president Anthony Anatolla?"

"Present," said Anatolla who leaned forward and wiped his glasses to get a better view of Miss Stone. Lucky for him, his loud mouth wife Marian was out playing Mahjong.

"Secretary/treasurer Desiree Stone?"

"Here, uh...I mean present." said Desiree, tugging on her skirt in mock modesty after noticing the attention she was getting from the men in the group. They were all part of her fan club, adding cash to her coffers by driving up the hits to her website where her main sponsors were Trojan and KY Warming Gel. For the thousands of dollars they made her every month, she could tolerate a little slobbering from the dirty old men in her audience.

"Lori McSmalley?" Concerned about having enough votes to support her super-secret agenda, Glitzsky searched the room for her missing board member. "Lori McSmalley?"

"I think she's at the rehab center with her granddaughter," said a woman in the back. "Her granddaughter's best friends with

Crazy Tracy." A wave of twittering swept the meeting as attendees bantered back and forth about the drunken antics of Crazy Tracy at the Delmar pool last week.

"Albert Wasserman?" Glitzsky looked toward the far end of the table where Wasserman was busy texting a message to a dating site. "Al, are you here?" she repeated.

Red-faced, Wasserman looked up from the photo of the girl on his phone like he'd just been caught with his hand in the cookie jar. "Oh...yeah. Here!"

"Thanks, Al. Glad you could join us," quipped Glitzsky. Counting enough board members for a quorum, Glitzsky was anxious to get on with the meeting and turned to her esteemed adult-film protégé. "Desiree, will you please read the minutes to our last meeting?"

Remembering the president's promise to defend her in-home video activities, Desiree was delighted to oblige the president with whatever reciprocity she required. The secretary/treasurer cleared her throat and began rambling through the list of endless minutia brought up at their last monthly meeting. Unfamiliar with financial terminology, she stumbled through the treasurer's report that had been so artfully crafted for her recital by Dyson Stampaugh.

The meeting attendees were quite entertained with her report. Many were already aware that her unfamiliarity with accounting practices hadn't prevented her former boyfriend from appointing her to several of his mob-controlled corporate boards. Treasurer's report concluded, she turned to her president. Glitzsky opened the meeting to the discussion of new and pending business. In response, Mrs. Karcass's hand went up, and Glitzsky reluctantly recognized the most cantankerous of the board member wannabes.

"Margaret, you have something you want to bring up?" she asked, pulling her mike closer, "...like maybe a new bathroom scale capable of accommodating livestock?"

"Can you be nice, Sarah?" countered Karcass. As the snickering subsided, she and husband Craig prepared to bring up an idea designed to increase her sagging popularity.

"Looking at the expense report, we think the common area electric bill is way outta wack," said Karcass. "Every time we're in the clubhouse and restrooms, we see the lights left on." A wave of twittering went through the rows behind her as she twisted around in her seat to encourage residents to speak out and galvanize more support for her idea. Karcass straightened up, sucked in her belly, and continued with her agenda. "We'd like to move that Delmar install automatic timers for the lights in the clubhouse and restrooms to bring the electric bill down."

"Move?" asked Glitzsky. "Are you referring to a bowel movement, Margaret?" Glitzsky frowned and corrected her. "You mean you'd like to make a motion to open it for discussion, don't you?"

Karcass made a face at the president's indelicate reference to her limited knowledge of parliamentary procedure. "Whatevah, Sarah. By the way, where's your painted vinyl shower curtain today?"

Glitzsky ignored her question, locking eyes with her adversary as she readied her retort. "So, after destroying the sea grape hedges and turning our lawn into a wetlands marsh area by disabling the sprinkler timers, now you're looking to save the planet, Margaret? Really?"

"As head of the landscape committee, I only had them cut back"-

"Yeah...to what-about three inches high?" quipped Glitzsky, scanning the room to fan the flames of discontent. Several of her supporters were nodding their heads in agreement. "Damn near looks like the surface of Mars, wouldn't ya say?"

"Speaking of cutting things illegally," countered Karcass, "... why is it that you refused to fine Stephan Calkings for illegally cutting the sea oats on our dunes? We have the photos on our phone."

A new wave of twittering swept through the meeting as the president slipped into her well-practiced dumb blonde act. "Why would Mr. Calkings ever do something like that?" she asked with feigned innocence.

Incensed at Glitzsky's refusal to admit the truth, Karcass struggled to get her immense body into a standing position as she wagged her finger in Glitzsky's face. "Apparently, because *you* couldn't see the beach from your chair on the patio, so you pressured him to cut our sea oats. Isn't that right, Sarah? Fess up!"

Glitzsky remained seated as she pounded her gavel on the table. "Sit down Margaret or I'll have you removed from the meeting," she shouted, "...if I can find a forklift large enough!"

The president pointed her gavel at Craig Karcass. "By the way, Mr. Karcass, two months ago you promised to bring the Board your documents to prove that your second-floor unit is in compliance with our condo rules on cork sub-flooring. Based on all the noise complaints coming from your neighbors, we're going to ask that you comply. So, where's the proof you promised?"

Karcass squirmed in his chair. "Well, our daughter, who's our attorney, deleted the photos and advised us we don't have to comply." His response was met by a chorus of disapproval.

Glitzsky looked disgusted. "So you lied to everyone about this, didn't you Craig Karcass?" she said accusingly as she watched him continue to squirm in his chair. The president knew there wasn't a soul in the room who believed the Karcass's stories, especially when it came to matters of compliance and cooperation. She knew the Board was weary of the noise complaints from their neighbors. The president looked left and right to gauge support as she prepared to voice her next motion.

"Motion to vote on levying a twenty-dollar-a-day fine on the Karcass unit until they comply with our cork sub-floor rules."

Stampaugh looked expectantly up and down the row of seated Board members for a response, and Anatolla spoke first. "I'll second the motion."

Glitzsky was confident it would be a unanimous vote. "All those in favor, please say 'aye' and raise your hands. Wasserman, Stone, Glitzsky and Anatolla joined in a chorus of "ayes" and raised their hands in support of their president. "It's unanimous. Motion carries," pronounced Glitzsky, pounding the table with her gavel and pointing it at the Karcass couple. "That's six hundred a month you owe us until you install the cork sub-flooring."

Defiant to the end, Margaret Karcass retorted angrily; "Good luck collecting. Our daughter's out of rehab now, so she has all the time in the world to file court motions. See you in court, you pompous"-

Knowing she held the high ground, Glitzsky pointed her gavel at the couple and responded sternly. "No payment after thirty days, we'll file a foreclosure lien, Margaret. Then you can move back to your trailer!" Karcass was fuming, ready to leave the meeting.

After the noise subsided, Glitzsky addressed the group. "Okay, anybody else got anything they wanna bring up?"

Carol Nutter had been sitting calmly in the middle of the group, waiting for her opportunity. Stretching toward the ceiling with her upraised arm, she waved furiously to be recognized. Looking to draw attention away from the conflict with Karcass, Glitzsky acknowledged her.

"Carol, you have a question?"

"Yeah. On the landscaping issue, Mark told me they specifically landscaped the grounds with foliage that's environmentally friendly to protect the shoreline." Many at Delmar knew the Boca Raton shiny sheets were strewn with articles portraying the McAllisters as supporters of environmental causes.

Annoyed, Karcass turned in her seat. "Carol, you're such a little gold digger. Their family's not even on the board any"-

"Their family still owns four units here," she shot back, "…and they pay a larger percentage of condo fees than any other owner," she added, winning the support of a majority of the attendees. "Shall we talk about your Slip 'N Slide, Mrs. Karcass? And your Wild Turkey parties on the second floor?" Embarrassed, Karcass was caught with her mouth open again as another wave of chatter swept the room.

"You go girl," someone commented.

"Probably ate her twin in the womb," added another with a nod toward Karcass.

"Okay, people." Glitzsky banged her gavel. "Getting a little off track here. Let's move forward," as she glared at Karcass. "The board has already voted to stick with the original landscape design. Are there any seconds on discussing the installation of automatic timers in the common areas and restrooms?" she asked, scanning the room for a response.

From the back row, Big Mike Rosenberg was anxious to make his presence felt. "I'll second the motion to install," he said, smirking at Glitzsky from the relative safety of his seat in the rear of the room. Big Mike was easy to spot, decked out in his trademark cargo shorts and Tommy Bahama size XXXL floral shirt.

"Hey, Mike, where's your beer tankard?" teased Lillian Peltz from the other side of the aisle.

"It's upstairs," answered Big Mike with a grin. "Shall I bring it down, along with some guacamole chip dip for you, Lillian?" he asked, winking at her. Lillian smiled back, playfully fanning her chest with her hand.

"Okay, okay people. Getting off track here. We have a second from Mr. Rosenberg," said Glitzsky. Not wanting to miss an opportunity to embarrass him, she added, "And, for God's sake, Mr. Rosenberg, will you please refrain from kicking your swim trunks into the silk trees in our clubhouse? I hope the lights are *out* the next time you decide to streak the clubhouse. I mean, my God, you looked like an oversexed gorilla!" There was a raucous round of laughter from those who'd heard about the balls-out confrontation.

"Cheapest thrill you'll have in a while," he countered. With Big Mike sitting in the same room with her, Glitzsky seemed clueless about how close she was to the wood chipper. Those who knew him better were more respectful, aware that most of Big Mike's friends were well-connected in New York and Chicago with families whose names contained more vowels than a scrabble game.

"A little too much chlorine in that gene pool," added a resident taking a jab at Glitzsky.

"Did you have something to add, Mr. Rosenberg?" asked Glitzsky, perturbed that he seemed to have more supporters in the meeting.

Big Mike stood to deliver his retort. "Yes, I've got something to add. A few of us were commenting on the genealogy of certain individuals and how they're prone to erroneous conclusions," he explained, certain that her feeble mind lacked the sufficient grey matter to grasp what the hell he was talking about.

"Ya think?" responded Glitzsky with a puzzled look on her face.

"All the time! You should try it!" replied big Mike, delivering his slam dunk as he jumped up and play-acted shooting a basketball. "Nothin' but net!" Hearing this, the entire room lit up again. Margaret and Craig Karcass snickered in amusement from the first row, while Glitzsky looked ready to crawl under the table as she turned her head and wiped her nose in embarrassment. As she opened her hand, she noticed the smeared remains of the dead fly that had been adorning her nose during the entire meeting. Beet red with embarrassment, she covered her mike and held out her hand with the fly's remains as she leaned over to huddle with her manager.

"Dyson, please tell me I didn't have this fly on my nose the whole time," she said in a low voice with her hand over her microphone. Embarrassed for her, Stampaugh looked away discretely while the Karcass couple in the front row continued to snicker. Desiree looked out the window in bewilderment while Anatolla took the opportunity to wipe his glasses for a better view of their in-house adult-film star.

"Don't worry about the fly, Sarah. We all love ya anyway," said Stampaugh as he reached for the Steinberg storm window bid. Grouping it with the two other fake bids to make the presentation look as routine as possible.

Recovering her composure to address the group, Glitzsky double checked to make sure her hands and face were free of the fly's body parts. In a calmer voice she said, "I'd like to call for a vote on installing timers in the common lighting areas. All in favor?" A row of raised hands on the board went up as they voiced "ayes" in unanimous support. "All opposed?" She paused, and seeing no more hands go up, she continued. "Motion is approved," said Glitzsky, bringing down the gavel with all the power and drama of a Judge Judy episode.

"Before we move on to the next item on the agenda, is there any more new business?" she asked, scanning the room. Carol Nutter raised her hand again. "Yes, Carol?"

"Ah...yeah, Mrs. Glitzsky," wiggling in her seat. "For those who actually swim in the pool and not just wash their soiled clothes in it, could we get the pool guy to double up on the disinfectant?" Everyone turned in their seats to see what Carol was about to say next, fearing what might follow.

A puzzled look came over the president's face. "And your reason for that would be...what, Carol?"

"A couple of days ago, Mark and I were relaxing, um...well, *kissing* and relaxing at the pool, and saw a lady holding a baby in diapers by the arms and dunking her baby up and down in the pool like a big teabag." There were disapproving sounds from the group before she continued. "Then, she changed the baby's diapers on the lounge chair...and we noticed they looked...well...you know... quite crapped in."

Director Al Wasserman slid his microphone closer. "Wait. Not sure I heard you, dear. Did you say '*quite crapped in*'?" he asked in a tone serious enough to address the dire issue of baby poop. Wasserman went into his diatribe. "Everyone knows that babies in diapers are strictly prohibited." He paused after reciting the pool rules and scanned the room for support before turning his attention back to Carol Nutter. "And you said they looked 'quite crapped in' Miss Nutter?" sounding like a prosecutor in a murder trial making a summary closing argument.

"Yeah, well, I was trying to be polite."

All five seated at the directors' table stared at her incredulously. "Okay, Miss Nutter, we'll look into that with the pool poop-I mean pool contractor," said Stampaugh as his mind drifted off course and into an intimate fantasy of Carol in her leather shorts. Forcing himself to focus, he continued with the thing that was most dear to his heart; the storm shutter contract with the huge super-secret bonus.

As Stampaugh readied the next item on the agenda, Big Mike leaned over to Stan Gelding in the seat next to him. "Exactly why I think twice about goin' in *that* pool. Too many unidentified bodily fluids floating around," he whispered. "I mean, damn, Stan. You know some o' the bigger ladies *do not* leave the pool for purposes of bladder drainage."

"Okay, okay everybody. We'll have the pool guy run some extra tests on the pool water and check it for...ah...stuff,' said Stampaugh. "Are we ready to vote on the storm shutter contract?" The manager was hoping it was a rhetorical question as he passed copies of the construction bids down the table. With his hand over his microphone, he held up the Steinberg bid to Glitzsky and pointed at the letterhead. In a hushed voice he said, "This is the one we talked about last week, Sarah-the best one for *all* of us." She nodded and looked furtively around the group to see if anyone had taken notice. Once again, Glitzsky banged her gavel to quell the noise and address the unruly group.

"Next item is the vote on our storm shutter contract," said Glitzsky in an exaggerated official tone. "We have reviewed three bids from certified state contractors, all with excellent references, and we're recommending the lowest bidder, Steinberg Storm Windows. They did a great job on our parking garage last year, and our condo manager is also recommending that we give the contract to Steinberg." Sarah was seeing dollar signs, and with her sixty grand 'bonus' hanging in the balance, she looked to the board members to her left and right for expected approval. "Is there any further discussion before we vote on this?"

Big Mike stood up in the back row. "Yeah, I got a question or two. Who are the other two bidders and why aren't we talking with them before we take a vote?"

"I'll answer that one, Sarah," offered Stampaugh as he gathered the three bids together with a troubled look.

With a pained expression, Stampaugh responded to Big Mike sitting in the back row. "Mr. Rosenberg, to answer your question, we've had interviews with all the bidders for the new hurricane-proof shutters, including Window Man and Boca Storm and Shutter, and we've discussed these bids in our last two meetings," said Stampaugh with a hint of arrogance. "If you had bothered to attend those meetings, you would know this," said Stampaugh with a smirk. "Also, we've checked their credentials and recommend the lowest bidder here, Steinberg Storm Windows," he said, shifting in his seat nervously. He'd made up his mind he wasn't going to let some rag-tag former fight promoter ruin his eighty thousand dollar payday. Stampaugh figured he'd earned it putting up with this bunch of flaky fruitcakes over the last few years.

"If you say so," countered Big Mike standing in the back row. "Three million dollars is a big expense for us and we want to make sure our money is being pissed away as prudently as possible." Several residents were chattering in agreement and a few patted him on the back in support of his challenge to what they all suspected was a padded bid.

"I *think* I know where you're going with this," responded Stampaugh with another pained expression. He could feel his blood pressure spiking over Big Mike's insinuation. "We're looking to save us *all* some money-"

"Uh huh. Well, we've been hearing rumors of padded bills and kickbacks from condo contractors up and down Boca Beach," countered Big Mike, laying his cards on the table, "and we-"

Losing his temper, Stampaugh interrupted and pointed a finger at Big Mike. "I can assure you that *none* of that is going on here at Delmar, Mr. Rosenberg. We run a tight ship here."

Hitting on a touchy subject, all fifty-one residents present joined the brouhaha and broke into a heated discussion as the meeting spun out of control. Nervous about her complicity in the kickbacks, and not having a clue as to what to do next, board member Desiree Stone acted like a monkey on speed chewing on a fly swatter, nervously crossing her legs twice. At the other end of the table, vice president Anatolla leaned forward, craning his neck to see around the ponderous president to get a better view of Miss Stone. Wasserman continued to text message a hooker he'd just met online, while Stampaugh looked expectantly at Sarah Glitzsky to defend their fake bid in the middle of the rising pandemonium. In the center of it all, Glitzsky knew she had to do something before complete chaos ensued.

"Let me remind everyone that Mr. Stampaugh and our board have worked tirelessly to save us hundreds of thousands of dollars, Mr. Rosenberg," said Glitzsky. "How dare you imply we'd take any money from our own condo. Shame on you!" Her act had been well-rehearsed from scores of previous insinuations and seemed to momentarily stay the angry residents.

"Yeah, well, ideally, *that's* the world *I* want to live in," Big Mike added sarcastically. "Just wanna make *sure* that's where we are today." His retort was accompanied by a twitter of "yeahs" and several "go get'um Big Mike" encouragements from the back of the room.

Refusing to buy into any more of Big Mike's taunts, Glitzsky moved toward a vote and scanned the room again for dissenters. "Any more discussion on the storm shutter bidding?" she asked in a calmer voice. Seeing no hands go up, she said, "Call for a vote. All in favor of choosing Steinberg Storm Windows, raise your hand and say 'aye'." All the board officers and directors present raised their hands. The vote was unanimous as she brought the gavel down hard enough to make Desiree wince and cross her legs again.

"Motion approved. Our contract goes to Steinberg Storm Windows."

As the board celebrated in restrained exuberance, Glitzsky, Stampaugh, Anatolla, Wasserman and Stone ignored the grumbling and turned to each other to exchange congratulatory fist bumps and high fives as dollar signs filled their eyes. Each of the directors had mistakenly assumed they had locked in an equal portion of the kickbacks. Little did they know Stampaugh had generously put himself at the top of the list for the lion's share.

"Meeting adjourned," said Glitzsky, banging her gavel one last time, turning a deaf ear to the grumbling.

For the Delmar Board of Directors, it looked like it was going to be a great holiday season after all.

NINE

The sun had set an hour ago, and Michael Steinberg was barreling south on I-75 toward the turnpike entrance at seventy miles an hour in his big V-8 Tundra. The building contractor was returning from Shands Medical Center in Gainesville, reportedly one of the best Alzheimer's treatment centers in the country. Many of the Century Villages residents in Deerfield Beach where his mother lived sent family members there for treatment-at least the ones who could afford the higher costs of care there. Knowing that Medicare paid most of the bill, he was less concerned with the expense than with getting the best care that money could buy for his mom. He liked the intern who had given his solemn promise to take good care of his mother, but he couldn't figure out why she kept calling him Melvin.

Steinberg had just stopped off on his way back to Boca to check on his elderly Aunt Miriam who lived in The Villages south of Ocala. His aunt had become the undisputed Mahjong queen at the condo community, and he'd just spent the last half hour patiently listening to her gripe about her arthritis, bladder control issues, the outrageous cost of Manischewitz and hearing aid batteries, and how the country is going to 'hell in a handbag'. Widowed three times in the last ten years, Aunt Miriam had survived the passing of all three husbands, each of whom were retired personal injury lawyers, two of whom sold their practices in Miami Beach and Hallandale years before. As a result of her extended term of life on the planet, she was reputed to be worth over six million dollars, which was six million reasons for Mike Steinberg to stay in her good graces.

He reached to turn up the volume to AC/DC belting out the last few bars of *Highway to Hell*, took another toke off his joint and drifted into a review of all the Star Trek movies he'd seen. A hardcore Trekkie since he was a teenager, he was stringing the movie titles together in his pot-ravaged gourd as he reflected on the last six years of Alzheimer's treatments for his mom.

That's when he saw the flashing blue lights in his rear view mirror. He knew the traffic stop wasn't for speeding because, whenever he was stoned, Steinberg had a habit of slowing down to a speed well under the limit. Maybe he'd swerved, but in his current state of mind, he couldn't be sure. Quickly stubbing out the roach in the ashtray, Steinberg chewed it up and swallowed it as he rolled down the window and came to a stop on the shoulder of I-75. With a DUI on his license from last year, he couldn't afford another ticket and frantically waved the pot smoke out his open window. Silently, he said a prayer in Hebrew before he saw the deputy sheriff exit his cruiser in his mirror and walk toward him, flashlight in hand.

The Marion County deputy was a fairly young-looking guy with a buzz cut, not much older than Steinberg's son. The deputy stood back from the driver's door as he shined the flashlight around the interior of the Tundra. Seeing no obvious contraband, he asked Steinberg to step out and produce his driver's license, and the contractor obeyed.

The good ole boy deputy sheriff checked his license before asking the age-old question; "Sir, do you know why I stopped you?"

Steinberg never knew how to handle this question, and the high from the grass made him want to add some levity. "Ah…'cause it's a dark lonely road and you needed someone to talk to?" he ventured.

The deputy shot him an icy stare as he shined the flashlight in Steinberg's face, already suspicious of South Floridians-especially those from Boca Raton. "Sir, I noticed you were driving erratically. Have you been drinking tonight?"

Steinberg was elated over what appeared to be a routine traffic stop. "Nothing to drink, but I *was* swerving a bit. I dropped my cigarette on my seat."

Unconvinced, the deputy cocked his head. "Mind taking a Breathalyzer?"

"No, not at all."

"Because I definitely smell something funny."

After the field sobriety test, the deputy was still suspicious and got on his radio to check for outstanding warrants. After Steinberg came up clean, the deputy walked back to the pickup and gave the Tundra a thorough inspection with his flashlight before the beam settled on his toolbox in the back of his truck.

"Mind if I have a look inside?" the deputy asked.

"Well, yeah, I kinda do mind," answered Steinberg.

"Watcha got in there, Mr. Steinberg? Drugs?"

"Just tools, officer."

"I can bring in a K-9 unit, Mr. Steinberg. If you wanna do this the hard way."

"K-9s? In The Villages, deputy?" marveled Steinberg. "Really? What're they sniffing around for, officer, bootleg DentuCream?" Already an hour behind schedule, he decided it was best to comply with the officer's request. He certainly didn't need the deputy on his case and calling for back-up.

After the deputy did a thorough search of Steinberg's toolbox, he found a pair of chrome-plated hemostats in the top tray and held them up. "Whaddya use these for, Mr. Steinberg?"

"Mini clamp."

The good-ole-boy deputy gave him a skeptical look. "Uh huh. Tell me, why they got burn marks on the tips?"

"Musta been a hot day, officer."

"You're a regular wise guy, aintcha?" tossing them back into the tool box. Finding nothing else to justify a much-needed drug bust to meet his quota, the deputy resigned himself to making corporal the hard way and let him off with a warning about the dangers of drugs and driving erratically. As the officer wished him a good night, he unleashed a spit wad of thick tobacco onto the pavement, inundating a lone scorpion in the process. Still baked from the weed, Steinberg watched from inside the truck as the tobacco-covered scorpion crawled off the pavement into the grass in search of safer ground.

Humming along again at seventy-five miles an hour, the contractor figured to make the drive from the Villages to Boca in under five hours, barring any further encounters with good-ole-boy cops or tobacco-covered scorpions. He tossed the warning ticket out of the window along with an empty Burger King container as he thought about his visit with his mom, still confused about why she kept calling him Melvin.

A few more miles further south on Florida's Turnpike, he noticed a flatbed semi up ahead stacked high with loosely-chained crushed cars. As Steinberg pulled closer to the overloaded eighteen wheeler, the crushed cars teetered and the truck began to swerve. As he came up alongside, he could see the truck driver was busy texting, likely sending a message to a hooker at the next rest stop, he thought. At his current speed, Steinberg calculated that the truck would likely block his exit onto Glades Road unless he could get around it fast.

Seeing the SR 808 sign that marked the exit a quarter mile ahead, he switched off the cruise control and pressed the accelerator to the floor. It was always a thrill to hear the deep-throated roar from the big V-8 as he pushed the truck hard to get around the teetering load of crushed cars.

Without warning, the big flatbed drifted left, forcing him into the emergency lane just as he began to pass. "What the hell?" he blurted as he struggled to keep the Tundra under control. He found himself straddling both lanes as he continued to accelerate with the gas pedal pressed to the floor. Just as he squeezed in front of the truck and prepared to swing back into the far right lane to exit the turnpike, he saw the Glades Road exit ramp zip by on his right.

"Sonofagun!' he yelled. Madder than a one legged man in an ass kicking contest, Steinberg pounded on his wheel in frustration. Hitting his horn, he flipped the flatbed driver off in his rear view mirror, resigning himself to exiting further south on Sample Road in Pompano Beach and pony up another buck for the extra toll. As he slowed the Tundra back down and breathed a sigh of relief, he knew just how close he'd come to rolling his rig. His cell phone rang, and he instantly recognized the 561 area code and office number from Delmar. He took a deep breath before answering.

"Working late, huh Dyson? How'ya doin', partner?" he asked.

"It's Maria, Mike. Can you hold for Mr. Stampaugh?"

"Wait. Maria, did we get the contract?" asked Steinberg anxiously, thinking there was still a chance that something might go right for him today.

"I'll let you talk to Mr. Stampaugh. Hang on. He's right here." There was a click and a pause as Steinberg waited to hear the news that would make or break his year. He heard the voice of Dyson Stampaugh.

"Mike, how are ya?"

"Pretty good, except for a truck full of junk cars that almost creamed me. Just now heading back to Boca from a hospital visit with my mom. Did we get the hurricane shutter contract?"

"Yessir, you did, just like I promised." Stampaugh paused as he thought about how to best phrase the change in their bonus arrangement. "To get your bid approved though, Mike, I had to promise the board members that you'd pay them in one cash lump sum at the start."

Steinberg struggled to contain his annoyance with the condo manager as he passed a sign telling him he was five miles from his turnoff onto the Sample Road exit. "Dyson, you know that's not what we agreed on. We agreed to tailor the bonus money for the board members as the construction draws are paid. Remember? That was our deal."

Stampaugh's eyes narrowed as he prepared to deliver his crafty deception. "Well, that's out the window, so to speak. That's not gonna happen 'cause the other bids were actually a little under yours, Mike…but I pushed hard for your contract on the basis of delivering higher quality and having less follow-up expense for Delmar." Stampaugh paused to let his deception sink in. Sensing the contractor's reticence, he added, "Tell ya what, Mike. If I can get you more business from the residents over the next year or two, can we agree on these terms?"

"Next you're gonna tell me you can parallel park a train, Dyson." Steinberg hesitated, playing it cool as he pulled abreast of a car load of college girls partying and smoking pot in a BMW 735i with the interior lights on. Steinberg slowed down and matched speeds while he craned his neck for a better view. At the same time, he was determined to stay calm and focused in his conversation with the condo manager, aware that the details of his contract could net him a bunch more money.

"How much more business?" he asked.

Stampaugh knew a buying question when he heard it. He smiled and thought about his upcoming eighty grand payday as he confidently crossed his feet on his desk top. "Oh, probably another half-million in mirror and glasswork that I could swing your way.

These geezers maybe old enough to be original investors in apple...the fruit, I mean...but they got the bucks, Mike, and they're not afraid to throw some around and glitz up their interiors. After all, this *is* Boca."

Still a little skeptical, Steinberg thought about it. "Okay, I'm in, as long as Delmar will add an exclusivity clause for me on all related work for the next two years and lower the follow-up limit on warranty work to no more than three percent of contract." Steinberg knew that the manufacturer would reimburse him for up to ten percent on warranty work, allowing him to pocket the difference of seven percent for another hundred grand.

"Okay. We can do that, Mike," replied Stampaugh as he recrossed his feet and leaned back in the leather chair in his office.

"I'll need a few days to get the cash together, Dyson. I'm only going to deal with you on this, so I trust you'll distribute the, ah... *proceeds* to the others, right?"

"I'll take care of everything," said Stampaugh. "Call me when you have the cash and we'll sign the paperwork at my office."

"Okay, Dyson. I'm counting on you." As they hung up, Stampaugh did a fist pump in the air in his office, suddenly giddy with the thought of an eighty thousand dollar payday.

The wild student party in the BMW continued to hold Steinberg's attention like a live episode of *Girls Gone Wild* as the two vehicles hurtled down the turnpike at seventy-five miles an hour separated by five feet of pavement. For a moment, his thoughts drifted to his petit college girlfriend, raven-haired Leslie Paulen. Leslie was far and away the most sensual girl he'd ever dated, and he wished she could be sitting next to him in the Tundra right now. Totally absorbed in his fantasy, he flew right by the Atlantic Boulevard exit ramp.

"Sonofagun!" he exclaimed again. Forced to drive to the next exit at Coconut Creek Parkway nine miles further south, at least he'd have some entertainment along the way.

Michael Steinberg had a lot to be grateful for as he raced toward Boca, grinning from ear to ear. He'd just landed the most lucrative construction job in his company's ten-year history.

⇒╬⇐

Tommy Tomlinson was fanatical about keeping his name off any official records or government forms, living small, off the grid, down low and under the radar. Paranoid about having his cover blown, he would avoid using his alias David Callahan in print whenever possible, even putting the utility bills in his landlord's name and reimbursing Lance Meyer monthly from his moldy stash of cash when he paid the rent. Even his rented home at Greenwood Mansion was leased in the name of a shell corporation, Neptune Holdings, created solely for the purpose of keeping his pursuers off his trail.

The treasure hunter who cheated his business partners out of over a hundred million in gold was always very cautious about having contact with strangers in Boca, trusting only his landlord whenever a contractor needed access to the historic villa on South Boca Beach. Since no one really knew who he was, Tomlinson wasn't a total recluse, often venturing out to restaurants and shopping at Walmart with his girlfriend Andrea. They kept a low profile wherever they shopped, paying in moldy cash for canned oysters, tuna and sardines, canned salmon, black olives and boxes of saltine crackers. It was a diet that he developed from spending weeks at sea during his salvage operation, and it had stuck with him.

The two-foot thick stone walls that kept Greenwood Mansion cool but damp had been built long before air conditioning was even invented. Callahan remedied this by setting up a portable AC unit in the basement where he spent most of his time. Once in a while, his paranoia would get away from him, and he would think about transporting his $170 million in moldy cash and crated gold coins to a new hideout. But until things got really dicey, he planned to stay put and entertain himself with the online obituaries while meticulously cleaning his three assault rifles.

⇥⊦⇤

That evening, alone in the clubhouse, Anthony Anatolla had been sitting on the toilet in the men's room, delighted with the privacy. Just as he was about to finish the magazine article about all the strange new ways to enhance his virility, the lights went out.

"What the hell?" he whined out loud. Sitting in the darkened bathroom stall for a moment, he listened for the sounds of anyone that might be present before he stood up to fix the problem, girlie magazine in one hand and tissue paper in the other. In the dark, Anatolla pushed open the stall door with his elbow and shuffled over to the wall-mounted timer with his pants around his ankles, oblivious to the three-foot long piece of tissue paper that was stuck to the heel of his shoe.

"Damn timers!" he complained out loud. "How ya supposed to take a crap and pleasure yerself in five minutes?" He fumbled for the switch on the wall, turned the timer dial to the full five-minute maximum and watched the lights come back on. Still holding his magazine, and trailing the toilet paper from the heel of his shoe, Anatolla did an about face toward the stall to finish his disgusting deed.

"Glitzsky, you witch!" he exclaimed out loud. "Who the hell puts five-minute timers in a men's room for God's sake?"

TEN

Dressed in his Bora Bora tank top and khaki shorts, Mark sat on a barstool at the outdoor patio bar at Shooters in Ft. Lauderdale, hanging out with his favorite bartender. As he and Rob watched the party animals parading past the boats rafted up five abreast, many were oohing and aahing Mark's forty-four- foot twin turbo catamaran "Multiple Ohhhs..." moored a hundred feet from the bar. It was mid-afternoon on Saturday, and Mark was on his second margarita, thoroughly entertained by the comments. Earlier, he slipped the dock valet a fifty to moor his showboat within sight of the outside bar, directly in front of the huge hot tub teeming with the best crop of gold diggers that South Florida had to offer.

"So, Mark, what's the craziest date you ever had?" asked Rob as he prepared two daiquiris for a couple sitting at the end of the bar.

Mark thought a moment. "I met this one girl at Mezzanottes one night. Smokin' hot, very feminine, a great dancer. Turns out she was a *shemale.*"

"Yeah, and you found out how?" Grinning, Rob was all ears.

"Well, luckily, she told me before we got too romantic and even invited me to feel her…ah, implants"-

"You didn't!" said Rob.

To keep him in suspense, Mark took a sip of his margarita before continuing. "Well, when we sat down at the bar, I saw something stirring that made me nervous."

Rob broke out laughing. "So, marriage was out of the question?"

"Well…I guess. So, later, I took the shemale thing off my bucket list," said Mark with a dead pan look.

"I took the bucket list off my bucket list," quipped Rob.

Mark continued. "Uh huh. So after that episode, my confidence took a hit and I decided to stop even thinking about love on the first date."

Rob gave him a skeptical look. "So, how'd that work out for you?"

"I decided to skip the first date."

"Uh huh." Rob knew there was more.

"But that didn't work, so I just stopped dating."

Rob didn't look convinced. "Yeah, right."

"For two whole days," added Mark.

"Heard that." Rob waited to hear more as he polished a highball glass behind the counter while Mark contemplated his dry spell, realizing he'd been stranded between wives and sailboats for far too long.

His introspection was interrupted by a heavy-set girl with a gold tooth, leopard-print bikini, straw cowboy hat and a "See Rock City" button pinned to her sumptuous bikini top as she made her way like a linebacker through the crowded bar. With her gaze fixed firmly on Mark, she was fanning herself with the color brochures from the Yankee Clipper Hotel as she sidled up to him.

"Hi, honey. I'm Tammy from Knoxville. What's *yer* name?" she asked in a hillbilly Tennessee twang as she looked him up and down like he was the flavor *du jour*.

Mark winced from the unwanted attention. He had perfected a whole bag of tricks he used to deflect such unwanted advances and put them in play. Scowling at her, he said, "They called me 'Hannibal the Cannibal' in the slammer."

Tammy wrinkled up her nose in distaste, but didn't take the hint and moved in closer, seemingly unaware of the important concept of personal space. "That's so, ah…cute…I guess," doing her best to look beyond his faults. "What were ya in jail fer, Hannibal?"

With a deadpan look, Mark said: "I was driving drunk and hit a deer, ah…well…a dear old man…with my car."

"Oh, dear."

"Exactly."

"Whad'ya do?" she asked.

"Well…I left a note, and…"

Tammy laughed so hard she snorted like a wild boar. She was convinced that Mark would sure make a big hit at her trailer park and began to plot a way to get him to come home to her next pig roast at her double-wide in Nashville. Determined to clear Tammy from his field of vision, he tried again to discourage her with another attempt to get her to move on. Frowning at her sternly, he held up a napkin from the stack on the bar.

"Tammy, do you think these bar napkins smell like chloroform?" A horrified look crossed her face, and Tammy's maternal instincts finally took a back seat to fear for her safety. Clueless as to what to say, she finally got the message and opted to keep on moving down the row of bar stools toward the next available hunky guy.

Relieved, Rob was chuckling in amusement. "We have a *wiener.*"

"Jeez. Thought she'd never leave," said Mark. Exasperated with the woman's perseverance, he sighed, took another sip of his margarita, moving on to less weighty issues.

"You know you're a redneck if your home has wheels but your car doesn't," joked Rob.

Mark chuckled as he glanced over at Tammy putting the moves on one of the regulars he knew from the dive shop. "Ten bucks says she thinks that professional wrestling is real but the moon landing was faked," he said. Temporarily freed from the tyranny of plump redneck girls in bikinis wearing "See Rock City" buttons, Mark and Rob returned to their favorite game.

"Think I see a '10' out there Rob," said Mark, looking toward the dock and shading his eyes.

"You sure she's not an LDB?"

"LDB?" queried Mark.

"Long distance beauty," explained Rob as Mark studied the girl on the dock from his barstool.

"Yup. Looks like a '10'," confirmed Mark.

"No way," said Rob skeptically, taking a break from the pina coladas he was blending for the two oddly-dressed gay guys sitting near Mark at the bar. The men were feverishly texting back and forth while trying to catch his eye. "Last time you spotted a '10' you were so drunk you bit your hand eating a sandwich. Remember stud nuts?"

"How could I forget?" said Mark. "It was a Sunday, and I was wearing the same clothes from a party in Deerfield Beach from the day before...*while* I was having breakfast with a girl that said her car was still parked at the Shooter's valet from three days before that. What was her name?"

"Valerie. And they say you can't party," said Rob as he poured two pina coladas from his blender into glasses for the gay caballeros in the patent leather vests, blue Mohawks and nose rings. He set the drinks on the counter and garnished them with sliced pineapple and the dainty pink umbrellas they'd specifically requested. Mark noticed one of the men wore a ring imprinted with the words 'LET'S RODEO'. Intrigued with his ring and thoroughly entertained with their get-up, and against his better judgment, Mark decided to risk a friendly conversation with the one sitting two seats over.

Mark leaned in with his best Hollywood smile. "Hey guys, what's with the matching outfits today?"

The limp-wristed man with the rodeo ring sitting closest turned to him with a big smile, pleased with the attention. "We're part of a gay country-western act on our way to Miami for a show," he said with a lisp.

"Great! Love the black vests and blue Mohawks," said Mark taking a sip of his margarita. "Always curious about niche marketing. What's your target market?"

"Depends," answered Mr. Rodeo. "Do you enjoy a girl's body?"

"This a trick question? I sure do," answered Mark.

"Well, then not *you!*" pronounced Mr. Rodeo abruptly as he turned back to his partner who was busy twirling his pink umbrella in obvious annoyance over the attention his partner was getting.

Mark leaned forward and lowered his voice. "Rob, what the hell's with the leatherette twins with the blue Mohawks and facial hardware?"

Rob gestured with his thumb toward the men. "Those girls? Strictly dickly. Looks like you caught their eye, handsome." Rob winked at him. "Make you wonder where life on this planet is heading?"

With a pained expression, Mark took a sip of his margarita and sat up higher, raising his glass to make a toast. "As a nod to the new era of sexual liberalism, why don't we just go ahead and replace Alexander Hamilton's portrait on the ten dollar bill with a shemale? Think that'd satisfy the pervs out there?" he asked with a hint of sarcasm.

Rob chuckled as he cleaned the counter top. "Sure, for about five minutes. He nodded at Mark's glass. "'Nother margarita?"

Mark shook his head and drained the rest of his drink. Slipping a twenty under his glass, he took a moment to preen himself in the mirror behind the bar. "Yeah, well, not in your lifetime, pal," said Mark to no one in particular as he straightened his collar and smoothed his hair. "Girls are way too interesting." He checked over his shoulder to see if the pretty girl admiring his boat was still standing on the dock.

Rob knew the drill. "Good hunting there, skipper."

Drawn to the stunning blonde in the black sheer cover-up, thong, high heels and black Mercedes Benz cap, Mark left his bar stool and meandered casually in her direction. When he got closer, he stopped to check the power hook-up and wastewater stream that poured from his boat's air conditioner through-hull. If everything was still the way he left it below deck, "Multiple Ohhhs…" would be nice and cool inside with a pitcher of margaritas waiting in the fridge. Busy planning the details for his own intimate episode of *Love Boat,* he watched her admire the boat's sleek lines and sparkly black lacquer paint with the red and orange flames and yellow lettering all custom-designed by a local artist. Mark sidled up to the girl with his best Hollywood smile.

"Love your heels. Jimmy Choo, right?"

She turned away from the catamaran to size him up, shading her green eyes from the bright sun, her smile as beautiful as a morning sunrise. Her plan was paying off, and she was curious about the man with an appreciation for designer shoes who'd just joined her on the dock. "You a shoe salesman or something?" she asked.

Mark chuckled. "Hardly."

"Game show host?" she asked, grinning.

Mark liked her sense of humor. "Sexy shoes are just a hobby," he said, extending his hand. "Mark McAllister."

"Amanda Peterson," she said, shaking his hand demurely. "This your boat? Talk about sexy!" Still shading her eyes, she swept her gaze from bow to stern in unbridled admiration.

"Yes, ma'am!" said Mark proudly. "Just had the engines tuned and blueprinted." He watched her eyes light up as she imagined how fast it would go. Her French-manicured nails ran daintily over the leading edge of the bow as she pointed to the boat's name scrawled across the hull.

"Gotta be a good story behind a name like that. How'd you come up with 'Multiple Ohhhs…'?"

Knowing he was being tested, Mark opted to play it cool and gave her the PG-rated answer. "It's what I always hear from my passengers," he said with a wink. That earned him the smile he was hoping for.

"You're funny." Entertained by the man with intelligence and sensitivity, Amanda was beginning to feel more comfortable with him. Intrigued with his confident playfulness and disarming humor, he seemed a refreshing change from the pumped-up muscle-bound meatheads that she so often encountered. She shot him a quizzical look. "Just out of curiosity, Mark, what sign were you born under?"

"Keep off the grass."

"No, seriously."

"I don't believe in astrology. I'm an Aquarius and we're very skeptical." He tried hard to keep a straight face.

"Really." She looked him up and down again, thoroughly amused with the irony and decided it was her turn to tease. Enthralled with his high-performance catamaran, and now his beguiling humor, she turned her attention back to the boat. "She's beautiful. How fast will she go?" giving him a look that could melt glaciers as she did a graceful pirouette like she was performing at the Met.

Mark was entertained by her moves. "She'll do a hundred and twenty-five on a flat sea. Looks like someone's had some ballet."

"You've got a sharp eye for ballet moves, said Amanda. "I'm with the Boca City Ballet. You should come see our performance of 'The Nutcracker' next Saturday."

"I just might hafta to that, Amanda." He knew a thrill-seeker when he saw one. "You like fast boats?"

"I *love* fast boats!" She snugged her cap over her blonde coiffure as if she were already onboard and moving at warp speed. As he watched her running her manicured fingers along the stainless steel bow rail, Mark's mind drifted, imagining those fingers dancing up and down his torso.

Out in the middle of the channel, three men aboard a Super Scarab passing slowly by were waving and trying to get her attention. Ignoring their drunken antics, she returned her attention back to Mark. "Your name sounds familiar. Are you related to Lloyd McAllister, the developer?"

"He was my dad. I'm the President of Mizner Park Development, when I'm not raising donations for the Save-Our-Turtles Foundation." He waited to see how she would respond to his reference to charitable causes. Guessing she was more about the money and less about the charities, he shifted gears. "You know where Delmar is on Boca Beach?"

"Isn't that the tall round building that looks like a giant gold-colored vibrator?" she asked with a smile.

Mark was amused. "Yup, that's the *one*. It was our biggest beach project, a scaled-down version of the Gherkin Tower in London. I have one of the penthouses there."

Amanda seemed pleased with his explanation, leaning with her back against his boat as if daring him to make a move. "That's my all-time favorite condo on Boca Beach. I'll bet your view there is gorgeous," she said.

"Not as gorgeous as the one in front of me right now," responded Mark with as much sincerity as he could muster.

Amanda blushed at his compliment and giggled like a school-girl, throwing him a playful jab to the shoulder. "Aw, c'mon Mark," she teased. "Tell me the truth. I'll bet you say that to all the girls you meet."

"Nope. Just you, girl."

She raised her eyebrows in flirty skepticism, wanting to know more about him and changed the subject to something safer. "I heard Mizner Development's one of the biggest developers in Florida. That true?"

"Thirty-two million in EBIDTA last year."

Amanda looked puzzled. "EBIDTA? That a character from *Star Wars*?"

Mark chuckled, unable to tell if she was messing with him or just unfamiliar with the term. "EBIDTA's an accounting term-earnings before income, depreciation, taxes and amortization. Income from operations, more or less."

"I know. I was messin' with ya. I was a business major before joining the ballet company. You sound smart, Mark. What do you do there again?"

"I took over our family business as President after I lost my dad." He was proud of his family's success and hoped he hadn't sounded too arrogant with his response. "Boring stuff. Let's talk about you, Amanda. You here by yourself?"

"I came with a coupla' girlfriends," she said, gesturing toward the bar at the two attractive brunettes huddled together, smiling and waving from their barstools. "We were admiring your boat from the bar. I wanted to get a closer look," she said coyly.

Like a politician running for office, he waved at her friends to assure them everything was okay. "Are all three of you performers?" he asked.

She tugged on her cap and smiled. "We're all dancers in the same company."

Sensing she was ready to take it to the next level, he asked, "Can I show you around inside, Amanda? Got an ice-cold pitcher of margaritas ready," he said, extending his hand expectantly, "... and a mink-covered master cabin berth," knowing women loved the feel of mink on their bare skin.

"Mink, huh? Well, this I might hafta see!" Not wanting to make it too easy for him, she pretended to need more persuasion, trying to hide her desire to get better acquainted. He seemed nice enough. She looked back toward the bar at her companions for approval.

"Don't worry about your girl friends," Mark reassured her. "I've known the bartender since high school. Rob's a gentleman-he'll take good care of them."

"Sure, why not. Love to see what you have down below, captain," said Amanda as she did a flirty sweep of his torso. She took his hand to steady herself, slipped off her Jimmy Choo heels and stepped aboard in her bare feet. As he slid back the cabin door for her, she caught her reflection in the polished black gel coat and adjusted the straps to her top, pretending not to notice that he was completely captivated by her every move.

She turned and gave a final wave to her friends at the bar as they headed below to explore each other's worlds.

After a quick lunch at Margeaux's "Hot Bikini Dog" stand, Dominick grabbed his car keys and the envelope with two grand in cash and headed for his Mercedes to hook up with Dr. Barry Levenson. Dr. Levenson was professor of chemistry at Florida Atlantic University and his former high school professor. Fifteen minutes later, he pulled up to the Starbucks at Glades Plaza. Pushing the big brass door open, he had a twinge of *déjà vu* as he remembered proposing to Margeaux at the very same coffee house years earlier. Scanning the bistro, Dominick quickly recognized the professor with his bushy grey hair and thick black glasses, the nerdy Albert Einstein look that his students used to find so hilarious.

"Barry, good to see you," said Dominick, shaking hands with his former professor as he took a seat across from him in the booth.

Removing the cash-laden envelope from his pants pocket and laying it on the table, his stomach emitted a loud gurgling sound. Embarrassed, he patted his belly. "Sorry. Wolfed down some leftovers from my girlfriend's 'Hot Bikini Dog' stand," he explained. "Just two corndogs with hot mustard fighting for kennel space down there, professor."

Amused, Dr. Levenson unfolded his hands and eyed the envelope. "Dominick, with those squared-off glasses, you know you look a lot like the hairless version of Walter White from *Breaking Bad*." He smiled and paused. "You know, with your grades in chemistry, I sure didn't figure you'd ever become a chemistry teacher."

"Nowadays it's more of a hobby," responded Dominick, his hand resting on the envelope. "So, whad'ya got for me, Barry?" Before he could answer, an attractive barista in her twenties with short-cropped brown hair and white apron arrived at their table.

"Professor Levenson, right?" she asked. Levenson nodded, gratified that he'd been recognized. "What can I get for you two today?"

"Large triple espresso mocha, no cream, please," said Levenson.

"Okay, sure thing." She looked up expectantly at Dominick. "And for you, sir?"

"I'll have the same, only with whip cream and *lots* of privacy. Okeydokey, smokey?"

"Sure thing," she said. "Be just a coupla minutes, guys. We're just finishing up on a big order for the FAU football coaches." She headed back toward the bar to prepare their espressos.

Dr. Levenson sat up and leaned forward. "I'm assuming this is all off the record," said the professor as he adjusted his glasses.

"Correcto mundo." Dominick slid the envelope across the table without taking his hand off it. "We never even had this meeting. Agreed?"

"Agreed." The professor gestured toward the envelope. "May I?" Dominick nodded. After running his thumbnail across the bills inside to do a quick count of the cash, Levenson stuffed it inside his coat pocket and pulled out several folded pages of lab instructions as he checked his surroundings again to make sure no one was eavesdropping.

Levenson lowered his voice. "To get the methylamine yield you want, there's two ways we can go here. I'll start with the cheapest, but also the most hazardous," said the professor as he unfolded the illustration and inverted it so Dominick could follow. "There are several ways to make the compound, and you could probably synthesize it right in your kitchen sink. Chemically speaking, methylamine is just ammonia with one hydrogen atom swapped out for a methyl complex-a carbon atom with three hydrogen atoms." Dominick looked puzzled, so he paused to make sure his student was following. "You could bubble ammonia gas through liquid methanol that's been laced with silica gel, which is a common ingredient in packaging material. But, like I said, it is *very* dangerous."

"Where's the easiest place to pick this stuff up?" asked Dominick.

"You can buy these chemicals at most industrial outlets and do-it-yourself hardware stores," explained the professor. "Maybe Home Depot's got it. The packages of silica gel are commonly found in shoe boxes and electronic packaging to keep them dry. We get our supplies through the state university wholesalers."

"Buying methylamine in bulk would probably attract a lot of attention, wouldn't it? Definitely don't need the DEA on my case."

"The authorities do keep an eye on this stuff, so there is that risk," acknowledged Levenson. "Smaller quantities shouldn't draw much attention. Even when our procuring agents buy it for our lab classes, there's a fair amount of red tape." He paused and removed a business card from his attache. "Or, you can do this, the safer but more expensive method and buy it ready to use," sliding the business card across the table. Dominick picked it up and studied it. The card read CARMINE CARREAUX, Chemical Engineer, Dow Chemical, Baton Rouge, Louisiana. There was a phone number written on it in blue ball point pen.

Dominick squinted at the card. "Who's this guy?"

"Your methylamine contact in Baton Rouge. Cost you thirteen grand a gallon. With total discretion. Black market price. I got him down from fifteen grand only because FAU gives him so much business."

"Why's this stuff so expensive?"

"Very hard to synthesize safely. Lotta folks get killed trying. Usually done in complex processes in large chemical plants," explained Levenson. "So, I saved you twenty grand on your ten gallon order."

"You buckin' for a raise here, Barry?"

"I'm good with the two grand." Levenson paused to clean his glasses. "Unless you're feeling overly generous." The professor smirked and leaned forward, lowering his voice. "Be careful with Carmine. I vouched for you, but you should know this guy's a heavyweight. Well-connected. Treat him right."

Not one to be intimidated, Dominick ran his hand over his clean-shaven head and put his elbow on the table. "Yeah, well, gotta few heavyweights playing on my team, too, Barry."

"You won't need them, Dom. Carmine's a businessman. Don't bring any firearms with you either-he's a pretty straight-up guy. Just treat him like a businessman and everything will be fine." Levenson had a feeling this would be the best piece of advice he would ever give his former chemistry student.

"Here we go, guys," interrupted the barista as she set their drinks on the table. "Two triple espresso mochas, one with cream, and one without." She smiled, tucking her tray under her arm and set the check down, along with two plastic to-go caps, straws and napkins. "Enjoy!"

"Thanks, Natalie." Levenson watched as she headed back to the bar. "Nice lookin' girl. Too bad she's a carpet muncher."

"How do you know?" asked Dominick.

"Former student," explained Levenson. "She ignored the guys and paid more attention to the girls than she did her assignments." The professor shrugged. "Maybe that's why she's waiting tables now."

ELEVEN

A former Playmate of the Month a few years back, Erin Griffith spent an hour a day at Gold's Gym in Boca. It was the perfect place to pursue her hidden agenda. The lavish gym was a known attraction for muscle heads, beefcake cops, well-to-do stockbrokers, gold diggers, wealthy real estate moguls, as well as her favorite prey-the millionaire sugar daddies looking for their next trophy wife.

Few actually knew of her secret ambition to set herself up with a half-million a year in income without having to work for it. Erin considered work and careers appropriate for the working stiffs, but far too mundane for herself. Her plan was to have a full-time nanny raise her kids after choosing only the most affluent of fathers before kicking them to the curb after she had their baby. After divorcing them, she would collect egregiously large child support payments that would provide her with enough extra income to gallivant around the globe with her boy toys, free of the responsibilities of motherhood.

With three marriages and three divorces already in her rear view mirror, and one child from each marriage, her plan was working. It was no secret that Erin loved men, but only just long enough to bear them one child each. Her criteria for sharing her body and intimacy were actually quite simple; as long as they were good looking, weren't shootin' blanks, had a high sperm count, net worth over ten million and could afford a minimum child support payment of twelve grand a month, nothing else really mattered. She was definitely all about the money, right down to her personalized Florida license plate that read 'FUN ONE'.

While the conditions for allowing men in her bed were fairly unique, her female playmates were subject to an entirely different set of criteria. Erin Griffith was truly a rich man's nightmare dressed up to look like a daydream. A big fan of Betsy Salkind, Erin believed in her immutable quote; "Men are like linoleum floors. Lay 'em right, and you can walk all over them for thirty years."

This morning, she was working out in her Under Armour skin-tight pink tights with her personal trainer, Demetrius. As he watched her bending backward over the exercise ball to do her tricep extensions, the Jamaican-born body builder was spell-bound, transfixed by her well-defined midriff and super-toned body.

"There, three sets of twelve," announced Erin, huffing and puffing. She extended her arms over her head and unceremoniously dropped the fifteen pound dumb bells onto the rubber matt. "Demetrius?" As she looked up, her trainer appeared hypnotized, his eyes riveted to her pelvis.

"Oh, yeah, great work, Erin," said Demetrius in a strong Jamaican accent, regaining his composure. "Now, we rolllllloxxx… breathe in…stretch out," extending his arms outward and making an arc in the air.

As she sat in recovery mode on the exercise matt, out of the corner of her eye she noticed the handsome man in a black tank top taking an interest in her as he stood at the squat machine.

Erin turned her head nonchalantly to check out the man who was checking her out. She remembered a friend pointing him out in the gym one day as the son of a wealthy developer. She noticed he was well-built, with dark brown hair and wearing a black Mercedes Benz cap. Their eyes met as she cocked her head, flashed her twenty-five-grand dental work and touched the tip of her tongue to her sensuous Botox-enhanced lips. The subliminal gesture had its desired effect as the hunky guy gave Erin a big smile.

"Are we done for today, Demetrius?" she asked. Demetrius knew it really wasn't a question. He'd seen Erin weave her web many times as she prepared to clear her dance card to make room for the new sugar daddy interview.

"We're done, pretty lady. See you again Friday," he said with a final appreciative look at his favorite client. Demetrius knew she was out of his league, but it wouldn't stop him from dreaming.

Clearing the deck for the next set of *cojones* to come her way, Erin dismissed her personal trainer with a fist bump and a smile, anticipating a prompt visit from the handsome man in the black tank top. Of all the things in the world that she best understood, at the top of her list were men.

Mark knew she was putting on a show for him and continued to watch her from the corner of his eye, entertained with her performance as she got on all fours on the workout matt. Her next move was to extend her shapely derriere as far as she could in an exaggerated spinal stretch. She followed that move with a flip onto her back, thrusting her legs up high as she began her air bicycle exercise. Practiced on how to tease a guy into taking action, she was confident that her next move would bring him crawling over to her as she increased the tempo and extended her legs up as high as she could to keep his attention focused on her.

"Mercy," said Mark under his breath as he watched her show. Mesmerized by her workout, Mark could feel his juices flowing, compelling him to abandon his last set of squats and meet the girl who proved to be so artful at teasing him into submission. He adjusted his cap and sauntered across the floor to meet the most beautiful girl in the gym.

"Where you pedaling to in such a hurry, gorgeous?" Mark stood over her in admiration, up close for the first time as she lay suggestively on her back, sure that her blue eyes had the power to melt icebergs. She sat up and wrapped her arms around her knees, shaking her hair.

"Well, hey there, handsome. I was just pedaling over to see *you*," she said flirtatiously.

"Anyone ever tell you that you look like Pamela Lee Anderson"? Mark's brown eyes sparkled with obvious flirtation.

"Yeah, right," she said, fluffing her hair. "I'll bet you say that to all the blondes at Gold's. Like your tank top with the manta ray on the back. Bet you didn't get *that* at Walmart."

"Can ya tell?" as he pulled his tank top out in front of him to emphasize the logo. "Got it at the *bon marche* in Bora Bora last year."

"*Bon marche?*" she asked.

"An outdoor food and art market in French Polynesia," he explained. "The manta is a symbol of strength and intuition in Tahitian folklore. Ever been there?"

"No, but I heard it's beautiful," said Erin as she shook her hair again. "Love to go someday. A friend told me one time that French Polynesia's so colorful it makes the Bahamas look like they're in black and white." She paused to ask him a question. "What's your name, anyway?"

"Mark. Mark McAllister." The warmth from her smile made him feel like he was basking in sunshine.

"Are you one of the McAllisters that developed Boca West, Mizner Park and Delmar?"

"Guilty as charged," holding up his hand.

"No kidding? You related to Lloyd McAllister?"

"He was my dad. I took over when he passed away a year ago," he said with a hint of sorrow.

"I'm so sorry. He's practically a legend in Boca. I interviewed your father when I was a reporter years ago. I can see where you get your good looks." Quickly deciding he met all the criteria to father her next child, Erin didn't hesitate to place him at the top of her list. As she stood up, she pretended to smooth the wrinkles out of her close-fitting Under Armour tights and extended her hand. "I'm Erin Griffith."

A surprised look came over his face. "Oh, that's right. The former Playmate," he said, grasping her hand respectfully as if they were standing at a Hollywood Red Carpet event. "I remember hearing we had a former playmate living here in Boca."

"And working out at the same gym! What are the chances?" she asked with feigned innocence.

"Didn't you used to work for WPBT, the local TV station?" he asked.

"That was years ago. They couldn't afford me, I guess, so I moved on to bigger things," she explained.

"I think I remember. You were the reporter who helped clear my dad's name years ago when the accounting firm was accused of embezzling all that money." He was immediately sorry he'd made any reference to the two million dollars that went missing from the Save-Our-Turtles Foundation. The media had a field day with the scandal even though his dad made good on every dime of the missing money from his own pocket, even adding an extra half-million dollar donation to quell the media frenzy.

"Yeah, that was me," admitted Erin. "I thought your dad handled it like a real gentleman." Bored with the small talk, Erin was ready for his next move. She ignored the exaggerated grunting, clinking of weights and stares from the meatheads doing their squats and bench presses.

"I worked on Wall Street back then, and I remember watching you in the TV interview and wondering who that gorgeous woman was," hoping his compliment hadn't gone too far afield.

"There you go again, Mark. All those compliments. What's a girl to do?"

"Well, here's what we *could* do," offered Mark. "You could come out with me on my twin turbo catamaran for dinner. I might even let you drive." He was smiling as he imagined her standing at the helm with his arms wrapped around her. "I could, ah...give you a lesson."

There it was, the invitation she'd been expecting, but yet not exactly what she came to expect from men of his standing. At least she wouldn't have to put up with any candles or awkward small talk like a typical, boring Match.com-type first date. The way she saw it, they could get right down to business in the cabin and she could be headed down the yellow-brick road toward another fifteen grand a month in child support.

"Wow! That sounds great. I've never driven a go-fast boat before," said Erin. "Does it have a cabin?" she asked coyly.

"Air conditioned and upholstered in mink." He watched her eyes light up and could see she was definitely on board with the idea.

"Mink? That sounds...um...kinda sexy. Where do you keep your boat?" she asked demurely.

"Bimini Boatyard, just across the C-15 canal in Deerfield. It's a dry storage-"

"I've seen it. I heard it's really nice. Is it true the staff wears white gloves?"

He was amused with her *naivete,* reverting to the image of his mechanic covered in grease as he emerged from his boat's engine compartment two weeks ago. "Not sure about that, but...are you free Friday night?" He could sense she was weighing his invitation, certain that she was thinking about her social calendar.

Actually, Erin was secretly calculating how close she was to ovulating. Three to five days from her next ovulation, Erin knew the timing would be perfect to maximize her chances for conception.

"Sure! Shall I meet you at the marina?" she asked.

"How about five p.m. That way we'll have time for a sunset cruise before dinner."

"That sounds really nice, Mark." As she extended her hand to say goodbye, he planted a kiss on the top of her hand. Giggling like a schoolgirl while she strutted and flounced her hips, Erin headed toward the front door, waving at Demetrius, along with a host of other admirers on the way out.

Former playmate Erin Griffith had a pretty good feeling Mr. Mark McAllister was in the bag.

⇥⊹⇤

Two days later, after a romantic Friday night seafood feast at La Scala's on the water, Mark and Erin were hand-in-hand, cruising up the Intracoastal toward Lake Boca. The popular anchorage was sprinkled with luxury yachts filled with quiet couples and party animals cavorting their way into the hearts and minds of Boca's social hierarchy. In the light of a full moon, the catamaran was a colorful standout from the surrounding boats as Mark eased it westward at idle speed toward the less-traveled side of the lake with Erin at his side. The soulful sound of Amy Winehouse drifted across the moonlit water from a nearby sailboat as he steered away from the crowd. Small ripples from the twin hulls softly roiled the mirrored surface as they approached their anchorage. His catamaran was well-known, so Mark opted for the added privacy of an isolated spot and dropped anchor a good hundred yards from the nearest yacht. Erin looked up at him approvingly and rewarded his choice with a kiss.

Their date was unfolding exactly as she planned. Erin made a point to include assurances of responsible birth control in their hot pillow talk to ease his concerns over pregnancy, and she was hoping that Mark had a taste for narcotics when she showed him the baggie. She was surprised to see him pass on the gram of snow she brought to spice things up. Her feminine instincts told her she was ovulating, and Mark was playing right into her hands. She'd gotten so excited about making love on the luxurious mink berth that she'd almost worn him out, hungering for every drop of his seed.

After hours of many memorable moments and unending screams of joy, something about it began to feel a little off to Mark. His intuition told him things weren't quite right. Though it was just a feeling, experience had taught him the greater the emotional investment, the more likely it would be that things would run off the rails. Acting on a hunch, he grabbed his bathrobe and headed to the head where Erin had parked her purse. He needed to clear something up.

"Honey, where ya goin'?" she wanted to know as he left their mink-lined love nest for the first time in their marathon event.

"Drain my lizard," he said, remembering that Erin had stashed her purse in the starboard cabin locker above the stainless-steel sink. "You want another margarita while I'm up?"

In a coquettish move, she raised herself off the bed to tantalize him with her uncovered breasts. "Sure. I love your margaritas." After Mark left the cabin, Erin made good use of the intermission by lying on her back, pulling her knees up to her chin and rocking from side-to-side to increase her chances of conception while her next daddy-to-be was busy making her margarita.

Mark's intuition told him he was getting smoked as he flipped on the overhead lights in the head and turned on the water to mask his moves. He could hear the twelve-volt water pump under the sink kick in as he found her purse and rummaged through it to find what he was looking for.

Methodically, he set the items on the counter, one-by-one. There was her leather-bound checkbook, with a balance of $156,000 (no surprise there), Oakley sunglasses, pink Chanel lipstick, keys to her red AMG Mercedes, a half-eaten egg McMuffin, an unopened pack of condoms, her divorce attorney's business card with a smeared kiss in pink lipstick, a container of Tic Tacs, eleven Florida State Lottery tickets dated over the last two years, an empty prescription bottle of Prozac, a Snickers wrapper, an empty baggie with cocaine residue, Maybelline mascara, a latex glove, a bottle of Visine, a pair of roach clips, and-on the very bottom of her purse-a gold-plated monogramed Tiffany case the size of a packet of birth control pills.

Bingo.

From the forward cabin, she moaned, "Mark, I need you. Come back to bed and warm me up, honey!"

"I'll be there shortly, baby." Mark was getting closer to the truth as he flushed the twelve-volt toilet to add more background noise and popped open her gold-plated Tiffany birth control pill case. There, he got the answer he feared most. Every single pill was still untouched in the blister pack, dating back to the beginning of the month two weeks ago. Sick to his stomach, he realized what her game was, and it wouldn't be the first time a hot-looking bimbo was looking to get knocked up by the only heir to the Mizner Park fortune.

Disgusted with his lack of good judgement, Mark starred at himself in the mirror, berating himself for not spotting her game earlier. "C'mon, Mark, you're smarter than this," he said out loud. He should have known better when she begged him not to use a condom.

He had to figure out a way to dump her before she ruined his image as Boca's most eligible bachelor.

TWELVE

Everyone knew that Craig and Margaret Karcass were the oddest couple at Delmar. Neighbors could plainly hear the sound of bouncing basketballs in the Karcass condo whenever bathroom fans were turned on in adjoining condos. The obese couple used the noisy basketballs to punish their neighbors whenever the least little sound was heard. The lack of proper sound deadening material between floors at Delmar was a major source of aggravation, so the condo board had passed new regulations last year that required the installation of cork insulation.

Of course, these regulations were blissfully ignored by the Karcass couple, and there was also a lot of gossip about another of their bizarre hobbies; stretching out their Slip-N-Slide on the living room floor, coating it with baby oil, and sliding naked wall-to-wall. According to nearby residents, the bizarre Slip 'N Slide antics usually took place after the couple consumed eight to ten shots of Wild Turkey while watching the latest episodes of "Naked and Afraid" on their big screen teevee. Bouncing basketballs and a blaring teevee could often be heard in the wee hours of the morning, and Delmar residents were perplexed about why the couple worked so hard at being everyone's worst nightmare.

On Saturday morning, the couple had just cleaned their cat's litter box. A frustrated Craig Karcass stood in his tidy whities and knee-high stretch socks as he stood at the bathroom sink to wash up.

"Margaret, what's wrong with the water pressure?" Pandora sat quietly in the hallway, licking her paws and watching the household drama play out with the typical disinterest of a full-grown Persian.

"Margaret?" he called out again, "...we don't have any water. Did you remember to pay our condo bill?"

Annoyed with his question, Margaret made her way up the hallway, sidestepping Pandora and peering inside the master bath where her husband stood at the sink. "Of course I paid the bill. Stop treating me like an idiot, Craig." She lifted the lid on the white wicker waste basket and used the pooper scooper to unload the flying saucer-shaped chunks of cat litter. Then she stripped off the latex gloves and began to lecture her husband.

"Should'a used the gloves, Craig-O," she said. "Didn't they teach you anything at that silly Catholic high school in New Jersey?" Margaret was tired of hearing about her husband's high-brow education, convinced that Ebenezer Carver High School in Palatka had given her all the education she would need to conquer today's world.

Ignoring her taunt, Craig reached for the handle on the toilet, hoping to see water flow. Again, nothing happened. "Can't flush the toilet either," he complained with a frown. "How am I gonna take a leak, Margaret?"

"Oh..., that's right," she said absentmindedly. "There was that notice in the mail room about having to replace some of the sewer lines. I think it said the water'll be off for the building until after one o'clock." Confessing her oversight, she wished she'd remembered to fill their tub with water the night before and hoped the water would be back on before it was her turn to use the toilet.

For a moment, Craig entertained the idea of relieving himself off their balcony, but the thought of exposing himself in broad daylight made him wince and reconsider. Instead, he rummaged through their linen cabinet to find the box of Depends and prepared to strap himself into one of the thick diapers, but the box empty was empty. "Are we out of Depends too, Margaret? I thought you were gonna pick some up."

Annoyed with his whining, Margaret defended herself again. "Well, I didn't wanna pay full price, so I was waiting for a two-for-one sale, just like you always tell me to do, Craig-O."

"Ya got a pile of those "50% OFF" coupons in your top drawer, Margaret. Use one of those."

"They're all expired, Einstein."

"Well, that's just great!" he said, crushing the empty Depends box in his hands and tossing it in the trash. Disgusted with his wife's flip attitude in light of his dire need to relieve himself, Craig bent over to pull up on his knee-high compression socks and continued with his rant. "Who the hell turns off the water on a Saturday morning?" He pushed lightly on his bladder, measuring how much longer he could wait. "I swear, if that idiot Glitzsky gets re-elected I'm gonna *hang* myself!"

"Do us all a favor and drain yer bladder first, Craig-O," responded Margaret. She'd patiently dealt with her husband's over active bladder and BPH for years, often pleading with him to have the surgery. But Craig was reluctant, fearing that the surgery would lead to total erectile dysfunction and deprive him of the pleasure of experiencing the one erection he was able to muster once a year on their wedding anniversary.

"You could pee in the cat litter box," she said. "When it clumps up, you can toss it off the patio." Craig looked skeptical. "It's biodegradable," she added.

"It's raw sewage," he countered.

She shrugged her shoulders and made a face that would've made a gargoyle proud. "Hey, it's their damn fault for turning off the water. Nobody'll notice if you toss it in the grass." She stood face-to-face with her skeptical husband. "Remember our trip to Disney World last year when we got lost and couldn't find an open restroom? You peed in the cat's litter box in the back seat. It worked for ya then, didn't it?"

"Did ya hafta bring that up, Margaret?" Craig was hesitant about the idea, remembering that Pandora had refused to use her litter box for days afterward, preferring instead to relieve herself inside Craig's golf bag for most of the trip. Later, Margaret made him throw it out due to the foul smell, and Craig was forced to temporarily use a large Army/Navy surplus duffel bag for his clubs, which worked well until Pandora peed in it.

Margaret pointed out their second floor patio window at the storm clouds gathering in the distance. "Look. The rain'll wash the cat litter into the grass before noon."

With his bladder about to burst, Craig knew he had to do something fast and was beginning to think his wife was actually making sense. Damn BPH! He made a face at the prospect of having to relieve himself in Pandora's litter box. With his bladder feeling the effects of a night of drinking Wild Turkey and beer, the four hundred pound man shuffled reluctantly into the laundry room in his tidy whities and knelt down alongside the cat's litter box.

"Aaaaahhhhhh….ohhh…that feels good," he groaned, looking over his shoulder at the family cat. "Sorry, Pandora. Gotta wait your turn."

Pandora was oddly entertained by her master's grunts and groans as she sat studying his strange behavior from the doorway. Over the years, Pandora had gotten used to the Karcass's odd behavior. Watching them slide across the living room on the Slip 'N

Slide in their underwear was particularly entertaining to the big Persian.

"Margaret!" he yelled as he finished his disgusting deed. "How long does this stuff take to clump up?"

"Just a coupla minutes," she answered from the living room.

Craig hoped it could be sooner so he could dispose of it over the patio railing and get it out of his sight as soon as possible. He grabbed the air freshener and thoroughly sprayed the room with citrus-scented Renuzit as Pandora ran and hid under the bed.

An hour later, the Karcass condo was still without water, and it was Margaret's turn to drain her engorged bladder, now sorry she had indulged herself with five cups of coffee earlier. She made her way to the laundry room where Pandora lay with her paws crossed in her imitation of the Sphinx as she guarded her two-by-four foot litter box against any further incursions. The big Persian cat still couldn't figure out all the sudden interest in her once-private kitty facility as she watched Margaret preparing to unzip her size 22 tennis skirt.

Uncomfortable with Pandora's stare, Margaret said: "What're you lookin' at, you pussy?"

Pandora reluctantly repositioned herself in front of the washer as she watched another huge human preparing to urinate in her private sanctuary for the second time this morning. Positioning her ponderous three hundred pound frame precariously over the litter box, Margaret struggled to maintain her balance as she straddled the box.

Confused, the big Persian watched in amazement. Didn't they have their own litter box? Why didn't they scratch around and bury it like they're supposed to?

"Oh, yeeaahhhhh…" Margaret closed her eyes for a moment to enjoy the pleasure of her long-awaited relief. Suddenly, she lost her balance and fell backward into the litter box. "Whoa!" she called out, landing heavily, accidently wedging her rotund rear end snugly between the two sides.

"Crraaaaig! Come help me up. I'm stuck!" she called out, flailing her arms like a chicken in distress. Frightened, Pandora scampered to the safety of the guest bedroom to hide under the bed again.

"Where are you, Margaret?" he called from the couch where he was watching a new episode of "*Naked and Afraid*". "Margaret?"

"I'm stuck in the cat box and I can't get up! Gimme a hand, will ya?"

Craig bounded down the tiled hallway in his tidy whities and knee-highs like a dinosaur on crack, grabbing the laundry room door jamb to stop his slide. Peering through the doorway, he beheld a sight heretofore never imagined. There was his obese wife with her rear end stuck in the cat litter box as she flailed her arms like a wounded bird, scattering soiled cat litter all over the room.

"What the hell d'you do, Margaret?"

"Don't just stand there! Help me out of this damn box for God's sake!"

Craig grabbed both sides of the litter box, trying to separate it from his wife's rear end while Margaret grunted and pushed against the sides. "Be a big help if your ass wasn't so damn wide, Margaret."

"Look who's talking, Jabba the Hutt," she retorted.

With a loud grunt, Craig jerked the box loose from his wife's butt, scattering the mushy cat litter all over the tiled floor. Margaret stood up, naked from the waist down as the chunks of semi-hardened cat litter began to fall from her derriere and disintegrate as they hit the floor.

"Now there's somethin' ya don't see every day," said Craig standing lamely as he held the empty litter box and tried not to laugh.

Upset with her ordeal, Margaret panned the room in disgust. Clumps of smelly cat litter were strewn all over the floor, on top of her sewing machine, all over her Tupperware-even on top of their vintage 1950s collection of Jell-O molds passed down from her mother's estate. She turned and gave her husband a repugnant look.

"Craig, you are such a moron."

—⊰⊱—

A few minutes later, Sarah Glitzsky was keeping an eye on the storm clouds building on the horizon as she busied herself with her daily inspection of the Delmar common areas. This time she was prepared in case the skies opened up. Out and about on the Delmar grounds wearing her signature J.C. Penney clear plastic wrap with the painted gold fish, the condo president was prepared for stormy weather. Glitzsky was more than a little OCD about the litter that often went overlooked by their groundskeepers and staff. From lip balm to condoms, sun screen to used Depends, cell phones, tampons, keys, handcuffs, bottles of Viagra and KY Warming Gel, she found all kinds of strange things on her morning inspections.

As Glitzsky ambled past the pool deck, Big Mike Rosenberg spotted her from his lounger. Surrounded by his entourage, the group was entertaining themselves by holding up large paper cards with numbers sketched in Magic Marker to rate the outfits worn by those parading past the pool today.

"Hey, Sarah, they had a big sale at The Dollar Store. I was gonna call you and tell you about it," he taunted.

She stopped to respond to his razzing from across the pool. "You know I don't shop there, Rosenberg!" she retorted, glaring at the cards that were aimed in her direction. There were two "0s" and one that read "-1." Glitzsky kept walking, pretending it didn't matter.

Big Mike wasn't going to let her off the hook. "Oh, that's right. Now I remember. J.C. Penney's, for fashionistas that can't afford the Humane Society Thrift Shop," taunted Mike. Frowning in disapproval, Glitzsky was trying hard to think of a way she could have him shot in front of a firing squad, or maybe used for target practice by F-16s with laser-guided bombs. She walked quickly to get as far from him as she could.

"So anyway, at the Dollar Store there on Federal Highway...," he shouted, "...I picked you up a couple of No Pest Strips to wear around your neck at the next board meeting. You know, to keep the flies away!" That earned a chuckle from the group as they recalled the hilarious night she presided over their meeting with a dead fly stuck to her nose. A week later, Glitzsky found photos of the embarrassing event displayed in the Delmar clubhouse scrapbook and tossed them in the garbage in disgust. Mike watched until her until she waved him off and disappeared around a hedge of sea grapes.

Now safely out of range of her antagonist, Glitzsky put Rosenberg out of her mind as she reflected on her reasons for choosing a cheaper first-floor condo for herself years ago. She enjoyed having easy access to the gas grille and sprinkler controls on the grounds conveniently located just steps from her patio door. She considered the grounds part of her domain and obsessed over the condition of the common area landscaping outside her condo. With Craig and Margaret Karcass living just one stack over and one floor up, she went out of her way to patrol the area nearest to her least favorite residents, always hoping to find a violation she could nail them with.

Emerging from behind a stand of palm trees beneath the Karcass condo, one of the last things she expected to see was a saucer-shaped clump of flying cat litter the size of a small mango flying from the sky.

THUPP! The soft chunk struck Glitzsky on the side of her head and broke apart all over her plastic J.C. Penney Designer cover-up. Picking pieces from her hair, she bent down to examine the strange debris that had come flying out of the sky. Thinking that it might be something hot off the grill, she squatted and sniffed the evidence for clues to its origin, pinching her nose at the unmistakable smell of urine. Clearly, this was a condo litter encounter of a whole new kind. Shading her eyes, she looked skyward for more clues just in time to see another saucer-shaped object come flying down and crash-land in the grass near her feet.

Glitzsky scanned the Karcass patio one floor up but saw no one. Hunched over the broken pieces, she inspected the second clump of strange material that lay on the ground at her feet, prodding it with the gold-colored toe of her J.C. Penney slippers. What the hell was this? *Invasion of the Cat Litter Saucers?* Insulted and annoyed, she brushed the cat litter from her J.C. Penney designer wrap and focused on the Karcass balcony. Cupping her hands around her mouth, she yelled skyward toward the patio.

"All right, Margaret. I know it was you! Littering the grounds with cat litter? That's a double fine! I'm fining you *two* hundred dollars, you horse's ass!!"

THIRTEEN

Why couldn't she stop thinking about Officer Rodman? His muscled body in particular. Wasn't he just another stud muffin in her lineup? Desiree lay baking on the beach in front of Delmar as she sprawled on her aqua-colored beach lounger in her black bikini. She was plugged into Pandora with her earbuds, oblivious to the looks she was getting from admirers as she fantasized about her boy toy's talented appendages. The last time she'd become emotionally attached to a man so adept with his appendages it had nearly gotten her killed.

Back then, the appendages belonged to a man named Antonio Ferraro. Unfortunately, Desiree was unaware that all his baggage included lots of booze, pharmaceuticals and some mob connections. But what she did know was that Antonio had a buff body and was quite talented in his use of those appendages. He was nice enough to shower her with cash and jewels almost daily, which meant she quickly fell in love with him and moved in after knowing him only six days.

As it turns out, Antonio wasn't well. He took lots of self-prescribed pharmaceuticals, notably Xanax and Percocet, washing them down with an abundance of SKYY vodka. Sometimes, he was the happiest person in the world and a joy to make love to. On other days, he was preoccupied with moving money from one fake corporation to another while he dodged Federal subpoenas. And some nights, he was an absolute monster-abusive, paranoid and gun-crazy. Especially when he thought the Feds were closing in.

Desiree had never known a man who was so infatuated with semi-automatic handguns with silencers. Sometimes he shot at the telephone; sometimes, he would shoot at the TV. Once, when she made the mistake of telling him about a flirtatious man at the grocery store, he got angry and shot the bagel toaster while Desiree was making breakfast. The counselors and therapists who tried to straighten him out all found Antonio to be the epitome of stability and consideration-even responsible, self-aware and repentant. One of the happiest patients they'd ever treated. But of course, they didn't have to live with the man.

To Antonio's credit, he never tried to shoot her, but there were a few times when he'd almost shot her by accident. So, why did she stay with him, knowing her life was in constant danger? As she daydreamed about the similarities between Antonio and Officer Rodman, she realized just how addicted she was to super-hunky men with talented appendages who made her feel exceptionally alive. Her fatal attraction to such men who were also quite familiar with the use of deadly force was yet another example of her own flawed judgment, but she just couldn't help herself.

Tapping her fingers on the arm of her chair in rhythm to the soulful lyrics of Adele, she felt the perspiration trickle down her body and was about to cave in to her two-day vow of chastity and give her boy toy a call. She felt a shadow move across her and opened her eyes to see a bald Dominick Martorono standing over her, cigar in hand, his Tommy Bahama suit doing little to hide his hairy pot belly that was suddenly providing her with so much unwanted shade.

"Desiree, you see what washed up on our beach?" he asked. "Never a dull moment around here, that's for sure." Shading his eyes, he turned to point down the beach. "C'mon, Des. Ya gotta see this. You won't believe it."

She sat up in her beach chair. "What are you talking about, Dom?" She could see a small crowd gathered about a hundred yards further south staring at something at the water's edge as she adjusted her Forty Niners cap to shade her eyes. "Where's Margeaux?" she asked.

"At her Hot Bikini Dog stand. Saturday's usually her best day. C'mon. Take a walk with me." Insistent, he held out his hand to help her up as she put aside her earbuds. "And for the record, Des, you look so much better without that damn pink ski outfit you wear all the time." He'd always entertained secret fantasies about her but was careful to keep them hidden.

Desiree could tell he wasn't going to take no for an answer. "This better be worth interrupting my Adele concert," she said, heading toward the crowd with Dominick as they heard the far-off sound of ambulance sirens getting closer. Apprehensive over what Dom wanted to show her, sometimes she wished she *was* wearing her trademark pink ski parka; it served so well to insulate her from the stares of onlookers in the crowd. As she drew close enough to see what was floating in the water, Desiree covered her mouth in horror.

"Oh my God," she exclaimed as she and Dominick stopped to take in the grotesque scene.

"Looks like he got run over by boat propellers," said Dominick, leaning over the body lying at the edge of the surf. The severely lacerated remains of a man in a plaid bathing suit rested on the beach, and the cork screw gashes of an outboard's props were unmistakable. Dom and Desiree were horrified to see that the dead man was missing half his face, making his identification difficult. Everyone in the crowd was clueless about the man's identity.

"You think it coulda been a shark?" asked an older man with a mustache and wearing a white linen Ralph Lauren beach outfit. Though the victim had bled out long before, he took a step back, careful not to stain his pristine clothing as he stood over the body.

"Na. Shark would have taken chunks out of him," said a surfer inspecting the body. "His flesh would look more ragged from the bite." The surfer glanced up at the older man, amused by his outfit. "Friend o'mine got bitten a few years ago, and his leg was all chewed up from the teeth."

A beach bunny from a nearby condo wearing a sequined bikini stood back, creeped out by the lifeless body. "Does anyone know who he is?" she asked.

The paramedics and Boca Raton police pulled up simultaneously, and the first responders hurried down the dune from A1A to examine the body and start their investigation. A crowd was gathering as more rubberneckers continued to circle the body to see if it was anyone they knew.

"What an awful way to go," said Desiree as she glanced toward the approaching officers, hoping her favorite motorcycle cop might be among them. In the crowd, she noticed a slender, scruffy-looking man with a beard, floppy canvas hat and tattered cargo shorts who looked a little out of place in the group of affluent rubberneckers. She remembered that the guy lived a few houses further south in the old Mediterranean villa that sat high on the dune. Their eyes locked as Desiree caught him staring.

"David, right?" she asked as she sidled up to him. She was a little creeped out by the way he stared, but her curiosity got the better of her, feeling more emboldened with the crowd surrounding her.

"Yeah, David," answered Callahan. Doing his best to blend in with the crowd and avoid attention, he did a double take on

Desiree, trying to remember where he'd seen her before. "Aren't you the girl who usually wears the pink ski outfit?" Callahan looked her up and down like Desiree was the flavor of the week. "You're on the web, right?"

"I have an internet business," she explained without offering any details. From a distance, the man always managed to make her feel uncomfortable, but up close, Desiree couldn't help noticing that his eyes looked eerily black and lifeless. Her intuition told her he might know something about the body. "I'm Desiree. Don't you live around the corner?" she asked.

"Yeah, I rented a house several years ago with my two dogs 'Dub' and 'Butch'," dragging his toe through the sand in a somber mood. Callahan thought playing the sympathy card might get him somewhere with her. "Butch got stolen and Dub was killed by a car on A1A a week ago."

"I'm sorry to hear that, David," said Desiree. "So now you're without a dog, huh?"

"'Fraid so." He paused and looked toward the body on the beach again, curious about her, but cautious about having contact with outsiders. Callahan was unable to resist the urge to flirt and bask in her attention. "You look so much better without your pink ski outfit, Desiree. You remind me so much of my girlfriend Andrea."

"Is she an actress?" she asked with a touch of professional pride.

"No…but…it's the way you move. Very feminine," said Callahan, trying hard to charm her, but seeing his comment wasn't having the effect he'd hoped for. He turned his attention to the body the paramedics were loading on the stretcher. "Helluva way to go, huh?" he asked in a patronizing tone. He watched her nod silently, then turn to walk back toward the pot-bellied cigar smoker in the Tommy Bahama suit who had accompanied her to the crime scene. A spitting image of Walter White from *Breaking Bad,* the man gave him an icy stare as she returned to his side.

Dominick said, "Hey Des, I'm gonna skip the Q and A from Boca's finest and head back. Pretty gruesome. You feel like stopping up for a drink or somethin'?"

"No thanks, Dom. I'm a little creeped out by all this," she said, turning to walk back with him as she pulled her hair back, tuning in to hear what the crowd was saying about the body on the beach. Her intuition was telling her to be careful. "Think I'm gonna head upstairs and take a hot shower." Dominick tried to console her by putting his arm around her, but she moved away.

"You're in a strange mood, Des."

She nodded toward the emergency vehicles lined up along A1A. "All this makes me feel kinda dirty for some reason." Dominick thought about how it was that an adult film star could feel dirty about *anything.*

Feeling insecure, she wrapped her arms around herself and looked back toward the crowd to see if the creepy bearded man was still watching. She was surprised to see him still staring. Locking eyes with him again gave her a chill and her gut instincts were telling her something just wasn't right about the guy.

Callahan stood silently in the crowd for a few more minutes, furtively watching Desire from a distance as the paramedics loaded the mangled body into the waiting ambulance. He listened carefully, straining his ears to overhear the questions the police were asking of the remaining bystanders. For the condo commandos, sun worshipers, surfers and gawkers alike, he had surely provided them with a lot to talk about. From what Callahan was hearing from the rubberneckers around him, it sounded like the cause of death would likely be characterized as "a boating accident". Hearing this, it made Callahan breathe a little easier.

According to his research on Wikipedia, there were 5,115 boating accidents in the U.S. last year, resulting in 742 deaths nationwide, and most of those victims drowned as 85 percent had not been wearing a life jacket. Too bad, so sad, he thought. Shoulda worn a life jacket. Shoulda left me alone. Now you're a looking for things to do in Boca while you're dead.

Finished with his eavesdropping, Callahan watched a news reporter's van pull up and a reporter step out, followed by a video cameraman. The reporter was checking his microphone and the cameraman popped the lens cover off his camera as they prepared to stir up enough drama to raise the ratings for the local ABC affiliate. Not wanting a starring role in the upcoming newscast, Callahan decided it was time to quietly slip away.

From his experiences years ago at the Sumter County Courthouse when he filed his treasure salvage claim under his real name Tommy Tomlinson, he knew just how aggressive TV reporters could be. A news van with a camera crew had chased him across town at speeds up to ninety-five miles per hour in their reckless quest to get an exclusive interview. He had outfoxed them by hiding in a bank drive-thru lane as he watched them speed by on their way to what they surely thought would be a Pulitzer Prize-winning interview.

In his quest to continue living the life of a fugitive, Callahan knew what he had to do. He would find a way to erase any evidence of Lance Meyer and their visit to Boca Boats, Tire and Hair Care Center on Federal Highway. He felt uncomfortable with the desire he felt for Desiree during their chance meeting at the crime scene, reminding himself that his unmet need for intimacy was still his Achilles heel.

He would get his fix by paying a visit to Solid Gold on Federal Highway where he could enjoy an anonymous intimate encounter with far less risk to his $170 million stash.

FOURTEEN

E arly Thursday morning, Carol was out of town at a swimsuit fashion show in South Beach, so Mark had spent a rare night alone. Pulling a coin from his jewelry box, he thought about the powerful storm that passed in the wee hours of the morning as he held the centuries-old silver piece-of-eight. He imagined what it must have been like in the brutal hurricane of 1715, the huge storm that had blown the Spanish treasure fleet onto the reefs along the Florida coast three centuries ago. Turning the coin over, he admired the distinctive stamp bearing the Royal Spanish coat-of-arms. He was fortunate to have collected a few of the historic coins minted in Havana in 1715 by the same Spanish sailors that had lost their lives on the Florida reefs that same year.

As Mark sipped his morning smoothie, he thought about the time he spent as a treasure hunter, now glad that he'd decided to accept the silver pieces as payment one summer when he worked for Real Eight in the Florida Keys. Ever since his unexpected discovery of the bale on Boca Beach weeks earlier, Mark had grown more eager to hit the beach at the crack of dawn, wondering what the storms and tide would bring him next.

At 5:50 am, his phone rang. Who the hell was calling so early? He glanced at the display and recognized Carol's number. He figured she had to be calling to check up on him. *C'mon, girl! It's 5:50 in the morning!*

Once, when she suggested text messaging, he remembered what he'd said to her; texting is a brilliant way to miscommunicate how you feel and misinterpret what other people mean. He pressed the voicemail button to keep her guessing and slipped on his Surf Walkers and Bora Bora cap.

In the bathroom, he stopped to read the pink Post-It note decorated with the imprint of her kiss that she'd stuck to his door two days ago. In her lilting, feminine handwriting, it read "Stop by for a nightcap?" with a winking smiley face. He mused on what a little hottie she was and stuck the invitation back on his bathroom mirror to remind himself to call her after his run. Grabbing his aqua-tinted Oakleys, he entered the marble hallway and spotted Mrs. Seidelbaum ambling toward him with her newspaper and a sad look on her face. Uh-oh, he thought, here comes the S.S. Melodrama.

"Hi, sonny. You're up early," she said. "You know my grand-daughter is back in the hospital again. Did I tell you about her yesterday?" With a sorrowful puppy dog look, the grey-haired grandmother who had survived three husbands waited expectantly for a touch of sympathy.

"Sorry to hear that, Mrs. Seidelbaum," he said as he locked his door. Anxious to avoid the depressing monologue that always seemed to follow her around like a toxic cloud, he headed for the stairway. "Gotta run! Hope your granddaughter's better." His dad always used to remind him that he was the face of Mizner Park Development, and although it was his nature to be polite, sometimes the whiners grated on his nerves.

He thought of a way to cheer her up. "Hey, Mrs. Seidelbaum, next time I see you, maybe we could drop some acid and play 'Twister'!"

Speechless, she stood in her bathrobe with her hands on her hips and a puzzled look on her face. "Ah...uh huh," she mumbled. Then she cracked a smile as she realized he was messing with her, thoroughly entertained by the idea of playing "Twister" and dropping acid with her younger neighbor.

Mark bounded down the stairs, then past the sea grape hedges to the walkover where he began to stretch in preparation for his run. The sun began to peek over the horizon, a brilliant orange glow with the intensity of a fireball that slowly filled the blue-grey sky as brilliant streaks of sunshine outlined the clouds on the horizon in majestic golden hues. Other than a few sea gulls diving into a school of bait fish and a few fallen palm branches on the beach, there were no signs of the fierce storm that had ravaged Boca Beach during the night.

He was alone as he hit the beach with an even stride, deftly stepping around the broken shells and pieces of sea glass in his path as if on autopilot. He headed south toward the coastal coral formations of Deerfield Beach. The Greenwood Mansion loomed on his right as he drew abreast of the old stone villa sitting high on the dune. He thought about David Callahan and his two bulldogs, wondering if Callahan was even his real name. He recalled the fruitless internet search that he'd done on his neighbor a few weeks before, and after the dream he had, his intuition told him something just wasn't right about the guy.

In his dream, Callahan was the scoundrel and thief who had cheated his business partners out of their fair share of the loot, the same businessmen who had financed the robotic technology used in the undersea search and recovery of over $170 million in gold bullion and newly-minted gold coins. Intrigued with the possibility of a fugitive treasure hunter living right in his own backyard, Mark made a mental note to do another web search.

As the rising sun brightened the beach, he stepped around a pile of empty Corona bottles before settling into a modest pace as he focused on his to-do list at work. There was another meeting with city planners over the firm's proposed new mid-rise at Mizner Park, lunch with the ad rep from *Boca Magazine*, and an interview with a new candidate for a management position at Boca West.

Scouring the horizon ahead, his attention was captured by a grey rubber dinghy lying on the beach a hundred yards away. Curious, he picked up his pace. Drawing closer, he could see that it was an inflatable Zodiac with a missing tow ring from the bow. He scanned the beach in both directions for clues to the owner's whereabouts, figuring the tow ring had likely pulled out during the gale-force storm last night as the dinghy was being pulled behind a larger boat. Without a soul around to claim it, Mark was excited about the prospect of taking it home and took the opportunity to examine the Zodiac more closely.

The twelve foot inflatable couldn't have been more than a month old. There were a few inches of seawater inside, and it sported a bow cover, hardened keel, a varnished wooden seat, and a transom with no signs that an engine had ever been mounted. It had twin seats amidships with a steering wheel, but he noticed no traceable registration or documentation anywhere. Something glinting in the bright sun caught his eye from under the bow. Cautiously, Mark reached under the bow cover and retrieved two spent nine millimeter shell casings from the coil of Dacron line.

Studying the brass casings, he thought about the arsenal of weapons he used to carry on his sailboat, including a NATO-version fully automatic M-16, stainless steel Mossberg twelve-gauge pump and his trusty stainless steel Smith and Wesson Model 659 sidearm. Mark sold the firearms years ago along with his last sailboat, no longer needing the weapons that accompanied him on his circumnavigation fourteen years ago. It was an arsenal made necessary by the cutthroat pirates who operated out of third-world countries along his route that made the passages so dangerous.

Tipping the dinghy up on its side to empty the water, he felt like Boca's stormy seas were becoming his new best friend. With no need for an inflatable to clutter the deck on his sleek 44-foot catamaran, he thought about a possible buyer. Craig Beloff, their in-house architect at Mizner Park, had just taken delivery of a 54-foot Bertram fly bridge cruiser with stern-mounted dinghy davits, but no dinghy. The former owner of the Bertram had transferred the inflatable to his new yacht, and it seemed like the stars were lining up for Mark yet again.

After rigging the Dacron bow line to form a harness, he opted to finish the second half of his workout by jogging through the shallow surf toward Delmar. With his new found prize in tow, he thought about all the fuel he could buy for his gas-guzzling catamaran with the extra cash.

With his eyes set on the gold-colored Delmar tower in the distance, he jogged briskly through the shallows as the morning sun climbed higher in the sky. He pulled the tow line tighter and brushed the sweat from his brow, working up a thirst as his mind drifted to the last time he shared drinks with Carol at Mezzanote's. Pushing himself into a faster pace, he was determined to cover the last two hundred yards in record time. Suddenly, he felt something move under his foot, followed by a sharp pain.

"*Damn!*" he yelled in agony as he felt something penetrate his heel. Grimacing in pain, he knew he'd stepped on a stingray's barb or a dogfish in the shallows. Trailing blood in the water, he pulled the dinghy up onto the beach, limped over to a fallen palm and sat down dejectedly on the trunk to inspect his wound. He could see the tip of the barb buried about a quarter-inch into his heel. Squeezing the wound to try to expel the poison, he cursed at his carelessness as he rocked back and forth in anguish, annoyed with himself for not seeing the stingray in time.

"Need some help?" The shapely young girl in a red one-piece Boca Raton lifeguard suit stood over him with a first aid kit tucked under her arm. "Saw what happened from my tower," she said in a soothing voice. "Stingrays come in to the shallows this time of year to mate," she explained with a sympathetic look from her blue eyes as she unslung her first aid kit from her shoulder.

"Yeah. Think I found one, mate," he quipped, wincing. From experience, he knew that the ammonia from urine could be effective in neutralizing the toxin, but decorum made him dismiss the idea of asking her to pee on his foot. "You got any ammonia in your first aid kit there?" He couldn't help noticing his angel of mercy looked like she'd just walked off the set of Baywatch, practically a clone of Carmen Electra.

"Think so. Let me see," she said, pulling her brown hair back around her ear and squatting down to examine his foot. She set her blue plastic first aid kit on top of the palm trunk and rummaged through it to produce tweezers, ammonia, antiseptic and a bandage. Preparing her gear, she looked up at Mark. "This may hurt a little," grasping her tweezers and waiting for his permission.

"Do it," he said, holding his foot up for the extraction. In a flash, she'd dug in with the tweezers and yanked it out expertly just like she'd done it a hundred times. "Son of a beach!" he yelped.

"Got it!" she proclaimed, displaying the barb. She cleaned the wound with an antiseptic wipe, added triple antibiotic ointment and tenderly applied a large butterfly band aid to his heel. "There ya go," she said, admiring her handiwork as she sat up on the trunk with him and clasped her hands together expectantly.

Admiring her handiwork, Mark took his shot. "Anyone ever tell you that you look a lot like Carmen Electra?" The resemblance was remarkable, and Mark was never in too much pain to think about romance.

"Thanks. I'm Becky," she said, holding out her hand with an air of formality.

"Mark McAllister," gently grasping her hand and displaying his best Hollywood smile, surprised by her formality. "Thanks, Becky."

In a professional tone, she said, "You're lucky. This ray was a baby. A bigger one might have put you in the hospital." She looked over at the dinghy. "Is that your inflatable?"

"Unless someone else comes along and claims it before I can get it home."

"I was watching you pull it down the beach. Most people ride *in* the dinghy."

"Yeah...well, I found it on the beach."

"I know," she said, smiling. "I passed it on my way to work." Becky pointed to the white 21-speed road bike leaning up against the lifeguard station. "That's my Trek 1500. Keeps me in shape."

"I'll say." Mark sat holding his foot and admiring her toned figure as another lifeguard began to make his way down the dune to join them from the tower. Without waiting for the second lifeguard to arrive, Mark went for the close. "So, Becky, are you free for a glass of wine this week? Maybe a boat ride?"

"In your dinghy?" she smirked. "No, not really, but thanks anyway," she answered coolly, packing up her first aid kit.

"No, I mean"-

She gave him a stern look. "Yeah, I know what you meant," she said. Snapping her first aid kit shut with an air of finality, she stood up. "Try to watch where you step, Mark. I think we're done here," she said and headed back to the guard tower.

Perplexed by her response, Mark was confused by this drop-dead gorgeous girl who seemed so completely immune to his charms. He thought about their conversation, trying to figure out what he may have said to offend her.

"What's with her?" he asked the young lifeguard who had cruised over to check on him. A nice looking guy, Mark noticed he looked a lot like a younger version of Sean Connery, making him wonder if the city of Boca was hiring all their lifeguards from the ranks of movie doubles.

"Becky?" He looked back at the beauty queen walking briskly toward the guard tower, then back at Mark. "Licker license," he explained as he stood over him with his arms crossed like he'd just caught Mark poaching on the king's private hunting preserve.

"Licker? Oh, you mean"-

"Yup. Carpet muncher," explained the lifeguard.

"Well, she's a beauty." Mark looked longingly toward the guard tower like he'd just missed out on a date with Carmen Electra.

"Tell me about it. I have to sit next to her in the tower all day. I'm Matt."

"Mark McAllister." They did a fist bump as Matt raised his eyebrows.

"Mark McAllister? As in Mizner Park Development?"

"Yeah. Have we met?" he asked.

"I saw you and your dad at the Save-Our-Turtles Benefit last year," explained Matt. "It's our Boca Lifeguards' favorite charity." Mark tested his new bandage to see if it would make it the rest of the way home. "I remember you had this smokin' hot blonde with you," Matt continued, "and I think you two stayed to watch that weird wildlife documentary."

"Oh, that Michael Moore film? I've seen better film on teeth," cracked Mark.

Matt chuckled. "Heard that. It *was* a little underwhelming, but your date sure had all the heads turning."

"That was Christa, my ex-wife," explained Mark. "Former Vegas showgirl. Now, well…I'm kinda in between wives and sailboats."

"Hah. We guessed she was a performer. She sure had the moves," said Matt, pausing to wave to someone on the beach. "What do you do at your firm?"

"I'm the President and CEO of the company," answered Mark. He thought for a moment. "But I really want to be a writer."

"Really?" Matt wasn't sure if he was serious, but he rolled with it. "What kind of writing you think pays the most?"

"Uh, hmm. I'm thinkin' ransom notes," joked Mark with a twinkle in his eye.

"Ha! You could be right." Matt was amused with the idea that a man born to wealth would actually consider such a thing.

Mark shrugged. "Development in Boca is all about who you know. Very political."

"I hear ya," said Matt. "But you've been pretty successful. Something tells me you could sell crack to a convent full of nuns." Matt squinted and looked down the beach, then back at Mark. "You know what I wanted to ask you? Why they used to call your dad 'Six Pack'?"

"Nothing to do with beer, I'll tell ya *that*," said Mark. "My dad had both shoulders, hips and knees replaced with implants. He was a competitive skier before he met my mom. Blew out his joints."

Matt tried to imagine what it was like to have six artificial joints made of metal. "Bet that played hell with the metal detectors at the airport, huh?"

"Yeah, well, he put up with it." His heel throbbed as he poked at his bandaged foot again to see if it was ready to travel on.

Curious about his new friend, Matt wanted to know more. "You going to the Save-Our-Turtles thing again this year? I think they're having it at the Boca Resort and"-

"Nah, probably not. Too many people died last year." Mark suppressed a smile.

"Funny," exclaimed Matt. "It *was* kinda dull. Anyone ever tell you that you have a dark sense of humor?"

"Yeah, Stevie Wonder. Told me I have a great face for radio, too."

Matt was entertained with his wry humor. "So, today, you scored a dinghy and stepped on a stingy, huh?"

"You know, that sounds a little like the lyrics to a Jimmy Buffett song," quipped Mark. "Wasn't that something that happened in Margaritaville?" Poking at his bandaged heel, his foot was throbbing, and he wasn't looking forward to limping back to his condo.

"You hear about that thirty-foot sailboat that washed up in Delray last year?" asked Matt. "This guy...didn't know anything about sailing, bought a brand new sloop, took it out for a spin in a storm, drank a bunch of rum, fell asleep and went aground on the beach three hundred feet from my tower. The guy ends up in a hospital and financially broke."

"Think I remember something about that," said Mark. "I heard the City of Delray Beach declared it abandoned and cut it up with a chain saw two weeks later 'cause they couldn't get a crane in there. Unbelievable. Waste of a good sailboat if you ask me."

"And the guy who grounded her disappears. They're still looking for him. Word is, he was a stockbroker who got depressed after the last market fiasco."

"Yeah, well, I spent twelve years on Wall Street. Lots of smoke and mirrors. The greed and corruption was unbelievable. Then my dad brought me onboard at Mizner Park Development. You trade the market, Matt?"

"I dabble. You know, win some, lose some. Hope for the best."

Mark looked back toward Becky in the guard tower. "Hope isn't much of a strategy," he said. "Where do you get your ideas?"

"I like to watch David Chu on CNBC."

"David Chu? Oh...the sandwich analyst," said Mark grinning.

"Right! Some kinda analyst I guess," said Matt. He gestured toward Mark's foot. "How far you gotta go with that?"

Mark pointed at Delmar further down the beach. "About three hundred yards to that round condo there."

Matt nodded. "The one that looks like a big gold vibrator?"

"Chew got it."

"Ya know, I've always liked that high-rise. It looks like one of those really cool round buildings you see in London. Your family built it, right?"

"Yup. Our biggest project on Boca Beach. A scaled-down version of the Gherkin Tower in London. Took us four years, start to finish."

They both stopped to admire the round gold-colored landmark that defined the Boca Beach skyline. Matt grew pensive. "You know, I don't want to be a lifeguard forever," he confessed. "You wouldn't have any openings there at your firm, would you?"

Mark had bowled on people like Matt most of his life. When he was younger, he was convinced that it stemmed from a genetic makeup of a superior design. But he had taken a liking to this lifeguard and decided to open the door for him. "We might have something entry level. I could check with my V.P. in Human Resources." He cocked his head. "You have any sales experience, Matt?"

"I sold cars for a year, 'til I found out the dealer was rippin' everyone off. The stuff I saw goin' on-wow! I mean, ya couldn't make the stuff up!"

"Well, if you can sell cars, you can sell anything," said Mark, impressed with his *ad hoc* resume.

Recognizing a possible opportunity for advancement, Matt smiled and pulled his lifeguard whistle and chain over his head, tucking it into the pocket of his shorts. Extending his hand, he said, "C'mon. I haven't had my morning workout yet. I'll pull ya home in your new dinghy." He pointed at Mark's injured foot. "That's why I always try to wear my Surf Walkers in the shallows."

"Sounds like a plan. Gotta meeting in Mizner Park in about an hour, can't be late," said Mark. With Matt holding his arm, Mark hopped on one leg toward the boat. "Startin' to feel what it's like to get old." He looked back toward the guard tower. "Be a lot more fun if we could get Becky to join me in the Zodiac."

Matt made a face. "And if the queen had balls, she'd be king, right?"

﹅╪╪﹅

For a buyer, one of the rules of better deal making was limiting the number of possible bidders. With that in mind, Craig Beloff was in a hurry to nail down the deal on the inflatable dinghy suddenly made available today before his boss had time to reach out to other buyers. Although Mizner Park's architect was anxious to seal the deal, he took a shot at saving an extra grand.

"So where's this Zodiac now?" asked Craig.

"At my condo," replied Mark.

"Since you found it on the beach, I'm thinkin' maybe...two grand?" ventured Craig as he leaned against the doorway. Mark scowled, but it didn't deter Craig. "It's not like you need the money or anything." The CEO shook his head, still refusing to capitulate to his tight-fisted employee. "Plus, there's no warranty," added Craig.

Mark uncrossed his legs and sat up in his leather chair. "Let's not forget about the hole I have in my heel from bringing it back," Mark countered. "By the way, that same model inflatable is priced at twelve grand at West Marine. Three grand is a steal. If that doesn't work for you, I could offer it to Steve in accounting. He just bought a new Hatteras, *and*...I don't think he's got a dinghy yet." Reaching for his phone, Mark had a feeling Craig was going to cave.

"Okay, okay," said Craig. "You win. Can you have it delivered to my marina slip?"

"Delivered? How the heck am I supposed to do that with my BMW M5?" asked Mark. "Aren't you the one with the giant SUV?"

"All right. How 'bout Debbie and I meet you at Delmar at six? Think the three of us could get it up on top of my Denali?"

"Piece a cake," he said as Craig turned to leave.

"Oh, and Craig."

"Yeah?"

"Don't forget the cash."

"I don't suppose you could just take it out of my paycheck? Make it a lot easier, don't you think?"

"It's not a 401-K, Craig. This is my play money we're talkin' about here. See you at six."

Craig stopped before leaving. "Hey, boss, now all you have to do is find me a 30-horse kicker for it, right?" he joked. "See any of those wash up on the beach, will ya let me know?"

"Dream on, Mr. Architect."

FIFTEEN

Delusional with avarice and often without a moral compass, the reckless condo commandos were drunk off the moonshine, seldom questioning the prudence of picking up a dime in front of a steam roller. At Delmar, there was a ton of money to be made by the unscrupulous who had the financial ability to flip in and out of beachfront condos quickly. And for those with no ethics and lots of cash, real estate swindles were becoming more commonplace in Boca Raton.

Conning the disabled and terminally ill into selling their most prized asset before anyone got wind and blew the whistle was tricky, especially when relatives got in the way. God forbid a son, daughter or grandchild should step up and voice objections to liquidating estate assets at a below-market price. In a waterfront real estate market that was in growing demand, condo flippers lurked everywhere, scouting out the most diseased and infirm owners like piranhas going after a side of beef.

The flippers could often be spotted feigning interest in their neighbors' personal medical condition as there was often a hefty pot of gold waiting at the end of such sad stories. Sometimes, even the descendants were onboard with the below-market deals if it meant they could pry the cash loose from the hands of their dearly departed that much sooner.

Chief among the opportunists were the members of Delmar's Board of Directors. Unscrupulous directors spent an exorbitant amount of time glad-handing and back-slapping, all in a clandestine effort to weed out the next below-market seller before anybody else got wind of a possible sale. The crumbling of the very fabric of Boca's glitzy society and turning the flesh of oldsters into ash mattered not; for they were members of a society that didn't understand boundaries, re-inventing them as they went, completely immersed in the never-ending pursuit of material greatness.

It was all about the money.

Delmar's condo manager had his own gluttonous hand extended deep into the trough of cash flowing in and out of the glitzy high-rise. Stampaugh had contrived his own way of participating in the flow of heavy coinage; he held the keys to the condo transfer approval process, the bureaucratic purse strings that controlled ownership for all the would-be Delmar investors. There could be no condo title transfer without his explicit approval as manager, making him the *de facto* condo gatekeeper, and Stampaugh wielded his bureaucratic sword with unabashed greed.

Once, while holding out for a five thousand dollar bribe from a would-be Delmar buyer, he held up the approval process for three weeks over a four-year old traffic citation issued to the would-be buyer for an expired auto tag, maintaining that the citation was emblematic of a person unworthy of Delmar ownership. Following weeks of threatened lawsuits, the would-be buyer finally decided that coughing up the five grand bribe was cheaper than litigation.

The absurdity and hypocrisy was out of control as directors and owners alike flipped in and out of the beachfront condo market, pocketing hundreds of thousands in fast money. But all that trickery left Dyson Stampaugh sitting squarely in the cat bird seat; he alone knew where all the bodies were buried.

⟞⊹⊹⟝

In her haste to visit Irving Lipschitz in the Oncology ICU at Boca Regional Hospital this morning, Margaret Karcass was weaving recklessly through the traffic on Glades Road in her Grand Cherokee at twice the posted speed limit. She knew Lipschitz was slipping in and out of consciousness as he lay dying of throat and mouth cancer. The verbal contract she discussed with Lipschitz on the phone earlier lay printed beside her on the car seat, ready for his signature. On the pretext of a "family visit", Karcass had made the appointment with Lipschitz's oncologist, and the only way she could pull it off during non-visitation hours was to impersonate the patient's unmarried daughter. Knowing that Lipschitz was heavily doped up on dilaudid following his surgery, she figured this was her best shot at a cool two hundred grand quick profit.

Also heading west on Glades Road this morning was seventy-eight-year-old Sidney Kornish. Mr. Kornish had just dropped his Pomeranian off at the vet's after his twelve-year old dog had barfed all over his Hush Puppies twice that day. Already on edge after having to leave his beloved pooch at the vet's for an overnight stay, Kornish went into a fit of rage when a white Chrysler Grand Cherokee suddenly cut him off, forcing him to swerve and narrowly miss a semi hauling construction equipment. He focused like a laser on the speeding SUV with a vanity plate that read "#1BEOTCH".

In a futile attempt to get around her in his eighty-four horse-power electric Chevy Spark, Kornish swung his tiny car into the passing lane and flipped her off from behind while he watched a McDonald's Big Mac carton fly out the SUV's window. Next came a paper napkin, followed by a plastic spoon, then a plastic fork that bounced off his windshield.

"Beotch, huh? Yup, and a damn litterbug too," he shouted angrily, banging on the wheel and stomping on the accelerator to push all of the eighty-four horses his Spark could muster. The electric motor whined in protest as he whipped in behind her and camped out on her rear bumper, intent on teaching this 'Beotch' a lesson in road etiquette. The heavy-set driver with the grey hair and bad haircut glared at him in the rearview mirror as she gave him the finger. Kornish wasn't about to let her shake him off her tail as she weaved back and forth in an effort to lose him, changing lanes aggressively in the heavy traffic like it was a game of bumper cars. Watching her sneer at him in the mirror, Kornish knew all too well about road rage. She just didn't know who she was messing with.

A year before, Sidney Kornish was forced to attend a court-ordered six-week road rage class resulting from an incident when he hurled a half bottle of Manischewitz at a senior citizen in a Lincoln Town car that had cut him off in traffic. Following his guilty plea, the judge gave him a 30-day suspended sentence, a $500 fine, and a ridiculous anger management class that he was still angry about.

Thinking about the anger management course got him riled up all over again as he edged closer to the #1BEOTCH in the Grand Cherokee. Kornish weighed his options and imagined what his therapist would recommend, what his mother would say, and what his podiatrist would likely suggest, but none of their advice could come close to quelling his anger.

Suddenly, the big woman in the Grand Cherokee veered recklessly to the far right emergency lane in an effort to escape him. Kornish followed right behind her, enduring the rapid thump-thump-thump of the speed bumps as he flew down the emergency lane at over seventy-five miles an hour. He stayed glued to her bumper like a gargoyle from hell, determined to teach her a lesson.

Unexpectedly, an emaciated Irish setter appeared up ahead beside the guardrail and wandered directly into the path of the Grand Cherokee. The SUV hit the dog so hard it bounced over the top and landed squarely on the driver's side of Kornish's windshield, cracking the glass and blocking his view of the road. Almost losing control, Kornish was forced to slam on his brakes and pull over. Jumping out of his Chevy Spark, Kornish was madder than a gay husband with tonsillitis on Valentine's Day. Drivers were whizzing by and flipping him off as they honked at the little red car with the crazy man and dead dog on the windshield.

"BEOTCH!" he screamed, shaking his fist in the air and pounding on the hood of his car as he watched the white Grand Cherokee disappear into the westbound traffic on Glades Road.

Kornish was saddened by the sight of the Irish setter that lay across his cracked windshield. He gently lifted the dog from the front of his car and placed him in the trunk, intent on giving the poor dog a proper burial. As he slammed his trunk lid, Kornish decided to ring up his buddy at the Florida DMV to track the owner of the plate that read "#1 BEOTCH". There was gonna be hell to pay.

Vengeance, he vowed, ought never to be served ambiguously.

⊰┼⊱

Thankful to have escaped the maniac in the red Chevy Spark, Margaret Karcass searched for a spot in the disabled parking lot at Boca Regional Hospital. She hung the HANDICAPPED hanger that she'd confiscated from an unlocked car at Town Center Mall last year from her rear view mirror. In a foul mood and weary from the road rage, the hanger would save her a few minutes of walking time. Karcass was all too happy to ignore the advice from her doctor who suggested that walking was great exercise, and a great way to lighten up on her hefty three hundred and twenty-five pounds.

The lot was full of griping oldsters making their way to and from the cancer center on walkers and canes. People dyin' to get in and dyin' to get out, she thought, turning toward the main entrance. Tucking the real estate file under her arm, she noticed a heavy-set uniformed security guard approach her from the guard post at the hospital's entrance. Staring at the front of her Grand Cherokee, he bent down to examine her bumper, then stood up as he hooked his thumbs in his duty belt and frowned at her.

"Excuse me, ma'am," said the guard. "You know you have blood dripping down your bumper?" The guard stood with his hands on his hips, waiting for an explanation. "Is there a body on the road somewhere that we should know about, ma'am?"

Annoyed with his insinuation, Karcass stopped to address the guard. "I think I may have hit someone's pet gerbil on the interstate or something," she said coldly. "No big deal. Right now, my father's in the ICU dying of cancer," pointing toward the entrance. She glared at the man who had the impudence to try and slow her down in her bid to score a quick two hundred grand. Like a runaway tank with no one to steer it, she bulldozed past the guard to get inside the ICU and get her contract signed before Lipschitz slipped back into a coma, or worse. She thought about that idiotic term that her real estate agent was always so fond of throwing around; "time is of the essence". Karcass wanted that quick flip more than the earth needed gravity, and no one was going to stand in her way.

Bellying up to the third floor nurses' station in her size 20W denim overalls, Karcass noticed the duty nurse bore a strong resemblance to Nurse Ratched from *One Flew Over the Cuckoo's Nest.* Her name tag read SALLY MCVEY, R.N. "Hi, I'm Leslie Lipschitz, here to see my dad, Irving Lipschitz," said Karcass in an act of solemn family concern. "He's expecting me. Is he awake?" she asked in her best imitation of a concerned daughter.

Nurse McVey looked her up and down, confused about the absence of even a shred of family resemblance. "His BP's a little low, and we're keeping him sedated," said the nurse. "I'm not sure he's awake at the moment. The surgery was hard on your father." She glanced at the file folder Karcass was carrying. "Regular visitation is over. May I ask the reason for your visit today, Mrs. Lipschitz?"

"Uh, got some urgent family trust business," said Karcass, holding up her file. She was thankful that the nurse didn't ask to see it.

"He's very weak and may not be coherent enough to make any business decisions, so you'll need to keep your visit short." Karcass nodded in agreement. "Follow me, Mrs. Lipschitz." Karcass followed the nurse down a hallway that reeked of disinfectant as they passed rooms full of intravenous bottles, myriads of tubes plugged into machines with emaciated cancer victims and patients moaning in pain. Hoping she wasn't too late to catch Lipschitz before his death rattle, she hurried the nurse along as she followed close behind. She wanted that deal. Finally, they stood at the entrance to Lipschitz's semi-private room.

"Wait here while I check to see if he's awake," said Nurse McVey. Bending over her patient, she shined a penlight into each eye and turned to her visitor standing in the doorway. "He's conscious, a little woozy from the dilaudid, so his speech will be very slurred."

"I'll only need a minute," said Karcass, flipping through the documents in her file. The nurse removed her glasses and took a step forward so they wouldn't be overheard. "Mrs. Lipschitz, you *do* know that they had to remove most of his tongue and part of his mouth, and his speech is-"

"I know. Too bad, so sad," said Karcass as she stared at the floor with as much melodrama as she could muster and pretended to wipe a tear from her eye. "I'll always remember riding on dad's knee when I was a young girl." The nurse studied her immense frame as she struggled to imagine Karcass sitting on her father's knee without putting him in traction.

"Can you give us a little privacy, nurse?" asked Karcass, dabbing at her eye with her handkerchief.

Nurse McVey nodded in sympathy. "Please don't be too long. He's very weak from the chemo and surgery. I'll be right outside the door if he needs me," she said. Karcass shut the door and approached her victim.

Sensing danger, Lipschitz heard the door shut and opened his eyes. Fear forced him to emerge from his narcotic stupor, and his eyes widened in alarm when he recognized his visitor. Still heavily sedated, Lipschitz had a vague recollection as he recalled his Delmar neighbor's dark intentions from their earlier phone call.

"Eh toe yeh eh wo sigh eh, aggi." Ignoring his rejection, she held the contract closer, unsympathetic to his tongue-less mishmash.

"Irving, don't give me that crap," she said coldly. "You know you've only got to the end of the month." She looked at her watch. "Today's the twenty-eighth. You're dying, and *I'm* making you a great deal here, so live it up while ya can! Think of your kids!"

Petrified, Lipschitz shook his head back and forth on the pillow. "Hep meh. Suh uh peezh hep meh," croaked the old man in a faint voice that was barely audible.

"Now, now, Mr. Lipschitz...I mean...uh, '*dad*', this'll only take a moment," she said holding the pen up and pushing the contract closer to his face.

"Ngoooh! Ngoooh wa...way! I gah emoozhezee eh heh," Lipschitz croaked as he shook his head back and forth against his hospital pillow. Fumbling for the call button, he was unable to find it but managed to raise his arm weakly in an effort to push her away. "Ngoooh! Hep! Peezh!" he yelled in a louder voice, hoping Nurse McVey would come to his aid.

Karcass glanced at Lipschitz's sedated roommate in the adjoining bed to make sure he wasn't conscious. To her relief, he was completely comatose, the heart monitor registering a pulse that could barely be heard. Knowing she only had a few more minutes alone with her victim, Karcass decided that more forceful action was needed.

"All right, then, Irving, if you won't sign our deal-the deal that *you* agreed to-I'll just go ahead and sign it for you." Lipschitz was horrified, unable to prevent her from signing his name to the sale agreement. The dying man watched helplessly as she leaned the file on the edge of his bed and signed his name to the bottom of the contract, shocked to see how closely it matched his own signature.

"Ah fugghh eh...I gaw die. Fugghh ew, aggie. Fugghh ew."

"And, more initials right here..." she said, as if they were in an office and routinely agreeing on the details. Her evil deed now complete, she gathered the pages together and exited the semi-private room, passing the nurse's station and checking the file to make sure she had the signature page.

As Karcass locked eyes with Nurse McVey sitting behind the desk, she said, "We're done, nurse. Would you mind witnessing my father's signature here, please?" Unwittingly, Nurse McVey complied. "Thank you, nurse." She folded the document into the folder and yet another demented idea occurred to her. "He said to tell you he's in a lot of pain and wants you to increase his pain killers so he'll be more comfortable. I think he wants to sleep now."

Nurse McVey began preparing another IV supplement, all too happy to put the old man back into a state of narcotic euphoria and bill it all to Medicare. Puzzled by her upbeat demeanor, the nurse watched as she headed down the hall to the bank of elevators with the file folder under her arm.

Unable to contain the wicked smile on her face, Karcass was now completely confident this would be the easiest two hundred grand she'd ever make.

⟩⟨⟩

Later that afternoon, Karcass sat in the Delmar office with her forged contract as she expressed her outrage with the egregious toll-charging scheme that Stampaugh contrived. She'd had numerous confrontations with the crafty manager, but she had yet to have one go her way. She imagined Lipschitz at the ICU, unconscious from the increased dose of painkillers she ordered after their confrontation. She needed to stay focused on having her bogus condo contract approved by Stampaugh if she wanted to close the deal. Secretly, she feared Lipschitz's son and daughter might uncover the bogus deal when they arrived for the funeral, but-so far-it was like taking candy from a baby.

"Cash talks and bullshit walks, Maggie," said Stampaugh as he read the contract. "We know your price is almost two hundred grand under market. You can damn well afford five grand to grease the gears a little." Stampaugh clasped his hands confidently behind his head and sat back in the padded leather chair to give her time to consider his unprincipled logic.

Her chair squeaking in protest, Karcass shifted her body, trying to get comfortable as she scowled at Stampaugh's arrogance. "You're a damn thief, Dyson. If I had a way to expose you, you"-

"Then you wouldn't be netting out your two-hundred-grand profit, would you?" he sneered. "Now, really, Margaret. Who's the thief here?" Stampaugh nodded toward the office computer sitting on the credenza behind him. "I've got his son and daughter's number right here. Whad'ya think they'd say about your deal? Think they'd go for it? Or make it subject to a new appraisal?" He studied her face and thought of another wrench he could throw in the works. "Even worse, what if they order a medical review of his competency? Or ask me about the latest selling prices?"

The two greedy condo commandos were squared off like vultures in their challenge to pick the bones of a road kill, neither willing to yield their share of the spoils. Smirking at Karcass, he was confident that she didn't have the pull with the board members to make good on her threat. Neither would she throw away a two hundred grand profit over a paltry two or three-percent bribe.

Frustrated, Karcass abruptly stood, smoothing the wrinkles on her huge overalls and pointed a finger at Stampaugh. "You're a real dick, Dyson." She paused with her hand on the doorknob before adding in a quieter tone, "Craig'll bring your money in the morning."

Stampaugh smiled demonically at his adversary. "Cash. No checks, please. *Then,* I don't see a problem with management approving your contract," twisting the knife ever so slightly as she exited. She threw open his door in a huff, surprising his secretary at her desk in the adjoining office who'd been eavesdropping on their conversation. As she stalked toward the outer door, she thought about hiring an attorney, if her opinion of them wasn't already so bleak. Karcass was convinced beyond reasonable doubt that attorneys believed their clients were innocent until proven broke.

"Everything okay, Mrs. Karcass?" Maria watched her exit in a fit of anger. The Sophia Viagra look alike took Karcass's stormy exit in stride, knowing that everyone at Delmar was usually upset about something after leaving her manager's office. She glanced over her shoulder at Stampaugh who had his feet up on his desk and his hands still comfortably clasped behind his head. Familiar with her boss' moods, Maria had no doubt that things were completely under control.

After Karcass's dramatic exit, Stampaugh got up and closed the door, sitting down to reminisce as he thought about his court-ordered sexual addiction course two years ago. What would his therapist have to say about the day's events? Dr. Doff had been fond of ending his sessions by saying the common thread in all his classes was greed and sexual aberration. He would often say some people will always see things for what they are, others for what they want it to be, and a small minority admit nothing at all. Getting psyched over taking his fair share of the spoils, Stampaugh refused to feel guilty. This culture of failure has got to stop, he reasoned to himself. He was an *American*, damn it! His country was blessed with boundless greed and the power to exterminate all forms of life as we know it. He would act like it, for God's sake!

It was all about the money, and it was time to get paid.

SIXTEEN

The man that called himself David Callahan dismounted from his bicycle and propped the two-toned Nel Lusso beach cruiser against a palm tree at Nautilus Realty. Squinting into the early-morning sun, Callahan was preoccupied with the possibility of having to plan a move from his hideout at Greenwood Mansion after receiving a mysterious call from an unknown air conditioning contractor. He was suspicious of the call because the stonewalled mansion was built a century before air conditioning was even around, and he'd shared his phone number with no one.

Knowing that cold callers had descended on Florida like a plague of hungry locusts, he considered the possibility that the call could have been a random phone solicitation. The call came in the early evening while Callahan was busy gloating over the online obituaries of former foes, and his paranoia compelled him to find a new hideout further north on the Treasure Coast where folks minded their own business. There, his secluded lifestyle would draw less attention and fewer questions.

Peering through the glass door to see if anyone was inside to write him a receipt, he could see a pretty young girl sitting up front at the reception desk. As he entered, Callahan was unprepared for the change in personnel that awaited him, unaware that the young blonde was Lance Meyer's replacement. The new receptionist was busy typing away on her keyboard and hadn't yet noticed him, which gave Callahan the opportunity to size her up.

In the middle of his fantasy, the receptionist glanced up from her computer. "Hi, can I help you?" she asked, feeling a little creeped out by the bearded man's black beady eyes seeming to fixate on her blouse's missing button. Alone in the office, she grasped the top of her blouse and locked eyes with her visitor. The last time she remembered eyes that black and lifeless was when they were attached to a twelve-foot tiger shark swimming less than a foot from her nose at the Monterey Aquarium in Northern California.

"Where's the guy who used to sit there?" he asked casually.

"He, um...well, did you hear about the accident two weeks ago?" she answered.

"What accident?" he asked nonchalantly. Callahan could see she'd become quite emotional.

"Lance was killed about a week ago in a boating accident," she said sadly. "He got run over by a boater. It was all over the news." She looked at Callahan like he'd been living under a rock on Mars.

"Well, ah...I've been out of town," he responded. "That's a shame. Lotta drunks out there drinkin' and drivin' boats. They catch the guy?"

The young receptionist shook her head. "Nope. No one seems to know anything." There was a moment of awkward silence for the dearly departed real estate agent who used to collect his rent.

"So, who're *you?*" he asked as he jerked the folded bundle of moldy Ben Franklins out of his pants pocket, spilling some bills on the floor. He made a neat stack of bills on her desk and squatted to retrieve the rest, trying to look relaxed.

"I'm Megan. Megan Rockwell. You must be Mr. Callahan," smiling weakly, searching for warmth behind the black lifeless eyes.

"Call me David," he said, grouping the stack of bills on her desk. "You must be used to men throwing money at you, Megan."

Megan frowned, uncomfortable with his insinuation. "Um... not really sure about that. I'll go ahead and count up your rent payment, Mr. Callahan."

"Really, Megan, please call me David," he reminded her as she pulled a folded piece of paper from the stack of bills. Before he realized what he'd done, she unfolded the invoice and was staring at a wrinkled receipt for a boat rental from Boca Boats Tire and Hair Care Center on Federal Highway. The receipt described a Boston Whaler rental dated from last week and had 'PAID CASH' stamped in red.

"Is this something you want to hang onto?" she said, holding up the receipt, feeling awkward at coming across something of a personal nature.

Callahan took the invoice from her hand to see what it was. As he read it, his heart skipped a beat. "Oh, this...uh...yeah, make a good tax deduction. Thanks," smiling weakly, nervously pulling on his beard.

"It was a fishing trip," she heard him say. Becoming increasingly uncomfortable with Mr. Callahan, Megan wished that her office manager was at her desk in the adjoining office. She glanced at the clock and realized Linda wasn't due in for another fifteen minutes.

Seeing the invoice again triggered Callahan's memory of Meyer floundering in the water and the sound of the man's screams just before impact. He remembered the hollow "thunk" sound when the hull of the Boston Whaler had impacted his skull. Callahan watched her carefully for any sign that she'd made a connection between himself and her predecessor as he stuffed the receipt back in his pocket.

"Just a fishing trip," he repeated lamely. Callahan hoped to hell she hadn't read it. "You wanna write me out a receipt so I can get back to my dogs, Slick?"

She'd never had anyone call her Slick before. Uncomfortable with his shifting back and forth, and creeped out by his attention, Megan couldn't get rid of him fast enough. "Sure, uh, let me get that," reaching for her receipt pad and hurriedly writing out a voucher for five thousand dollars. "Thank you Mr. Callahan," she said, adding an air of formality.

"Sure thing," he smirked. Upset with his carelessness, Callahan headed for the door and exited the office quickly. Outside, he took a deep breath and let it out slowly. Stupid, stupid, stupid, he thought as he grabbed his beach cruiser and pointed it south toward Greenwood Mansion. Pedaling furiously, he strayed out of the bike path momentarily and almost sideswiped a white Mercedes full of beachgoers.

Callahan wished he'd thrown that receipt away. Still spooked about the strange call he got earlier from the AC contractor, he felt like his carelessness was catching up with him. The sleepy little town of Vero Beach they called "The Hamptons of South Florida" was looking better and better. He figured he could make the transfer in two or three trips using a heavy-duty minivan to haul his $170 million stash of gold coins and cash. He pedaled faster, vowing to get serious about planning the details of his move.

Detective Klein sat in his car at Red Reef Park in Boca as he watched the two girls toss the Frisbee back and forth on the beach. He took a bite out of his Whopper and thought about the next move in the investigation of his brother-in-law's death, reminding himself that he'd promised his grief-stricken sister he'd find out what really happened. So far, there were few leads, and the Boca

Raton detective was feeling frustrated. Reaching for his ringing cell phone, he cursed as the meat patty slipped out of the Quarter Pounder and landed in his lap, spilling his French fries. "Sonofa-" With ketchup on his fingers, he pressed the talk button.

It was Anthony Costello. "Hey, Jim. Sorry to hear about your brother-in-law." Klein listened as he slipped his meat patty back between the buns and licked the ketchup off his fingers. "Just finished booking in two crack dealers. Scumbags tried to sell me a twenty dollar bag right at the entrance to Town Center Mall. What's up with you?" At twenty-two years old, Costello was the youngest undercover narcotics detective in the Boca P.D. Criminal Investigation Division, and Klein had been impressed with his record of arrests.

"Lunch break at Red Reef. Me and my Quarter Pounder that just landed in my lap when you called," he said in disgust. "Don't suppose you could have waited ten minutes to call me?" Klein set his burger down on the armrest as he gathered fries from his lap and scooped some from the sandy floor of the Crown Vic.

"Sorry, Jim. Just wanted to let you know Lt. Dickson's reviewing my application for transfer to robbery/homicide."

"Congrats." Annoyed with his clumsiness, Klein dabbed at the ketchup stain on his shirt with a napkin as an Arianna Granda look-alike sashayed past his cruiser. He watched her in his side mirror as she continued her animated Valley-girl conversation on her cell phone.

Costello wanted to cheer him up. "Hey, I heard Mickey D's new rat sandwich is all the rage in Bangalore," said Costello. "Heard it makes you wanna order it with cheese."

"Don't quit your day job just yet, funny guy. Rat meat's not on my bucket list. You grow up around a lot of lead paint or something?"

"Maybe," said Costello.

"Ranks right up there with drinking Mexican tap water and a rattlesnake with a 'pet me' sign." Hungry enough to eat a side of beef, angioplasty couldn't have been further from his mind as Klein took another greedy bite of his burger and chased it with a handful of sandy French fries. "Another thing you won't catch me doin' is letting O.J. Simpson show me his knife collection."

Costello chuckled. "Can't believe they ever let that guy walk. So, what's the eye candy report today at Red Reef?"

"Beach is here, bro. Wish you were beautiful," he answered wryly. "So, what's on your mind, Tony?"

"Had an idea that might help with your case. There's a little hole-in-the-wall marina just west of Federal Highway on the Boca side of the C-15 canal. They don't do much advertising, so it's mostly locals. Been there forever. Used to work there when I was a kid."

"Yeah, but that was last week, right?" Klein liked to tease his protégé about his age. The guys in CID joked that he looked like Matthew Broderick from his role in *Ferris Bueller's Day Off.*

Costello ignored the taunt. "Happens to be one of the closest marinas to where they found Meyer's body. And obscure enough if a perp wanted to stay low on the radar. You been over there yet, chief?"

"Ya know, for someone just startin' out in CID, you're on the ball, Costello. That's actually not a bad idea. My next stop, right after I finish my fries. Gotta go-Michael Jackson's doctor is calling on the other line with some prescriptions he wants me to try."

After the two detectives hung up, Klein entertained himself by watching two girls sitting on the restroom wall as they passed a joint back and forth. Conflicted about busting them, he almost ran over a kid with a surfboard as he backed out of his parking spot. More shaken than angry, the kid flipped Klein off and banged his fist on the trunk of his unmarked Crown Vic in protest. Klein ignored the kid's attitude and turned south on A1A to check out the marina. He didn't usually like working cases with partners, but if he had to, Costello would be high on his list of choices.

Minutes later, Klein pulled up in front of the three-story corrugated metal building. It seemed like an odd bunch of businesses to bundle together under one roof as he read the sign a second time. Boats, tires and hair care under one roof? Really? Definitely an out-of-the-way place to rent a boat, the place was older than dirt, the sign faded, and the building could have used a fresh coat of paint ten years ago. A page from Boca's past, he thought, stepping around the huge blooming hibiscus and making his way across the faded pavement toward the front of the building. The cavernous open entrance made it look like an old airplane hangar with two pink plastic flamingos guarding the entrance.

"Hey, pal...the owner or manager around?" asked Klein of a man behind the counter with his back to him.

The weathered grey-haired man in bifocals turned from his inventory duties to see who was asking for him as he wiped his hands on a rag. "Ya got Bob here, fella. Owner for the last thirty-seven years. Help ya with something?"

In a cheeky mood, Klein smiled. "Yeah. I'm trying to decide whether I should get a set of tires or a haircut today, Bob." He met the old man's gaze with a poker face, but it wasn't the first time the old man had heard this particular line. He glanced over the detective's shoulder and checked out the tires on his unmarked cruiser, then focused on Klein's hairless head.

"Well, sir, since you got good rubber on your cruiser, there, and don't need no haircut, how 'bout a boat rental, officer?"

"I can see there's no foolin' you, Bob." He broke into a grin. "Been awhile. I think I was still a patrolman last time I was here." He flashed his identification, and the old man leaned over the counter to check it out.

"Don't think I remember you, Officer Klein." Bob pointed at his head. "Early stage Alzheimer's," he said apologetically.

"Sorry to hear that, Bob. By the way, it's Detective Klein," he corrected. "We're investigating a boating accident. A Boca real estate agent was run over and killed." The detective pulled out a black and white snapshot of Lance Meyer taken during happier times and laid it on the counter.

"Well, Detective, don't wanna sound cold or nothin', but we're up to our asses in realtors. You think Boca's really gonna miss one?" he asked wryly.

"He was my brother-in-law."

The old man looked over the top of his glasses and met Detective Klein's steely gaze with a somber look. "Sorry. Didn't mean nothin' by it." Feeling obliged to make amends for his callous remark, Bob picked up the photo. "Nice looking young man. Think I saw it in the *Boca News*." He ran his hand through his hair to stimulate his memory. "Or maybe it was on TV," handing the photo back to Klein.

"You seen anything unusual, any boats come back damaged this past week?"

Bob scratched his head absentmindedly. "Not as I recall. Brain don't work like it used to." He winced and pointed again to his head. "Early stage Alzheimer's," he repeated.

"Yeah, I think you mentioned that already." Impatient with the old man's repetition, the detective forced himself to wait and hear if there was more information that Bob could provide.

"Well, I found out there's some benefits, though," said Bob. Klein was amused. "I get to watch the same great movies over and over 'cause I can't remember how the hell they end." Bob cracked a smile. "Oh, ah...by the way...had a outboard catch fire coupla weeks ago, almost cost me a boat, but nothing else really comes to mind. Not sure I can help ya here, detective." Bob returned briefly to taking inventory on gallon jugs of two-stroke engine oil and replacement parts before he turned around again. "Oh. Wait." He held up a finger as if it were dialing into what was left of his memory. "One of my two Whalers came back from a rental with some minor gel coat damage."

"When?"

"'Bout a week ago."

"Hull damage?"

"Well, gelcoat was chipped up on the bow. Guy said he thought he mighta hit a sea turtle or a oak pallet or somethin'. I kept a hundred and fifty bucks of his deposit and he didn't seem to mind. Paid everything with this moldy cash like he just dug it up or somethin'. Kept calling me 'Slick'."

"Slick? Moldy cash? Hmmm." Klein rubbed his chin as he thought about the old man's eye-witness account. "Can I see the boat?" he asked, trying hard to contain his exuberance.

"Sure. Follow me." The two men walked past the two-story forklift toward the first row of boats that sat towering on steel I-beams. There were over a dozen stacks of boats laid out in a crisscross pattern all the way to the building's roof. "Think it was this one right here. *Blew By You.*" Bob rested his arm on the gunnel as he watched Klein inspect the boat.

"*Blew By You?* Really, Bob?" Klein looked expectantly at the old man, waiting for an explanation.

"My wife's idea. She's a rag bagger from way back," explained Bob. "She used to charter out an old gaff-rigged schooner outa Key West." Klein responded with a grunt and squatted to examine the leading edge of the Boston Whaler's bow as it sat on the ground level support cradle. Peering closely, Klein noticed a tiny piece of organic material imbedded in the gelcoat that looked like it didn't belong there. He pulled a ball point pen out of his top pocket to probe the chipped area just under the tow ring.

"You haven't done any repairs on her, have ya, Bob?" Hoping the evidence was fresh and untainted, the detective waited for the old man to grasp the importance of his question.

Bob struggled to think back on when the scruffy-looking customer with the beard had returned the boat. "No sir, just rinsed her off with fresh water. Maybe a little bleach to kill the algae. Our gel coat guy only comes around once a month. Should be here on Thursday," he explained. "I had her on the list to"-

Klein stood up abruptly, his tone firmer. "Bob, don't touch this boat. I need to get forensics out here to recover evidence. This could help us solve a possible murder, and this whole area," waving his arms, "...boat included, is now a crime scene." He stepped closer to the old man. "Ya with me on this, Bob?"

Startled at the detective's sudden change in attitude, Bob gripped the top of the gunnel and straightened himself up. "Yes sir." Concerned about how long his rental boat would be part of a "crime scene", the old man was running the numbers, already trying to figure up the lost revenues, now regretting his cooperation.

Klein walked toward the metal building's entrance to get a stronger cell signal as he autodialed the Boca Raton P.D. "Yeah, hey Judy. It's Detective Klein. I need a forensics team out here. Got a good lead on that boating accident last week. Who's on duty now?"

"Peebles and Hightower. Which boating accident?" she asked, needing clarification. "The dive boat collision off Delray Beach, or the deceased realtor on Boca"-

"Yeah, the deceased Realtor on South Boca Beach. You know Lance was my brother-in-law, right? Got a boat here with gel coat damage and what could be some tissue and hair from our victim," said Klein.

"Sorry for your loss, Jim," offered Judy. "I didn't know that you were related to the victim."

"Let's keep that between us, okay?"

"Sure thing. Gimme the address there, Jim," she said as Klein walked with his phone to retrieve a couple of rolls of crime scene tape from his trunk.

"1920 S. Federal, Boca. You know, the old Boca Boats, Tire and Haircare Center there on Federal Highway."

"Roger that. Forensics team will be on the way in a few minutes. Oh, and Jim?"

"Yeah, Judy."

"Could you ask him if they have any specials on perms this week?"

━┼┼━

Years ago, Tommy Tomlinson discovered that there was a dark side to him that excited him. He loved to hear the sound of extreme fear in a human voice. Fury, panic, despair-the full cycle of primal desperation-turned him on. It was a latent emotion that he'd first noticed when he came close to strangling his girlfriend Andrea back in Chicago the first time she hinted about turning him in if he didn't share the loot with her.

Starting as his assistant, then living with him as his girlfriend for three months, Andrea made the mistake of confronting him one day over his greed, and the argument quickly deteriorated into a screaming match before it turned violent. Tomlinson grabbed her by the throat and almost choked her to death on the floor that day. The thrill of having the power to end her life with his bare hands aroused his darker side, and the rush of adrenaline he experienced acted like a narcotic, making him feel intoxicated. Even stranger, he noticed Andrea had gotten just as aroused as he did with his savage behavior. His uncontrolled rage sometimes upstaged their abusive foreplay, but not before an intense bout of sadomasochistic eroticism erupted.

There were over a dozen repeat performances of near strangulation that caused Andrea to realize that being a fugitive on the run was taking a toll on her boyfriend's state of mind. While she feared his violence, she would sometimes get so excited that her fear took a back seat to her inexplicable primordial feelings. Often, she would imagine herself as a wild animal in the jungle while he slapped and choked her during their lovemaking.

As a result of her boyfriend's bizarre behavior, Andrea began to fantasize about rough sex with strangers and people they'd pass on the beach or in public. She realized this was a side of her that was beyond her own control, satiated only by her boyfriend's sadistic fantasies. She knew she was putting herself in danger as he became more paranoid about being caught by the police. At the same time, she was sexually aroused with the increasing cruelty of his emotional and physical abuse, and the truth was that she enjoyed being forcefully held down during their lovemaking.

Drawn to danger like a moth to a candle, Andrea was convinced he was slowly becoming unhinged as she tried in vain to avoid major confrontations with him. Their most recent argument at a local restaurant had frightened her so much that it forced her to re-evaluate their relationship.

It all started when he had taken Andrea to Pisano's in Boca, one of their favorite seafood restaurants. While she was being ogled by a nice-looking guy sitting behind her boyfriend, she'd become so disgusted with Tommy's table manners that she couldn't eat. Tommy was slurping his three dozen raw oysters with such wild abandon that customers at surrounding tables had become quiet in silent disapproval. She had often accused him of being anal/retentive and OCD (the two disorders went hand-in-hand, she often told him). She thought about this as she watched him arranging the empty oyster shells around the rim of his plate, repeatedly stacking them into six identical piles of four. He was jabbering on and on, seemingly oblivious to his erratic behavior, completely unaware that his actions were embarrassing them both in front of other customers.

She thought about her disgust with his habit of chucking everything out the window of his Land Rover. From hamburger cartons and coffee cups to handfuls of junk mail-it all became litter along the roadway. Increasingly uncomfortable on their drives together, she was amazed at his callousness toward the environment and the unwanted attention it always seemed to bring them, including several incidents of road rage. Andrea wasn't clear about the clinical names of her boyfriend's disorders, but she was often annoyed with the symptoms; anything he couldn't drink, eat or control was thrown out the window of his SUV.

Then there was his temper.

"What's the matter, Andrea? You're not listening to me," he said.

"Sorry, honey."

"What're you gawking at?"

"Nothing."

He could tell she was upset. "Is there anything wrong with your scrod?"

"It's fine, Tommy."

"I *told* you not to call me that!" Irritated with her slipping up and using his real name, he turned and scanned the restaurant full of customers to see if anyone had overheard. Suppressing his anger, he leaned forward to admonish her. "How many times have I told you, it's *David* in public? C'mon, Andrea. Get it together. Just for that, you can pick up the check."

Weary of living a life in social isolation and his increasingly bizarre behavior, Andrea was fearful of setting off one of his abusive tantrums. But it was his unmitigated cheapness that annoyed her the most. "Let me get this straight. You got $170 million at home and you want me to pick up the dinner check?" she asked incredulously. "What's wrong with this picture, *David*?"

"Sshhh. *Dammit*, Andrea, somebody will hear you."

Frightened by the demonic look in his eyes, she lowered her voice to a whisper. "I don't want to fight again. I just think a man with your money ought to treat me better. I take good care of you. You owe me."

Her comment enraged him. "All right, Andrea, finish up. We're out of here." He turned toward their waiter who hovered a few tables away. "Waiter, bring me the check." She could see him fighting to control his anger and began to dread the ride home as she ran her hand over the bruises on her neck that were still visible from two nights ago. Fearful that his explosive temper was about to erupt again, she was afraid of what would happen once they were alone.

⚒

Three days later, Callahan had grown tired of sitting in his basement cleaning his AK-47 and watching movies on Netflix. Opting for a relaxing moment on Boca Beach as the sun sank lower behind Greenwood Mansion, he sat back in the swing on the dune in the growing twilight and thought about Andrea. The two fingers of Larresingle XO he'd just tossed back had a euphoric effect on him, and the smoke from the Cohiba trailed slowly from his mouth. He held it in for as long as he could, mimicking her last breath, reluctant to let it escape from his lungs as he savored the mix of aromas and flavors. The peaceful sound of ocean waves reaching their final destination on the beach below was lulling him into a reverie of recent events. He tried to put her screams out of his mind as he watched the dragon flies riding the swaying stalks of sea oats on the dune. He could hear a solitary single-engine plane practicing stalls and turns high overhead as it circled over the sea, watching it until it disappeared into the clouds.

She always had a way of bringing out the worst in him. Why did she have to be so confrontational?

Callahan had always had a hard time accepting responsibility for his violence. It was just so much easier to lay the blame at her feet. The large empty footings ready to fill with fresh concrete flashed through his head again, and thinking of her rolled up and motionless in the blanket took him to a place where he ached to go back. Though he missed her, he no longer questioned that he would do whatever it took to protect his $170 million fortune

He wondered if he would ever be able to trust anyone again.

SEVENTEEN

The water become cooler as he descended into the turquoise depths toward the reef below. In stealth mode for a blue water hunt, Mark wore a 3mm teal-colored nylon skin, an overfilled 120 c.f. steel tank with a 40% nitrox mix, and an assortment of hunting gear dangling from six snap shackles on his buoyancy compensator. With enough nitrox for a two hour hunt, his game plan was to fill his bag with only the choicest seafood from his favorite Florida reef.

Before he dove overboard, he had said his goodbyes to Carol laying nude on deck as she studied for an upcoming exam on her laptop. Before jumping, Mark had set the dive flag from the VHF antenna and tossed the Danforth overboard on site three hundred yards east of the southern tip of Highland Beach.

Diving on a beautiful reef wasn't only physical for him; it took on a deeper spiritual meaning as he surrendered to a consciousness that superseded his own being. It was God, life, and love all rolled into one beautiful kaleidoscopic experience as he became part of the reef itself. Fascinated by the vibrancy and colorful diversity of reef life, he felt protective, like all the living creatures were part of his family.

As he swam deeper toward the 75-pound Danforth waiting on the sandy bottom, his ear was tuned to the faint sounds of reef inhabitants as they scurried about in the never-ending struggle for food and survival. He thought about men who liked to hunt deer with a high-powered rifle. The hunter has grace, respect, and purity of heart. Pumping a .308 slug into a defenseless deer just didn't qualify as a sporting event in his book. Hunting only seemed sporting if the hunter was in as much peril as the hunted. His intuition told him that today, his philosophy would be tested, and he vowed to be extra cautious.

Thrilled with the water clarity, he estimated the visibility to be about 200 feet as he watched a large spotted moray slither along the coral wall thirty feet below. The moray was followed by a curious school of yellowtail that swam up from the depths to greet him. As the lead shot weights in his BC and his steel tank carried him deeper, he spotted the shank of the anchor that waited for him in the sand below.

The weather forecast had predicted an increase in wind and seas, and he wanted to place the Danforth on the windward side of the gigantic concrete slab set there two decades earlier by the Army Corps of Engineers. Resetting the Danforth would give it more holding power in case the weather worsened. His console gauges confirmed 3400 PSI of nitrox and depth at 70 feet as the heels of his flippers made contact with the sandy bottom.

Mark reached down and grasped the steel shank of the anchor with his gloved hand and pressed the BC inflator button for added lift, bouncing off the bottom and kicking forward like he was rebounding on the moon's surface with one-fifth the gravity. He kicked hard, moving man and anchor ten yards forward to re-position the Danforth under the edge of the massive concrete formation. After letting go, he heard it 'clunk' against the concrete and watched it settle behind the slab. Satisfied with the anchor's new position, he pressed the purge valve lightly to reach neutral buoyancy again to face the reef wall in perfect weightlessness.

It made him feel like he was in another world, almost as if he was unborn and still suspended in the amniotic fluid in his mother's womb. Floating weightlessly, he was mesmerized by the colorful soft corals swaying back and forth in the mild current. Mark spotted a medium-size nurse shark cruising in and out of rock formations halfway up the reef wall on a hunt. Cocking his three-band spear gun, he clicked the safety on and double-checked the lobster snare, game bag, mini-EPIRB and emergency regulator hanging from his BC. Tightening the Velcro fasteners on his gloves, he checked his compass bearings and swam due east. Slowly, he ascended toward the top of the reef wall, heading straight for the 20-foot cube-shaped tubular steel structure called "The Cage" as he went over the dive plan again in his head.

Positioned in the middle of the quarter-mile long reef among the greatest concentration of lobster holes, "The Cage" was the starting point of his planned dive. The huge metal structure was always the easiest of all the reef's features to identify on his boat's sonar screen. From "The Cage", he planned to head south against the mild current for the first half of his dive along the top of the western reef wall. Then, he would circle to the eastern edge and the reef's large crevasses that resembled giant fingers extending into the grey depths of the deeper water toward the open ocean. On the backside of the reef, he would visit the next landmark nick-named "The Rubble", chunks of odd-shaped coral formations located seventy-five feet down where he would likely find another cache of bugs.

Though dangerous and ill-advised by dive instructors, Mark had become adept at skip-breathing to extend his dive time. By controlling his heart rate and breathing, he could squeeze two and a half hours out of his overfilled steel tank at an average depth of sixty-five feet and still avoid having to decompress at the end of his dive.

From "The Rubble", he planned to turn north to ride with the current in the second half of his underwater hunt. He would come up over the top of the reef at about fifty feet and descend into a beautiful, sandy-bottomed underwater lagoon the size of a basketball court that he called "The Aquarium". There, the water was exceptionally clear and still, and a myriad of sea anemones and soft corals of indescribable colors marked the entrance as they waved back and forth in the current.

A great diversity of marine creatures, both divine and deadly, were known to hide in the holes along the perimeter of "The Aquarium". Often filled with a dangerous collection of competing hunters that included black tip reef sharks, lionfish, moray eels and barracuda, Mark liked to think of it as his own private seafood market. An occasional manta ray or school of tuna would sometimes find their way to the reef's edge and meander over the top in their hunt for a meal. One of his favorite sights were the groups of cuttlefish that would hover over the reef in formation like a squadron of aircraft suspended in midair.

As he swam closer to his first waypoint and "The Cage" came into view, Mark watched a large green moray eel slither through the structure at the top of the reef and continue north away from him. On the hunt for similar prey, the eel continued, unaware of the huge spiny lobster Mark had spotted at the entrance to a large hole about fifteen feet down the reef face. Releasing a stream of air from his inflator, he descended down to the sandy bottom, putting himself in a position ten yards directly in front of the monster lobster. Relaxing his breathing, he concentrated on reducing his heart rate and lowering his electromagnetic signature so he could get closer to the granddaddy bug without alarming it. To his delight, the lobster responded to Mark's approach by creeping forward a few feet out of his hole in a bid to challenge him.

Suddenly, out of the corner of his mask, he saw a gigantic octopus with tentacles six feet long emerge from the coral crevasse and lunge at him. Mark suppressed his instinct to unsheathe the dive knife strapped to his leg and dismember the beast as the animal's menacing beak pressed against the glass surface of his facemask, completely obscuring his field of vision. Surprised to feel one of the tentacles tugging at his regulator, he fought with the octopus to secure his air supply, but the creature managed to pull it out of his mouth and held it out of reach.

Holding his breath, he was in a dilemma as he knelt on the ocean floor with the creature wrapped around his head and shoulders. A previous encounter with an octopus on the Great Barrier Reef years earlier flashed through his brain, and he remembered the key to surviving the experience lay in showing the creature that he meant it no harm. With one hand on his still-sheathed dive knife, Mark struggled to remain calm. As he began to see stars from lack of oxygen, the immutable words of Dylan Thomas's famous poem about sinking through the sea and rising again echoed through his head.

He made a last-ditch effort to avoid bloodshed and firmly pushed the tentacles away from his body. He was elated to feel the creature respond as it released his regulator and softened its grip on him. As he was about to lose consciousness, he lunged for the regulator and reinserted it into his mouth, taking several deep breaths. Then, the huge creature squirted a massive cloud of black ink to cover its retreat. With a fresh supply of oxygen coursing through his veins, he watched the octopus rocket back into the crevasse from which it had emerged.

Unsettled by the attack, Mark maneuvered out of the black ink cloud into the clearer water behind him, thankful that he'd survived without having to kill such an intelligent creature. Relieved, he worked to regain his orientation, looking toward the surface seventy feet up and wondering what Carol was doing as he watched his air bubbles ascend. He pictured her sunning herself on the deck, floating far above him as she chatted away on her cell phone.

His desire to bag the trophy lobster returned. He peered through the crystal-clear water ahead to see if it was still around and spotted his trophy-to-be, still waiting twenty yards ahead behind a school of yellowtail. The spiny lobster seemed unfazed by the life-and-death-drama just played out as it continued to sweep its antennae slowly back and forth, guarding the entrance to its lair. Checking the reef wall ahead for any signs of the octopus, Mark moved in for the kill, now more determined than ever to bag the big bug. Extending his snare as he approached, he slipped the noose over the giant crustacean and jerked hard on the cable to tighten the loop. He could hear the huge lobster grunting in protest as he wrestled the creature into his game bag with gloved hands and imagined the surprised look on Carol's face when he presented his trophy topside.

Another ninety minutes of hunting lapsed, and Mark had snared fourteen lobster captured at "The Aquarium" and "The Rubble". As two playful porpoise emerged from the depths and swam up close to check out his bulging game bag, he pulled his bag closer to protect his day's catch. When he reached out to touch them, one of the mammals nudged his hand for a friendly hello. After circling a few more times, the porpoise swam into deeper water eastward in their hunt for an easier lunch.

The two-foot long lobster had torn his dive skin during his struggle to corral it, and Mark could feel his mac-daddy bug working hard to escape as he checked the lock on the bag. With enough air left for one final gamefish run, he flipped off the safety on his spear gun and began his final leg along the colorful soft corals on the top of the reef. His air gauge read 635 PSI, barely enough for what he had in mind. After encountering three large sharks earlier on his dive, he thought about the risks of leaving a blood trail from a wounded fish. With only enough room in his bulging bag for one or two large gamefish, he began skip breathing again to conserve his remaining air.

Cruising another fifty yards along the reef top, he passed a few medium-sized hogfish meandering through the soft corals before spotting a large black grouper darting between holes. Just out of range, Mark settled in behind a group of sea fans to hide his approach. Groupers were more elusive than hogfish, so he'd have to be on his toes to bag it. A trophy black grouper to match his monster lobster would be a nice addition to the menu, and the one in his sights looked to be about twenty pounds. He waited patiently and burned through another ten pounds of air before he saw the grouper emerge again. Mark descended below the edge of the reef and made his approach at a right angle for the best shot. As the grouper emerged ten feet away, Mark had a clear shot, took aim and squeezed the trigger. The stainless steel spear hit the fish just behind the gill plate. It was a perfect shot, and Mark pounced before the grouper could roll over on the bottom and push the spear out. Holding the prize fish against the sea floor, he extracted his spear and stuffed the grouper head-first into his packed game bag.

As he reloaded his spear gun, he felt something tugging on the line to his game bag. Mark spun around and suddenly felt a sharp pain in his forearm. Then he saw the monster shark and his own blood in the water, shocked that he'd accidently stuck his arm into its open mouth. Quickly, he jerked his arm back before the shark could close its jaws, ripping open the dive skin on razor-sharp teeth. As a diversion, he exhaled hard into his regulator, purging a lungful of bubbles to try and scare the shark. The shark turned away, then circled back toward him with pectorals extended downward in full attack mode. With the unloaded spear gun still in his grasp, Mark did the only thing he could think of-he flipped the gun around and hit the shark hard on the nose with the rubber stock as he exhaled forcefully into his regulator again to release another explosion of bubbles.

Mark was relieved to see the shark disappear into the depths as it swam into deeper water to the east. With the grouper's blood now dispersed in the water with some of his own, he was convinced the shark would return. A moment later he saw the shark circling from a distance, this time accompanied by a second shark.

Critically low on air and surrounded by blood, Mark knew he had to leave the area fast if he wanted to live to dive another day. In the excitement, he'd burned through another four hundred pounds of air and was down to 225 PSI. Then an escape plan took shape.

Reloading his spear gun, he strained to stretch the three bands and lock them into position before the sharks could attack again. Rotating 360 degrees to search, he saw three sharks lurking in the shadows about 200 feet away. The pain from the laceration on his forearm was growing more intense, and to slow the bleeding, Mark used his knife to cut a foot-long section of his dive skin away and tie it around the wound. As luck would have it, he spotted an adult hogfish swimming lazily among the sea fans a short distance from him, oblivious to the drama unfolding. Knowing that his very survival now depended on keeping a cool head, he struggled to keep his wits about him. Fear was the mind-killer that he had to overcome.

Down to only 150 PSI, he worked quickly to put his plan into action. Descending under the edge of the reef for cover, he swam parallel to the hogfish, got ahead of it and pivoted to set up a 90-degree shot. Mark fired, spearing the fish and worked quickly to remove the spear and run his stainless stringer through the gills, then anchoring it to a nearby coral outcropping. Tethered to the rock on the three-foot stringer, he watched the bleeding hogfish thrash around, knowing the distressed fish's vibrations would act like a dinner bell for the sharks.

When he saw the first shark attack the hogfish, he knew his plan would work, but he was out of air. He checked his dive computer for nitrogen saturation and the gauge indicated he was about to cross into the yellow warning zone. Having no air left for decompression, Mark knew he had to risk breaking the surface within seconds or he would drown. Looking over his shoulder, he could see the sharks fighting over the remains of the hogfish as he made his escape westward along the sea floor with his last lungful of air. Spotting his anchor, he followed the chain rode upward, the air in his lungs expanding as he angled toward the surface. His tank empty, his lungs screamed for air as he neared the top.

"Huuhhhhhhh," taking a huge lungful of air as he broke the surface, he was grateful to see the sky again. Without knowing if the sharks had followed him to the surface, Mark was eager to leave the water as he raised his mask. He could see Carol leaning over the edge of the bow, her sunbathing interrupted by his sudden breach of the water's surface.

"Honey, are you okay? You were gone a long time." Carol was kneeling on the foredeck and peering over the edge of the boat from her sunbathing perch, her breasts dangling six feet above him like beautiful ripe peaches in the morning sun.

"Nice view! Meet me at the stern and drop the swim ladder," he sputtered, spitting out sea water. "Got us enough seafood to last us for a month." With his fins on the bottom rung of the swim ladder, they managed to lift the over-stuffed game bag into the boat. Almost weightless in the water, he estimated it contained over a hundred pounds of seafood as they hoisted it aboard.

When Carol saw the blood, she got upset. "Mark, you're bleeding. Honey, your wetsuit's torn. What on earth happened to you down there?" she asked, helping him up the swim ladder. He sat down heavily on the aft bench seat, banging his tank against the bulkhead, tearing off his mask and breathing a huge sigh of relief. Blood dripped from his forearm onto the white deck as he wriggled out of his BC and harness. "What the hell happened to you?" she repeated, grabbing a towel and wrapping it over his bleeding forearm.

"I just wanted to score some fresh seafood," explained Mark. Carol stood over him with her hands on her hips, waiting to hear more. He gestured at his bloody forearm. "Just a little slice. I'll live," he said, exhausted, resting his head against the padded seat back.

"I was worried about you," she said with a pouty face. She knelt down in front of him and took a closer look at the makeshift bandage on his arm as a gentle breeze began to blow out of the east. "And what's this?" Peering over his shoulder, she peeled off an octopus sucker from the back of his dive skin and studied it in the palm of her hand.

"Not all the wildlife was friendly," he said. "Giant octopus and a shark turned my dive into," taking a deep breath, "...an encounter of the wrong kind." She stared at him in disbelief. "Can you bring me the first aid kit from the starboard cabinet under the galley sink?" he asked, stripping off his equipment and dive skin. "I need to rest for a moment."

Carol stood and pirouetted, the *au naturel* first mate sashaying toward the cabin entrance. Then she stopped. "Starboard is on the right side, right?"

"Chew got it, girl. And how 'bout a cold beer while you're up?" Mark smiled. "For medicinal purposes."

"Sure thing, captain," she said, saluting smartly as she disappeared below deck.

With his head laying back against the seat bolster, Mark looked into the sky. He said a prayer and thanked God for sparing his life. Moments later, Carol returned with a roll of paper towels, the first aid kit and an ice-cold Warsteiner. "Ohhh, this tastes sooo good," said Mark, gulping the beer. Carol went to work drying his wounds and applied butterfly bandages to the lacerations on his arm and hands, coating them with triple-antibiotic and covering them neatly in gauze. Checking his arm bandage, he was impressed with her triage.

"You know, you'd make a great nurse," he said appreciatively.

The thought made her smile. "Thanks, sweetie, but I'm not sure they could afford me. Besides, I'm on track to complete my PhD. and become the CEO of my own sportswear company. Got some great ideas!"

"Where you would actually wear clothing?" he teased. "Love to hear your ideas after we get back."

As she snipped the gauze bandage and tied the ends together in a square knot, Carol winked. "There ya go, skipper. How's that?"

"Good job, Nurse Carol. Anything interesting happen while I was down on the reef?"

"They all thought I was a hooker, laying out on the deck by myself."

"Who?" he asked as he took another huge gulp of beer.

"The two boats full of horny guys that stopped by. One of them even asked me how much for a blow job."

"What did you say?"

"Very funny."

"Well, you don't really look like a hooker."

"Gee, what a sweet thing to say," said Carol.

"You being sarcastic?"

"Shut up and kiss me."

"Gee, what a sweet thing to say." Ignoring the pain, Mark was trying hard not to laugh.

"You're making fun of me, aren't you?" she said.

"No I'm not. I think you're amazing. I could search a million years and not find a girl who could perform triage in her birthday suit on a pitching deck." A boat with three standing divers in full gear was idling slowly by at a safe distance while they pretended to look away.

"All right. That's it." She took the beer from her wounded warrior and set it on the deck. After the dive boat had passed, she climbed on top of him, lifted his hands and placed them on her bare breasts.

"Listen up, Mister 'Multiple Ohhhs…' I've been waiting for you for hours," she said. "You dragged me out of bed at six this morning and told me you were going to make wild crazy love to me."

"I did say that." He could tell Carol was beyond randy, and he was having fun teasing her.

"You notice what I'm wearing?" asked Carol.

"I sure do, honey. It's a really terrific outfit."

"Tell me what I'm doing," she said.

"Um…straddling me in the nude?"

"Exactamundo, mister. And where are your hands?" asked Carol.

"On your gorgeous, ah…peaches?"

"And are you enjoying," she asked, "where my hand is?"

"I most certainly am." Her touch was having a tumescent effect on him, and her hair smelled divine.

"Then what are you waiting for?" In a more demanding tone she added, "*After* you've taken me to the moon three or four times, you can tell me all about the wild creatures who tried to eat you. Right now, it's *my* turn."

"Okay."

An hour later, Mark was smiling again as he thought about their wild day on the water. The wind and seas sea had started to pick up, and with the approach of changing weather, he was ready to call it a day. After engaging the electric windlass and winching in the anchor line, he doused his dive flag and fired up the two 775 horse power turbocharged engines to get underway.

With her bikini back on, Carol buckled herself snugly into the captain's lap. Brushing her hair with a big grin, she mused about their last hour of lovemaking. Within minutes, "Multiple Ohhhs..." was soaring over the six-foot seas at ninety miles an hour and Carol was having goosebumps as Mark nuzzled her neck in the windy cockpit while he kept a firm grip on the wheel and throttles.

Excited by her captain's affection as they flew over the ocean, she shouted over the whine of the engines. "I think Einstein was right!"

"About what?" he shouted back.

"We're moving so fast I feel like I'm actually getting *younger*."

He thought a moment, then shouted back: "God I hope not, honey. I could get twenty years for screwing a minor."

"Don't worry, sweetie. I'll get you off!"

Mark nuzzled her earlobe again. "See? That's *exactly* what I'm worried about!"

As the fast-moving catamaran approached the inlet, he anticipated the narrow entrance would be perilous for all but the largest of vessels as the rapid outgoing tide collided with the incoming breakers. With Carol still securely strapped in between his legs, Mark eased the throttles back as they rounded the outer marker, angled the bow up with the trim tabs and prepared for the dangerous combination of waves and currents that had earned Boca Inlet its reputation as one of Florida's most treacherous channels.

Pressing his lips against her ear, he said, "For your own safety, I want you to buckle yourself into the seat next to me. Water's gonna get a little rough in a minute." Carol obediently buckled herself into the port side chair as Mark threw the wheel over, bringing the cat in behind a sixty-five foot Hatteras that was blazing a path for them seventy yards ahead. The beamy Hatteras was riding on a half-plane with the bow up high as the captain maneuvered the big sportfish from the upper helm in the tuna tower. Mark squinted into the afternoon sun to figure out the wave action in his path, but the big Hatteras was obscuring his view of the turbulent waters ahead. His boat speed dropped to under eight knots before he saw the huge hydro that had formed at the narrow first turn of the inlet.

"Hang on, Carol! This may get a little dicey."

Suddenly, before he could increase his speed and bring the bow up higher, a huge incoming breaker rolled up under them and pitched the catamaran's stern up. Restrained by her four-point harness, Carol pushed hard against the grab rail as the entire boat pitched forward. With the engine's lower units out of the water, Mark had no power or steering. Passengers on the Hatteras ahead stared in disbelief as the big cat was sucked into the hydro. The bow submerged under the outgoing tide and hundreds of gallons of water poured over the deck into the cockpit, threatening to flood the entire boat.

Terrified, she shouted, "Mark! What do we do?" In the grips of the hydro, the cat was taking on more water than the scuppers and bilge pumps could handle. All three bilge pumps kicked in simultaneously as they worked to pump out the excess water. In the insanity, Mark was gripping the wheel so tightly his knuckles were turning white.

As the next big breaker passed under the boat, the stern settled back just enough to restore power. Quickly, he angled the trim tabs downward, reversed the boat's engines and hit the throttles to wrest control of the boat away from the hydro. The bow came up, but the cat's stern submerged under another incoming wave and water poured in over the engine covers, flooding the cockpit with knee-deep water. They were in danger of sinking unless he could quickly rid the boat of hundreds of gallons of sea water. Terrified of losing power and steering again, he reversed direction, put the engines into forward and angled the trim tabs up. As they gained momentum, the bow rose higher and hundreds of gallons of seawater swept past them and out of the big cat. Within seconds, the water level decreased from knee deep to ankle deep and Mark knew they had a fighting chance to escape disaster.

Carol hung onto the grab rail as she watched the torrent of water sweep past her legs and into the scuppers. Amazed at his last-ditch maneuver, she yelled, "Screw me sideways on a pogo stick! Where'd you learn how to do that?"

"Don't tempt me. I'm pretty good on a pogo stick!" he yelled back over the engines. "I had a fifteen-foot boat with a twenty-five-horse Johnson when I was a kid," he explained. "I was wave surfing off the Coca Beach pier when I got caught in a hydro. Almost sank me!"

With most of the excess water now out, the brightly-colored catamaran slowly made its way up the inlet against the current, and Mark and Carol breathed a sigh of relief. They spotted a group of onlookers cheering from the Boca Inlet Bridge looming fifty yards ahead. Joyful as a kitten pouncing on a bag of catnip, Carol vaulted on top of the engine covers and began cheering with the crowd as she waved. "Yeeehaaa!" she yelled. Over the catcalls and whistles, Mark heard a familiar voice.

"Mark! Over here!" They could see Dominick and Margeaux leaning over the draw bridge railing forty feet off the water and waving frantically. Pointing at her cell phone, Margeaux yelled down to her friends; "We got you guys on video, you crazies! We're gonna post it on You Tube!

Dominick cupped his hands and yelled, "What did you catch?"

Carol jumped down from the engine covers to open the cargo bay hatch cover. Pumped with adrenaline, she grabbed the over-stuffed game bag and hoisted it over her head like a Bulgarian weight lifter in a clean and jerk contest. "Check it out!" she shouted.

"Gimme summa that for dinner!" yelled an admirer from the bridge.

"All right, you wise guys," shouted Mark. "Meet ya at Delmar in about an hour. Gotta put my cat away," waving his cap to the crowd as they passed under the bridge.

"MERRROOOOOOOWWWWWW!" howled Carol in a feline appeal to her rowdy audience.

As he made the turn to port and headed south down the Intracoastal toward the marina, Mark cast an admiring glance at his first mate.

For the first time, he was wishing his favorite PhD candidate wasn't a kept woman.

⚔

Big Mike Rosenberg loved fresh lobster. Eyeing the layout of seafood on the pool deck below from his third floor balcony, it took him back to the good times at his favorite seafood store, Famous Fish Market off West 145th Street in The Big Apple. He headed downstairs to check out the day's catch. To his housekeeper, he said, "Maria, gonna get us some fresh seafood. Be back in a few minutes." By the time he made it downstairs, a crowd had gathered.

"Dude, nice catch!" said Big Mike. Concerned with Mark's bandages, he took a closer look at his forearm. "You get into a tussle with a barracuda or something?"

"Actually...a shark. He was after my game bag," said Mark matter-of-factly. "I offered him a hogfish snapper instead. Headin' up to the clinic at Glades Plaza when we get done with our seafood fest. Coupla stitches. I'll live," returning his attention to his filet of the black grouper.

Big Mike offered him a fist bump. "You're a gladiator." Mike took a closer look at the bugs laid out on the deck. "Any of these guys for sale? Got an empty freezer upstairs," giving Mark a puppy-dog look. The twelve-pound monster caught his eye as it made a feeble attempt to escape, clawing its way forward on the concrete deck. "How 'bout that big feisty one there?"

"For our very own TV rock star, sure," said Mark. "That one put up a pretty good fight. Whad'ya have in mind, Mikey?"

Big Mike took notice as Carol handed an ice-cold Warsteiner to Mark. Switching gears like he was back wheeling and dealing at Famous Fish Market, he said; "Okay. Have I got a deal for you! I have two cases of Warsteiner upstairs for two medium-size bugs, and I'll give you a hundred bucks for that big guy there," pointing at the monster lobster and holding out his hand. "Deal?"

Wanting to keep the TV celebrity happy, Mark adjusted his cap as he thought about Big Mike's offer. "Okay, deal. Only one condition. How 'bout a cameo appearance for us on your TV show?" nodding toward Carol.

Big Mike rubbed his chin and studied the couple as he considered Mark's idea. He could tell Mark was serious. "Have either of you had any acting experience?"

"Some modeling, and I know Carol has been in a few video shoots for her company's sporting line," turning to Carol who winked and nodded enthusiastically as she turned on the charm for her boyfriend's celebrity buddy.

Big Mike smiled in approval. "Nice. I can see you'd both dress up the set." Mike nodded toward his wound. "After you get yourself stitched up there, big guy, how 'bout I have my teleplay girl write you in for a scene or two? We can meet upstairs and go over the paperwork." Big Mike reached in his pocket and peeled off a C-note for the lobsters, giving him a pat on his shoulder. "We're *all* gonna be superstars!"

He yelled upstairs to his housekeeper watching from the third floor balcony. "Maria, bring me two cases of that Warsteiner down here, will you please, honey? We are having *king lobster* tonight!" Turning back to Mark, he said, "Thanks, brother!" Enthusiastic about having fresh lobster for dinner, the fight promotor scooped up his big trophy from the pool deck.

Back upstairs, while Maria was busy with dinner, Big Mike checked on the scene below from his balcony. He spied Sarah Glitzsky in the shallow end of the pool holding court with a group of elderly condo commandos, and his mood took a mischievous turn. Grabbing the liveliest of his medium-size lobsters, he took careful aim and tossed it off the balcony, watching it land in the pool directly in front of Glitzsky. Shocked back to life by the chlorinated water, the spiny crustacean took off and darted smack into Glitzsky's belly.

"Look out below!! Runaway lobster, Sarah!!" he yelled.

Glitzsky screamed and lunged toward the steps in a bid to exit the pool before the big bug could make another run at her. Everyone else in the shallow end panicked, running at the sight of the lobster darting around in the water like a ricocheting billiard ball on a pool table. Glitzsky pointed an accusatory finger at Big Mike laughing three floors up.

"That's a hundred-fifty dollar fine, Mr. Rosenberg!" she yelled in anger. Picking at a snag in the middle of her polyester granny suit where the lobster had hooked her, she added, "A hundred for the lobster and another fifty for my ruined swimsuit!"

Mike shrugged and yelled back. "Sorry, Sarah. Our dinner crawled off the balcony when we weren't looking! Lucky for you, Penney's having a tent sale, so you can save some money on your next granny suit!"

Residents standing around the pool were thoroughly entertained, and Mark was laughing so hard his bandages were loosening. "C'mon, honey," urged Carol as she grabbed his arm. "Been a wild day. Let's stash the beer and seafood and get you over to urgent care before you get abducted by aliens- or something crazier happens."

⊷┼┾⊶

Fresh from his trip to the walk-in clinic on Glades Road, Mark took a few moments to collect himself as he sat back on his couch and inspected the new bandage on his forearm. Cold beer in hand, he flipped on the TV, switching over to the local station just in time to catch the local six o'clock news update. Following a gory story about the latest terrorist attack, he was surprised to see the video of his catamaran in the hydro suddenly appear on TV.

"Carol, we're on TV! Check it out!" Reliving the white-knuckle experience from the comfort of his Roche Bobois leather couch was a welcome change. The banner caption at the bottom of the screen read: "WILD ROLLER COASTER RIDE ON BOCA INLET". Mark reached for the remote and turned up the volume as the weekend announcer described the images; "Some tricky maneuvering and a lively first mate helped a local skipper avoid disaster this afternoon as the Boca Inlet lived up to its reputation as one of the most dangerous inlets on the east coast."

Carol ran from the kitchen and stood behind the couch, mesmerized by the dramatic footage taken by Margeaux on her cell phone only hours earlier. Excited, Mark speed-dialed Dominick in the north penthouse to let his buddy know his wife's video was being aired on the local TV station.

"I'm watching it now," said Dom. "Your video already got over forty thousand hits on You Tube in the last hour."

"Unbelievable." As he hung up, Mark looked up at Carol, still spellbound by the scene on TV, amazed at the speed that news traveled these days. "Dom says our video got over fifty thousand hits on You Tube," he said as she leaned over him to get a better view.

"Honey, I'm glad I put my suit back on. Can you believe that?"

"Yeah, well, otherwise we'd be locked up for indecent..." stopping mid-sentence as Carol removed her bikini top.

"Aren't these the prettiest peaches you've ever seen?" she asked with a mischievous smile.

"As pretty as they might be, honey, it's a family station," he said. "For mature audiences only." He knew what she wanted. "Here, bring those over to daddy so he can give 'em some proper lovin'," reaching for her. "Let's start our seafood fest with some dessert," he said with a twinkle in his eye.

Excited by his suggestion, Carol's smile broadened to a grin. "Okay!" She tossed her bikini bottom at him and playfully ruffled his hair as she gently pushed her wounded captain down on the leather sofa.

"Dessert is served," she said.

EIGHTEEN

Dominick was dreaming about Margeaux in a beauty contest. He dreamt that the first prize was one million dollars a month for the rest of their lives. In his dream, he was suddenly aware that the crowd applauding his wife onstage consisted entirely of dead SWAT team officers and deceased drug dealers who resembled the zombies from *Walking Dead*. Terrified, he began running toward the beach and calling out for Margeaux as he looked over his shoulder. Dominick ran as fast as he could, fearful the crowd of zombies would catch him as he searched for a path between the gleaming high-rises and condominiums to make his escape. But there was no way out. The sprawling mass of huge concrete buildings blocked his view of the sky, and there was no road, no alleyway, or even a beacon of light to lead him to safety.

In the dream, he ran frantically as the sand beneath his feet was disappearing rapidly beneath waves of cold ocean water rolling in, slowing his escape. When it reached his ankles, he realized the tide was coming in much faster than usual. When the water reached his waist, it was no longer possible for him to run and he ceased moving his legs, immobilized by the freezing water. Continuing to pump his arms, he feared the icy water would become his grave unless he could keep moving.

He looked skyward for warmth and salvation from the sun, and there was his answer: the water had turned frigid because the sprawling condos had become so massive that the sun's rays were being blocked out by concrete buildings thousands of stories high.

His dream morphed into a nightmare, the frigid sea water rising up to his neck as he fought to catch his breath and make his escape. He felt stabbing pains throughout his body from the shockingly-cold ocean. Floating all around him were the corpses of SWAT teams and the cadavers of dead pelicans and seagulls. He cried out for help as he pushed away what he thought was a hand from one of the cadavers. It wasn't a cadaver, but Margeaux's touch that caused him to awaken and open his eyes.

"Honey, you were having a bad dream. It's okay, just a bad dream," she said softly, caressing his cheek.

He reached for her hand and kissed it. "Margeaux, don't ever leave me." He kissed her hand again. "Promise you'll never leave me."

She ran her fingers gently across the lines of his face, thankful that she'd been rescued from a life of lap dances by a man who was forever devoted to her happiness.

"I'll always be here for you, Dom. You know I love you." He closed his eyes and felt her kiss on his forehead. She'd been waiting for just the right time to spring her idea.

"Dom, honey, I've been thinking. "Shooters" is offering twenty-five thousand in cash for their next bikini contest, and Desiree, Carol and I want to enter. Mark says we'd be shoo-ins. It's only a hundred bucks apiece. Whad'ya think, honey? Will you sponsor me?"

Returning from a Vero Beach scouting mission, the man who called himself David Callahan drove up to his rented Boca Beach mansion and activated the remote control for the outer security gate. He noticed the side pedestrian entrance was open and he swore under his breath for leaving it unlocked. After securing the gate and pulling his car up into the brick paver courtyard, he aimed the garage door remote and eased into one of the three parking spaces. After driving for two hours on I-95, it seemed like everyone in Palm Beach County was in a hurry to either cut you off or flip you off.

The inconspicuous wooden wedge he used to detect entries was still in place between the door's edge and the weather stripping. The house was dark and silent as he entered, and the place didn't feel the same without Andrea. He had avoided entering the front door, using the service entrance just in case that damn detective was spying on him again. With the lights off, Callahan cracked the dining room blinds for a peek across the street.

In the dim light of the street lights, he could see the grey unmarked Crown Victoria parked on the other side of A1A in the Esplanade Condo visitor's spot. Focusing his binoculars, he adjusted the low-light setting to confirm his suspicions. It was that same bald-headed detective sitting in the car on his cell phone, slumped down in the front seat, trying look inconspicuous in the drizzle as he watched the stone mansion from his rear view mirror.

The unwanted attention made his stomach tighten. He'd been so careful to keep a low profile and live an anonymous lifestyle off the grid. Lowering his binoculars, he vowed to accelerate his moving plans and find a new hideout before they could gather enough evidence to get a warrant.

<hr />

Ever since Klein's last partner retired early and opened a landscaping service he named *Lawn Enforcement*, the detective had needed a new partner. If he had a voice in the selection, he preferred an undercover cop who was good at infiltrating younger crowds, and someone who was good at navigating social media. Though he was a rookie detective, Anthony Costello was a master at both and rounded out these attributes with the unassuming physical appearance of a hip-hop techno geek. The detective was unassigned when Klein approached his boss in CID, so it hadn't been too difficult to get him re-assigned as his junior partner.

Since finding blood and tissue evidence last week that might link the rental boat with Lance Meyer's death, the newly-teamed detectives had been working the case together as a homicide. Klein and Costello were frustrated with the lack of leads but refused to let Callahan slip from their crosshairs.

In spite of his tech savvy, Costello had been unable to find anything on social media or the grid about the mysterious man who lived in the Greenwood Mansion. The only connection with their case came from the fact that the guy faithfully paid his rent to Nautilus Realty on A1A where Meyer had worked before his death- but so did eleven hundred and sixty-seven other renters in Boca. It was a slim lead, and there were no connections to Callahan with phone calls, credit cards or bank accounts. Even the utility bill was listed under the name Neptune Holdings, LLC, which was owned by yet another shell corporation. Klein decided it was time to pay a visit to Nautilus Realty.

"Hey, partner." On his phone, Klein hunched down in the front seat to stay out of sight as he spoke to Costello in a low voice. "Sorry to interrupt your hot date, buddy, but I'm on a nocturnal mission of my own here. Whad'ya find out?"

"What nocturnal emission?" joked Costello, leaning back from his laptop and taking a break from his internet research.

"Stop playin' with yourself for a minute," said Klein. "You said Callahan has a girlfriend, right? What's she look like."

"Blonde, shapely, about five foot sex"-

"Costello, get your mind off sex and help me out. You said five foot sex."

"Sorry. Long night."

"Whatever."

"Five foot *six*, mid-to-late twenties, blonde, nice lookin'"-

"When's the last time you-or anyone else-saw her with our suspect?" Klein crouched lower in his Crown Vic. He thought he saw someone peering out from the window of the Greenwood Mansion. In a flash, the figure was gone but the blinds were swaying.

"At Publix. Maybe a few weeks ago. Why?"

"'Cause I haven't seen anyone with him that fits that description, and I've been watchin' this guy on and off for days. Plus, this guy likes to skulk around in the dark. Somethin' a little off with this dude," adjusting his mirror for a better view of the mansion.

"Let's push the State Attorney to persuade Judge Rosencranz to get a search warrant," suggested Costello.

Costello lacked experience with the internal workings between law enforcement and the court system, so Klein was patient. "Already tried that. State Attorney says we haven't met the probable cause threshold. He doesn't see it as a capital case, so Rosencranz doesn't feel the urgency. And do me a favor, don't mention to anyone that Lance was my brother-in-law. I don't wanna get pulled off this case for some bullshit conflict of interest." He let out a big sigh. "I promised my sister we'd put this perp away."

"Okay. Got your back, partner. What did forensics say about the tissue sample from the rental boat?

"Oh, forgot to tell you," said Klein. "Forensics said the sample could be human tissue, but it was contaminated with bleach the idiots used to clean the boat. So, we got zip. And, since the perp paid in cash, we got no way to connect *those* dots. Plus, now the old man at Boca Boat Rentals, Tire and Haircare there on Federal Highway suddenly can't seem to remember what he looks like."

"You showed him photos?" For procedural reasons, Costello hoped that his question was rhetorical.

"Of course, in a group with four others. The old man couldn't pick him out. He's got Alzheimer's. And, without a warrant, we can't even force Callahan to answer the damn *door.*" Klein paused as he watched a car pull up in the parking lot and an obviously drunk middle-aged couple in party mode exit the vehicle and enter the condo's wrought iron gate together. Slumped down in the seat on his stakeout, Klein ignored them. "My gut tells me this guy's behind two murders."

"Two? You talking about his girlfriend? Maybe she left him."

Klein looked out his window. "Just a hunch." The rain had let up and Klein rolled his window down partway for some fresh air, ignoring the light patter of raindrops on his armrest.

"Where are you, partner?" asked Costello, tossing back the last of his cabernet and closing his laptop.

"Surveillance. Across the street from the Greenwood Mansion." Klein scrunched down further in his car seat, studying the mansion's first floor windows in the dim glow of the Ocean Boulevard street lights for signs of movement.

"Look. I have a feeling this guy knows he's got heat. He'll slip up," assured Costello.

"He could also decide to disappear in the middle of the night," countered Klein. Glancing in the mirror, he saw movement again at the window and the reflection from what looked like a pair of binoculars. "Think I've been made, partner. I'm gonna call it a night," turning the key to start the car. "We need to amp up our game plan."

"Okay." Costello felt like a light bulb suddenly flashed in his head. "Hey. Just had an idea. Gonna work on it tonight. Can you meet me at CID in the morning?"

"Okay. I'll buy ya a cup a coffee," responded Klein. "For now, I'm headin' home."

"Copy that, big spender."

Deep in the bowels of the old stone mansion, the dampness in the dimly-lit basement was wreaking havoc on Callahan's nerves. The dankness was unbearable, and the outbreak of hives on his face and scalp had gotten worse. His nerves were a mess, and he couldn't stop scratching the itchy blotches. While he searched on-line for a new beachside rental in Vero, he could feel the air getting progressively mustier with the rainy weather.

He reached to turn up the power on the small Mitsubishi portable air conditioner to its highest setting as the machine whined in protest. Callahan blamed the mildew for giving him a raspy throat and watery eyes, and he hoped like hell it wasn't toxic. He tossed back the last sip of cognac, wiping some from his beard, and poured another two fingers of his favorite XO. His throat was starting to feel better. The euphoric effect put him in a reflective mood as he looked back on how he'd come to live the solitary life of a fugitive on the run. Andrea had always warned him about 'gaining the world and losing your soul.' Deep down inside, he knew it was already too late.

Years ago, when he was known as Tommy Tomlinson, Callahan moved around a lot to escape from bad situations, situations that always seemed to get worse when he stayed. The boat rental invoice that he stupidly handed over to Megan Rockwell with his rent payment a few days ago bothered him, and he had a hunch that she wouldn't hesitate to throw him under the bus if she had the chance. Now, he was faced with yet another loose end to tie up and decided to find out as much as he could about her online-where she lived, where she shopped, and what restaurants she frequented. Her Facebook site told him everything he needed to know. Loose lips sink ships. Just take a look at the *S.S. America*, he thought.

Callahan had a gruesome sense of vengeance that he liked to entertain by playing one of his favorite games; hunting online to find out which of his past acquaintances had recently bought the farm. For hours, he took almost as much pleasure in the pursuit of his morbid obituary searches as he did counting his cash and coins.

One of his favorite bookmarked obituaries described the tragic death of Professor Bruce Hardwick. Hardwick had been one of his instructors at Appalachian State College, Tomlinson's *alma mater.* The professor had a well-known mean streak; a nasty habit of exposing and embarrassing any grad student who strayed even the least bit from his strict rules on properly annotating sources in the research papers written by his students. Tomlinson had learned later that his professor had flunked twenty-three of them in the last two years, accusing them of "plagiarism" even though most of them were later exonerated when the charges were overturned by the dean's office as an exaggeration of the facts.

One day, Professor Hardwick had disparaged Tomlinson in front of his classmates so thoroughly that he had left the classroom in utter humiliation. Matters became far worse when Hardwick sent him an email threatening to expose him on the internet, accusing him of plagiarizing the marine archeology thesis he'd written on the proposed underwater salvage operation of the *S.S. America.* Tomlinson had pleaded with his professor to reconsider because the fallout would likely destroy any opportunity to attract enough investors to fund his salvage of the gold-laden ship. Knowing that the accusation would likely put an end to Tomlinson's career as a marine archeologist if it went public, Hardwick refused to budge.

Though it was true that he had played a little fast and loose with some of the credits, Tomlinson knew Hardwick was already disliked by most of his students and counted on the professor's unpopularity to deflect attention from what he was planning.

Before the professor could make good on his threat, someone took it upon themselves to cut the hydraulic brake lines on his Ford Taurus, and the resulting catastrophic brake failure caused him to lose control of his car on a hairpin turn on his way home. Professor Hardwick wound up careening through a guard rail in the dark and flying off a steep cliff. The next morning, a passing motorist had alerted the West Virginia Highway Patrol who later found his car at the bottom of the two hundred foot ravine. The car had been demolished, and the lone occupant burnt to a crisp. The body was burned so badly that the forensics team was forced to use dental records to positively identify the professor.

In the investigation that followed, there were no arrests, and the suspected homicide had gone unsolved. Any suspects seemed to have up and vanished like a fart in the West Virginia mountain wind. In the two weeks that followed, Appalachian State College wasted no time in finding a suitable replacement for Professor Hardwick, and the newly-installed professor of marine archeology proved to be much more popular with his students and staff, thereby likely avoiding a similar fate.

After reading the obituary for the third time, Callahan grinned and raised his cognac snifter to toast his former professor. "Here's to you, *perfesser*," taking another sip and leaning back against the pile of cash with his feet propped up on his desk.

"Payback's a bitch, ain't it Hardwick?"

NINETEEN

It was a sunny day on Boca Beach as Mark watched the Frisbee floating up high in the sky and hover in the air. It was a perfect toss. He'd lofted it so it would catch the onshore breeze before angling down the beach toward Carol, his intended target. She ran to get under it as Dom chased after her for the block, catching it right before he grabbed her playfully around the waist. The game of touch Frisbee had Mark and Carol matched against Margeaux and Dom. Desiree was watching from her beach lounger, applying a layer of SPF 50 while she listened to pop music on her earbuds.

"So, Dom, how's the headache?" yelled Mark as he made another toss from down the beach "Heard about your late night party from Rod Rodman at the gym this morning. You know it's a good party if you hear about it from the Boca P.D., right?"

"Feel like I had an unrequested colonoscopy," Dom complained, "...that reached all the way to my brain." Recalling the night's wild events, Dominick felt fortunate that the Boca police hadn't insisted on stepping inside during their visit. There could have been a slew of embarrassing questions about some of his laboratory-grade

Pyrex equipment, industrial chemicals, and the three oversized stainless steel fume hoods adorning his kitchen.

"Heard *that*, brother," shouted Mark. Margeaux was giggling as she chased him, and he'd purposely slowed down to tease her into thinking she had a shot to block his catch. Laughing, he caught Margeaux around her waist in a pretend tackle as he reached out to snag the return shot from Carol.

"Gotta leave those roofies alone, bro," he shouted to Dom.

Dom was quick to counter the idea. "Yeah. Well, the eight or nine shots of Cuervo mighta had something to do with it." Dom liked everyone to believe he was a drinker, but Mark knew better. Dom liked his chemical highs better than anything you could buy at the local ABC Liquors. They just didn't talk about it much. Secretly, he hoped there would come a day when Dom would no longer be blinded by the huge sums of money he made from his meth business and come to acknowledge the harmful effects of highly-addictive drugs.

Dom paused to catch his breath, glancing over at Desiree reclining in her lounger. "Hey, Dez, c'mon over. Jump in here. How about some two-on-one action?" His invitation grabbed the attention of a couple walking by who seemed interested in her response.

Desiree sat up and pulled her hair back. "You sound like one of my videographers. Always with the two-on-one stuff." She adjusted her Wayfarers and straddled her lounger. "Think I'm gonna have a cold one instead," reaching into the cooler. She was joined by Carol and Margeaux who'd worked up a thirst after a half hour of play. The score stayed close at seven to six in favor of Mark and Carol.

Mark took the opportunity to grab Dom's ear about something that was bugging him. Expecting to come across some mention of their mysterious neighbor in yesterday's online search, he'd found only a bunch of mishmash and concluded that the internet may have just collectively thrown up on the name David Callahan.

"Hey, whad'ya know about, ah…what's his name?" asked Mark. "You know, the guy at Greenwood Mansion. Callahan, the scruffy-lookin' guy that rides the two-tone beach cruiser up and down A1A."

"Yeah, always with the ragged clothes," offered Dom. "Doesn't even look like he could afford the place." Dom took a moment to remove his sunglasses and wipe the sand and perspiration from around his eyes as he wondered where his buddy was going with this.

Mark leaned over with his hands on his knees to catch his breath. "See, that's what I mean. There's just certain things that don't fit."

"Some of the richest dudes I know walk around looking like bums, trying not to be noticed. No big deal really. Look at Jimmy Buffet."

"Yeah, probably strung out on meth with no money left to buy clothes," ventured Mark, dropping a tongue-in-cheek hint about his buddy's avocation.

Hearing this, Dom looked at him thoughtfully. "Interesting to hear you say that. I've been kicking around the idea of opening a drug rehab center."

Surprised, Mark's eyes widened as he looked at his buddy with new found admiration. "Seriously?" he asked. Dom nodded. "That is music to my ears, brother," giving him a manly hug. "Maybe it *is* time to move on and get out while you've still got your girl, your cojones, and your money, right?"

"Hear ya. Margeaux's idea at first, but I'm onboard with it now," added Dom. He looked back toward the girls lounging and sipping their beer, then back at Mark. "The numbers look good, and I'm thinking I'd like to leave a better legacy. You know, something to help people improve their lives."

Mark took a moment to study his friend. "Let me know what I can do to help," he said. "Got a coupla connections in the drug

rehab business. Been there, done that, and it's all good." Dom nodded in agreement. Mark reached for his toes to stretch his hamstrings
and glanced back toward the girls sitting on the ice chest. "Hey, you
remember that guy Callahan said he had a girlfriend, right?"

"Vaguely," said Dom. "Haven't seen her in a while. Or his dogs."
Dom thought a moment. "Ya know, 'bout a week ago, Dez was say-
in' he really creeped her out when she ran into him on the beach.
Weird dude."

"Well, Dez gets a lot of looks…she knows she's gonna attract a
few weirdos here and there." Mark checked on Desiree, busy rocking out and soaking up the sun while she was jammin' on her earbuds, oblivious to the attention she always attracted.

"Sure she does, but she said this guy really made her feel *super*-
creepy," said Dom, running his hand over his bare head. "It was
the day they found that realitor's body on the beach. Remember?"

Mark squinted. "Lance. His name was Lance Meyer. Rest in
peace," crossing himself. "He used to collect rent money for my
dad there at Nautilus Realty. Helluva nice guy. You thinkin' there's
a connection?"

"Who knows?" said Dom as he shaded his eyes. "But Dez was
saying it was the *way* he looked at her that got her panties in a twist.
Said he had these black lifeless eyes of a shark. For her to mention
it to her motorcycle cop oughta tell ya somethin'".

"She told Rod about Callahan?" asked Mark.

"Apparently."

"Funny, Rod didn't say anything about it to me at the gym," said
Mark with a lisp as he swished his wrist.

Amused with his gay charade, Dom chided him. "What, like
he tells you all his police stuff? You know, you do that swishy thing
real well, bro. You sure you're not…ah…maybe just a little bit…you
know…" teased Dom.

"How bad ya wanna know?" added Mark with an extra-sweet
lisp.

Dom redirected the conversation. "Plus, he's a cop, Mark. And Desi's his girl."

"Yeah, I get it. Thought I had a shot 'til *he* showed up with his six shooter," said Mark with a wince.

"Dez said Rodman passed it on to the detective handling Meyer's case. He's getting' kinda protective if ya ask me."

"Look who's talking," said Mark. "A man so much as *farts* in Margeaux's direction and you're ready to take his head off," play-punching Dominick's shoulder.

"Yeah, okay. Whatever." Dominick punched him back. "Check this out. Two nights ago, around midnight, Margeaux and I were comin' home from Mezzanotes, and we see him cruisin' down A1A in his black Range Rover with his lights off. Looked kinda creepy, like he was up to somethin'."

"Maybe he was drivin' drunk," suggested Mark, but they both knew there was something not quite right with Mr. Callahan. "Yeah. He is a little out-of-step. It's like…life is a game of chess… and he's playing video games."

Dom stepped closer and put his arm around his bud's shoulder. "If you're done playin' detective, there Marky-Mark, let's go pop a coupla beers with the girls and I'll tell you more about my new drug rehab business. Get your take on a coupla things."

Mark looked at his buddy and grinned, giving him his best Ross Perot impression. "I'm all ears."

Early the next morning, Detective Anthony Costello turned into the Boca P.D. parking lot as he thought about his latest idea to advance their investigation of Lance Meyer's death. Parking his black Chevy Malibu, he removed his 9mm Glock from the glove compartment and stuffed it back into his waist holster. Driving was more comfortable with his Glock in the glove box, and having it tucked away out of sight added to his street cred. The twenty-five caliber automatic with hollow points he carried on his ankle was all he needed for undercover work.

Spotting his partner's car, Costello checked his watch. It was seven forty-five a.m. and Klein was already at work. As he hung his badge around his neck, he wondered if Klein had a life outside the CID. Inside the building, he pushed through the bullet-proof glass door and waved to the duty officer as he swiped his ID through the security slot. He spotted Officer Rodman on his way out to start his shift.

Costello nodded at his buddy. "Hey, Rod. Heard about your new part-time gig. How're things at, ah...what is it? Stallion Productions? Sounds like some nice work, if you qualify."

Rodman grinned, tucking his motorcycle helmet under his arm as they shared a hardy handshake. "Yeah, the interview was to die for. So, you heard about that, huh? Haven't seen you since your promotion, Tony. Congratulations."

"Thanks." Having known each other since high school, Costello had finished at the top of their class at Boca High, but the two police officers had taken radically different paths to get to the police academy. Rodman was a star athlete, while Costello was active in MENSA, their high school chess club, and home economics. Costello remembered how Rodman used to make fun of him in their senior year over his passion for cooking, baking and needlepoint.

The two officers couldn't have presented a more dissimilar appearance as they stood together at the entrance to CID. Rodman's muscle-bound leather-booted physique contrasted sharply with Costello's techno-geek, wispy grunge look. Costello's Warby Parker glasses suggested a sensitivity that disguised an inner strength in him which often took people by surprise. Most of the time, they never saw him coming, and he would often use his boyish appearance to his advantage in situations where gaining trust and information was key.

Rodman had a habit of flexing his bicep before making an important point, and he did so as he spoke. "By the way, Tony, I gave your partner a lead in the Meyer investigation. It may be nothing, but I thought you might want to check it out."

Costello looked at him thoughtfully. "Appreciate it, Rod. Curious, who's the source?"

"Confidential," he answered with a poker face. He was thinking about Desiree a lot these days.

Costello smiled. "You mean personal, right?"

Rodman winked. "Okay. Yeah, a personal source. Talk to Klein. I gotta head out for my shift."

Costello shared a fist bump with him before entering the CID section, where he found his partner pouring a hot cup of coffee in the concession area.

Klein looked up as he stirred in a heavy dollop of creamer. "Sup, Tony? So, you mentioned you had an idea."

Costello leaned against the counter. "I ever tell you about my ex-girlfriend Megan? Used to model lingerie for Macy's." He smiled at the memories. "Well, she still does, only part-time."

"Any pictures?" joked Klein as he leaned back against the counter and took a big sip of his café latte, always amused with his partner's long list of ex-girlfriends. Klein waited patiently to hear about what possible connection there could be between a lingerie model and his brother-in-law's murder.

Costello helped himself to a cup of coffee. "You'll meet her soon enough. She's a temp now, and you'll never guess where she's working."

"Ah…Snap On Tools?" Klein was grinning from ear-to-ear.

Costello gave him a stern look. "Anyone ever tell you you're warped? No, actually she's a temp at Nautilus Realty."

Klein's grin disappeared and he stopped stirring his latte. "No shit, Sherlock. The branch on Boca Beach?"

"Yup. I think she misses me. She called me last night about this weirdo Callahan drooling all over her when he was paying his rent. With moldy cash."

Klein made a face. "Okay, we know he's a little weird, a possible perv with moldy cash, but you still haven't told me about your idea, junior."

"She says she saw something he didn't want her to see."

"Was his fly zipped up?" Klein tried hard to suppress his grin.

Costello ignored his taunt. "It was a cash receipt for a boat rental."

Hearing this, Klein stiffened and set his cup down on the counter. "From where?" he asked in a serious tone.

"She's not sure."

"Where's the receipt now?"

"She said he stuck it back in his pocket before she could finish reading it. From what she said, he got real nervous about it." Costello could tell that the importance of the details weren't lost on Klein. "You think it's enough for probable cause so we can get our search warrant?" asked Costello.

"Probably not yet, but that's gotta be our guy, Tony." Pausing, the senior detective ran his hand over his bare head to ponder their next move. "All right, let's go talk to her." His resolve firming, Klein focused like a laser on the game plan. Impressed with Costello's angle, he was developing a whole new level of respect for his junior partner.

"Better if I do it," offered Costello.

Klein nodded in agreement. "You do it. I'm a little light on experience with lingerie models." Klein winked. "Bet they never see *you* comin', though." Secretly, Klein was envious of his partner's under-the-radar approach with women.

Costello listened to his senior partner as he continued to stir his coffee. "Let's figure out a way to get this guy's prints. I'd be surprised if Callahan's even his real name. We get his prints, we'll know."

Costello nodded in agreement. "I'm with ya. If David Callahan's not an alias, there's no way his name wouldn't be *somewhere* on the web."

Klein nodded. "Yeah, that is strange. He'd have to be on the grid somewhere. We'll track him." Klein cocked his head. "Think Megan'll help us?"

Costello's face lit up. "*That* was my idea. Let's go find out."

TWENTY

Distracted with her thoughts, Erin Griffith stared out the window of her central Boca Beach condo overlooking Red Reef Park as she watched a group of surfers carving up the waves. They reminded her of the young men she'd been engaged to in her twenties when she naively pursued men for love instead of money. As she took another sip of chardonnay, her thoughts drifted to the terms of endearment often used to gain her favors over the years, as well as the gifts of diamonds and jewelry. The diamond rings she'd returned without remorse, with the exception of one she kept out of sentimental feelings. It was a ring given to her by a guy named Jack Shamway, one of the few guys she'd almost been in love with.

Always broke, Jack Shamway struggled for years as a singer in bars and restaurants, almost starving until he started doing voice overs for political campaigns. His fortunes changed, and he became quite successful with his new-found career of vocal art, as he called it. Gradually, he made his way onto the airwaves on prime-time television doing voice overs for campaign commercials. It was ironic, given the fact that Shamway couldn't stand politics and held the senators and congressmen in such low esteem that he refused to vote for them. She had come to admire Jack for recognizing the hypocrisy in what he did and admitting that he hated his job. Erin thought it took a man with integrity to recognize there were few things in today's world that were as deceptive and underhanded as a sixty-second campaign commercial.

After living a dichotomous life for years, Jack Shamway began to develop deep psychological issues with the hypocrisy, even entertaining suicidal thoughts that he sometimes shared with Erin. As she watched a man she admired squander his God-given talents as a singer to provide a wealthy lifestyle for her, she began to realize that she was at least partly responsible for his conundrum. Often, she faced the same self-inflicted dilemma; she could be idealistic, or she could be wealthy, but she didn't see a way to be both. It was a sad realization for her at such a young age, and certainly no coincidence that all her lovers had been quite well-off.

Earlier in their relationship, she felt guilty about the jewelry, the Benz, the waterfront house on Biscayne Bay, and all the extravagant shopping trips- all provided by a job that Jack hated. After their break up, Erin saw her choices with even greater clarity when she learned of Jack's suicide the night he put a shotgun in his mouth. It made her sad, and although she missed him, she'd already made the decision to move on to greener pastures with men who were filthy rich and immersed in political power.

After surviving the Jack Shamway fiasco, Erin decided that she was indeed a player and set out on a new path to secure her own financial independence. Given the irrational valuations that Americans placed on beauty, Erin took the easy road and set out to monetize her looks and sex appeal in the easiest way she could; by using the internet.

With her new pay-to-play web enterprise in its early stages, she taught herself to grow thicker-skinned and deflect the never-ending accusations from all of her ex-husbands. She assumed they were

commiserating with each other when they all began to simultaneously refer to her as "the platinum gold digger" in court filings.
Screw them. Let them talk. Such mudslinging would only help her
cause, especially since three-fourths of the presiding judges were
men. Florida's laws on child support were crystal, and there wasn't
any getting around them. Erin really didn't care what they called
her as long as her egregious child-support checks were wired each
month to her seven-figure Zurich bank account.

In her court filings, she listed her expenses with the Las Olas
mansion, her Ferrari and Mercedes Benz, and the frequent shopping trips to the Galleria on Sunrise Boulevard as absolutely necessary to maintain her lifestyle as a professional model and actress.
And, of course, income that was essential to provide childcare.
Her collection of seventy-six Hermes, Luis Vuitton and Coach
handbags was the envy of every woman in her narcotics anonymous class. She needed lots of cash for the two full-time nannies-
the caregivers that gave her the freedom from the daily grind of
raising her three toddlers. In her mind, she wasn't a bad mom, she
just wasn't crazy about any of the responsibilities that went with
the job.

Today, she was ready to implement her lucrative plan to perform "private dances" for older men of power and wealth; men
whose carefree use of Viagra as a recreational drug made them so
incredibly eager to make appointments on her website. She played
on their need to reinvigorate their dwindling sex lives, and her
business plan consisted of hooking up with the octogenarian mil-
lionaires whose gigantic egos demanded the intimate company of
a former Playmate of the Month.

Ever since her recent failure to snag what would have been
her fourth monster child support check from her tryst with Mark
McAllister, she felt compelled to enter the wild world of cyber dating and cash in on her Playmate status in a way that would guarantee her financial success.

It had been especially difficult for her to face the truth about failing in her latest bid to make McAllister the unwitting father of her next child. After uncovering her deception, he had unceremoniously dumped her, and her ego had taken a bruising. When her pregnancy tests came in negative, the experience had put her into a tailspin that morphed into a depression. Following the weeks of self-pity, drugging and drinking, Erin came to the realization that nothing seemed to work better than cold hard cash in restoring her spirits. Convinced her charms were totally irresistible, Erin was off and running in her latest venture to milk the millionaire condo commandos dry.

And so Erin's path to financial independence changed course with the easy money she figured to make by hooking up with elderly "generous gents". The private dances would not only free her of the burden of carrying her unborn child around for nine months, but her convenient new service would eliminate the pregnancies that were taking their toll on her centerfold figure. After giving birth to two boys and a girl over a five year period ($64,800 a month in child support checks!), Erin decided there was an easier path to cashing in on her looks. The way her publicist described it, it all came down to sexy photos, great marketing and a little hot pillow talk.

On the net, Erin came across an old geezer named Anthony Anatolla. Mr. Anatolla had described himself as a "generous gent who enjoyed private parties". He posted photos of himself on "ManlyMillionairesClub.com", photos that Erin guessed were likely taken shortly after his college graduation. After spending ten minutes with him in a private chatroom, he expressed an ardent desire for a private show after Erin emailed him a link to her website, complete with a digital collection of photos from her Miss September layout. When Mr. Anatolla began babbling on about doubling up on his heart meds, she was quick to dismiss it as a cheap attempt to get her to reduce her fee.

'How do I know you're not some violent lunatic psycho?' she'd asked him in the online chatroom, a question that had become standard in her qualifying process. Turns out that Mr. Anatolla had developed a deep infatuation with the former Miss September and wouldn't take no for an answer. A master at acting hard-to-get, she knew how to play a man like a finely-tuned piano. When she succeeded in enticing him into doubling his offer from five to ten grand, she was all in with a "lap dance to die for". With his wife away for a week at a spa in Palm Beach, they decided to hook up at his luxury high-rise at Delmar for their first tryst. Anticipating lots of security, she went in wearing a disguise using her stage name "Sherry".

After clearing the security guardhouse in her bright red S550, she found a shady out-of-the-way spot in guest parking. Scanning the security marquee for Anatolla's listing, she picked up the entry phone and pressed the talk button as she peered into the security camera in her Dolce Gabbana sunglasses, Donna Karan floppy black hat, red wig, seven-inch Jimmy Choo heels and *faux* fur coat. As it rang, she checked her Rolex to make sure she was on time. It was exactly 7:59 p.m.

"Yes? Can I help you," asked her date in a thick Brooklyn accent.

Erin made eye contact with the camera and waved. "Sherry. Miss September. For our eight o'clock appointment."

"Ah…wait a second. Miss September's a blonde. You're a red-head. Who're you, honey?" Anatolla seemed annoyed.

"Honestly, Tony. I thought it would be fun to wear a disguise. C'mon. Loosen up a little."

With the Viagra beginning to have its desired effect, Anatolla acquiesced. "All right. C'mon up. Apartment 808. End of the hallway."

What a toad, she thought as she hung up the phone. She heard the electronic lock release and pulled the door open, entering the glitzy marble-columned lobby. Riding the mirrored elevator to the eighth floor, she noticed two more cameras from under the brim of her hat and avoided looking directly into the lenses. As a tease for whomever was watching, she opened her fur coat to straighten the seams of her fishnet stockings. Exiting the elevator, she spotted her mark standing two doors down the hallway. The portly board member was dressed in a blue smoking jacket, red and white striped boxer shorts, and wearing the worst toupee she'd ever set eyes on. For God's sake, she thought, she'd seen better rugs at Family Dollar Store.

Anatolla stood expectantly beside his open door at the end of the hallway chomping on a huge stogie. "C'mon in, *Sherry*," waving her in. The portly man gloated over his trophy date as she stepped past him into his living room. Inviting her to get "more comfortable", Erin placed her coat, hat, wig and sunglasses into a nearby suede chair. The Delmar director removed his jacket to reveal a wife-beater tee shirt as he dropped his ponderous rear end into the suede couch and prepared for a "lap dance to die for."

As she checked out the Louie XIV décor, she couldn't help noticing a tall stack of hundred dollar bills sitting on the green marble end table. "That for me?" she asked.

"Make me a happy guy and it's all yours, honey," flicking the ash off his stogie in the marble ashtray. "Can I fix you a drink?"

"Thanks, Tony, but I had three before I left," she said, smiling. "You know, to get in the mood."

"Well, okay. How 'bout a dance to start things off?" He sat back with his arm on the edge of the couch to admire her tight-fitting thong, fishnet stockings and high heels as she set her I-pad down on the coffee table and pushed the play button. A sexy saxophone tune by Boney James started up, setting a sultry mood. As the sensual music filled the room, she began a slow, grinding pirouette.

Erin put on her best erotic dance, a sexy routine she perfected during her years as a pole dancer in a burlesque club before becoming Miss September. A few minutes into her dance, she couldn't help noticing something stirring in his shorts, and wondered how many Viagra pills he'd popped to jump-start his manhood. As she placed her hands on his bare thigh and squatted down suggestively on his knee, Anatolla's face suddenly turned bright pink, and the big man lurched forward, clutching his heart, dropping his lit cigar onto the marble floor.

"AARRGGGHHH!" Anatolla's eyes glazed as he grabbed at his chest, his head slumping lifelessly over her shoulder, pinning her in an awkward embrace.

"Oh my God!" Shocked, with both arms Erin pushed the huge man off her onto the back of the couch and stood over him in her high heels, bending to see if he was still breathing. The huge man gurgled slowly, and she thought she could hear him faintly moaning her name.

"Tony???" Desperate to revive him, but knowing nothing about CPR, she straddled his body in her high heels and began bitch slapping him across the face to revive him.

"Tony, wake up!!" grasping his jaw and shaking it back and forth, a maneuver she'd learned from an online tutorial on National Geographic Channel about training gorillas. "Wake up!" From her experiences with guys who liked it rough, Erin bitch slapped him a few more times before stopping at the sight of foam forming in the corners of his mouth.

Frozen with fear, Erin was clueless as to what to do next. She was desperate for a way to avoid being blamed for his heart attack. With still no response from her date, Erin panicked, dismounted the unconscious condo director and straightened the seams on her fishnet stockings. Hurriedly, she put on her wig, fur coat, hat and sunglasses. Pocketing the tall stack of hundreds from the coffee table, she looked around the condo for a phone and found one on the kitchen counter. She dialed 911.

"911.What is your emergency?' asked the female dispatcher.

Erin was in a panic. "I think Mr. Anatolla is having a heart attack!" she blurted. "*Please* send an ambulance to Delmar on Boca Beach! For God's sake, he has foam coming out of his mouth!"

"Please calm down, ma'am. Can you tell if he's breathing?" asked the dispatcher. Erin could hear shouting on the dispatcher's phone in the background.

Flustered, she approached her unconscious date and began bitch slapping him again. "WAKE UP, TONY!" she yelled, getting angry as she thought about the prison term for manslaughter, or even worse-death by lap dance. By now, she was out of her mind with fear and considered hanging up, but the dispatcher came back before she could end the call.

"Hang on," said the dispatcher. "We got someone off their meds here. I need to confirm the address there, honey."

"I don't know exactly," said Erin in a panic. "South on A1A. Delmar. Just look for that round condo that looks like a big gold vibrator on the beach. Number 808...I think," as she picked up his lifeless wrist to check for a pulse. "Please hurry!" She heard another round of loud voices in the background.

"Okay," said the dispatcher. "I got Delmar, South Boca Beach, number 808. Stay with me, ma'am. What's your name?" Erin's heart raced with fear. "Ma'am? I need your"-

There was a click as Erin ended the call. Petrified, she wiped her prints off the phone with the edge of her stockings and slid it across the marbled counter where it fell, clanging into the empty stainless steel sink. At that moment, she was startled to hear a very strange voice coming from the bedroom that sounded like a little old lady singing "Rock of Ages" in a falsetto.

"Rock of ages...cleft for meeeee....rock of ages, cleft for meeeee! SQUAWK!"

Dressed in her Jimmy Choo high heels, fishnet stockings, fur coat, wig, Dolce Gabbana sunglasses and Donna Karan floppy hat, Erin crept cautiously down the travertine hallway toward the bedroom, fearful of who or what she was about to confront and petrified at the thought of a possible witness.

"Hello, is someone there?" her voice cracking. Peeking through the bedroom doorway, she could see no one. Then the singing repeated.

"Rock of ages…cleft for meeeee….rock of ages, cleft for meeeee! SQUAWK!"

Her heart beating out of her chest, Erin stepped inside the master bedroom where she saw a gilded cage hanging from the ceiling that contained a white cockatiel. She watched the bird's crest stiffen as he turned around on the perch to face his visitor.

"Scored a lap dance to die for! Lap dance to die for!" squawked the bird. "Hi, I'm Perry. Perry's a rock star! Perry's a rock star! What's yer name? What's yer name? SQUAWK!"

Things had taken a turn toward the surreal for Erin. Not believing what she was seeing and hearing, she lowered her sunglasses in amazement as she leaned against the door jamb. "Oh my God!" she said in amazement.

"Oh my God! Oh my God!" repeated the cockatiel. "Wake up, Tony! Wake up, Tony! SQUAWK! Got some cash for ya, honey! Take the cash! Better send an ambulance! Need a date, honey? SQUAWK!"

Erin grabbed her purse and I-pad and ran to the front door as fast as her Jimmy Choo high heels could carry her without managing to break a heel.

"Perry's a rock star! Take the cash! Better call an ambulance!" squawked the cockatiel from the bedroom as she slammed the door behind her.

Minutes later, after exiting in her S550 through the service entrance, a very distraught Erin Griffith drove north on A1A at double the posted speed limit, wanting to get as far from Delmar as fast as she could. She felt like a character in a Stephen King novel as she nervously checked her rearview mirror for any signs of cops in her bid to distance herself from the insane asylum. An entire pitcher of margaritas wouldn't be enough to calm her nerves.

Directly ahead, a red and white Palm Beach County ambulance raced toward her at high speed, sirens wailing and lights flashing. She was guessing it was Anatolla's ride to the ER. The ambulance was followed by a black and white Boca police car as she slowed her Mercedes and yielded to the emergency vehicles passing her, almost running over two teens with surfboards just south of the Boca Inlet Bridge. It was only a lap dance, for God's sake. Didn't mean to kill the poor bastard.

After the emergency vehicles had passed, she punched the accelerator and the big Benz lurched forward. Crossing over Boca Inlet, she thought back to her last five thousand dollar booking at Delmar on the day that big oaf Karcass had booked her nude performance last week. The words that kept repeating in her head were "…a lap dance to die for," the same words that formed the new banner at the bottom of her website.

Speeding north on A1A, Erin thought it might be a good idea to limit her future liabilities by adding a disclaimer to her website recommending a recent EKG before booking a lap dance. *That* oughta get her some eyeballs. That idea triggered thoughts about adding liability insurance to cover future lap dances, and Erin decided to call her agent and get some quotes.

Then, Perry's performance of "Rock of Ages" popped back into her head as she freshened her lipstick in the rearview mirror at seventy miles an hour and checked again for cop cars. Unable to get the tune out of her head, she began to sing the lyrics out loud again, trying to mimic the cockatiel's falsetto.

"Rock of ages…cleft for meeee."

TWENTY-ONE

Early on Tuesday morning, the scruffy-looking man that called himself David Callahan pedaled his Nel Lusso two-tone beach cruiser north on Ocean Boulevard on his way to Nautilus Realty as he cruised in and out of the high-rise shadows. Locals passing by him in their Beemers and Bentleys were preoccupied with their shopping trips to the Town Center Mall or spending the afternoon at Waterstone Resort, paying little attention to the fugitive in their midst.

Callahan was trying to figure out why Megan had left him a voice mail telling him she needed more money. Had he mistakenly underpaid his rent? She'd given him a valid receipt for his five grand. Although she didn't seem like the type to extort money from one of her company's own tenants, he thought it would be wise to agree to another meeting to find out what was on her mind. Uncomfortable with the added attention he was beginning to attract, he'd decided to accelerate his plans to find a new safe house. With only a few days to go before completing his disappearing act, he was getting antsy.

Nautilus Realty's most dangerous tenant turned into the parking lot and propped his beach cruiser against a palm tree. As he did so, he noticed a familiar van with heavy window tint, curly-que antennas and grey primer coat. It was parked at the far end of the lot, and he remembered seeing the van the day they found Lance Meyer's body. It made him suspicious.

Entering the office for their eight-thirty meeting, Callahan spotted Megan sitting behind her desk typing away on her computer. Impatient, he shuffled up to her desk as he tugged nervously on his beard. "Hey Megan. Got your message. So, did they raise my rent or something? "

Megan stopped typing and calmly looked up. "Won't you sit down, Mr. Callahan?" gesturing at the empty chair next to her desk. He looked around the office to see if they were alone as he took a seat. "You must be thirsty from your bike ride. Would you like an ice cold Coke?" she asked.

"Sure. Why not." Callahan was determined not to let her stunning beauty distract him from the business at hand.

She held the door open to the mini-fridge stocked full of canned soda. "Please. Help yourself." Still wary of her agenda, Callahan grabbed a can of Coke from the top shelf, popped the top and took a big swig. Megan smiled and leaned back in her padded leather chair to size him up as she took a sip from her coffee mug.

In a confident tone that seemed unfamiliar to him, Megan said; "Got a deal for you." She placed her folded hands in her lap and cocked her head as she recalled her coaching. "I know how much you like your privacy, Mr. Callahan, and *I* could use some extra income." Uh-oh, here it comes, thought Callahan. "For a thousand a month in cash, I will help you keep things quiet," she said in a calm clear voice. "If you *are* who I think you are, the money won't matter."

His eyes narrowed as he struggled to contain his temper, annoyed with her pathetic little shakedown. Surprised by her boldness, he thought her proposal sounded a little too canned and took a deep breath before responding. "Whatever do you mean?" he asked, keeping a lid on his emotions to buy some time, finding it hard to believe this was the sweet young lady he'd met last week.

"I think you know what I mean," she said. "The boat receipt." Taking another sip from her Starbucks coffee mug, Megan watched him start to fidget as his calm demeanor began to dissolve.

"So that's what this is, a shakedown?" he asked in a hostile tone.

"Look at it this way, Mr. Callahan. I'm a divorcee' with no one to support me. I need some extra cash to get started with my new business and I have a lot of expenses." She waited for some sign he understood but doubted she would see it as she set her coffee down. "Tell me. The boat on the receipt. Was it the one that that ran over Lance Meyer?"

He was startled by her directness. Just two more days, he told himself. Two more days. Poker faced, he said, "Maybe. Maybe not. Who knows? Be hard to prove, wouldn't it?" He paused to look around the office once more to make sure they were alone, checking to see if there were any security cameras. Spotting no cameras, an awkward silence followed before he leaned forward.

In a low voice, he said, "Okay, Megan. Say I make a thousand dollar monthly contribution to your new-career kitty fund. What do I get in return?"

"My undying silence," she said with a straight face.

Undying was the only part he wouldn't guarantee, he thought, glaring at her. "All right. Done. I can bring you the cash tomorrow."

With Detectives Klein and Costello listening in the van outside, armed and ready to intercede, she knew she could push him. "I need it today...as a sign of good faith. You can do it." Seeing no reaction, she continued. "I need to make a bank deposit to cover some checks," she explained, "...so, shall we say, in about an hour?"

He glared at her and checked his watch. It was only eight forty-five. If he agreed, it would give him plenty of time to pedal home and grab some cash from the stack in his basement. He knew he needed to be conciliatory, and it would be some cheap insurance to buy him the time he needed before he disappeared. "Okay," he said reluctantly, "...but I'll need a receipt from you." He watched her face for clues. "As a sign of *your* good faith."

"Not a problem," said Megan. She watched him drain his Coke and set the empty can on her desk. "Let me toss that for you," she offered, reaching for the empty Coke can. She realized she'd been a little too eager.

Callahan beat her to it and snatched the can from the desk. Standing abruptly, he said, "That's okay, Slick. I'll drop it in the bin on my way out."

But he didn't.

Megan watched Callahan walk out and give her an evil look from outside the glass office door as he headed for his bicycle. She breathed a sigh of relief. It was almost over. She reached behind her back and tapped on the microphone that was taped to her back, the pre-arranged signal.

"Interview is over, guys. He has the Coke can with him. Sorry I couldn't get his fingerprints."

⊰⊱

It was Wednesday, and the beachfront house in Vero that Callahan rented a few days earlier was scheduled to have the electric turned on before nightfall. An older beachfront home in Vero's Central Beach area, this time Callahan had found a rental with all the modern comforts-including central air conditioning.

As he studied it from his SUV, he realized how much his new hide-away resembled Greenwood Mansion, with its Mediterranean-style red terracotta roof and gated security protecting the front entrance. With the AC running full blast inside his Range Rover, the outside temperature gauge read ninety-two degrees as he enjoyed the cool air. Surrounded by the latest high-tech surveillance gadgetry in his mobile office, he enjoyed listening on the police scanner and watching on his laptop all the locals passing by his home in Boca an hour-and-a-half away.

Callahan calculated that the cargo capacity of his new commercial minivan should accommodate his special cargo of crated gold coins and cash in only three trips. The minivan decorated with the magnetic "ABERNATHY PLUMBING" signs would help him blend in with the more sedate Indian River County culture. Moving over three hundred ninety cubic feet of U.S. currency in large bills, plus thirty-two crates of gold coins and a body in a blanket would pose no problem. After coordinating logistics for twenty-six different companies during the $170 million salvage operation of the *S.S. America* more than a decade earlier, this move up the Florida coast ought to be a cake walk. But the timing had him worried.

As luck would have it, he spotted a brand new group of seaside townhouses going up on A1A in Vero Beach only a mile from his new Central Beach hideout. He couldn't believe his good fortune in finding a new construction project so close to pouring the large concrete seawalls. Callahan's daytime inspection revealed there were two or three sections of the plywood forms fifteen feet or deeper that would be very useful in helping him tidy up loose ends. From the contractor's notes written on the building permit, he knew they planned to pour fresh concrete within three days. He remembered Megan worked late on Wednesdays and Thursdays in preparation for the Friday staff meetings. If she really was a struggling divorcee who needed cash, Callahan had plenty of it to offer, and since she was single, he hoped her absence would go unnoticed until he was long gone.

His situation made him think back to the first time he had to deal with a greedy would-be blackmailer. Ten years earlier, he'd planned to hole up at an old bed and breakfast in a sleazy suburb called Aurora, just outside Chicago. The little working-class town was located right on SR 56 about forty miles west of downtown Chicago. There, he'd come upon a bed and breakfast called "Lucie Daze", and the off-the-beaten-path location was perfect for him. The B&B wasn't much more than a bunch of old wooden hunter's cabins strung together by planked boardwalks and run by a grumpy old spinster named Lucie Kerroux.

The first time he'd set eyes on Mrs. Kerroux, the seventy-year-old widow reminded him of a large black widow spider, with a personality to match. Callahan made the mistake of pulling out a wad of Franklin's big enough to choke a horse when he'd paid her for a month in advance on the afternoon he arrived. The old lady got suspicious and decided she wanted a larger chunk of it.

Little did Callahan know that Mrs. Kerroux suffered from incurable insomnia and had a habit of staying up all night drinking absinthe and playing with tarot cards. From her office at the front of the B&B that night, she spotted Callahan moving his crates of coins and cash from his big panel truck at three in the morning. Unfortunately for Callahan, the widow had a nose for outlaws and saw an opportunity to make what she thought would be some easy money. The cranky old spinster had left him a nasty little note demanding he pay her for "a year in advance" and slip the cash under her door the next day or she'd call the cops.

After reading the note she'd left, Callahan decided to try and talk some sense into her. Early the next morning, he took a walk down the rickety boardwalk to have a chat with the old lady. He hopped up the porch steps that day and knocked on her front door where they had a brief but very unsatisfactory conversation through her screened door. Mrs. Kerroux had gotten quite nasty and stuck to her demands for a cash payment of ten thousand dollars in exchange for "lookin' the other way", as she called it. Although Callahan was outraged with the old lady's demands, he stayed calm and agreed to bring her the money before the day was over.

But he didn't.

As it turned out, the old wooden turn-of-the-century B&B was in such a state of disrepair that Callahan stumbled upon more than a few maintenance issues that posed a serious fire hazard. Focusing on one such safety issue, he noticed that the old cabins had wooden floors built on stone pilings with exposed copper gas lines underneath. He knew just how often those exposed copper gas lines could freeze up, rupture and leak.

As fate would have it, a little after ten o'clock on a night of sub-freezing temperatures, Callahan had loaded up his big panel truck and hidden it a half-mile down State Road 56. Right after that, one of those gas lines just happened to rupture. The resulting explosion and fire incinerated Mrs. Kerroux, her tarot cards, her absinthe, and all the office records that may have held any incriminating information about her guests. The investigation by the City of Aurora Fire Department classified the cause of the fire as "a gas leak with explosion caused by poor maintenance."

Following the terrible tragedy, Callahan drove like a scalded gerbil for two-and-a-half days straight, all the way to Boca Raton, Florida to find his next safe house; the Greenwood Mansion.

⊷⊶

As the sun was about to set behind the condos and office buildings on the west side of A1A, the 21-speed Schwinn hybrid flew along like a silver bullet on the eighteen-mile trip to Highland Beach. Mark liked listening to the soft humming of the 28-inch alloy wheels speeding over the super-smooth bike path as he pedaled faster in top gear, pretending he was about to get airborne.

Like an aircraft about to take flight, his front and rear LED lights were blinking brightly as an extra precaution. He was fully aware that some of the half-blind condo commandos that passed him in their Bentleys and Beemers were quite capable of turning him into a hood ornament without even noticing for a week or two. Pedaling fiercely, he enjoyed watching the shocked looks of passengers as he passed them on his silver bullet. In twenty-first gear, Mark continued north on Ocean Boulevard at warp speed toward the Boca Inlet Bridge. His digital speedometer registered a steady twenty-nine miles an hour as he reveled in the feel of the sea breeze on his face.

Riding at dusk when it was cooler and less congested was more enjoyable. Flying along A1A on his bike was an experience so unlike hurtling across the ocean on his twin-turbo catamaran at 100 miles an hour. The absence of loud noise and vibrations made cycling different from flying over the ocean with enough speed to distort facial features into gargoyle faces. The excitement of moving so swiftly under his own power took him back to his childhood when he used to jump from the roof of his house in his early attempts to fly.

Once, when he was six years old and lived in Naples, Little Lloyd had ordered a new washer and dryer delivered for Mark's mom. The day they arrived, he carved up the two shipping boxes to craft a pair of cardboard wings that he bound together with glue and twine from his dad's utility room. Back then, he'd been experimenting with designing homemade wings for weeks, using the illustrations from his mom's Encyclopedia Britannica to create an effective airfoil. While other kids his age were flying kites, six year old Mark was taking his wings to the seashore for test flights.

When he was finished with his latest creation, he used his dad's stepladder to climb up on the roof of the two-story house, confident in his design and determined to prove he could soar with the birds. Fearlessly, he jumped, soaring across the back yard, crash-landing into a chain link fence and catapulting into the neighbor's pool head first. After suffering a mild concussion, bruised ribs and sprained ankle, his parents forbade him to make any more attempts at flying without a pilot's license.

Ripping north through Boca Beach on A1A, he was startled to see an older man up ahead wobble, then stumble and fall hard to the pavement. The man lay motionless in the grass, and Mark hit his brakes hard, coming to a grinding stop as he pulled over. A middle-aged woman on her cell phone with a big beach bag ambled toward Mark on the pedestrian walk, seemingly unaware of the crisis unfolding in front of her. Mark dropped his bike and grasped the man's shoulder to roll him onto his back, and he recognized Al Wasserman, one of Delmar's board members. Wasserman lay motionless, bleeding from a gash on his head as Mark reached to check for a pulse.

"Al, buddy, talk to me. Can you hear me?" Feeling no pulse, Mark quickly pulled off his Under Armour biking shirt and folded it under the man's neck to open his airway and begin CPR.

"Is he okay?" asked the concerned woman as she bent over them, still holding the phone to her ear. "Should I"-

Mark held his hand up, stopping her mid-sentence. "Ma'am, please, hang up and dial 911! Tell them a man is unconscious on the east side of A1A a hundred yards south of the Boca Inlet Bridge." He looked around for something to prop up Al's legs. "Ma'am, I need your beach bag."

"For what?" she asked, clutching it close to her body.

"To help save his life," he said, reaching for the bag. "He's going into shock." The woman hesitated. "Don't worry, you'll get it back." After removing a long round object stuck inside a sock that she quickly slipped into her slacks, the woman sheepishly handed him the bag and Mark tucked it under Al's feet. He continued CPR as the woman finally dialed 911.

"This is 911. What is your emergency?"

"911? Yes, this is Sadi Hadid. Can you send an ambulance to," putting her hand over the mouthpiece, "...where'd you say we were again? I'm not from around here," she said apologetically.

Mark looked up from his CPR and took a deep breath. "Boca Beach, A1A, just south of the inlet bridge," he said slowly. She repeated their location to the 911 dispatcher as Mark pressed on Al's chest in rhythmic intervals.

"They said the ambulance should be here in a few minutes," said Sadie, frowning at their unconscious patient. A crowd of onlookers began to gather as traffic backed up on A1A, and Mark was beginning to feel light-headed from the CPR. A black and white police cruiser pulled up with lights flashing, and an officer emerged.

Seeing Mark performing CPR on the man, the officer spoke into his shoulder mike. "Two forty-six to dispatch. Need an ambulance sent to A1A in Boca, just south of the Boca Inlet Bridge."

"Copy that, two forty-six," said a female voice. "EMS is already on their way. ETA is about three minutes."

"Copy that." The uniformed officer looked a lot like James Gandolfini, and his nameplate read "OFC. N. DEMILLE". He hooked his thumbs in his duty belt as Mark looked up, anticipating a question. "What we got here, sir?" he asked.

"Probably a heart attack," responded Mark between breaths. "You got an ambu bag in your cruiser? I'm getting dizzy."

"Sure do." Addressing the crowd that had gathered, he said, "You folks wanna stand back and give us some room here?" Another Boca police cruiser pulled up, and the second officer hopped out and began directing traffic. Officer DeMille retrieved his emergency equipment kit and laid it out on the grass, extracting the ambu bag. "You a doctor?" he asked Mark.

"No, but I'm trained in CPR. I'll do the cardio if you can do the ambu bag."

Nodding in agreement, Officer DeMille squatted to fit the mouthpiece over the victim's airway and began a steady pumping action. As Sadie leaned over them to check on their patient, a loud humming sound could be heard coming from her pocket. Embarrassed, Sadie turned away and reached inside her pocket to switch off the power to her appliance. Mark and Officer DeMille exchanged knowing glances.

"EMS should be here in about two minutes," said DeMille, nodding at their patient. "You know who he is?"

"His name's Al Wasserman. He's on our board at Delmar."

"That big round condo that looks like a giant vibrator?" he asked, squeezing the ambu bag and glancing at Sadie.

"That's the one," said Mark, not bothering to explain it was a rendition of the Gherkin Tower in London. When he checked again for a pulse, he felt a faint heartbeat just as he heard a siren coming from the other side of the bridge. "Praise the Lord, we have a weak pulse," as Mark wiped his brow in relief and said a silent prayer, thankful that Al's heart was beating again. They watched the ambulance pull up and the paramedics hop out with their life-support equipment.

Officer DeMille looked at Mark. "Good job. You may have saved this man's life. By the way, I'll need your name and address for my report."

"Mark McAllister. From the big gold vibrator...uh...," glancing at Sadie, "...the one down the road big enough for people to live in." It was the first time he'd smiled during the ordeal. As the paramedics stepped in to take over, they attached an IV and lifted Wasserman onto a gurney while Mark stood and stretched. Flanked by EMS personnel, the Delmar director was placed into the waiting ambulance as Mark asked the lead paramedic for a prognosis.

"He's got a weak pulse, but I'd say his chances are fair to good," said the young EMS tech. "We have a cardiologist waiting at Boca

Community. Gotta fly." He hesitated at the open door of the ambulance. "By the way, are you the one who stopped and gave him CPR?"

"Yessir."

"Good job."

"Al would have done the same for me," said Mark. He watched the paramedic jump in the front seat as the vehicle's lights and siren came to life again, and the ambulance sped off toward Boca Community Hospital on Glades Road.

Sadie Hadid was back on her phone as Mark stood with the group of onlookers and Officer DeMille. "Are you one of the McAllisters of the Mizner Park group?" asked DeMille.

"Yessir," answered Mark as if it were a routine traffic stop.

"I thought I recognized you from the Boca shiny sheets. Call me Nelson."

"Okay. By the way, in case you have time, Al Wasserman has a wife named Naomi. I'm sure she'd want to be by Al's side."

"As soon as we get this traffic moving again, that's where I'm headed next, partner," responded DeMille.

"If you see that lunatic Rodman down at the cop shop, tell him I said hi," said Mark with a smile. "He's my work-out buddy at Gold's."

"Motorcycle patrolman, right?"

Mark nodded. After exchanging a fist bump with Officer DeMille, he got back on his bike to finish his trip to Highland Beach, said another prayer for Al Wasserman, and thought about a movie he watched last night.

It was so true, he thought; in order for it to be real, happiness needs to be shared.

TWENTY-TWO

At nine-thirty on a partly-sunny morning, Klein and Costello approached the Greenwood Mansion to pose a few questions to Mr. David Callahan. For the Boca Raton detectives, Callahan had proven about as easy to corral as the ghost who was rumored to haunt the century-old mansion. The BEWARE OF DOG sign seemed out of place in the affluent Boca Beach neighborhood. Pausing with his hand on the wrought iron security gate, Klein noticed that the padlock was unlocked.

"Looks like someone forgot to lock the gate, Anthony," said Klein in a mocking tone. Costello glanced at his partner and nodded his approval as Klein lifted the latch and the two detectives entered the courtyard. They headed up the walkway to the front porch where the concentric semi-circles of artfully-laid Chicago brick spoke volumes of the old-world artistry that set the mansion apart from the upscale contemporary condos on either side. The front door was crafted of thick, antique tongue-and-groove oak with oversized cast iron hinges, and the doors were rounded at the top in Old Mission-style and coated with several layers of varnish.

"This guy lives pretty high on the hog," said Klein, grasping the huge cast iron knocker and banging loudly on the door. Klein stared up at the security cameras and wondered if anyone was staring back. He had an eerie feeling about the place. Both of the large thermo-pane windows on either side of the entry door were covered with sun-reflecting tint, offering no clues as to who or what waited inside. The front of the huge mansion was protected by ultra-high definition security cameras equipped with LED lights, motion detectors and night vision technology. It was an expensive set-up, and the detectives couldn't help wondering why Mr. Callahan felt the need to spend so much on security.

After knocking for the third time and hearing only silence, Klein smoothed a hand over his bald head in frustration. "Even if this guy's home, he's not gonna answer the door," he said.

"He knows he doesn't have to without a warrant," responded Costello. Klein retraced his steps down the Chicago-brick porch.

"C'mon, Tony. Let's take a peek inside the garage."

"Betcha this guy drives a Range Rover," said Costello as he bounded down the steps toward the three-bay garage.

"Nice neighborhood," commented Klein as he watched two girls leisurely bicycle south on A1A.

"Long as you got the coin." Saying it out loud made Costello feel like Captain Obvious.

The two detectives approached the side-entry garage door to take a peek through the oval-shaped glass windows. Klein cupped his hands and leaned in for a better view.

"Son of a gun has black film or paint over them," said Klein. "Can't tell what's parked in there." Klein scanned the courtyard again. "This guy sure loves his privacy."

Costello pointed to another set of cameras on the far corners of the house. "Looks like he's prepared to repel boarders," he said, analyzing the security hardware. "Pretty high-tech. Infrared motion-detecting cameras with night vision. Expensive stuff. Probably watching us right now."

"This guy must have a coupla bucks," added Costello as he glanced at his partner. "What're you thinkin'? Another drug dealer?"

Klein smirked. "If we're lucky."

On their best behavior just in case they were being recorded, the detectives discretely scoured the front of the house for more clues about their suspect. Klein shaded his eyes from the morning sun as he studied the cameras, unable to escape the eerie feeling they were being watched as the cameras panned back and forth to track their movement.

Costello echoed his partner's intuition. "Betcha the perv's watching us right now on his laptop."

"Screw him. I don't care if he is. I'm gonna check around back," declared Klein.

The detectives made their way around the side of the house to the brick paver patio in back. The two scanned the terracotta roof, stone exterior and mirrored glass sliders for more clues about Mr. Callahan before their attention was drawn to the drop-dead view looking out over the ocean.

Costello and Klein stood in awe of the huge expanse of beach that formed the gorgeous panorama from the back of the house. A thin line of joggers and beachgoers made their way up and down the beach as the surf broke in a measured cadence at the shoreline. The tide was out, and sea gulls were taking turns diving into the surf in their quest to pluck a quick breakfast from the water. The chirp of sandpipers could be heard as they scurried back and forth in their search for minnows and sand fleas brought by the surf's ebb and flow.

"I could get used to this," said Costello, enjoying the sea breeze. The two stood mesmerized by the sounds of the seashore, forgetting for a moment they were there to investigate a murder.

Klein was drawn to the bamboo swing-for-two perched in the sea oats at the edge of the dune. "Yeah, I could get used to this, too. Wonder what this guy pays for rent," making himself comfortable on the Sunbrella cushions as the sun warmed his face.

"Megan said the rent's five grand a month, and he always pays with the same moldy cash in large bills," answered Costello. "I don't see any AC units anywhere outside the house. I'm bettin' that's why the cash stays moldy."

Klein nodded. Temporarily hypnotized by the sway of sea oats waving in the breeze, he focused on a round red wrapper lying in the tall grass and got up from his perch to investigate. Retrieving the item that lay at the top of the dune, he looked over at Costello. "Check this out," he said, holding up a paper band from a Partagas Series D, No. 1 cigar. "At least we know he's got good taste in cigars." Klein smirked, resentful of the man's lifestyle.

Spotting something else in the sea oats ten yards away, Costello stepped deeper into the dune grass to retrieve a yellow and white band of paper. It was faded from the sun, and he squinted to make out the markings. Barely legible, on it was printed "$10,000." He walked it over to his partner so Klein could confirm his find.

Klein studied it closely. "It's a $10,000 money band issued by the Federal Reserve Bank in Miami. This guy sure gets around."

Costello nodded and slipped into an improv of Larry the Cable Guy. "Don't he, though? Like a bad case'o heartburn. Think we know how he can afford them there expensive *C-gars* and this here high-dollar view, right Hoss?"

Amused with his partner's impression of a celebrity redneck, Klein turned toward the closest camera with his best fake grin as he held the money band up, just in case they had an audience. The detective was well aware of the rules on illegal search and seizure and sure that the sand dunes were beyond the private property lot line. "*Now* maybe that liberal rights activist Judge Rosencranz will agree to grant our search warrant."

"I dunno, Hoss," continued Costello with his impression of Larry the Cable Guy picking his teeth with a toothpick. "Guy's been playing checkers while the rest o'the world's been playin' *Grand Theft Auto* on their dad gum Xbox."

＊＝＋＋＝

Sitting comfortably in his idling Range Rover in Vero Beach, Callahan watched the show on his laptop in air-conditioned comfort. Chuckling at the frustrated detectives, he hit the zoom-in button to give him a close-up of the bits of trash they were holding up. Clueless as to what their names were, he nicknamed them Mutt and Jeff. He was getting a kick out of watching them on his new HD internet camera system, tickled pink with his new toys from Best Buy. Using the 50:1 zoom-in feature, he was beyond entertained as they fumbled around outside his Boca mansion looking for evidence. Two weeks ago, he was wondering if his plans to move to a new hideout were premature. But with the heat he was getting lately, he knew his decision to move quickly was a good one.

Though the Federal Reserve Bank money band and cigar wrapper were hardly damning evidence, Callahan nonetheless made a notation in his daily planner that the two officers had just performed an illegal search of his grounds. Just in case Boca's Keystone Cops ever did catch up with him, he wanted to be ready to turn the tables. The two detectives had been poking around the Greenwood Mansion for a half hour before climbing back in their grey Crown Vic and heading north on A1A. Callahan was feeling pretty smug as the first internet episode of "The Mutt and Jeff Show" came to a close.

Callahan clicked back onto the Macy's women's apparel website and scrolled down to the seductive images of Megan Rockwell in sheer lingerie. The sensual images of Megan posing in skimpy negligees and thongs got him so wound up he was starting to have second thoughts about his plans for her. An idea took shape as he suddenly remembered the twenty tabs of GHB in the center console of the Range Rover. At the bottom, he found the amber vial buried under a pile of fake licenses and passports and held it up in the light to check the contents. A fantasy was forming as he grinned and stuffed it into his pants pocket.

Callahan got out of the SUV to stretch his legs and get more familiar with the new neighborhood in Vero Beach. He'd been cooped up in his mobile office for the last forty minutes doing remote video surveillance of his place in Boca. The web pages of a scantily-clad Megan Rockwell modeling for Macy's had made him lose track of time.

To his left were a couple of Q-tips walking arm-in-arm on their way to the Jaycee Park boardwalk, and to his right a golf cart full of high schoolers were ogling his Range Rover as they whizzed by in the opposite direction. He activated the security gate remote to check to see if the utilities were turned on yet and was pleased to hear the hum of the motor as the gate retracted.

With the utilities now on, everything was working according to plan as he drove in and parked his SUV inside his new digs. Looking around the triple garage, he liked what he saw. The absence of windows would keep prying eyes from invading his privacy and made the garage a safe place for items that might otherwise attract the wrong kind of attention.

Callahan popped the hatch and gathered his power tools from the back of the SUV, carrying them into the large dining room. The room's elevated pine floor provided the perfect spot to build a hinged trap door that would give him easy access to his stash of cash and gold coins. Along with his new ten by twelve Persian rug to cover the opening, concealment of the door to his stash would be a done deal. After spending a few minutes diagraming the opening with a Sharpie and six-foot level, the circular saw's high-pitched whine filled the house as he went to work on the pine floor.

❯❮❯

The sun had set a half hour earlier as Callahan tightened the last screw in the piano hinge and adjusted the recessed stainless latch for the trap door. With his tools back in the Range Rover, he drove north on A1A to check on the seaside townhouses going up. The site was right where the old Surf Hotel once, stood only a mile north of his newly-rented villa. Nothing proved as useful to Callahan or seemed quite as permanent as freshly-poured concrete for hiding his dirty little secrets.

He parked in the guest parking at the office building across Ocean Boulevard to keep a low profile. It was dusk, and the traffic along A1A in the sleepy little beach town had slowed to an occasional passing car or bicyclist. Just dark enough for him to blend into the shadows, he cautiously made his way across the sandy lot, sidestepping two wheelbarrows and several stacks of rebar. He needed to make sure they hadn't already poured the footers for the huge seawall.

Peering inside the structure with his mini-Magna light, he heard nearby voices. He switched off his light and froze as he watched a young couple through the privacy fence walking on the beach a hundred feet away. Laughing and talking on the phone, they seemed oblivious to his presence. When the couple was out of range, he switched his Magna light back on to illuminate the steel rebar wired in place. Callahan was overjoyed to see that the twenty-foot deep plywood form looked ready to be filled with truckloads of fresh concrete. It was the perfect spot for what he had in mind.

Seeing the huge empty form waiting in the darkness made Callahan's heart sing. In his glee, he switched off his Magna light too soon, forgetting about the wheelbarrows in his path and tripped. He fell onto a stack of rebar, cutting his wrist on the jagged edge. Cursing under his breath, he got back on his feet, holding his wrist tightly to stem the trickle of blood as he snuck back across the lot, hoping like hell he wasn't leaving a trail of traceable DNA.

Disgusted with his clumsiness, he saw no one as he crossed A1A to his Range Rover to retrieve the first aid kit that he kept behind the back seat. Stupid, stupid, stupid. In the dim light of the inside dome light, he found an antiseptic wipe to clean his cut and, for a moment, considered stopping by an urgent care center for a tetanus shot. Then he thought about all the paperwork. While Callahan had an unhealthy disregard for his own safety, he disliked filling out personal medical forms even more and knew the Medical Information Bureau would create a paper trail that could be accessed by law enforcement. Angry with himself for being so careless, he pressed the square band aid onto his wrist and scanned the area to make sure no one had seen him.

Then, the fugitive who was wanted in seven states started the engine for the ride back to Boca to check on his stash and tie up some loose ends.

Night had descended on Boca Beach, and the rain had diminished to a light drizzle. Inside the Nautilus Realty office, Megan Rockwell sat at her computer in her purple tank top and khaki shorts as she organized sales figures into neat little columns on her screen. Earlier, she'd promised her boss to have the report finished in time for their Friday morning sales meeting and had returned to the office to wrap it up. Sometimes she wished she wasn't always so accommodating. With only her black Labrador for company, the part-time lingerie model was planning to stop by PetSmart after she finished. She was out of Bailey's favorite dry dogfood and wanted to pick up a large bag for the most deserving male in her life, and maybe a few new chewy toys.

For weeks, Megan had been trying to convince her boss to update the software since coming onboard with the firm. Unfortunately for Megan, her manager's bonus was based on net profits, and Mrs. Lafferty wasn't crazy about laying out the money for a software upgrade. The older version Excel program had always been a challenge for Megan, and combining the quarterly sales and listing figures for all three branches and getting it in the right columns wasn't easy. Frustrated with her progress, she was comforted by Bailey's wet nose nuzzling her bare knee and leaned down to stroke his head.

"Hey, Bailey. I know you're ready to go home." Bailey absolutely adored having his ears rubbed. "Mommy'll be just a little while longer. Hey, ya wanna go to PetSmart? PetSmart, Bailey?"

He didn't have to be asked twice. The black Lab wagged his tail in anticipation of a visit to his favorite store. Watching the finches and parakeets in their cages was intoxicating to him, and sniffing all the gerbils, hamsters, toys and treats was always a hoot. To Bailey, PetSmart was heaven on earth, and he rolled his tongue and licked his lips at the idea of roaming through PetSmart with her at his side. She smelled so wonderful! With one hand on her keyboard, she continued to stroke his head, and Bailey was torn between a wild romp at PetSmart and his craving for more love and affection from her. Couldn't he have both? The faint sounds of footsteps outside made his ears perk up, triggering an immediate need to explore as he exercised his primal urge to prowl and investigate.

"What is it, Bailey?" She watched him trot to the back of the office where he scratched the door with his paw. Usually, it was Bailey's way of telling her he had to pee.

"Okay, Bailey, hang on. Let's get your leash." She reached for the leash lying on the credenza, grabbing her keys and umbrella.

Peeking out the side window to check on the rain, she noticed a black Range Rover parked close to the back of the office. Oddly, it was backed in and the hatch was open. She thought it was strange that she hadn't heard the vehicle pull up in the drizzle. It seemed a little late for a sales associate to be unloading yard signs in the back of the building. Concerned, she walked toward the back door to check on Bailey and take a peek outside.

As she reached for the doorknob, the big metal door suddenly flew open. It all happened so fast. She was shocked to see a ski-masked man dressed in grey sweats toting a black backpack burst through the door and thrust a semi-automatic with a silencer in her face. Stunned, Megan suppressed a scream and covered her mouth with her hand. Bailey had an unsavory habit of passing gas whenever he was surprised. With the man's sudden appearance, the dog's haunches grew taut and Bailey farted loudly, bolting past the gunman and out the door like he'd been shot out of a cannon.

"Bailey!" she yelled. Vaulting across the rear parking lot, the big Lab continued to fart as he ran while the gunman confronted Megan. With the gun pointed at Megan, he slammed the door and locked the deadbolt.

"Guess that solves the dog problem," said the man in a voice that sounded vaguely familiar. He lunged at her and held the gun in her face. "Your dog always fart like that?" Megan was frozen with fear, too stunned to speak. He grabbed her arm and pressed the gun to the side of her head. "I like a girl who's quiet and follows instructions. Just do what I say and you and your gassy dog just might make it."

"Please don't"-

"Shut up!" he yelled, increasing the pressure on her arm.

Megan nodded, breaking down in tears. The gunman said: "Lay down on the floor, face down." Thinking he had the worst of intentions, she hesitated. The man pressed the barrel hard against her temple and cocked the gun.

"NOW!" he commanded.

Fearing for her life, she complied, laying down on the tile floor. The gunman sat down hard on top of her, pulling her arms behind her. She had a fleeting thought of trying to break free and reach for the cell phone lying on her desk, but the gunman was stronger than he looked and gripped her arms tightly. His black backpack dropped to the floor next to her head, and her attacker unzipped it with one hand and pulled out a roll of grey duct tape.

Sobbing, she said, "Please don't hurt me! I'll do anything you say!"

"I know you will," he said in a threatening voice. Now *shut up* before I put a bullet in your head!"

She'd been robbed once before at gunpoint. It happened when she'd taken the subway to a photo shoot for Macy's in Battery Park last year. Deep down, she hoped her passive compliance would bring her mercy from her attacker, just as it did with the assault in New York. She heard the gun clack against the tile floor as he set it down to peel off a section of tape, tearing it with his teeth and wrapping it tightly around her wrists. Then he tore off another piece and wrapped it tightly in the opposite direction.

"Please, mister," she pleaded, "...I have a bag of really good Jamaican bud and three hundred dollars in my purse." She'd had been saving the pot and cash for her high school reunion party next week. "Just please"-

"I told you to shut up!" he said angrily. "Don't want your money, Megan."

There was that voice again. Where had she heard it? How did he know her name? In her desperation, she tried to remember. Then it came to her. The black, lifeless eyes like a shark circling its prey, and that strange, depraved voice. Fearing this was payback for cooperating with the two detectives, now she was sorry she had underestimated his brutality. She felt something cold poking her in the back of the neck and assumed it was the silencer that pinned her to the tile floor. Having never seen a 9mm semi-automatic with a silencer, she instinctively feared her attacker had done this before. Her arms ached from having them restrained behind her, and the weight of his body ground her pelvis painfully against the tile.

Hope began to fade for Megan as he lifted her head and wrapped the tape tightly around her mouth before she could utter another word. Squeezing her eyes shut tightly, she looked down at herself from somewhere up high, the out-of-body experience causing her to lose track of who she was. This can't be happening, she told herself. Her inner voice was telling her to comply and do whatever he said, to keep him busy, to keep him from killing her. Things would get gruesome, but she would do anything he wanted to stay alive.

Callahan thought about moving his pretty hostage onto the padded office carpet to have some fun. He lost interest when he noticed it was covered in dog hair, preferring sex that wouldn't require a top-down combing with a lint brush and hot shower afterward. He imagined her without her shorts and top, lying helplessly in the privacy of his basement where there would be no cameras and no chance of someone barging in to interrupt. There, he could take his time with her, his very own Macy's lingerie model for his private amusement. He reached inside the backpack for the squeeze bottle and paper napkins.

Her nostrils flared from the strong stench of a chemical she hadn't inhaled since her high school chemistry class as she felt the wet paper smother her face. Instinctively, she tried bucking him off her and strained to raise her head but the pressure from the gun against her neck and the weight of his body held her down.

Gagging from the fumes, she tried to cough but the tape across her mouth pushed the air out her nose, forcing her to take in a lungful of the noxious chemical. Dizzy from the chloroform, her head began to spin, drifting, sounds becoming echoes in her head, fainter, reverberating and fading into the distance. She felt herself slipping away as if she were being carried down a river, then spinning effortlessly as she floated above the clouds.

A dream took hold, unlike any other dream in her twenty-four years. She was being carried aloft, higher in the sky by some unknown force, up inside a rain cloud from where she looked down and saw a funeral procession in a green cemetery below.

In her dream, she was being placed in a wooden coffin. She screamed and tried to reach out to prevent the lid from closing but couldn't move her arms. Her screams trailed off, muffled at first, then fading away altogether.

Suddenly, everything became deadly quiet as the heavy wooden lid of the coffin closed and locked in place. As she pressed her face up into the soft inner lining and gasped for air, darkness descended.

His wet nose quivered and twitched at the many delightful scents in the air, tantalized by so much to smell and taste tonight. The fresh sea breeze not only felt great on his face, it smelled *fantastic*. Bailey loved to romp free, especially after a hard downpour. It was such a thrill! His master didn't give him many chances to explore the seashore without his leash, and he took full advantage of his freedom, stretching his legs in a full gallop as he headed toward the sound of the breaking surf.

Bailey had fleeting thoughts of her but was distracted by all the taunting smells, a buffet of aromas filling his senses that demanded his immediate attention. He detected the distinct aroma of fresh crab, the audacious odors of seagulls and pelicans, the musky scent of rodents running loose, a faint whiff of fresh fish, sunscreen and cigars, and even the scent of barbeque-flavored potato chips that someone had kindly tossed into the swale for him.

Eagerly, he gobbled them up, relishing the piquant smoky flavor of hickory-flavored barbeque potato made soggy by the rain.

The freshly-scrubbed night air called out for Bailey to investigate every nook and cranny in his path, and the black Labrador heeded the call without reservation.

⚔

She awoke with blurred vision and a nasty headache, trying to adjust to her dank surroundings. Megan leaned against a bed-sheet that partially covered what looked like a huge stack of cash wrapped into bundles with yellow and white paper bands. The soft moonlight poured in through the two tiny basement windows as she struggled to figure out where she was.

Cold, naked, and chained to the floor, she was gagging on the smell of mold and chloroform. Helpless and petrified, she tried not to imagine what he had planned for her. She remembered the chloroform but had no memory of him removing her clothes and shuddered to think of what he was up to. Her ankles and wrists were bound with multiple layers of thick duct tape which she was unable to tear with her teeth because her mouth was also taped.

On the far side of the room, she could see a small desk with a laptop and stretched to see if she could reach it. She tried to inch forward like a caterpillar, but her wrists and ankles were bound by the leather straps and chains tethered to the floor. Above her, a small air conditioner was mounted on a shelf, and she was thankful it wasn't running. Unable to get the bedspread to wrap around her, she huddled against the pile of cash for warmth.

She heard footsteps outside and trembled at the thought of him touching her again.

TWENTY-THREE

The condo was dark and silent. As Marian Anatolla removed her key from the stainless steel deadbolt, she realized the door hadn't been locked and no one had set the alarm.

"Tony, I'm home." She flipped on the foyer overhead light and called out his name again. "Tony, honey...are you here?" She picked up an empty discarded package of anistreplase from the floor that looked like it was torn open in a hurry, along with a short piece of clear plastic tubing. "Tony?"

Concerned, she flipped on more lights before checking the patio and guest bedroom where Tony liked to sleep to get away from Perry, their pet cockatiel. Her husband wasn't home. She checked the kitchen, where she found her husband's cell phone sitting in the sink. Thumbing through the text entries, she found his last message had been sent to an Erin Griffin. It read: "See you at 8."

"That son-of-a..." Livid, she wanted him to sit down and tell her exactly what the hell he did while she was at the spa for the weekend. She wandered back to the living room where she found his half-smoked Fuente and a diamond earring on the floor under the suede couch. Upset, she managed to pour herself a vodka and soda from the sidebar.

"I'm gonna kill him!" she exclaimed out loud before making her way into the master bedroom. In his cage, Perry ruffled the feathers of his crest and stiffened as he looked over his shoulder at the lady of the house.

"Scored a lap dance to die for! Lap dance to die for! SQUAWK! Better send an ambulance! SQUAWK!"

"Perry, shut up! You damn bird brain! Before I roast you for dinner!" tossing the rest of her vodka back.

The cockatiel turned on his perch to face his adversary, crest bristling. "Perry's a rock star! Perry's a rockstar! Take the cash, honey! Better send an ambulance! SQUAWK!"

Marian threw her Luis Vuitton purse on the marble counter and stood in front of the master bedroom mirror to take stock of herself. Leaning on the edge of the granite counter, she studied her face, hallow-eyed. In spite of a three thousand dollar makeover and a weekend at The Breakers, she looked like hell. Her hair was frazzled from the humidity, and now she had to find out where her damn philandering husband had run off to. The Mahjong Queen of Delmar confronted herself in the bright vanity lights, leaning in toward her image in the mirror to stiffen her resolve.

"*I am* going to shoot him!" she said with renewed determination.

The fugitive watched the lights in the high-rises twinkle on and off around him as he walked north in the darkness along Ocean Boulevard to retrieve Megan's SUV. He was annoyed with himself. The twisted fantasies he entertained about her were muddying his mind, confusing him as he toyed with the idea of letting her live. The idea of keeping a beautiful lingerie model chained up for his personal amusement was becoming harder to let go.

On the other hand, he thought about the closing window of opportunity at the construction site and knew he wouldn't have much longer to figure it out. The empty footers offered a chance to bury his problems in Vero forever. After completing the first trip with a van full of crated gold coins, Callahan had loaded up for a second trip, and there was plenty of room for her body rolled up in a blanket. He felt he was in control, and his darker side toyed with the fantasy of playing God a little longer.

The nighttime drizzle had diminished to a mist as he peeked out from under his umbrella at the passing cars. He tried to blend in beneath the dim streetlights, unnoticed by anyone watching from the high-rises. With latex-gloved hand, he patted his pocket to make sure her keys and phone were still there, better prepared this time for the rain in his black foul weather gear.

Callahan stopped across the street from the real estate office to measure the mood of the neighborhood. He could see the blue-grey Highlander was still parked at the far end of the lot, illuminated by the building's dim footlights as he scoured the area to make sure no one was watching. He stood still for a moment as a black Mercedes turned into a driveway in front of him. Waiting for a break in the traffic, he crossed the street quickly and clicked the remote button to unlock it. As the keyless entry on the SUV chirped in response, he noticed the black Lab waiting on the office porch sit up and take notice.

There was that damn dog again!

⤞╬╠⤝

Where'd she been all this time? Had she forgotten he hadn't had dinner? Hearing the chirp of her car, Bailey stood up, yawned and stretched from head to tail, sure it was time to head home with her as he trotted agreeably toward the SUV. He was hungry after spending the day sniffing, exploring, chasing birds on the seashore, dodging cars and generally being a pain in the ass to folks who looked like they might have something to eat. At first, it seemed like the bearded stranger approaching wanted to make friends as he reached inside his coat pocket.

"Here, Bailey, got something for you…" said the stranger as he walked toward her car. Bailey cocked his head, never once taking his big brown eyes off the stranger's hand. Licking his lips and rolling his tongue in anticipation, he hoped to see him pull a Beggin' Strip or an egg McMuffin out of his pocket. As the stranger got closer, Bailey sensed danger, detecting that same scent of moldy perspiration. He realized it was that same man with the mask and gun that ran inside with her earlier. But why was her scent on the stranger?

The man's hand reappeared, holding something metallic and shiny, and the hope of a snack faded. His survival instinct told him to run.

"That's it. Run you mutt, before I put your gassy ass out of misery!" yelled the stranger as he slipped the shiny metal thing back inside his pocket.

Spotting a friendly couple on the sidewalk who looked like they might have a snack, he trotted amiably toward them. He knew they couldn't resist his big brown, hope-filled eyes. Tail wagging, he was hoping they had something really good to eat as he made his way across the lawn, sniffing the ground for clues about his master.

Didn't she know it was time for him to eat?

Callahan folded his umbrella and climbed in the Highlander while her black Lab was occupied with the geriatrics on the sidewalk. Even with the silencer, he didn't want to have to put two in his chest right on Ocean Boulevard in full view of condo commandos passing by on their dog walks. He started the engine and glanced over his shoulder, backing the SUV out carefully before noticing the large metal cage in the cargo bay and the bag of Beggin' Strips on the seat beside him. The pungent smell of a dog badly in need of a bath filled his nostrils as he adjusted the rearview mirror, watching the annoying canine pander to the elderly couple on the walkway.

Perfect, he thought. While that damn dog was distracted, he would make his getaway.

━≼┼┼≽━

The nice folks were rubbing his ears as her car passed, and Bailey looked up for her. He missed her. Did she forget it was past his dinner time? Surely she would stop for him at the next corner. Thinking it was a game, the black Lab suddenly gave chase, cutting across the street and in behind the SUV.

Bailey sprinted up to a girl walking her poodle on the pedestrian path, stopping for a moment to give the poodle's stuff a good sniffing and let the nice-smelling girl pet him. He thought of dinner again and gave chase. Her SUV stopped behind a row of cars, and Bailey expected to see the door open so he could hop in next to her. Instead, the window rolled down and he was overjoyed to see a hand empty an entire bag of Beggin' Strips out the driver's window. Yum! What a great game this was!

As he stopped to gobble up the tasty treats scattered in the road, Bailey ignored the honking cars and the angry people yelling at him and wondered if there was more in her car. He looked up to see her turn into that driveway with the big house and gate. As soon as he was finished with his roadside treat, he would catch up with her for more great snacks-unless he found something better on the way.

━≼┼┼≽━

Callahan parked her Highlander inside the last garage bay, beside his new commercial van with the "ABERNATHY PLUMBING" signs. As he switched off the engine, he checked his watch. Ten twenty-five. He knew he'd have to get rid of her car. That half bag of Beggin' Strips she'd left on the front seat had sure come in handy.

Just as he stepped out of the SUV, her phone began to ring. In his haste to outrun that damn pesky dog of hers, he'd forgotten to drop the pink phone into a public waste container on the way back to his house. The incoming call display read ANTHONY COSTELLO. Where had he heard that name before? Not that it mattered. Say goodbye, Mr. Costello. She's mine now. He popped the back of her ringing phone off and extracted the SIM card, crushing it between his fingers. He pocketed the battery and placed the phone on the concrete floor where he stomped on it with the heel of his Nike cross-trainers until only small pieces remained.

Callahan exited the side door of his garage with the pieces of her phone in his pocket and headed outside to give it a proper burial. The full moon shone brightly as he carefully checked the beach in both directions for any passersby. Although the drizzle had stopped, he wasn't expecting to see anyone out on the beach at this late hour. On his way down the dune, he patted the outside of his foul weather jacket to make sure he hadn't dropped his semi-automatic in the excitement. When he was close enough to the water, he hurled the pieces of her phone as far as he could, watching them sparkle in the moonlight before falling into the surf.

With one last loose end to tie up, he headed back to the rear patio of Greenwood Mansion to make sure the motion-activated security lights were working. As he approached, the lights illuminated the entire grounds and stone façade of the house. Perfect, he thought. Entering the six-digit code, he heard the electronic lock release and slid the glass door back, stepping inside to check on his houseguest. He hoped she was conscious. Leaving the lights off, he aimed the mini flashlight's beam on the oak steps leading downstairs to the basement and descended the stairway.

He was overjoyed to hear her muffled moans as he approached his pretty houseguest, illuminating her body with the flashlight. She was his new project, the beautiful lingerie model who had given him such heartache and so many new problems to solve.

Her blue eyes widened in terror at the sight of her attacker standing in the dark with his flashlight trained on her body. She tried to cry out but her sounds were stifled by layers of duct tape still tightly wrapped around her mouth. As he drew closer, he found himself aroused by her muffled screams and the sight of her kicking and thrashing against her bonds. The darkest of joys swept over him as he stood in silence, sweeping the narrow light from head to toe.

"You wouldn't be here if you just minded your own business, Megan," he said in a soft voice as if to console her. "Tryin' to shake me down and get my prints off a Coke can. Really? Who you think you're messin' with?" Her only answer was a frightful stare.

Callahan switched off his light to admire her beauty in the pale moonlight, the tinted basement windows letting in just enough light to make out the soft curves of her body. Immune to the frightened look on her face, he was unable to resist temptation and stooped down to caress her bare breast. Lifting a strand of her blonde hair to his nostrils, his perverse intimacy triggered another round of kicking and muffled screaming from Megan.

Reaching into his side pocket, he fished her license out and studied the photograph in the moonlight. "I like the page boy better. It's a hot look for you."

She wanted to tell him what she really thought of him as her hope continued to fade away. Shivering in fear, Megan stared out the tiny basement window as a tear made its way down her cheek.

In a business-like tone he said, "You know, if you could be a little more cooperative Megan, we might be able to work something out. Like for the rest of your life, maybe." Pretending to be a nice guy and saying the words almost made him feel normal, and for a moment, Callahan even felt like he was a regular guy. He noticed her shivering and reached inside a cabinet for a sheet to cover her. Feeling protective, he spread the sheet over her.

Megan shuddered at his depraved fantasy, preferring the thought of dying rather than being molested forever by this insane creep. She tried desperately to raise her legs and kick at him, but felt weak from being restrained for two days with only granola bars for meals.

"Calm down," caressing her hair. "Daddy likes a quiet girl." Disappointed with her lack of appreciation for him, he would be patient with her. "Daddy'll be in the other room when you're ready to make nice." Grinning demonically, Callahan decided to forego any further gratification with her until he could tie up one more loose end. He reached for the squeeze bottle of chloroform.

By the time they found her SUV, he would be long gone.

The weird sound her phone made on his last call to her was bugging him. Costello was concerned and decided to drive by Megan's apartment on 4th Street, the same apartment where she lived when they dated last year. When he called her three hours ago, her phone had made a strange, high-pitched squeal like a mouse having its head smashed in a trap before her line went dead. There was no response on the next two calls he'd made, and her voicemail wasn't picking up.

As he pulled up in front of her apartment complex, he noticed her parking space was vacant and the lights were out. He checked his watch. Eleven thirty-five. Costello stepped out of his Chevy Malibu and walked to her front door. Knocking, he spotted Bailey's empty dog bowls through the window sitting on her kitchen floor.

He knocked again, listening for any sign of Megan or her dog, but it was deadly quiet. Wherever she was, Bailey must be with her.

He knew she liked the complimentary drinks on ladies night at Mezzannotes three miles away, so he decided to swing by the popular nightclub. Before he could reach his Malibu, a car pulled up in the adjoining parking spot and a young, well-dressed couple stepped out. Costello ventured over to see what they might know and noticed they were both barefoot and dripping wet.

"You guys seen Megan anywhere?" he asked the couple. The disheveled man held a half-empty twelve pack of Budweiser under his arm and tried to focus on Costello's face.

"She left before we went out," answered the intoxicated young man as he steadied himself. "Hey, anyone ever tell you that you look like that movie star guy, um…Matthew Broderick?"

"No, you're the first one," Costello answered sarcastically. The detective watched as the girl leaned against her date to put her shoes back on. Obviously, this was a man who had little respect for Florida's laws on drinking and driving, and Costello had no patience with kiss-ups. He pressed for an answer. "Now, when was it that you saw Megan leave?"

"You mind if I ask, ah…why you want to know?" in a confrontational tone, his bravado bolstered by the beer.

Costello stepped closer and flipped open his I.D., holding it up close. "Detective Costello. It's police business," he said matter-of-factly. "So, when *was* the last time you saw her?"

The man stiffened, trying suddenly to appear sober, glancing at his date who had also become more attentive to Costello's question. "Ah…maybe a little after six. Is she in some kinda trouble?"

"No, but you might be," he said with a steely glare, pausing to let it sink in. A fearful look swept his date's face as the prospect of a night in jail for her boyfriend became a reality.

After putting the fear of God in them, Costello continued. "If you see her, have her call me right away," he said sternly, handing him his card. As he walked away, he pointed skyward for emphasis. "And don't drink and drive!" he yelled. Without waiting for a response to his admonishment, the detective walked quickly toward his Malibu, shaking his head in disgust. He hopped in his car to head east and check the party scene at Mezzannotes on Palmetto Park Road, fervently wishing he'd never gotten Megan involved in their investigation.

At nine o'clock on an overcast morning, Detectives Klein and Costello entered the front door of Nautilus Realty on South Ocean Boulevard on official business. Concerned over the whereabouts of Megan Rockwell, the officers hoped for the best but feared the worst. Costello was especially uneasy over the possibility that her disappearance was connected to their hapless investigation of the man who called himself David Callahan. Hampered by the lack of a search warrant or any proof of Callahan's involvement, a murky set of circumstances had them bogged down. The detectives needed evidence that would help them connect the dots and move their investigation forward.

As they entered the office, a half-dozen salespeople were busy on their computers or on the phone. Looking for someone in authority, they approached the middle-aged woman in the blue floral dress sitting at the largest desk.

"Morning, ma'am. I'm Detective Klein, and this is my partner Detective Costello. We're looking for Megan Rockwell." Klein held up his I.D. and badge as Costello nodded at the woman.

She adjusted her glasses and nervously checked her watch. "Megan was supposed to be here at eight-thirty. I've called her, but she's not answering her phone this morning. I'm hoping she's on her way in."

Costello said: "And you are…"

"Linda Lafferty. I'm the office manager," she said, standing and extending her hand. As she introduced herself, Costello surveyed the office surroundings and noticed several dog chewy toys and a dog bowl lying on the floor. One of the toys had "Bailey" scrawled on it with a Sharpie.

"What's this about?" Lafferty asked, focusing on the older detective.

Klein was nonchalant. "We'd just like to talk to her."

Costello bent down and picked up a dog chewy as he noticed a layer of black dog hair on the carpet. He showed the chewy to Klein. "Looks like she and Bailey were here recently. She has a black Lab," he explained to his partner.

"She brings him in sometimes to keep her company when she works late," added Lafferty. "Let me check something," holding up a finger. She walked to the front desk and opened the Excel spreadsheet on the PC. "From the looks of things...she was working on our sales report but," scrolling through the program "... looks like she never finished it."

Something wasn't adding up to Klein. "Does she normally leave her dog's toys here overnight?" he asked.

Lafferty removed her eyeglasses and nodded toward the dog toys on the floor. "No, she usually cleans up before she leaves." She thought for a moment. "I hate to say this, but I *am* a little worried. This is the first time she's left without completing her reports."

Klein removed his notepad from his pocket and flipped it open. "Anything else you can tell me, Mrs. Lafferty? Notice anything different in her work habits or demeanor lately? Anyone threaten her?"

Lafferty bent over the PC again, reviewing the spreadsheet. "The time stamps in her Excel program indicate she was here until about seven forty-eight last night. The app is still open and she left the computer on," she explained. The office had grown quiet as the sales associates were ending their phone conversations one-by-one and tuning in to hear what the detectives were saying about their part-time lingerie model.

"Was anything else out of place? She leave her cell phone, purse? Any signs of a struggle?" asked Klein.

Clearly alarmed now, Lafferty answered slowly. "No...not really." She paused and remembered something. "Oh, wait." She turned to face the rear of the office. "Doug, didn't you say something about the door being left unlocked?"

One of the younger salesmen spoke up from a desk in the back. "Uh, officers, that's right. The back door was slightly ajar when I came in at seven-thirty this morning, but it didn't look like anything was missing."

Klein and Costello looked at each other. "What make, model and color of car does Megan drive?" asked Klein.

"She has a blue-grey Toyota Highlander," said Lafferty. "Maybe four or five years old."

"When's the last time anyone saw her, or her SUV?" asked Costello casually as he bent down to examine Bailey's empty water bowl.

"Yesterday," answered Lafferty. "She left around five but told me on the phone that she was coming back after dinner to finish her sales report."

Klein was busy jotting down the details. Costello continued. "Does your firm rent that big stone beach house to a tenant named David Callahan?"

Lafferty stepped up to answer. "Yes we do. He rents the old Greenwood Mansion on the beach south of here."

"What can you tell me about him?" asked Klein. "Please be candid. Any details might be helpful."

Lafferty hesitated. "Why, is he a suspect?"

"Let's just call him a person of interest," said Costello.

Lafferty was concerned over potential liability to her firm and guarded with her answers. "Well, he's been a good tenant. Kinda peculiar, always pays his rent on time, in cash. Likes to ride his bicycle here."

"Did he give you any I.D.?"

Lafferty said: "Yes, I saw a copy of his Florida driver's license that said 'David Callahan'."

"Can you make me a copy?" asked Klein.

"Sure," she answered, turning to a girl behind her. "Cheryl, can you do that for me?"

Klein grew pensive and scanned the associates scattered throughout the office. "Who handles his account since Lance Meyer's no longer around?" Looking for dissension in the ranks, Klein was already aware that Callahan had already chosen Megan.

It was Doug who answered from the desk in the back. "Uh, don't know *why*, but he specifically asked for Megan to handle it for him," with a hint of sour grapes. Lafferty gave him a reproachful look.

As the two detectives eyed Doug at the desk in the back, Costello continued his line of questions. "Anybody know if Megan has a boyfriend?"

Doug shifted nervously in his seat as Lafferty answered. "She's a pretty girl and gets a lot of attention, but I don't think she was dating anyone. I think she mentioned once that her ex-boyfriend was a police officer." Klein gave his partner a knowing look while Costello looked at the floor and shuffled his feet.

"Ma'am, you know what her email address is?" asked Klein, pen in hand.

"Sure, let me get it…" walking back to her desk and scrolling through her desktop PC. "It's, ah…Baileysfavmodel@gmail.com." She watched Klein make a note.

"Does she have a Twitter account?" asked Costello.

Lafferty shrugged. "Don't think I've ever seen her tweet anything. She was a little shy about using social media. I think she was afraid of the wrong kind of attention."

Costello thought about her answer. "Okay, if you hear from her, or think of anything else that might help us find her...anything at all, call my cell number right away. Thanks for your help," handing her his card.

Klein closed his notepad and the detectives exited through the back door, stopping to examine it for any signs of a forced entry. Finding nothing out of place, they headed for Klein's Crown Victoria.

"Let's put an APB on Megan's SUV," suggested Costello.

Klein opened the car door and looked over the roof at his partner. "Done," he said. "If she *has* been abducted and you were the perp, where would you hide her car?"

Costello climbed in and shut the door, pointing up and down the row of condos through the windshield. "Any of these condo garages without a security gate would be a perfect"-

"Exactly." Klein hesitated before starting the car. "Let's split up. I'll take you back to the station to pick up your car. Put a trace on her credit cards and phone calls while you're there." Klein noticed his partner getting emotional. "What's up, Anthony?"

Costello continued to stare straight ahead. "I have a bad feeling about this. What if we find out this nut job's a bad ass serial killer or something?" He looked away, out the side window as he wiped his eye, then back at his senior partner. "We need a search warrant, Jim," he said emphatically.

Klein sympathized. Frustrated, and now remorseful over involving Megan, they were more motivated than ever to find the girl. "Not sure we have enough evidence to get one, but I'll give it another shot."

It was Klein's turn to get emotional. "Damn liberals treat us like we wanna put handguns in every child's hands in America." Pausing again before starting the car, Klein continued to vent. "Been at war for fifteen years, carrying the mantle of democracy and freedom to savage people in a land full of barbarians, but we can't seem to get a damn search warrant to prevent a murder in our own hometown!" Disgusted with the bureaucracy holding them back, he turned the ignition key and put the car in drive.

Costello nodded, surprised to hear more out of Klein than he'd heard in days. They were both weary of keeping their frustrations bottled up.

"Let's try again. I'll check social media, and send her an email from CID," looking for agreement from Klein, "...where we can track her I.P. address. I have a hunch it'll go unanswered."

⟪━┼┼━⟫

Two hours had passed since the statewide APB was issued by the Boca Raton Police for Megan Rockwell, and the patrolmen in the three squad cars that were assigned to search twenty-seven condo and public garages on Boca Beach had failed to find her car. Megan and her dog Bailey had gone missing, and both had disappeared under suspicious circumstances. Computer checks of her phone calls showed the last incoming call was made by Detective Anthony Costello the prior evening, and there was no new activity reported on any of her credit cards.

Costello called a buddy at the Broward Sheriff's Office to see if he could unofficially expand the search area into Deerfield Beach. The clock was ticking and the detective knew he could save time by calling in a favor. Costello made the call from the parking lot at Mulligan's on Boca Beach, and Patrolman Bradley Doppler answered. "Brad, what's up? You still workin' traffic for BSO over there in Beerfield Beach?"

"Hey, Anthony. Yeah, for the time being. Got my app in for sergeant. Running a radar trap out here on West Hillsboro right now. By the way, congratulations on making detective. What can I do ya for?"

"Workin' a possible missing person case. You remember my ex, Megan Rockwell?"

"Of course. Who could ever forget a…ah…face like hers? She still doin' the underwear ads for Macy's?"

"Well, yeah, part time. We think she may have gotten caught up with a perp in an investigation and may be in trouble."

Realizing his buddy had a personal interest, Patrolman Doppler grew somber. "How can I help, Anthony?"

"Be a big help if you can swing by those two high-rises on Deerfield Beach just south of here. We think there's a possibility that the perp may have hidden her SUV there. The two biggest ones with no security gates."

"Ya mean Crossways and Sea Watch?"

"Them's the two."

"Tell ya what. Soon as I finish inhaling these two hot bikini dogs out here, I'll swing over there. You can owe me one." Patrolman Doppler set his hot bikini dog down on his armrest and reached across the computer to grab a pen. "Hang on…okay…gimme the vehicle description, VIN and plate number, Anthony."

Costello read the description from the computer mounted in his Malibu. "Late model blue-grey Toyota Highlander, plate number tango victor bravo six thirty-four." Then he read the VIN number.

"Got it. By the way, next time you feel like slummin' it and gettin' outa glitzy town there, ya gotta check out this Hot Bikini Dog stand just east of Hillsboro and 95. Ask for Margeaux. She'll knock your socks off."

Where had he heard that name before? "Thanks for the hot tip, Brad. Let me know what you find in those garages. We gotta locate this girl. Tick tock."

"You got it, bro. Check back with you in an hour."

At six fifty-five p.m., Detective Anthony Costello got a phone call from the Broward County Sheriff's Office. Deputies had found Megan Rockwell's blue-grey Toyota Highlander parked on the second floor of a high-rise parking garage on Deerfield Beach, a half mile from the Boca Beach city limits. Although there was no clear evidence of foul play, BSO Forensics was treating the vehicle as a crime scene. Following the on-site investigation, deputies arranged to have the SUV towed to the forensics lab for further analysis.

The forensics team had combed the contents of her SUV. Inside, they found thick layers of dog hair, a dog brush, crushed dog chews, empty bags of Beggin' Strips, a box of latex gloves, eye shadow, waterproof mascara, a small bottle of pepper spray, a pair of fishnet panty hose, a pamphlet on how to control dog flatulence, a vibrator with dead batteries, and a set of Ben Wa balls. The only fingerprints found inside the SUV belonged to Megan Rockwell.

No one had seen or heard from the part-time lingerie model or her black Lab for two days, and a GPS trace of her last cell phone conversation indicated her last known location was South Boca Beach on A1A, near the Nautilus Realty office.

TWENTY-FOUR

After kissing his still-sleeping girlfriend, Mark McAllister stepped into the marble hallway and quietly shut the door to his Delmar penthouse. It was a few minutes before sunrise on a cloudy Saturday morning in Boca Beach, and he was careful not to wake his sleeping neighbors. The forty-year old President of Mizner Park Development was unshaven and slightly hung over after sharing a vintage bottle of Grand Vin Lafite Rothschild 2009 last night with Carol to celebrate the grand opening next week of her new line of sportswear. Not in the mood to deal with Mrs. Seidelbaum's drama, he crept quietly past her doorway on his way downstairs for his four-mile morning run south to Deerfield Beach.

Feeling good about the way things were going lately, he was pleased to be Carol's partner in their new apparel venture she named "OMG". A catchy name, it was well-received by advertisers. A talented designer, she had the inside scoop on the booming fashion sportswear business, having already turned down offers from both Under Armour and Nike. Mark had helped her secure a lease with three thousand square feet of prime retail space just inside the main entrance to the Town Center Mall. It was a prime location with lots of foot traffic, and she was ecstatic about sharing the venture with him. His love for her drove him to use his influence to help her create a more promising future.

Mark could never forget what she'd said to him one day with that magical look in her eye. "Peasants marry for love, and royalty marries for a cause greater than themselves." Sometimes he felt like a peasant, sometimes a patrician, and sometimes he was lucky enough to be treated like royalty.

Boca Beach was waking to a new morning as he watched the seagulls floating on the incoming breeze, chirping their mournful cries of insatiable hunger. Bright orange streams of light broke through on the horizon, outlining the light blue clouds in gilt like the entire eastern sky had caught fire. The sun broke above the ocean's horizon with the spectacular brilliance of a thermonuclear detonation as he stretched with his foot on the top railing. The fresh scent of seashore filled his nostrils, and an inner voice was telling him this would be a propitious day.

As the sun rose higher behind the gilt-edged clouds, he lengthened his stride and fell into a comfortable rhythm, running past the outline of a large heart drawn in the sand just as the incoming tide began to erase the fading epitaph. A quarter mile up the beach stood the foreboding Greenwood Mansion, and he wondered if Callahan had ever found his two missing bulldogs as he listened to the sound of a dog barking in the distance.

Ghost crabs darted about along his path as he sprinted another three hundred yards, bringing him abreast of the distinctive Spanish barrel tile roof and stone walls of the mansion. From the corner of his eye, he spotted a black Lab making his way down the dune through the sea oats, past the bamboo swing. The dog trotted toward him, barking up a storm, the Lab's tail wagging eagerly as he got closer. The Lab looked familiar, and he sensed the dog was trying to tell him something. Squatting on the beach and bracing for a friendly greeting, he remembered seeing the Lab around the neighborhood. Embracing the dog, he noticed the name "BAILEY" printed on the tag along with an email address that read "Baileysfavmodel@gmail.com".

"Hey, boy, you're up early," hugging his neck and rubbing his ears. "Anybody fed you yet this morning, Bailey?"

Excited, Bailey began another round of barking, tail wagging fiercely as he started back toward the villa on a sprint, then stopped after a few yards. The dog looked back, big brown eyes begging for understanding, panting away to see if Mark was going to follow him. Like a child pleading for his father to give chase, Bailey repeated the exercise, trotting back to Mark for another hug and ear massage, then barking his appreciation and racing full speed in the direction of the villa before stopping to see if Mark would follow him.

"Okay, boy. I get it. You got something you wanna show me, right? All right. Let's go." Mark felt a mysterious bond with the dog as he chased after him toward the villa. Reaching the base of the dune, he stopped to catch his breath, watching the barking canine sprint up the dune and turn at the top. Bailey looked back expectantly like they were playing King of the Mountain.

As he scaled the dune to find out what Bailey was up to, Mark thought about his first conversation with Callahan. At first, he had him pegged as a dog lover, and it made him wonder if Callahan had brought Bailey home as a replacement for his missing bulldogs.

When he got to the bamboo swing-for-two, he stopped. He could see the dog was clearly disturbed, barking and whining loudly as he pawed the mirrored sliding glass doors at the back of the mansion. Even more peculiar, Mark noticed the security cameras panning in his direction as he walked toward the patio. What was Bailey was trying to show him? Was Callahan inside operating those cameras?

Then he heard the faint sounds of a woman's muffled screams coming from inside the stone walls. With his ear against the glass, he couldn't tell if it was real or a movie. At first, the screams sounded like a woman with her face in a pillow being pleasured from behind. Bailey was zeroed in on the muffled sounds and began pawing at the base of the rear wall where there were two small basement windows. Debating over whether he should be a nosy neighbor and knock, Mark was guided by his intuition.

"It's okay, Bailey. I hear ya boy." Not knowing what to expect, he knocked loudly on the mirrored glass door as the dog joined him at his side, still barking away. After a third round of knocking, he was about to give up and leave when he saw a light flicker on the keypad and heard the door latch release. The glass door slid back just enough to reveal a scruffy-looking shirtless man in soiled cargo shorts standing inside the darkened room.

"Mark, isn't it?" The scrawny bearded man with the black lifeless eyes looked annoyed with the intrusion.

"Sorry to bother you, Mr. Callahan, but when I brought your dog home I heard screaming and, well…"

Callahan opened the door wider, giving them both a disgusted look. "He's not my dog, and if you wouldn't mind, I'm watching a movie."

Instinctively, Bailey reacted to the muffled screams coming from the basement. His haunches grew taut as he coiled and the dog farted loudly as he shot through the doorway past Callahan.

"Jeez, not again!" exclaimed Callahan, with a scowl. "That damn dog!" As Callahan spun around to try and stop the dog, Mark saw the semi-automatic jammed in the waistband in the back of his shorts. With a quick scan of the interior, he noticed a pink cell phone, a woman's purse and a roll of grey duct tape sitting on the teak dining table. Turning to face Mark again, Callahan removed the semi-automatic from his waistband and pointed it at the floor, enjoying the look of fear on his visitor's face.

"Wasn't sure who was at my back door," Callahan explained lamely. "Can't be too cautious these days." Mark was fervently wishing he'd just kept running.

"Uh huh," said Mark to buy himself some time. He cocked his head to catch another series of muffled screams coming from downstairs. Worried about the dog's safety, and the likelihood of a female captive in the house, Mark thought of an angle as he tried on the role of a concerned neighbor. With an unhealthy regard for his own safety, he took a step forward to test Callahan's reaction.

"Let me help you corral Bailey. I'll take him back outside," volunteered Mark. "Sorry about the intrusion, Mr. Callahan."

It was a tense moment as Callahan grew pensive, pursing his lips, the gun still pointing at the floor. He stepped back to let his uninvited guest inside. Mark entered the dimly-lit dining room, his eyes adjusting to the low light as Callahan closed the sliding glass door and locked it firmly behind him.

Mark was surprised to feel the cold barrel of the silencer pressed against the back of his neck as he heard the click of the gun's hammer cocking. Fear took over, freezing in his tracks, not wanting to provoke the man as the muffled screams continued to float up from the basement.

Callahan said: "Too bad you didn't postpone your investigation until tomorrow, slick." He pressed the gun harder against his neck. "*I* wouldn't be here, and *you* would have been a lot better off," he said grimly. "I may not shoot you if you do exactly what I say." Callahan prodded him with the gun again. "Hands behind your head. On the floor, face down. Now!"

Mark raised his hands, pretending not to notice the woman's phone, purse and roll of duct tape on the table. "Look. I'm sure none of this is any of my business"-

"Shut up!" pressing the silencer firmly against his neck.

Doing as he was told, Mark got down on his knees on the tile floor as his will to fight took over, now certain that the crying and muted screams were coming from a girl being held captive downstairs. With his back to Callahan, he drew his left hand into a fist and tried to calculate the distance to Callahan's face.

"Now, now. Let's be cool here," cautioned Callahan. "You can be a live prisoner, or you can be a dead hero. Up to you, slick," prodding him again with the semi-automatic. Mark opened his fist and laid down on the floor. He felt the steady pressure of the gun at the back of his head, then the weight of Callahan sitting on him.

"Hands behind you. That's it." Mark felt the thick tape circle his wrists four times. Callahan tore it with his teeth as he wound another strip of tape tightly between his wrists. Then he wrapped the tape twice around Mark's mouth, forcing him to breathe through his nose.

Callahan said: "Now get up. We're going through the living room to the stairway downstairs, where you'll meet a lingerie model. But first, we're going to make a stop in the kitchen. Let's go." Mark grudgingly nodded, getting to his feet awkwardly with his hands bound tightly behind him. He felt the barrel of the gun jammed in his back as Callahan gripped his arm firmly, pushing him forward. He could hear Bailey barking excitedly downstairs, along with the moans and muffled screams of a very distraught woman.

Callahan maneuvered his captive into the kitchen, stopping at the fridge to grab a slice of roast beef before they continued through the darkened living room decorated with black-out curtains.

"You don't behave, then I shoot you, the girl and that damn gassy dog before I leave here today. Nod if you understand," commanded Callahan.

Mark nodded as he navigated the darkened stairway with the gun in his back. Stepping from the bottom step, they entered the basement where he could see a large open room that had the look and smell of a dungeon. What he saw next shocked him.

A nude young lady was lying on her back on a soiled bedspread, bound in grey duct tape and leather straps chained to eyebolts in the floor. Her cheeks were streaked with dirt and mascara from hours of grief as Bailey whined and licked her face affectionately. The entire scene gave Mark an eerie feeling-a surreal funhouse feeling like he'd just stepped onto the set of a B-rated horror film that existed entirely outside of today's world where there was a brand new order of unknown moral laws.

Bound, gagged and unable to help, Mark locked eyes with her in sympathy, her blue eyes pleading for his help. He wanted so desperately to be able to comfort her and tell her help was on the way, but with his mouth taped shut, he was unable to offer her any words of encouragement. Fear was the mind killer, and he struggled to keep his fear in check in the face of their dismal plight.

As Bailey continued to whine, the gunman lashed out. "Shut up you mutt!" kicking the dog viciously in the hind quarters with his Topsider. Bailey yelped from the pain, scampered out of harm's way and ran quickly up the stairs before stopping to look back at them from the top step.

Callahan prodded Mark again with the gun. "Okay, slick. Sit down right here next to Megan with your back to me," as he reached for a section of chain and a padlock from the credenza. Keeping the gun pressed to his neck, Callahan threaded the chain between Mark's wrists, padlocking the ends together through the eyebolt in the floor before pocketing the key. "You guys go ahead and get acquainted while I go take care of that damn dog." Callahan stuck the semi-automatic back into the waistband of his cargo shorts and headed upstairs.

Fearing the worst for Bailey, Megan emitted another muffled scream in protest, kicking at her restraints in frustration. Chained to a second heavy-duty steel eyelet mounted in the concrete floor next to hers, Mark watched helplessly as they listened to the gunman baiting Bailey upstairs.

"Here, Bailey. Look what daddy's got for you," trying to coax the Lab outside where he could hose off the mess. He caught up with the Lab in the dining room, dangling the slice of meat in front of the dog so the sweet flavor of fresh beef could waft through his nostrils. Callahan slid back the sliding glass door, tossed the roast beef onto the patio pavers and readied his semi-automatic. Bailey shot through the open door in pursuit of the meat, clueless about the gunman's evil intentions.

"Go boy. All yours, Bailey," aiming the semi-automatic with his right hand at Bailey's head at point blank range. Gripping the gun tightly, the oil on his hand from the meat caused the gun to slip just as he fired.

FFFFUPP! The bullet missed the dog's ear by inches, hitting the concrete patio pavers and ricocheting off toward the beach. After slurping up the delicious slice of roast beef, the dog took off like he was shot out of a cannon as the bullet flew by. Bailey had learned that a gunshot meant he was supposed to run!

Callahan swore, wiping his hand off on his shorts for a better grip and took aim to fire again just as he noticed an older couple walking on the beach directly in the bullet's path. Quickly, he slid the glass door shut before they could spot him, still not believing his bad luck with missing the dog at point blank range. Exasperated, he crouched at the back door to locate the pesky canine as he waited for the couple on the beach to clear from his line of fire.

Crouched for another shot as he waited for the black Lab to reappear in his sights, Callahan heard scratching and barking coming from his front door.

That damned dog!

Enraged, and more determined than ever to put Bailey out of his misery, Callahan chambered a fresh round in his semi-automatic as he bolted toward the front of the house, an unspent bullet falling from his gun. Ever so quietly, he eased open a front window to avoid spooking the dog and positioned himself for a clear shot.

⫘

Now wise to the ways of men with guns, especially those ripe with the pungent scent of moldy perspiration, Bailey heard the window slide open. The black Lab stopped pawing and barking as he sniffed the air cautiously, looking up for approval with that adorable expression of huggable innocence that was so well known to owners of Labs the world over. Bailey instinctively knew he would succeed in winning forgiveness for whatever misconduct he had committed. Then, his craving for another chunk of that delicious roast beef took over. Certain there would be more snacks waiting on the back patio, he scampered to the rear of the house for his reward. What fun he was having! What a great game it was!

⫘

"That damned dog!" yelled Callahan as he ran back toward the rear glass doors to finish him off, not seeing the unspent bullet lying on the tile floor. The sole of his Topsider rolled across the unspent cartridge like it was a large ball bearing, and Callahan catapulted backward. He landed hard on the tile as his gun hand hit the floor with his finger still on the trigger.
FFFUPP-PING! The gun fired, sending a bullet flying through the front window of Greenwood Mansion and straight across A1A.

"Damn!" he yelled, rubbing his backbone, hoping he hadn't broken anything. Lying painfully on his back, he looked over his shoulder and eyed the bullet hole in the front window. Disgusted with his clumsiness, and completely ignorant about the exact location of that particular projectile, he was hoping it hadn't lodged anywhere it would be noticed.

While Callahan was upstairs playing "Shoot the Dog" like a drunken sailor at a carnival arcade, his lone male prisoner was downstairs laboring with every muscle of his body to separate the hardware he was chained to. After managing to loosen his ankles, Mark squatted over the eyebolt like a weightlifter in a clean and jerk contest, pulling and jerking on the chain with all his strength, determined to pull it out of the concrete floor with both arms still taped behind his back.

Lord, give me the strength to stop this madman.

Megan cheered him on from behind with frenzied muffled squeals, glad for the only glimmer of hope she'd felt in her three-day ordeal.

⤙⤚

DISPATCHER: "911. What is your emergency?"

CALLER: "God, please help me!"

DISPATCHER: "What seems to be the problem, sir?"

CALLER: "I got shot in my ass!"

DISPATCHER: "Sir, are you in any immediate danger?"

CALLER: "You idiot! I was screwing my wife lazy-dog style and got shot in"-

DISPATCHER: "No need for insults, sir. Calm down. Try to hang on. We have a unit available. Do you need help?"

CALLER: "Well, HELL YES I NEED HELP!! I'm bleeding with a bullet in my ass!"

DISPATCHER: "Sir, can you move? Can you get to"-

CALLER: "I'm tied down. I can't move! She used my neck ties! I can't…move, dammit!"

DISPATCHER: "Sir, are you in a safe place?"

CALLER: "Safe? I'm tied up on my bed, for God's sake, then I got shot in my"-

DISPATCHER: "Well, sir, if you're tied up, how did you call"-

CALLER: "My crazy-ass wife dialed my cell before she"-

DISPATCHER: "Sir, is your wife there with"-

CALLER: "She ran out, screaming…she gets freaked out by minor things"-

DISPATCHER: "*Minor* things? You mean, like the sound of gunfire, people getting shot, and the sight of blood, sir? Sir?"

CALLER: "Yeah, like that kinda stuff. *Please* send an ambulance!"

DISPATCHER: "Hang on, sir (unintelligible voices). Sir, what is your wife wearing?"

CALLER: "Nothing!"

DISPATCHER: "And you live on Boca Beach?"

CALLER: "Yeah…how did you"-

DISPATCHER: "Sir, I have to put you on hold. I have another call about a naked screaming woman with a knife running down A1A."

CALLER: "Wait! Please wait! Don't hang up on…aaagggghhhh!"

TWENTY-FIVE

N o one had seen or heard from Megan Rockwell in three days, and Klein and Costello were beginning to fear the worst. For all they knew, she could be abducted, stuffed in a trunk, or drowned somewhere. After being denied a search warrant in their investigation for a second time by Judge Rosencranz, the detectives headed back to CID in a dour mood, once again disappointed that the State Attorney's office hadn't pushed the Judge harder.

Unfortunately, the State Attorney, James Harbaugh, was up for re-election and needed the Judge's endorsement to clinch the ballot. As it turned out, the 'good ole boy network' was alive and well in Florida politics, gumming up the wheels of justice as usual. Unfortunately for Megan Rockwell, the 'good ole boy network' had reared its ugly head at the most inopportune of times.

They had just finished a special meeting in chambers, which was unusual for Judge Rosencranz on a Saturday because he was also preoccupied with his own re-election campaign. With the liberal electorate of Palm Beach County hanging in the balance, Rosencranz couldn't afford to appear callous when it came to the personal rights and freedoms of alleged criminals. The detectives and officers at CID were convinced that the judge's supersecret agenda included avenging the infamous Bush-era "hanging chads", delivering the county back to the liberal electorate on a silver platter.

Klein and Costello were tired of getting the run around and frustrated with their lack of progress. Stymied by a liberal judge, and weary of being repeatedly told there was "lack of probable cause" to support the issuance of a search warrant, they were on their way back from the judge's chambers. The two detectives were turning into their Boca Raton Boulevard headquarters when they heard the "shots fired" call come over their police radio.

"Hey, that address is right across A1A from our weirdo at Greenwood Mansion," exclaimed Costello.

Klein gave his partner a knowing nod. "Brilliant, Captain Obvious. Let's roll." Hoping this could be a big break in their case, he reached for his radio. "Roger that twenty. Shots fired, man wounded, screaming naked woman with a knife, 1901 S. Ocean Boulevard, Boca Beach. Twenty-seven responding." Costello leaned forward to activate the dash-mounted blue police beacon and sat back in his seat as Klein made a high-speed turn onto Palmetto Park Road. As the cruiser sped east toward the beach, Costello grabbed the radio to request a forensics team to meet them at the scene.

The detectives rolled into the parking lot at the five-story Esplanade Condominium on Boca Beach just in time for the show. A small group of condo commandos had gathered for the spectacle, the crowd pointing upward at the bullet hole in the mirrored glass façade on the fourth floor. An ambulance rolled up, and the rear doors sprang open as the paramedics unloaded a gurney and headed upstairs to Apartment 408.

As Klein parked the big Crown Vic, Costello checked his Glock for a full clip and holstered his gun, exiting with his partner. From the crowd, a heavy-set woman dressed in pink Lululemon tights pointed at him.

"Hey, Matthew Broderick is here!" she yelled. Embarrassed, Costello waved sheepishly to the group of geriatrics, trying to ignore the woman in the tights. He grabbed his notepad and scanned the group of rubberneckers to try and spot any potential witnesses. So far, there was no sign of the press, and for that he was thankful. Reporters always seemed to hinder his investigations with their grandstanding, often turning crime scenes into a three-ring circus, all in the pursuit of a headline on their way to that elusive Pulitzer Prize.

"Anybody here see anything?" he asked the group gathered at the portico. The Q-tips all shook their heads, returning their attention to the bullet hole in the window four floors up, clucking like a group of hens speculating about the bullet's origin.

Recognizing one of the paramedics wheeling the gurney in the front door, Klein followed him inside the atrium-style building just as a black-and-white police cruiser pulled up with lights flashing. A heavy-set patrolman stepped out of his cruiser, and Klein gestured for him to set up a crime-scene perimeter to keep the rubberneckers out.

Entering the wrought-iron security gate, the two detectives came face-to-face with an elderly male resident who was slowly pushing a wheeled walker across the tiled courtyard, oblivious to the clatter it made. Klein continued inside to catch up with the paramedics while Costello stopped to see what the old man might have seen.

Studying Costello with a confused expression, the man said, "Somebody sa…said there's a…screa…screaming…crazy," scratching his head, "…have you seen my wife, Mil…Mildred? Mildred Numbchucks?"

"If I see her, old timer, I'll let you know," patting him on the shoulder. "Right now, I got a shooting to investigate." The old man stood there, scratching his head, seeming to forget where he was. Costello strode briskly past the ornate landscaping and marble fountain toward the glass elevator to catch up with his partner.

Klein caught up with the paramedic in charge. "Who's the victim, Ron?" he asked over the clatter of the gurney's plastic wheels.

He checked his docket. "Male, age forty-seven, guy named Ryan Uzem," said Ron as he pushed the gurney stacked with equipment toward the elevator.

"How bad?"

"Took a bullet to the right buttock. He'll live. Lost a little blood," he said in a casual monotone, as if a man getting shot in the buttocks in bed was an everyday occurrence in Boca Beach. "Claims he was tied up doin' his wife when the bullet came in through the bedroom window."

As if on cue, the second paramedic began to sing a Beatles tune from the Abbey Road album. "She came in through the bedroom window..." Ron gave him a reproachful look. "Really, Jimmy?"

Ron continued. "Mitch is up there treating him right now. Nice lookin'."

"Who?"

"Crazy-ass wife."

"Where's she?" asked Klein.

"She's sitting by the pool, no clothes, covered in a blanket. Refuses to go upstairs to get dressed."

"She still have the knife?"

"Yessir," said Ron. "She's a little out there," twirling his finger around his ear to describe her mental state. "Won't put her clothes on. Claims there's blood all over them."

Content to let his partner lead the investigation until now, Costello overheard the conversation and stepped up to the men just as the elevator door opened. "I'll go talk to her and get *her* statement," turning to head toward the pool as he cleaned his Warby Parkers with his shirt tail.

"Yeah, thought you might. Don't miss out on *that*," quipped Klein as he boarded the elevator with the two paramedics and gurney. "Be sure to give her your 'Matthew Broderick' autograph there, Ferris." Costello gave him the finger over his shoulder. He didn't get a chance to question too many naked, crazy-ass wives running down A1A in Boca right after being so rudely interrupted during sex.

Klein ascended with the paramedics in the glass elevator, admiring the atrium's interior. The condo's peaceful Zen-style garden landscaping and two-story waterfall in the center of the courtyard seemed to contrast sharply with the violence of the shooting upstairs.

Klein continued his Q&A. "The vic say where the bullet came from?"

"Nope. He's conscious, so you can ask him yourself in about thirty seconds," said Ron, organizing the equipment on the gurney as they approached the fourth floor.

"I will."

Klein spoke into his hand-held radio. "Twenty-seven to base. Where's our forensics unit? We're gonna need a laser bullet trajectory kit here *yesterday*."

"Twenty-seven, base. Should be arriving now, Jim," responded the dispatcher as the two paramedics rolled the gurney in through the open double door of Unit 408. Looking east through the living room window as they entered, Klein spotted the forensics unit turning off A1A into the condo parking lot below. He stepped into the master bedroom to interview the victim.

⟞⟨┼⟩⟝

Nervous as a cat in a room full of rocking chairs, Callahan peeked out through the blackout drapes at the three-ring circus across the street just as a news truck from WPEC-TV pulled into the guest parking area at Esplanade. It was a beehive of activity as the reporter and cameraman went into action. Checking his watch, he figured he had about twenty minutes to get out of Dodge before they traced the origin of the bullet back to the hole in his living room window. With the expected grandstanding by officers on the scene, he was hoping the reporters scrounging for their next headline would muck things up just enough and give him a chance to make his escape in his "ABERNATHY PLUMBING" van.

Callahan knew he was out of time as he stopped to check the clip from his .380 auto and counted four rounds remaining before heading downstairs to take care of his witnesses. Two rounds apiece oughta do it. His face contorted with a twisted smile as he remembered the fun he'd had with Megan. The smile disappeared from his face as he thought about the eight crates of gold coins that still needed loading.

To speed things up, Callahan dug the amber vial of coke out of his pocket. He unscrewed the top and snorted half into each nostril with his head tilted back, basking in a tsunami of euphoria that washed over him like a huge warm wave. Callahan's heart felt like it was pounding out of his chest as he thought about the window of opportunity closing at the construction site in Vero. He knew he had to hurry and hoped they hadn't poured the footers yet. Superman's evil twin was about to make his appearance downstairs, boys and girls.

With the cocaine kicking in, Callahan quickly rolled up one of the two five-by-eight Persian rugs and slung it over his shoulder. In his right hand he grasped the semi-automatic with four remaining cartridges and headed downstairs to cover his tracks.

⋙✦⋘

Mark's stomach tightened when he heard the sicko open the basement door at the top of the stairway. Glancing at the girl, he watched her muscles tense up and her eyes widen as a fearful look crept over her face. What they did not expect to see in the dim light was the rolled-up carpet the gunman carried over his shoulder as he descended the stairs. The carpet dropped to the concrete floor beside them as Callahan bent down to check the chains. Knowing what was to follow, Mark looked into the frightened girl's eyes one last time as if to warn her he was ready to take his last desperate shot.

"Too bad you two won't have a chance to get acquainted there, slick. She's actually a lot of fun once you get to know her," said Callahan, grinning demonically. "As much as I'd like to stay and chat, I'm on a deadline here. We're back to Plan B."

Mark felt his muscles tense as he waited for just the right moment. As Callahan turned to cock the hammer and kick the roll of carpet open, Mark sat back quickly, dragging the chain under his heels to bring his arms in front. With all the strength he could muster, he jumped up. The loosened eyebolt gave way, and Mark launched himself at Callahan, flipping the chain around the gunman's neck and pulling him backward over his knees in a desperate attempt to dislodge the gun.

A loud explosion detonated in Mark's ear as bright fireworks burst in his eye socket. He'd never known such pain, the entire right side of his skull burning white hot as he fought to stay conscious. Mark pulled as hard as he could on the chain to choke his adversary, cutting off the gunman's air supply. His blood made the chain slippery as Mark fought to stay conscious. Callahan gagged and clawed desperately at the chain around his neck, the gun clattering to the floor next to Mark's foot. He kicked the gun hard, sending it across the room and out of Callahan's reach as the girl's muffled screams and the pain from the bullet ripped through his head.

Suddenly, the basement window shattered and something whizzed by Mark's head, spewing a cloud of gas that set his eyes, nose, and lungs on fire. He felt Callahan's body go limp on top of him as he continued to keep pressure on the chain around his throat until there was no more movement and no more gasping.

He could hear muffled shouting and men running as the basement filled with the burning gas. With Callahan's lifeless body on top of him, he fell over. Barely conscious, he was blinded by the gas, seeing only bright stars. The thunderous clanging in his head continued like a burning locomotive running full speed through his skull. He raised a hand to explore the side of his head. It felt like hot molten lead; distended, gooey, his hand falling back to the floor limply.

He thought it was the beginning of a dream, the polished black boots in front of his face, men's muffled voices above him, orders being shouted. Then the voices faded and he no longer heard anything.

In the dream, he was slowly floating away, up into the sky, high above the ocean-front condos, until he was so high that the seagulls, people and cars stopped moving.

Then everything went dark.

TWENTY-SIX

The slow-moving flying-machine dream kept rerunning itself in his head like an old sepia-infused film flickering from the 1920s. In the dream, Mark shivered from the high-altitude cold, with nothing to cover himself, the huge machine lumbering through the clouds to gain elevation and escape the bullets ripping through the thin skin and clanking around inside, slowing his escape. The clouds seemed impenetrable and his eyes watered badly. It was difficult to see. He felt himself being dragged down as he struggled to breathe and free himself from the deadly grasp of large talons clawing at him, squeezing the life from his body.

Then a light shone brightly in the distance. The light grew brighter as the talons began to loosen their grip and he could feel air fill his lungs again. Blinded by the light, a verse he once memorized from Ecclesiastes when he was a boy was suddenly emblazoned across his mind's theatre, taking center stage;

"But woe to him who is alone when he falls and has not another to lift him up!"

Then a powerful force took hold of him, pulling him upward, out of the bullet-ridden flying machine, freeing him and restoring his vision. It was that crazy black Lab Bailey, the flying retriever, pulling him upward, releasing him from death's grip.

But then he realized it wasn't the black Lab lifting him up; it was Carol, who, with a gentle hand, held his head up to adjust his pillow. He opened his eyes wider to focus on her sensuous lips and inhale the sweet scent of her perfume. Reaching for her, he bent forward to give her a kiss but the massive pain from his head made him stop halfway. As he laid back, he noticed the IV drip and electronic monitors attached to his arm and fingers, dropping them back to the bed.

Carol was grinning. "Looks like someone's feeling better."

His eyes welling with emotion, he said; "Sweetheart...it's so good to see you again," gasping, leaning back against his pillow. "I thought I was"-

"Honey, don't try to talk. Or kiss me. You'll pull your stitches loose."

Ignoring her own advice, she held his hand and leaned over. "See if this helps," she said softly, delivering a slow, lingering kiss.

As their lips touched, a joyful tear crawled down his cheek and Mark began the painful process of piecing the recent events together. He wanted to smile, but pain ripped through the side of his head like he'd been hit with a meat cleaver. He raised an exploratory hand to touch the bandage covering the right side of his face, still tender from the surgery. Thankful to be on the right side of the grass and in the land of the living, another wave of emotion swept over him.

"Honey, I'm so sorry about all of this," said Mark, taking a fresh look at her. "You look fantastic."

She was surprised to hear him say this. She was wearing a snug-fitting aqua sundress (his favorite color) with spaghetti straps and a big ruffled hem. "I think the Vicodin's affecting your vision, sweetheart," she said. "I look awful. Haven't had time for the spa since you went on your rescue mission and wound up a hostage."

"Yeah, well…I'm back." Flirting without being able to smile was a new experience for him, and he'd lost all sense of time in the denouement. "What day is it?" he asked, still in a fog.

"Tuesday," she said, stroking his head. "You've been out of surgery in la-la land for three days, mister." Clearly, no one had brought him up to date. "So, how was your trip?"

"Nerve-wracking. I was getting shot at."

"Sounds familiar."

"So, what happened to the girl that was"-

"Megan, the girl you found chained in the basement?" Carol raised her eyebrows like she was describing a B-rated horror film.

"Yeah. What happened to *her*?"

"She stopped by earlier today to check on you, but you were still in la-la land. She had to get back to work."

"She leave any samples from Victoria's Secret?"

Carol gave him a disapproving look. "You *are* feeling better. By the way, she works for Macy's." He watched her step to a nearby table decorated with a large expensive floral arrangement and a gift-wrapped box with a big bow. She plucked the card from the top of the bouquet and handed it to him. "She's very grateful, Mark. The flowers and fifth of Hardy are from her. Somebody told her you like V.S.O.P. cognac," she said, with a wink. "By the way, she asked me if I was, ah…interested in a *threesome*, of all things." Certain that Megan's very private invitation would lift his spirits, Carol held back on her disapproval, waiting to hear what he would say.

Uncertain of her feelings in the matter, Mark's heart skipped a beat as he stopped unfolding the note. His feelings for Carol were stronger, so he was careful. "And you said…"

"I said I'd ask you when you were feeling better," she answered, poker-faced.

"Uh huh. Not sure that we wanna do *that*, honey, but I think I *am* feeling better." His brow furrowed and he grew pensive. "What about Callahan? Is he...?"

"Dead? No. I talked to that cop, you know, Klein...the bald-headed detective and his partner, Costello-you know, the one that looks like Matthew Broderick." Mark struggled to remember the details. "They moved him to a maximum security hospital in Miami. He's been charged with two murders and a coupla dozen felonies. You did a pretty good number on him, Samson."

"Like...what're you...oh, the chains?"

Carol nodded. "Those two talk like you're a hero," stroking his head, smoothing his hair back. "They've been here every day to check on you."

"Klein and Costello, huh? Sounds like a comedy act," said Mark. Then he got emotional again. "Just tryin' to keep everyone on the right side of the grass." A twinge of jealousy swept over him. "You sure it's *me* those detectives were checking on every day?"

Carol gave him a seductive look. She loved it when he got jealous. It happened so rarely she couldn't resist milking the opportunity. "Not sure about Klein, but Costello's kinda cute." She watched him make a face, then look behind her as someone appeared in the doorway.

"Hey, Marky-Mark, can't keep a good man down, right?" Wearing a big grin as he entered the room, Dominick was glad to see his friend awake and out of his narcotic cloud. "Just when you thought it was safe to run on the beach again, right buddy?" Mark smiled as they did a fist bump with his free arm. "Anybody tell you those scavenger hunts can be dangerous?" Dom laid a smutty magazine and a bottle of Courvoisier on his bed. "Brought you some entertainment."

Carol scooped it all up and laid the girlie magazine on top of the monitors out of Mark's reach. "Dom, really," she said playfully. "He knows I'm all he needs." She leaned over and gave her patient a quick kiss on his forehead. Mark knew a quick kiss wasn't a good sign and often preceded a departure.

"You leaving?"

Carol nodded. "I've got some new designs to go over with the factory manager, and I've gotta meet with the contractors for our new place. They all *loved* the name 'OMG'," she said proudly. "It's gonna make a great label, especially for performance sportswear." A young nurse scurried in to check his IV drip and move the magazines off the monitors, giving Carol a disapproving look on the way out.

Carol continued. "Honey, you'll be so proud." She brushed the hair out of his eyes and gushed with enthusiasm. "*We* are gonna do so well with our new store." She pulled her blond hair back and nodded at Dom. "I'll give you a chance to catch up with Dom. Be back later to check on you."

"You know I love you," Mark said dreamily, unsure if it was the narcotics or him doing the talking.

"I know, baby." This time she gave him a proper kiss on the lips. "Feel better," she said, sashaying out the door with his heart in tow.

The men watched the provocative sway of her hips without saying a word as she disappeared through the door. "Wow," offered Dom. "You got your hands full there, bro." Turning his attention back to Mark, he said, "Got some great news for you, Marky-Mark. Margeaux and I have signed a deal to start our own rehab center. Rehabbing a building on five acres right here in Boca." Dom was beaming, proud of his decision to do something positive for the community and turn some lives around.

Mark offered his former meth-cook buddy a fist bump before prodding his bandage with a thumb to scratch an itch. "Congratulations, Dom! I'm proud of you, but I'm thinkin' Walter White would probably roll over in his grave."

"Uh huh. Well, I wanted to right some wrongs...and leave a better legacy." He looked at the floor for a second, then added,

"It's the right thing to do." Mark was pleased that Dom had grown a conscience.

In the middle of their heart-to-heart, a tough-looking bald man in a polo shirt and Dockers appeared at his door, followed by a second man that looked suspiciously like Matthew Broderick with his shirttail out. "Knock knock," said the tough-looking guy. "Need a few minutes, Mr. McAllister," he said, glancing at Dom.

In spite of his narcotic fog, Mark could tell they were cops even before he saw the gold shields mounted on their belts. "Sure. C'mon in, guys."

Feeling a little clausterphobic with police officers crowding into the room, Dom glanced at the detectives, then back at Mark. "Gotta go check on Margeaux at the Hot Bikini Dog Stand. Glad to see you're doing better, Marky-Mark," patting his leg. "Enjoy the fruit-flavored condoms." Passing the two officers on the way out, Dom nodded politely and gave them a quick salute. "Detectives."

After Dom left, Klein closed the door and fixed his gaze on their patient. "Got a coupla questions for our star witness, and some news I think you're gonna like there, chief," nodding at his partner.

"Do I know you guys?" asked Mark. Their voices sounded vaguely familiar to him.

"That was a helluva gutsy thing you did, Mr. McAllister," said the younger officer, extending his hand. "We'd like to shake your hand. I'm Detective Costello, and this is my partner Detective Klein. We're the ones who found you at Greenwood Mansion. You know, the tear gas, the SWAT team and all that."

"That was *you*? I'm very grateful," said Mark.

Klein spoke first. "What we wanted to know is how the hell you found Tommy Tomlinson? He's been a fugitive from law enforcement for over ten years. Been on the FBI's Ten Most Wanted list for"-

"Who's Tommy Tomlinson?"

"The man who shot you and abducted you and Megan Rockwell," answered Costello. "His real name is Tommy Tomlinson. He's been on the run for over a decade and"-

"We think he may be responsible for at least three other murders," interjected Klein, "...including Lance Meyer. We'll need your statement when you feel up to it. Right now, we're tryin' to fill in some blanks here. So, what led you to him?"

"Well...that black Lab, Bailey, he...ah..." The infusion pump beeped softly as it sent another round of Vicodin into Mark's IV, raising him to a new level of euphoria. "Not sure if I can hold a pen right...ah...," his voice trailing off.

"No worries," said Klein. "I can have a court reporter here in twenty minutes to videotape your statement." The detective glanced at his partner. "Shall we go ahead and give him the good news, Tony?" Costello nodded.

"There's good news?" questioned Mark, touching his bandage again, wincing from the pain. With his eyelids beginning to droop from the meds, he looked first at Costello, then back at Klein.

"I think you're gonna like this part," said Costello with a smile. "As soon as we have your signed statement, the insurance company will cut you a check for ten percent."

"Check? For what?" Mark felt like he might still be in Vicodin dreamland. Klein and Costello exchanged knowing glances.

"For ten percent of what we recovered," explained Costello.

Mark squinted at the two detectives, trying to figure out what they were talking about. "What you recovered?"

"Yup. One hundred and seventy million dollars," explained Klein. Mark looked puzzled, so Klein broke it down. "The insurance reward. Ten percent of the one hundred seventy million in missing cash and gold coins that Federal marshals recovered from Tomlinson's two homes in Vero and Boca."

"That *we* and the Federal marshals recovered," corrected Costello.

"That *we* helped recover," reiterated Klein with a nod to his partner. "You made Tomlinson's original investors, *and* their insurance company very happy, Marky-Mark. They've been lookin' for that money for a long time. Even after your finder's fee, the appreciation in the gold added another thirty million to the haul." He waited for the news to resonate with his star witness as he watched Mark's expression for some sign that this was all sinking in.

"So, by rights, your end of that is seventeen million," said Costello. Mark's jaw dropped.

"So, you ready to move forward and give us your statement?" asked Klein.

Mark couldn't escape the strange feeling that he was still in la-la land, writing and directing his own movie while it was being filmed on the spot. As the narcotic steered him toward dreamland again, he touched his bandage as a reality check, still skeptical.

Fighting to stay focused, Mark offered his recap. "So, let me get this straight, guys. I give you my testimony about what happened at that beach house, with the dog, the girl, the pile of cash... Callahan-I mean-Tomlinson, the shooting, and the teargas and all...and they're gonna give me... *seventeen million dollars?*"

Costello looked at his partner, then back at Mark. "Chew got it, partner."

"After taxes, that would be...ah..." His eyes were drooping, and in his doped-up state, the math escaped him. "Well...what're we waiting for? Let's do it," said Mark enthusiastically.

He watched as Klein autodialed headquarters on his cell phone.

⊰⊹⊱

The rowdy crowd of Boca condo commandos was busy tossing back the free champagne, cold beer, and devouring the shrimp and lobster hors d'oeuvres like they'd just spent the last ten years in a Mexican jail. It was a catered Saturday afternoon Boca Beach pool party to end all pool parties, complete with spiffy bow-tied waiters.

Mark stood at the railing on the ocean side of the pool deck waiting for Carol to join them. He was wearing an aqua-colored shirt hand-painted by a famous Tahitian artist that he'd dug out of his closet especially for the occasion. The brilliant underwater scene he wore contrasted nicely with his Navy blue cargo shorts as he stood in the sun and surveyed the Delmar festivity that had drawn over two hundred party animals.

Also present to take advantage of the catered gourmet event were the inevitable freeloaders, the fifty or sixty boisterous party crashers from neighboring condos. It was a convivial event, with condo commandos busy darting about, pushing their agendas and slapping each other on the back as they congratulated each other on being masters of the universe.

The bow-tied caterers that Mark hired for the party had declined to serve refreshments in plastic glasses, insisting instead on serving in their traditional crystal glasses in defiance of the condo rules. The catering manager made it clear to Mark that 'they didn't do plastic'. After what he'd been through, he was at a point where he just didn't give a damn about the petty condo rules. He was happy to see his guests crowding around the two open bars and having a jovial time in a celebration of life on the right side of the grass.

A second round of plastic surgery had reduced his facial bandage to the size of a large Band Aid. For the first time in weeks since being shot by a serial killer, he was no longer feeling trapped inside the fog of a narcotic stupor.

A new day had dawned, and he felt like a new man, reinvigorated and blessed by God as he gazed out over the azure ocean from the pool deck, ready for the proverbial first day of the rest of his life.

The drone of hundreds of partiers faded into the background as his attention was captured by a large sloop on the horizon. The huge cutter rig was slowly making its way south along the western edge of the Gulfstream countercurrent, moving at about six knots on a beam reach five hundred yards out. He imagined himself at the helm, trimming the sheets and serving up margaritas to his passengers in the cockpit while Jimmy Buffett played in the background as the yacht headed for the Bahamian out islands.

Watching the wind fill the sails took him back to his past adventures in Bora Bora, Tahiti, Moorea, Fiji and the Marquesas, fueling his growing desire to explore French Polynesia all over again. He fantasized about trading in his turbo-charged gas-guzzler for a more comfortable stately craft of sizable length and girth; an elegant ship capable of taking his future family to faraway islands anywhere in the world. Maybe it was time for another circumnavigation.

"Hey, Marky-Mark!" His fantasy was interrupted by the unmistakable sultry voice of Desiree Stone as he turned to greet the girl he'd once had a huge crush on. She looked stunning in her classic black string bikini with matching sheer cover-up as she approached, a smiling, hunky motorcycle cop in tow. Brimming with joy, Desiree thrust her left hand out to show him a new diamond ring that sparkled with enough brilliance to make him squint.

"Guess what?" she gushed. "Rod asked me to marry him!"

Mark pulled her hand closer to admire the impressive fiery stone. "Nice rock there, girl," smiling at their beaming faces. "And, so, what did you say?"

Desiree gave him a kiss on his good cheek. "You're a funny guy, Marky-Mark."

"Sunny beaches," added Mark, shaking his head in wonderment at the ring. The two work-out buddies exchanged a celebratory fist bump as the jaw-dropping film star looked on approvingly, happy that her two favorite hunks could share her serendipity.

"Si. Sunny beaches, hombre, y huevos rancheros amigos," joked Rod. "There's more, bro," he said. In street clothes for the party, Rodman was sporting a green floral Tommy Bahamas outfit as he prompted his bride-to-be to bring Mark up to date on their future plans.

"And," she continued, "...I'm enrolled in nursing school at Lynn University. Changing professions. Gonna be an R.N. What do you think of that, *Mr.* McAllister?" Her blue eyes sparkled with joy.

A broad smile covered Mark's face. "I think the college would be very fortunate to graduate the sexiest nurse in the history of nursing," he said, giving her a congratulatory hug. "So what else is new, gorgeous?"

She waited for a private moment with him while her husband-to-be stepped away to greet a couple across the pool. Then, she leaned closer. "Are you ready for this? Dom told me he donated all of his lab equipment to the Spanish River High School chemistry department. He's using all the, uh...money he made to build a drug rehab facility."

"That's what I heard. Unbelievable, isn't it? Not sure *Walter White* would approve, but it's quite a formula for meth cooks the world over to follow." In his wildest dreams, Mark could not have envisioned a more welcomed transformation in a friend, with the added bonus of not having to worry about posting bail for his former meth cook buddy.

From behind him he heard a familiar Brooklyn accent. "Hey Mark, let me introduce you to Lillian Peltz," said Big Mike. The tough-looking fight promoter had found himself a date cool enough to soothe his savage soul. "Tomorrow we head to Hollywood to start filming the spinoff from my new hit series, *K.O.s For Kids*," he explained as they shook hands. Mark thought the two looked like they belonged on the red carpet together as Lillian stood beside him wearing an alluring Armani one-piece and cover-up, Dolce Gabbana sunglasses, and Ralph Lauren floppy beach hat.

As Lillian headed to the nearest bar to retrieve some refreshments for her celebrity boyfriend, Big Mike was looking to get caught up with his buddy. The two men watched her sashay toward the bar. "She's a keeper, Mikey. Isn't she the one who likes the, ah...chip dip?"

"Slurped, not stirred," answered Big Mike in an improv of James Bond. "Hey, have you given any thought to selling your crazy-ass story to a screenwriter or producer? Helluva story. It's all over the net and newspapers. Media's eating it up." He watched Mark for any sign he could be interested, unaware that his bandaged buddy was already busy weighing how much of his privacy he'd have to relinquish for putting himself back in the media spotlight.

Big Mike continued. "Now would be the time to cash in, during the media frenzy. So, if you're interested, I know a few good producers that would love to talk with you. Here, keep my card and let me know. I know you're still gettin' over your ordeal." Big Mike grew thoughtful. "Hell, if I'd gone through what you did, I'd probably be making a disability claim for post-traumatic stress disorder."

"Thanks, Mike. I'll give it some thought," pocketing the TV star's card as he watched Al Wasserman on his wheeled walker make his way through the crowd. While Big Mike headed over to the bar to corral his date, Mark shared a few high-fives and fist bumps on his way through the crowd to check on his recent heart attack patient.

Before he could hook up with Al Wasserman, a portly middle-aged brunette wearing a gold lame dress trimmed with sequins intercepted him. He stopped to admire her outfit, wondering if it came in her size. "Excuse me, but who here's got some coke?" she asked Mark with a pained expression.

"Uh...I...ah...you should know we've got several recovering substance abusers here just out of rehab." Hearing this, she frowned. "So, for *this* party, things don't *necessarily* go better with coke." She looked at him like he had three heads. "See someone I gotta say hello to," he said, pointing toward the crowd.

Politely blowing off the druggie in the skin-tight Liberace outfit, he turned to find Al Wasserman in the crowd when a totally baked Jason Glitzsky decked out in an Under Armour biking outfit intercepted him. Jason raised an oversized Phillies blunt and blew a smoke ring into the crowd as partiers backed up and gave the condo president's brazen son some room.

"Cool party, Mark! Hey, why do Kamikaze pilots wear helmets, man?"

"Beats the hell outa me, Jason," as he kept moving, "...but don't let your mom catch you with that blunt unless you wanna wind up back in rehab."

Working his way through the crowd, Mark finally caught up with Al Wasserman. "Al, good to see you up and around. How's it hangin'?" His question clearly amused the frail condo director who was sporting a nasal breathing tube attached to a miniature green oxygen tank on his walker.

Al looked up at Mark, his face lighting up as he recognized the guy who rescued him from his near-fatal heart attack on Ocean Boulevard. "Oh, hey...nice party. Well, young man...that's just the problem. That's all it does; it just *hangs* there."

Mark smiled and put his arm around the shoulder of the eighty-year old condo director. "Well, we can't be stud muffins forever, Al. As your in-house condo cardiologist, I'd advise you to go easy on the Viagra until your heart's a little stronger," he joked.

Wasserman offered some sage advice of his own. "Take it from an old condo commando like me, son," putting his hand on Mark's shoulder, "...revel in your time, 'cause who knows how long you have?" He scratched his head and continued philosophizing. "Who knows how long *any* of us have?"

Feeling his mortal nature becoming more fragile by the minute, Mark was ready for a lighter moment. He waved at Margeaux and Dom across the pool as they held court with a couple of residents clad in matching Ralph Lauren outfits. At the opposite end of the pool deck he could make out Delmar's jovial custodian. Jorge Hernandez was feeding his young wife jumbo shrimp dipped in cocktail sauce while his brood of five kids was busy chowing down on the salmon and lobster hors d'oeuvres.

Mark spotted Dyson Stampaugh toasting champagne glasses with his secretary. Stampaugh looked like he was three sheets to the wind with his arm around Maria's waist as he offered the crowd his take on the day; "It's a sick world, but I'm a happy guy," Mark could hear him say. The crowd watched in amusement as Stampaugh dropped an ice cube down Maria's well-filled halter top as part of his drunken buffoonery while she wiggled around like a braless Sophia Viagra. The tasteless act triggered a scenario in Mark's mind where Delmar was the respondent in a pending sexual harassment suit seeking a sum of money commensurate with the size of her chest.

His thoughts were interrupted by the screechy voice of Sarah Glitzsky. The condo president had just made her appearance as she stepped around the corner wearing the most hideous flaming orange-and-green-striped polyester pants suit Mark had ever set eyes on.

"Mister McAllister," she shouted arrogantly over the noisy crowd, "...do you not know it's a hundred dollar fine to bring glassware to the pool area?" Her remark was met with several 'boos' and defiant raised glasses from the crowd around her.

"Bill me, Sarah," he said, walking toward another group of party animals he wanted to say hello to. He couldn't resist stopping to address their prima donna president with more sage advice.

"And you might wanna think about hiring a new image consultant there, Hoss."

The next day, the sky over Boca Beach was filled with huge fluffy cumulous clouds looking like giant cotton balls that parted occasionally to let the sun shine through. Mark was on his first beach run since undergoing surgery from the gunshot wound ten days ago.

What would the tides bring him today, he wondered?

He was long-striding it at low tide, flying along the seashore like he was on wings, his feet barely touching the sand, joyous to have survived the gunshot and relishing the euphoria of endorphins again.

What was he was going to do with seventeen million dollars? He thought about the verse from Timothy written on his father's tombstone:

We brought nothing into this world, and it is certain we can carry nothing out.

Comforting, but leaving so many questions unanswered. Maybe he would donate a large part of it to cancer research in memory of his mother and father. For a moment, he pictured the image of a hundred-foot Hinckley cutter rig with a Navy blue hull and teak deck. He could see the name *Vitamin Sea* painted on her stern as his bare feet flew effortlessly over the sand.

As he ran, his thoughts shifted to yesterday's story describing the recent disappearance and likely abduction of yet another missing woman in Vero Beach. He thought about how the narrative seemed to blend with the eternal ebb and flow of mortal events, and how things are always building up and tearing down like the powerful currents that eroded the changing coastline.

The lyrics and melody from a sixties pop song floated through his head from the Procol Harum rockumentary he watched the night before; her face just ghostly, a crowd calling out for more, then, a whiter...shade of pale.

The words reminded him of Megan's face when he'd first found her, pale and streaked with mascara from her ordeal. He remembered the reporter who'd asked him if he would do it all over again when he'd answered "...I acted instinctively, using my God-given intuition."

From the photo in the newspaper, he visualized what the latest missing woman's face would look like today if he found *her*, how short our lives were, how there was amazement and cynicism, how lovers were lost, but love survived. And how some dreams can come true, and others that can't.

Mark thought about how the world was spinning out of control, how everyone seemed caught up in a virtual reality, often ignoring the real world around them. He remembered back to his childhood when he couldn't wait to speed headlong into the future, believing it was the place to be, and how today he wanted to slow things up, sometimes even stop time altogether, unsure of whether the future was where he wanted to be, but sure that God had a plan for him.

He thought about Dominick and Margeaux turning their lives around, Rod with Desiree, an adult film star that became a nurse. Big Mike hooking up, Anatolla, Glitzsky, Stampaugh, Wasserman and the entire wacky crew of condo commandos, all mired in their silly petty rules.

And although we are handiworks of our past, we don't have to be confined by it. It made him wonder if he had the balls to be a dad.

It was then his random reverie was suddenly interrupted by a barking dog, a bark that he recognized as the familiar black Lab ran up to greet him.

"Bailey! What are you doing out here, boy?" squatting to hug his favorite canine as the dog's tail wagged furiously, pounding excitedly against the sandy beach, then climbing up on Mark, happy to be reunited with the man who saved his master.

"Hey boy, good to see you too!" petting his head and rubbing his ears, prompting another round of barking and face-licking. Bailey took off, just like before, this time toward the weathered sky-blue house with white-tiled roof sitting at the top of the dune. The dog stopped and turned to see if Mark would follow.

"What's up, Bailey? What've you gotten yourself into now?" The black Lab pawed at the air and barked at him again, then panted heavily, waiting for him to understand. Instinctively, Mark knew what he wanted. He had a bond with Bailey that could never be described by words alone.

And he thought of Lance Meyer's body washed up on the beach, the serial killer Tommy Tomlinson in his hideaway at Greenwood Mansion, on his way to Vero, captured only minutes from a clean getaway. And finding Megan chained up in that moldy basement full of cash, Detectives Klein and Costello coming to the rescue, the tear gas, the gunshots, not sure if he wanted to get shot again, but sure that he wanted a family with Carol.

Who knew what the tide would bring?

Knowing she was in danger, he was driven to find her, the missing woman, as he slowly turned to face the mysterious house on the dune, always amazed at the people and things the tide would bring.

And the notion that nobody rings a warning bell when it's going to happen, praying to God it would be different this time.

Mark could feel his heart beating out of his chest, the adrenaline surging through his veins. He looked at Bailey waiting impatiently on the sand.

"Okay, boy. Ready when you are."

66761160R00193

Made in the USA
Charleston, SC
29 January 2017